HARRIS NECK DEAD

HARRIS NECK DEAD

JOHN WILSTERMAN

Harris Neck Dead

A Novel by

John Wilsterman

This novel is dedicated to Kira and Luke, life's gift of love, wisdom and adventure.

Harris Neck Dead is a work of fiction. Although real places are depicted, here they are given fictional treatment tailored to suit the story. All characters are drawn from the author's imagination and are not intended to represent any real person.

PART 1

"Have Patience with everything that remains unsolved in your heart... live in the question." from Letters to a Young Poet, Rainer Maria Rilke

CHAPTER 1

"Harris Neck Dead"

Fort Stewart, South Gate, a little past 10:30 PM:

"Merle, this should be an easy run," Ricky Lee had said. "Pick up the load and take it to the so-called yacht club. Don't be late and tell that idiot brother of yours to keep his mouth shut."

They were stealing from the US Army, smuggling it out in their truck and the guard had stopped them cold at the gate. No surprise Merle Cuthbert's heart pounded, and his gut sank faster than a lead weight.

Like he could keep Donnie's mouth shut.

The MP corporal handed back his paperwork.

"Sir, the regs say we have to inspect all loads after eighteen hundred hours. It's way past that... like twenty-two thirty."

Merle knew military time. He had served in the first Iraq war when he was just as young as this baby-eyed corporal, but he had never been a jerk about the regs.

"Corporal, It's scrap from your own recycling center. We've made these runs before, and we've done 'em at night. At all hours. Nobody told us we can't move a load at night."

The MP looked at the long string of cars waiting behind their truck.

"Well, stuff changes all the time, sir. I'll have to take a look inside those containers."

Merle let out a long breath.

In the truck's passenger seat, his brother Donnie pulled his earbuds out. God-awful music buzzed from the dangling cord. "What's the holdup?" Donnie said. "We're late."

Merle closed his eyes.

"Shut up, Donnie." Merle gave him a look. Donnie put his earbuds back in.

"Sir, tell your passenger to stay put. I just need you to step out and show me what you're hauling."

"He knows that, son. We've done this before. Many times." Merle's voice sounded old and tired. Just like daddy's he thought. When did I get that old?

The truck's door screeched. Merle stepped out and his knees buckled when his boots hit the pavement. He walked to the back of the truck and slowly hoisted himself up on the rim of the flatbed. There was barely enough room to stand.

Strapped to the bed of the truck were six dumpster-sized steel bins, each holding a little over two tons of scrap. At one time the containers had been painted a bright environmental green, with "Coastal Recycling" stenciled on the sides. In this climate paint didn't stay bright for long.

The MP Corporal climbed up as nimbly as a squirrel. He nodded to Merle to open the top of the first bin.

Merle undid the latch and lifted the steel cover, which gave out a metal-on-metal groan. He didn't have the strength to hold it open, so he shoved hard. The heavy steel lid arced and slammed against the bin behind it. He and the corporal both winced.

Together they looked down at the contents of the bin.

The US Government spent billions of dollars equipping their armed forces, the largest, most technologically advanced, best equipped fighting force in history. Most of it ended up overseas, some destined for war, some for training, some to have just in case, all of it shipped by military transport, the most reliable and expensive method possible.

In the battlefields of the country's current conflicts, hard to pronounce places in the Middle East, this equipment was destroyed by men armed with little more than small arms and homemade bombs.

Further risking American lives, the army collected everything it could from the battlefield and shipped it back to the United States lest something usable fall into the hands of the enemy. Back in the USA, the wreckage was dismantled, sorted, and scrapped.

The Department of Defense had mandated recycling programs, ostensibly to help the environment. To stimulate local economies, they hired nearby contractors to separate the debris into steel, aluminum, various copper-based alloys, plastic and glass. Local contractors then sold and shipped the metals to industries, usually in Japan, India, Brazil, Mexico and China.

The plan looked good on paper and was an easy sale to DOD Appropriations.

Under the streetlights Merle Cuthbert and the MP Corporal stared into the container.

Merle didn't like looking at the stuff. All the patriotism in the world could not keep the thought out of his head, we must be losing.

All that expensive technology lay bent, shredded and chopped up like corn stalks in a silo, discards from battlefield, still coated with the residue of fighting men on both sides, smelling of their blood, sweat, tears, and vomit. America's best and finest lay in tatters to be further rendered into something less demoralizing. And the quicker it was removed from sight, and crushed into blocks, the better.

Merle Cuthbert looked over at the MP. The young corporal's face had gone colorless except his cheekbones glowed with hot red circles. He darted his flashlight over the stinking pile. His training had not prepared him for undeniable evidence of how rough it was over there.

Merle thought, you fool… you probably voted for the idiot in the White House. I voted for the last one.

The corporal jumped down from the truck bed like a paratrooper. Merle closed the bin and secured the latch. Stiff knees and a hitch in his back forced an ungainly descent.

"The rest of these containers... same stuff?"

Merle bit off a sarcastic reply. "Yes, Corporal... like it says in the paperwork."

"Well, I guess I officially inspected it," the corporal said, and waved his arm to the other guards.

"Let 'em go!"

Merle folded the manifest and put it in his shirt pocket.

When he got back in the truck, Donnie asked, "What was all that about?"

Merle didn't look at him. "Shut up, Donnie."

He revved the diesel and let out the clutch. With twelve tons of scrap behind them, the big flatbed bucked and jerked into an uneasy motion that smoothed out as the they picked up speed.

Merle drove east on Highway 84, through the quiet part of Hinesville. At that time of the night, they encountered little traffic.

Donnie kept silent for a while, but Merle saw him fidgeting. When he took a deep breath, Merle shot him a look, but Donnie's impulses always trumped Merle's looks.

"Merle, how much longer we gonna..."

Merle spoke in an urgent whisper, "Shut your damn mouth!"

"I mean, geeze, we don't know who this stuff goes to... terrorists or drug dealers."

Merle fought his own impulses... the urge to backhand his brother like he had done when they were kids.

"Donnie. Shut. Up!" Merle twisted in his seat toward his brother. The steering wheel jerked following his move, and the truck's right-side wheels slid off the pavement. Both men bounced in their seats. Gravel gurgled under the tires. Viciously, Merle spun the wheel left. They both bounced again.

"Don't kill us, for Christ sake!"

The big flatbed staggered, smoothed out, and the darkness erased all witnesses. Donnie refolded his arms and slumped in his seat.

They took a couple of shortcuts onto smaller country roads. The cloudy, moonless night quickly swallowed the truck and its yellowing headlights. Only a few windows glowed along this lonely stretch. They eventually turned onto Highway 17, the US Coastal road that weaves along both sides of Interstate 95.

Up ahead the sky lit up as they approached an underpass for I-95. No fewer than five gas stations, a McDonalds and a Subway surrounded the exit, but darkness soon swallowed them again.

A mile later Merle slowed the truck to make the turn onto Harris Neck Road.

They headed east toward the Atlantic Ocean.

Harris Neck Road was even lonelier than Highway 17. The truck's headlights lit up a few Spanish moss draped Live Oaks and stretches of coastal marsh. The road dead-ended at a vine covered brick gateway that looked like a crumbling relic of the plantation era. Just beyond the gateway a giant tree grew out of the middle of the road. Merle carefully squeezed the truck around it.

He doused the headlights. They proceeded at a walking pace, and Merle peered through the bug-splattered windshield, trying to keep the truck on the road in near-total darkness. The road surface, corrugated by late winter rains, set up a rough vibration that the truck's aged sus-pension could not dampen.

The truck approached another gateway, this one offered a nautical flair, stout pilings wrapped in heavy rope and a perching plastic pelican. A sign announced, "Barbour River Yacht Club – Members Only."

The 'so called' yacht club.

Merle could barely make out boatyard buildings, scattered empty boat trailers, a few pickup trucks and cars belonging to the people who lived on nearby Barbour Island.

Merle pulled the truck on to a large concrete semi-circle next to the boat lift.

He checked his watch. They were thirty minutes late. He couldn't imagine what punishment awaited them, but damn, it wasn't his fault! He backed the truck up near the edge where the concrete met the dark Barbour River and shut off the engine.

They sat in silence for a minute. Absorbed in his headphones Donny laid his head back.

Out of the silence, Merle heard footsteps rushing toward them. He kept his eyes forward, staring at the nothingness beyond the glass.

Merle felt and heard minor vibrations from the back of the truck. Someone opened the hidden door of container number four, which was not the one he had opened for the guard at Fort Stewart. He heard number four's door slide shut.

Their instructions at this point were to wait and listen for the outboard motor, give it another fifteen minutes and then he and Donnie were free to go.

Someone came up and rapped his window. Merle jumped like he had been poked with a stick.

"Merle, you and Donnie get out here," said a deep voice.

Merle's heart hammered in his chest.

"What the...?" Donnie said.

Donnie's door flew open, and strong hands yanked him out like a ragdoll.

On his side a giant pulled Merle out, forced him to the concrete, and pressed a giant's foot against his backbone... heavy... irresistible. The air whooshed out of his lungs. He heard Donnie thump to the concrete a few feet away.

Donnie cursed but a muted thump silenced him. His heavy breath morphed into the staccato panting of a winded dog.

Merle knew they were in for it... being late, Donnie's mouth... he broke their very strict rules. Merle could do nothing... about Donnie, just a quick prayer they would survive.

The low voice spoke in his ear, "Merle. I don't want you to talk. I'll get the Barn to let up on your back a little but you got to be still. Okay?"

Merle nodded rasping his face against the concrete. The foot eased off his back. He took a breath.

"Jesus… God damnit…" Donnie's voice.

Merle thought, "Please, Donnie, shut up.

Thunk! Donnie fell silent.

"Donnie, don't talk or I'll whack you again. This is a genuine Colt AR 15 rifle, six pounds of the best gun ever made. A round from this old Colt can splatter your brains like a jar of salsa, and it's buttstock pretty good for bashing heads… like a teaching aid for them that don't know what 'no talking' means."

His voice… they both had heard it before, but they were more used to dealing with 'The Barn,' the big guy who had his foot on Merle's back. Nobody really wanted to talk to Ricky Lee.

"Donnie, I'm getting to where I just don't know what to do with you. Merle over here is a hundred times smarter. He follows rules. But you Donnie… Your brother tried to get you to shut up, but you don't listen. Now I got to tune you up a little.

"I have a rule about talking when you're on a run, but you just can't keep your goddamned mouth shut. You want to know how I know you was talking? I bugged your truck. I also put a tracker on it. I got to know where this truck is at all times. I'll need a head start if the Feds ever get on to you. Now listen up, you idiot. If I can bug your truck, so can the Feds.

"You-all's supposed to be carrying a load of scrap. Feds are gonna wonder why you're in a hurry, what's the rush, you know? So you can't go talking about being late. Can you understand why I don't want the feds thinking about it? They're going to wonder, where they going that's so important? Who're they meeting up with? That's why you can't say nothing. Don't give 'em nothing to think about.

"Now what is it I hear you say? You want to know about terrorists and drug dealers? Are you shitting me? You think we're stealing army blankets for the homeless? Don't say nothing.

"You boys got it pretty good. You think your daddy scrap yard made you rich? Hell, you Cuthberts ain't smart enough to piss and miss your shoes. I worked on this deal for two fucking years. Got you the money to buy the metal compactor and got you contacts to sell the steel. You're making out like bandits and you ain't had to do shit.

"Merle's sends his daughters to that fancy private school. And you Donnie, you got a new truck, a new boat and new piece of tail, that skanky broad with the saggy tits. You dumb-fucks didn't do a damn thing to earn it, and all that stuff could go away. What'll you do then, huh?

"So, stop thinking about drug dealers. All you got to know is you get paid lots of money for driving a truck and selling scrap.

"And Donnie, you're only in that truck because it's a federal contract and they want two people. Not one. If you want to be the guy in that truck, then shut your mouth. Now in a day or so, you'll meet up with Barn and he'll hand you a big wad of money. You can take your skank girlfriend shopping and we won't tell your wife.

"But Donnie, you're gonna need a little tough love. It's either tough love or Harris Neck Dead. You know what that is, Donnie? It's something old Hank Baxter dreamed up. He was sheriff when we was all in grade school, a real, old-time high sheriff. He ran this county and everybody in it. My daddy worked for him. From time to time he had to set an example, let people know who not to fuck with.

"I puked first time I saw it... I never seen a man's body all tore up like that. You get stripped naked and your hands tied behind your back. Then we stick your feet through a concrete block, wrap a float around your neck and drop you out in the marsh where the water don't get too high. The float keeps your head up, so you don't drown and your feet stay anchored to the bottom. Won't take the crabs long to find you. Crabs have been around millions of years. Humans are just a piece of meat to them. They go for the eyes and the balls first. Ever have a crab nibbling on your privates? It's quite a sight, a man covered up in crabs, all scrambling to find a piece of to hold onto. Blood oozing, innards spilling out. Soon the tide brings in the little sharks, not much longer than a couple of feet. They get all worked up and jump out of the water like dolphins. You can scream all you want. Nobody'll hear you. Not out on the marsh. You're dead and you know it... just takes a day or so. Then the word gets around that you fucked with the wrong dude.

"This deal is too good to have you bring it all down. So, we don't need Harris Neck Dead do we, Donnie? Don't say nothing. I know you can hear me."

"The barrel of this AR15 has a front sight that's like a little hatchet, perfect for notching your ear. There. You feel it, don't you? Cold steel against your earlobe?"

Donnie hissed.

Whack! A pause. Whack!

Merle winced but it wasn't his ear that got notched.

"Aarrraghhh..." Donnie fell silent.

"That's good, Donnie. You'll be quiet now."

Merle heard a faint scuffling of feet, and in another minute the start of a big outboard motor. A big boat zoomed off. The sound receded, and wake of the boat sloshed the river against the marsh grass waving unseen in the darkness.

Merle helped his weeping brother into the truck.

CHAPTER 2

"How did you ever find this place?"

Somewhere between Atlanta and Shellman Bluff, Georgia
From the Journal of Brendan Macbean:
"You're going to ask that question. Everybody does. Right after you turn off Highway 17 onto Harris Neck Road."

William Rawlings' words echoed in my head, and he had nailed the timing too... the question popped into my head just after I turned onto Harris Neck Road.

A few weeks ago, a cold, wet Saturday in February, I attended a literary conference where I shared a table with the bestselling author. We had met at this event several times before and enjoyed a good, "same time next year" friendship. Usually it meant an extended happy hour on Friday and whispering jokes to each other during the conference dinner the following night. Then he'd drive his silver Cadillac back to Sandersville, and I wouldn't see him until next year. We'd scatter a few emails in between, mostly him sending me an announcement of a new William Rawlings' novel or some award he'd won.

Our annual meeting took place at "Murder Goes South" organized by The Friends of the Smyrna Library in Smyrna, Georgia, a bustling suburb of Atlanta. To celebrate the genre, the "Friends" invited notable

Southern authors and fans of mystery and suspense novels. Although far from notable, they welcomed me at this event. I was semi-known as a local TV newscaster and because years ago I actually had written a 'true crime' book about a vicious criminal.

Rawlings and I shared the table in the conference bookstore. His novels took up most of the space, but he graciously allowed me a little room for my own out-of-print title.

I asked him, "This place of yours, is it that far off the beaten path?"

He pondered my question a little longer than necessary.

"You're missing the point, City-boy. It might seem a little out of the way when you'll realize how far out of your comfort zone you are."

"Really, Rawls? A three-hundred-mile drive across the state of Georgia won't do that?"

"Not hardly. When you leave Route 17, the Coastal Highway, you leave behind interstates, convenience stores and streetlights. You're no longer surrounded by five million people and you won't have the steady rap of traffic to lull you to sleep. At my place there's no phone, no cable TV, no internet."

I let my cynicism morph into derision. "And a moon on the bathroom door. Wow! I can't wait!"

He gave me a disgusted look. "No, Macbean. It's not primitive, just rural. There's indoor plumbing, running water, air-conditioning."

"It *is* the South. We need AC," I added.

"For many generations, our ancestors made do without it. My place is a comfortable little house in a lovely setting, but you have to drive on a dirt road to get there."

"Okay, Rawls. And why do I need this?"

"You're gloomy, Macbean. I don't know what happened to you since last year, but it's different. You're different. Your rapier wit has lost its repartee and your sarcasm has gone to seed. You're in a fugue of some kind. You keep drifting off into melancholy introspection, like you're trying to explain yourself to yourself. It's obvious to me, this city-life ain't working for you. You need a few days at my cottage.

Rawlings had peeled a key off his key ring and handed it to me. It felt hot and heavy in my hands, like a lump of kryptonite might feel to Superman.

His cottage was located in Coastal Georgia, in a no-man's land between Savannah and Simons Island, an unknown stretch of coast between two very popular destinations. In my former life as a TV reporter I had traveled all over the South but somehow had missed McIntosh County, the town of Townsend, or the seashells of Shellman Bluff.

Rawls may have hit the nail on my head, but I never appreciated being pegged, so for no good reason I dawdled for a couple of weeks before separating myself from my comfort zone in Atlanta, my Mac-mansion, as he called it, my bunker for gloomy introspection and sarcasm gone to seed.

Heading south on I-75 I left Atlanta driving my brand-new Toyota Land Cruiser, which had been specially prepared as a fire service command truck for the Smyrna Fire Department. The Smyrna Fire Department had ordered it as a fire chief's car and the enthusiastic engineers at Fouts Brothers had mistakenly built two for them. I got wind of it and bought the extra one. All Smyrna city logos and EMS lettering had been removed. I kept the red and white color scheme and gleaming gold pinstriping as well as the special equipment. The previous year I had fallen in love with a luxurious Mercedes sedan and had vowed to get myself one, but when this quirky opportunity came along, I jumped at it.

In Macon, I refueled and grabbed a hamburger from Five Guys. I couldn't eat more than half of it, so I re-wrapped the remainder for later.

I drove I-16 east toward Savannah, passing places like Dublin, Dexter, Vidalia, and Statesboro.

The Land Cruiser provided an exceptional ride, a commanding view high above the pavement, surprisingly quiet and extremely comfortable, and a bonus... the streaking red fire chief special seemed to be on a mission. The highway cops gave me a pass.

I approached I-95 feeling a temptation to cruise straight into Savannah. I could dine at Garibaldi's and get a sundae at Leopold's. I could stay at the Foley House Inn and listen to the creak of old ghosts prowling the place at night. I had enjoyed all these things in the past. Savannah was wonderful, picturesque… comfortable.

That word again. Staying in my comfort zone refuted the purpose for making this trip, whereas plunging on toward my destination seemed healthy and stretching.

So, plunging on is what I did, heading south on I-95, that great river of commerce stretching from Maine to Miami. But for the next thirty miles or so, temptation hit me again… the thought of continuing on to Saint Simons Island, another place of good food, comfort, and safety. But Rawls would never let me live it down if I didn't at least spend a night at his cottage.

I crossed a body of water identified as the Ogeechee River. The sunset splashed vivid gold and red on the wind rippled water.

Pretty.

Afterward clouds rolled in and the night fell hard. Overcast and moonless, darkness presided over my exodus from the civilized world. The landscape swapped shadows between coastal forest and miles of marshland. The interstate exits were well lit, but everything in between brooded murky and unknown. I drove across long, low bridges, their sole purpose to traverse what looked like vast swamps. And then another patch of forest, trees lit only by my headlights, seeing nothing beyond the range of their light. At one stretch, a mile off to my right a paper mill lit up the night like a Hollywood premier. My GPS identified the facility as "INT PAPR" and offered nothing further.

I finally saw signs for exit 67, "South Newport" and "Harris Neck Wildlife Refuge".

I wondered what South Newport was. Nowhere on the GPS screen did I see a reference to Newport, north or south.

The exit itself was a blaze of light with no less than five gas stations, plus a Subway and a McDonald's. Less than a half mile past the exit total darkness returned. I crossed a bridge with a sign that said, "South Newport River" so I figured there must be a North Newport River. My GPS said I passed a landmark called, "The Smallest Church in America" but when I looked, I saw nothing. It must be tiny and of course no lights.

Ahead a sign loomed, "Harris Neck Wildlife Refuge" and an arrow pointing left.

I turned left on Harris Neck Road, which stretched out into a dark and featureless unknown.

I said out loud, "Rawls, how did you ever find this place?"

And he was not there to say, "I told you so."

The Toyota's headlights showed little beyond their light, like the rest of the world had vanished. The darkness unsettled me. Rawls was right, city-boys were used to streetlights.

Nine miles of asphalt and glimpses of forest and marsh told me nothing about where I was headed. Occasional mailboxes, dirt roads leading off to nowhere.

I flashed past another paved road labeled by a sign that said, "Youngman Rd." and my silly brain started singing the old song by the Village People. Another road, dirt this time, said "Green Acres" and my brain lit up the theme from the 1960's TV series. I passed the entrance to the Harris Neck Wildlife Refuge and the road was suddenly overhung with live oaks trailing curtains of Spanish Moss. My GPS had run out of map, showing just the icon-car dashing over blue creeks and green landscape. Apparently, the GPS services didn't know the extent of Harris Neck Road.

But I knew I had to be getting close. Rawlings' instructions said, "The road veers right at the end of Harris Neck Road... That's Julienton Road, but you keep straight, okay? It's a dirt road, but it's a pretty good dirt road. You'll see an entrance to a place called Gould's Landing. There's a brick wall on both sides of the road. That's the way to the cottage. Another half mile and you're there."

I slowed the Toyota to a crawl. Ahead I saw the dirt road and the brick gateway.

The road and the vine-covered brick gateway seemed like relics from the set of a horror movie. I could almost feel the movie audience shifting in their seats, saying, "Don't go in there!"

I drove in there anyway. Just beyond the entrance, a large tree grew out of the center of the dirt road. Apparently, whoever built the road chose to flow it around the tree instead of cutting it down.

Good call, I guess.

As dirt roads go, this one wasn't too bad. Not too many potholes, but it did have ripples from rain and heavy use. The half mile went quickly. The road turned to the left. Immediately there was a high, white privacy fence with a gate.

My destination.

I pulled the Land Cruiser directly toward the closed gate and got out. I saw a sign on the gate showing a cartoon rendering of a Rottweiler at high alert. The caption said, "The dog can make it to the gate in 5 seconds. How fast are you?"

This was William Rawlings' sense of humor. He would put the sign up just to keep trespassers from opening the gate. But it made me hesitate. As I lifted the latch and opened the gate, I listened for the pounding paws of a large, snarling dog.

There was no dog. The gates swung wide enough for the Toyota to enter. I had been told to leave them open so the neighbors would know I was here.

Neighbors? If there were neighbors, I saw no sign. No outside lights. No inside lights shining through windows. Early to bed neighbors, maybe, but here I was in total darkness. Dark sky above and dark earth below. City-boys aren't used to zero light. In the city there's always some light somewhere. There's always some noise, too. Somewhere. But here and now, I heard nothing but the Toyota's engine.

I scrambled back inside the Land Cruiser.

Inside the gate it felt like I was driving through a tunnel. I crept along twin tire tracks over bare dirt strewn with fallen tree limbs. A utility shed appeared in shadows on the left and I slowed to check it out. Is this where I'm sleeping tonight? No, it couldn't be. Rawlings wouldn't send me totally across the state to sleep in a shed.

I continued down the path and wondered how far a Rottweiler could run in five seconds.

And then I saw the house.

From the Toyota's headlights, I could see it appeared to be a two-car garage with an apartment on top. It looked like someone had built it with a larger project in mind, maybe part of a multi-building compound, a grander house with a separate garage apartment for the in-laws. They never got around to the larger house.

But it looked neat and compact, as much as I could tell in the darkness. There were no lights on in the building. I parked with the Toyota's headlights angled on the door, got out and opened the place up using the key Rawlings had given me. Inside I found plenty of light switches and turned them all on.

Porchlights and interior lights blazed, and I felt immediate relief.

I returned to the Land Cruiser, retrieved my duffle, backpack and half Five Guys hamburger and took it all upstairs.

It was small but nice, the size of a modest hotel suite, kitchen on the right, living room on the left. The living room contained a large over-stuffed easy chair and ottoman and a loveseat of the same design. The far wall was dominated by bookshelves which included a plethora of books, and a small TV.

The kitchen had all the necessaries, including a side by side refrigerator. I opened the right side and saw that it was empty except... ketchup and mustard and a bottle of salad dressing and a whole shelf dedicated to Heineken.

Bless your heart, William Rawlings! A typical, stupid-guy-thing, I arrived having brought no provisions for staying here, like food. Or beer.

I grabbed a bottle and rummaged through a drawer until I found an opener.

That first swig was amazing. A sensation overwhelmed me... the relief of a marooned man who at least had a cold beer.

The kitchen had a breakfast bar, with a large rectangle in the wall opening to the living room. Lying on the breakfast bar was a red plastic three-ring binder with the commanding title, "Read First!"

I opened the notebook. There were about a dozen tabs, "Water, The Mule, Green with Envy, Harris Neck WMA" and something spelled E-

U-L-O-N-I-A. I had no idea about any of this, but Rawlings thought it important, red binder, exclamation point and all.

The first page said, "Friend, there is no guest book to sign. You are already rated among the few people deemed have enough sense to enjoy my place in all its glory. This notebook contains information about the area and a few points of interest. You may want to discover some of this on your own. Your choice, but you should read at least the first tab. Enjoy yourself and let me know what you think."

It was signed by Rawls himself, his book signing scrawl looking like he had writer's cramp.

Best Selling Authors' problems.

I flipped the page and read "Water."

"Water comes from a well located near the front of the property. The water from this well has been tested and is not only safe to drink, but actually good for you, healthy and full of interesting minerals.

"We turn off the water heater when the place isn't occupied, so if you're into hot water, go downstairs and turn it on. The water heater and electrical panel are on the southwestern corner of the downstairs. Breaker number seven, the only one tripped, I hope.

"Our water contains minute levels of sulfate, a naturally occurring combination of sulfur and oxygen. Sulfate tends to concentrate in the hot water tank when it's unused for a while. This means when you take your first shower or two you might notice a slight "paper mill" smell. This will go away very quickly, but I wanted you to know. It *will* go away.

"Water straight from the tap makes the finest cup of coffee I've ever tasted, so enjoy.

"Before you head home your penultimate act will to be to turn breaker seven off. Your last act will be to run out and take a final look at the marsh."

Rawlings was pretty optimistic about his guests liking the place. So, I went downstairs, found the electrical panel and the large-capacity water heater and got the whole thing operational with the flip of a switch. A hot shower sounded pretty good.

The water heater crackled with energy.

I gave the rest of the garage a brief survey. No room for a car but everything else seemed to be there. Present were all kinds of lawn equipment, another refrigerator, a large wine cellar, a laundry and even a shower and toilette built under the staircase. Anybody who gets all marsh-muddy can wash off before they go upstairs.

Back upstairs, I retrieved my half-consumed Heineken and headed for the bedroom.

I flipped on the light and immediately a ceiling fan began to groan and rotate like a Depression-era relic. The bedroom was compact and spotless. I felt a definite feminine touch with pale-yellow walls and white trim. I pulled back the silk comforter and discovered the queen-sized bed unmade. Well, my momma taught me how to do that. All I had to do was find the sheets.

The sheets were found in a coastal style, whitewashed armoire, full of high thread-count cotton bed-clothes of the best quality. I made the bed and began to feel my body's reaction to the long drive. Finish the beer, take a shower and hit the sack… sounded like a plan.

The bathroom seemed to be all Mrs. Rawlings, a woman I'd never met but now, for whom I felt a growing appreciation. Bold, gold fixtures, a huge mirror rimmed with dimmable Hollywood lights over a Travertine marble countertop. On my left was a beautiful Jacuzzi bathtub, big enough two, if they were friendly.

Rawls, you old dog!

The bathroom had been scrubbed and accessorized like it belonged in a posh bed and breakfast. Both the sink and tub held unopened boxes of *L'Occitane en Provence, Savon pur vegetal*, which from my vast Francophile experience, I knew to be the good stuff.

Back the bedroom, I took a peek into a walk-in closet and found a collection of Rawlings' summer clothes. On the eastern wall of the bedroom was French doors, presumably where one would find a marsh view, if there was one.

I unlocked and opened them.

With the bedroom lights on, whatever might be viewed behind the retractable screen was completely hidden. I went back to the wall switch and turned off the lights, plunging myself into total darkness again.

Well, not total darkness, but let's call it near-total. Some ambient light from an unknown source provided barely enough visibility to shuffle back to the French doors.

A heavy tree canopy below a moonless night, a gentle, cool breeze floated through the screen bringing the scent of the marsh, a sharp salt tang, mixed with a musky, acidic, somehow prehistoric odor.

But that wasn't the main event. I had heard tree frogs and crickets before, but never in such profusion. An amazing wall of noise battered my ears. Every voice in the amphibian and insect world and every noise on every pitch within and beyond human range: buzzes, chirps, yelps, screams, cries, staccato taps, and snaps, crackles and pops, loud in their urgency to be heard. Sounds more numerous than the stars in the hidden sky, everywhere, overreaching my ability to discern them.

Man, at the top of the food chain, suddenly confronted with millions of creatures utterly ignoring him, carrying on as they had for millions of years.

Okay, in a few seconds it went from confusing to interesting and eventually a pleasant white noise, calming... and besides, there wasn't a thing I could do about it. A great deal of my comfort came from the thin screen between me and the wilderness, my protection against the profusion of unknown beasts and critters outside.

A grand end-of-the-day ceremony followed: a hot shower in the fabulous Jacuzzi tub, a L'Occitane scrub-down and a rubdown with one of Rawlings' thick cotton towels. It was time to shut off the lights and slide into bed.

My head sunk slowly into a marvelous pillow that seemed programmed to erase gravity. My eyes stared wide into near total darkness with the tree-frog cacophony carrying on outside. The mild breeze had cooled and freshened the room considerably. The comfort of Rawlings' bed was gargantuan, a magical blend of firmness and support. I vowed to get one just like it if I ever returned to civilization.

Not when but if... where did that come from?

Rawlings... the guy was a genius, diagnosing my gloominess and ordering me to a change of scene, this place, and I had fought so hard to retain my gloominess and isolation with all the fear my timid soul could muster.

I give Rawlings credit. After scaring the city-boy crap out of me, he had delivered what he promised.

I felt better than I had in months, and in total cozy comfort, I slid into sleep with a smile on my face.

Something woke me an hour later... maybe two... who knew? It had brought me out of a real deep sleep... something had alarmed my subconscious. I felt it.

The room retained its near-total darkness. And quiet. The frog symphony had ended. Only the sound of the gentle breeze rattling a few leaves remained.

No, there was something else, a sound any city-boy would be familiar with, only out of place here.

A diesel engine. Just one. Idling, clattering away somewhere nearby.

Approaching? Maybe.

The truck seemed to be barely moving. My eyes scanned the darkness of the room for reflections of headlights flashing across the walls and ceiling.

Nothing. No light bounced off the walls. Yet the sound grew louder... a big truck coming.

I had heard that sound carries over water. Maybe the truck was too far away to see the headlights. No, that couldn't be it. There was nothing to the east but marsh and ocean, and this wasn't a boat. I could hear the tires crunching on gravel and the blowing of a radiator fan.

I remained in bed, holding on to my comfort and safety. With nothing to see outside but utter blackness, why get up?

And now louder, the sound of the big diesel.

I reached over to feel my black nylon backpack. It hung on the bedpost, exactly where I put it.

I chided myself. The boogie man wouldn't come in a diesel truck. I didn't know who it was, but it didn't sound like it was pulling into the driveway. In fact, the noise receded a little, grew fainter and finally stopped... like the truck had gone out of earshot.

Or it stopped and the driver turned the engine off.

Well, I was fully awake now, wondering if I would ever go back to sleep. My curiosity was like a machine. Trucks in the night were common in the city. The city never sleeps, but out here in the country?

Some time passed. Rawlings didn't keep clocks in his bedroom, so I don't know how much time.

Then I heard the sound of another engine, this time I was pretty sure it wasn't a truck. Maybe a big outboard, a modern smooth-running engine. The boat motor idled for a few minutes and then roared away like the devil chased it.

And the explanation came to me.

Barbour Island. Two miles away on the Barbour River. The only way to get there was by boat and airplane. Somebody drove up to the Barbour River Yacht Club, got in their boat and headed for the island. At night? I guess so. What did I know about the comings and goings of the locals?

Then I heard the diesel start up and slowly drive away. Again, no lights. Curious.

So, someone dropped someone else off, who got into their boat in the middle of the night and headed out to the island. The truck driver kept the lights off and drove slowly so as to not wake up the neighbors.

Except me. Maybe, because I was a little spooked by being in a strange place. And all the neighbors were familiar with the comings and goings of the Barbour Island folks.

And maybe because the truck didn't want to attract any attention.

Humans must have an explanation for everything.

CHAPTER 3

"On-again, Off-again"

Gould's Landing, Townsend, Georgia
From the Journal of Brendan Macbean:

Again, something woke me... but not quite "awake" awake.

More a state of drowsy relaxation, eyes closed, shallow breathing, no tension. My body nestled deeply into that marvelous mattress and pillow as if I had been melted down and recast during the night into a new me. I didn't open my eyes but lay there enjoying total comfort and an absence of agenda, worry or responsibility.

Rawlings had been right. I needed this. Somehow the night had refreshed both mind and bod, and I felt eager to see a new day. Perhaps a day of exploration and adventure.

I could allow myself a healthy dose of both. I was in Rawlings' cottage, the little house on the edge of the marsh on a part of the Georgia coast that neither Google Maps nor Garmin knew much about.

Maybe nobody could find me, but I didn't worry about that. I could stay lost for a few days.

I breathed deeply the cool air blowing in from the open French doors, that spicy smell I sensed last night, forest and marsh.

It was still dark, but I could see the outline of objects in the room, the open door, the armoire, unmoving ceiling fan above me, but little else that was familiar and where no phone, cable TV or internet could reach me.

The sun was coming, but it was not up yet.

I made a quick decision to go watch the dawn over the marsh. And I had no idea if the lay of the land would even allow it.

But first I needed coffee. My warm feet hit the cold floor, and I stumbled on stiff legs into the kitchen. The wall-switch gave me a fanfare of light. I spied a coffee maker on the counter with a coffee grinder sitting next to it.

Fresh ground coffee! Excellent, Rawls!

I opened up the freezer and saw an entire shelf devoted to his coffee collection, which seemed to represent every continent... Central and South America, Asia, Africa, all marked with bold names like Yirgacheffe, Tarrazu, Altura, Double A and Triple A. I saw one plain, paper bag on which the word "blend" had been scrawled in thin pencil. I don't know what "blend" meant, but wondered, could Rawlings be hiding something?

I threw on sweatpants, baseball hat, shirt and my Nikes and then studied the big map on the wall while the fancy Breville coffee maker gargled the brew. "Blend" gave out a marvelous aroma.

The map showed a good portion of the surrounding area, including the Harris Neck Wildlife Refuge, the South Newport River, the Barbour River, Barbour Island, and Sapelo Sound, where Saint Catherine's, Blackbeard and Sapelo Islands framed the very large inlet.

The coffee maker beeped at me.

My backpack had too much stuff in it. I took out my Yeti rambler and my laptop. I left the Redhawk in the backpack where it belonged.

I filled the Yeti with "blend" and headed for the marsh and the dawn.

Outside, the pre-dawn gloom showed Rawlings' yard had plenty of trees. The path from the house to the marsh was visible, but the yard was in terrible condition. Fallen limbs, brush, leaves and uncut grass as high as my knees cluttered the yard. A giant limb twenty feet long and a foot in diameter lay across the path. It was too large for me to move without a chain saw. Briefly I wondered if this was Rawlings' purpose in sending me here… yardwork as repayment for a few days in paradise. Probably not… this place never heard of yardwork.

The marsh stretched out as far as I could see. A tiny sliver of red-gold sun peeked over the tree line on Barbour Island, two miles away.

The water's edge of Rawlings' property had no water. Instead there was a mud hole fully one hundred feet long and fifty feet wide and about four feet deep. I assumed it was low tide. I wondered what it would look like at high tide. A lake? The mud hole seemed to be alive with… well, in the dim light it took a minute to sort out what it was. There were hundreds of little black crabs scurrying around, crab-walking all over the mud.

Just a few feet off the path there was a wooden porch swing suspended from stout wood beams. I brushed the twigs and leaves off the swing and sat down facing east.

During my long career as a television journalist, I had traveled all over the state of Georgia, but not so much on the Georgia Coast. Certainly, I had visited Savannah and further south, Saint Simons Island, but here between those two destinations lay the heart of the Georgia salt marsh. And I really didn't know much about it. But as the Earth turned toward the sun a portion of the vast expanse of marsh lay revealed before me. It was a huge area… the distant tree line of Barbour Island was miles away and in between was nothing but marsh grass, mud channels, creeks and lagoons.

In its simplicity the marsh was quite beautiful. And kind of dark and forbidding. Man could not cross the marsh without a boat. The tall grass gave the marsh a uniform appearance, but it had to be a tough plant living in salt water.

The sliver of sun rising over the distant horizon showed pink and then gold. Wisps of mist floated over the sea of grass like lost cloudlets. The light racing across the marsh turned the mist to shades of red and then gold and then… poof! It vanished.

Wow.

To my right a flock of birds, maybe fifty of them flew in a ragged V formation, white wading birds, their legs stretched out behind them. As they flew overhead, I could hear the strain of their beating wings, whines of feathers cutting the air. Flying through the changing light changed them as well, pink then gold. And then they were white again. And then they were gone.

Wow.

I took a sip of "blend" from the Yeti. Smoky, salty, exquisite brown nectar, a most perfect coffee flavor spread across my mouth like a sensuous dream. I felt like a trespasser, like I accidently wandered into some kind of opium den where coffee fanatics lay about in a haze sipping "blend" from tiny porcelain cups staring at me bleary-eyed with caffeine dreams rippling through their cerebellums.

Rawls had cleverly tried to hide this concoction by putting it in a plain bag, but he must have spent a fortune on each bean. Which I had pilfered.

I took another sip and smiled. "I'll never get invited here again."

The first half of the sun lifted over the marsh bathing the brown-green tops of the grass with warm light. Water seeped into the mud basin from the right.

It seemed like nature was putting on a show for my benefit. It was working. I couldn't remember when I have felt so strong a sense of well-being.

I heard a loud "Huff!" It sounded exactly like a guard-dog coming to high alert, a prelude to a snarling, furious charge. The sign on the front gate with a picture of a Rottweiler, sprang into my head. "...from the house to the gate in 5 seconds" and I wondered how long it took to get from the house to the marsh.

But the sound wasn't coming from behind me but more toward the marina, where the Barbour River came close to the land. I looked in that direction

In the sparkling water, I saw two glistening, finned backs break the surface. Another "huff!" sounded and a misty plume rose from their exhales."

Oh, dolphins. Bettye loves dolphins.

And before I could stop it, my left hand reached out to touch the woman who wasn't there.

Bettye, the on-again, off-again love of my life.

I met Bettye years ago and we fell in love, a love so powerful it swept us away, despite the obvious design-flaws in our relationship. She was a beautiful, sophisticated Parisian woman, while I, born and raised in Atlanta, a card-carrying member of the middle class. Love made us ignore differences of class, nationality and geography. Every trip across the Atlantic was like a honeymoon and when we had to return home alone, we burned up our phone minutes like there were no limits. Our reunions were endless hugs, kisses and love-making, our separations painful and tear-stained.

But the real world has a way of wearing down such intensity as if it didn't matter. As if it never mattered.

What were we thinking? I couldn't ask Betty to leave Paris any more than Bettye could ask me to leave the red clay of Georgia. The frequency of our trips and phone calls diminished like the blips on a terminal patient's heart monitor. The day came too soon when our love flat-lined. We both must have seen it coming but failed to mention to each other. The day came when the phone calls ended. We both waited, expected, needed the other to make the call.

My spectacular morning became quiet and still. I stared at the marsh-grass and reviewed my poorly constructed euphoria of just a few moments ago. How fragile it was, my feeling of well-being. How short it lasted.

To combat the gloom after Bettye and I broke up, I focused on my career. I was popular television reporter, at least to the Atlanta TV viewers. Even the best TV journalists struggle to remain independent from station politics. My efforts to practice free, unbiased journalism often resulted in a layoff, but my popularity usually got me rehired.

Eventually. Sometimes. Who can count on eventually and sometimes?

It was during the time of my deepest sorrow over losing Bettye that I achieved the biggest scoop of my career: the opportunity to interview the most despised man in America, Ray Suffield, the disgraced CEO of the giant petro-conglomerate, InCorps, who with his CFO, Wylie Schram, pulled off the biggest stock swindle of the twenty-first century. Schram died in a car in car crash and Suffield went to prison for the rest of his life. Federal officials kept Suffield away from the media for several years but with pluck and persistence, I was granted access to interview him at the Federal Prison in Louisiana.

And I nailed the interview. On camera, Suffield eventually broke down, apologized, turned emotional and begged forgiveness. It was dramatic, sensational television.

I rook the video back to Atlanta feeling I had really accomplished something. Just like that I saw my career soaring, awards, fame, fortune.

But before the award-winning interview could be broadcast, Betty returned, and she was dying of breast cancer.

Not a word from her for two years... not a phone call, not a letter, not an email.

Now I knew why. She had been fighting her deadly disease for those two years. She had been through chemotherapy, radiation, mastectomy, infusions and finally defeat. Her doctors said further treatments would not work.

My reason for not calling her were cowardly. Of course, I could not know about her cancer, but I had been afraid. Fear is what made us part without saying goodbye. And all the time I nurtured my ego, Bettye fought for her life.

Alone.

Her last act of defiance against the disease was to beg me to come to Switzerland with her, to a special clinic where she could die while someone she loved held her hand and cried.

Did I have that kind of courage? What could I do? What should I do?

I stood on the brink of all the success I could dream of and suddenly had my priorities reset. My stunning achievement... I dumped it all in the lap of Shelby Chadwick, the stunningly beautiful, ambitious, local TV celebrity who everyone knew was destined for greatness. Video experts could edit her into my interview and erase me completely. America would love her doing the interview a lot more than me.

That afternoon, Bettye and I flew to Switzerland.

Bettye looked so bad, I didn't think she would make it to the clinic, but she did.

And Bettye didn't die. Whatever magic they worked on her at that clinic... well it worked.

While many women have survived breast cancer after their own doctors had given up on them, Bettye's recovery was meticulously documented. She represented the first success in a long line of specific experimentation, and doctors all over the world wanted to examine her.

Her body still bore the carnage the battle cancer had wrought, but she was still my Bettye, the on-again, off-again love of my life.

On-again. For a while.

Cancer had taken away her boobs, her beauty, her youth, but I didn't care because we were on-again and that's the greatest magic in the universe.

Except when it is not.

Our situation reminded me of Ray Bradbury's novel "Something Wicked This Way Comes," where the evil carnival master spun his victims around on a magic carousel. Each revolution aged a person a year. The two boys in the story were best friends, both thirteen years old. One of them was tempted onto the ride, and after a single revolution was forever changed.

Those of us who haven't been on the ride, well, we just don't know.

Off-again.

I came home. Back to Georgia. Back to unemployment and a house that lay vacant for nearly a year. I didn't keep track of the days since I left Bettye, the number of days with no phone calls, texts or email. It was just too depressing.

Nothing I could do except try to not feel so bad about it, and remind myself that just a few minutes ago, I felt happy. But then the universe had to give me a couple of dolphins, which brought Bettye back and then my mood drowned in a sorrow that would not go away.

But the universe wasn't through with me.

At the moment the sun cleared Barbour Island, I heard something sneaking up behind me.

CHAPTER 4

"Armadillo in Mourning"

Gould's Landing, Townsend, Georgia
From the Journal of Brendan Macbean:

I turned and saw what looked like a giant football advancing through the brush, pointy end first. Then I saw it had a head, little feet and a tail.

An armadillo, hell-bent on an armadillo's agenda, rush a few feet, pause, head darting, rush a few more feet. He closed the distance, totally unaware of me. Then suddenly he stopped and sniffed the air, not twenty feet away.

I held my breath. I had never seen a live armadillo before. In my travels, I had seen many of them lying on the side of the road. Evolution had perfected the armadillo design one hundred million years before man's ancestors climbed out of the trees, but back then nothing moved as fast as a car. Even more modern critters like possums and raccoons found ducking the automobile a challenge.

One of my former coworkers made a parody about it, from George Straight's paean to the rodeo cowboy, Amarillo by Morning, it became Armadillo in Mourning. "When the sun gets high in the Georgia sky, I'll be lying by the county road..." Well, that was the gist of it.

The armadillo didn't catch my scent and continued on his way. He angled toward the fence separating Rawlings property from the neighbor to the south. Rawlings' lot was fenced on three sides and open on the eastern end where I sat. The fence separating the neighbor to the south was covered by a dark green mesh fabric, probably for privacy. I could see the roof of the neighbor's house but nothing else.

The fence ended at the water's edge, except that at low tide there was four feet of unfenced land. That gap closed with the incoming tide.

The armadillo paused when he arrived at the end of the fence. He seemed to be totally focused on the neighbor's yard, perhaps looking for danger? Who knows what anxieties flow through that scale-covered head?

Apparently, he didn't see anything to worry about and proceeded at a deliberate pace. The armadillo got about five feet into the neighbor's yard when it exploded.

The next thing that happened... well I don't know what the next thing was. I found myself lying face down on the ground, my left hand grabbing leaves and dirt, my right hand inside the nylon backpack firmly gripping the butt of the Redhawk.

My eyes burned with the memory, the brown body of the armadillo rising two feet off the ground and coming apart in red chunks. I hadn't heard a boom or explosion. At least I had no memory of it, but my ears rang like someone had popped an M80 near my head.

Through the ringing I heard a deep male voice and another voice, softer, female. They were at some distance so I could not make out the conversation. And it came to me... the neighbor had shot the armadillo with a high-powered rifle.

I pushed off the ground to my knees, took a deep shaky breath. And another.

"Hey! Stop shooting! There's people down here!" My voice sounded high-pitched but I hope my anger reached the people on the other side of the fence.

Seconds of silence. Then the deep male voice, "Bill? Is that you? I didn't know you were coming down."

Bill? Doctor William Rawlings doesn't like the name, Bill. He prefers William.

I yelled back, "No, not Doctor Rawlings. I'm a friend of his. I'm staying at his place for a few days."

Silence, then a cough. "Well... Bill, didn't tell me anybody was coming."

Really? Does he have to clear it with you? I was beginning to understand the privacy fence. What did Robert Frost say? "Good fences make good neighbors."

The voice again, "You're a friend of Bills? Well, come on up to the house... let's have a look at you."

Huh? Why does he need to 'have a look at me?' On the other side of the fence, I'd have about the same chance as the armadillo.

"Come on. I won't shoot you." I heard a chuckle.

The guy was reading my thoughts. Okay, might as well make friends.

My Yeti had tipped over and leaked all its precious coffee. I put it inside the backpack where it clunked against the Redhawk.

The other side of the fence was a stark contrast to Rawlings' side. Most of the trees were gone, leaving just a few magnificent Live Oaks, their massive trunks surrounded in manicured flowerbeds. There was an expanse of grass that would have made Augusta National proud. A marble fountain percolated in the middle of it all. The house was a smaller than a mansion but very nice, a gray stucco with a silvery metal roof.

A wide, four-pillar porch stretched across the back. On the right side of the porch stood a couple, stiff enough to model for a Grant Wood painting, only this one would have been called, "Southern Gothic." The man cradled a scoped rifle in his right arm and dangled a cigarette in the other hand. The woman had a detached look, staring off at an angle into a realm of her own.

The rifleman was tall, barrel chested but a bit stooped with age. White hair over a mahogany face, tee shirt over cut-off shorts and flip-flops... casual morning dress for this part of the woods.

I really wanted the man to put down the gun, so I walked straight up to him, stretched my lips into a goofy grin and stuck out my hand.

"Hi, I'm Brendan Macbean."

The man looked perplexed for a moment. He could not shake my hand without putting down either the rifle or the cigarette. He decided to put them both down, laying the rifle on a low patio table and stubbing out the cigarette in a messy ashtray.

His big hand gave mine a squeeze.

"I'm Ralph Freeman. This here's Alice."

Alice's dreamy expression disappeared when she turned toward me. She apparently wasn't the hand shaking type. It took a second to figure out what was going on with her. She was about the same age as Ralph, but as thin as a rail. The jogging suit she wore looked like it had once fit a larger woman. Her crew-cut salt and pepper hair and sagging cheekbones told me the story. I had seen lots of women in the last year battling breast cancer. Alice was a survivor. A spark flashed from her eye to mine acknowledging my sudden understanding.

"Ralph, you sure have a beautiful place, a lot different than next door."

He snorted, "Bill's place is a mess. It would take a month and big crew to clean that place up."

Ralph's face formed hard lines talking about the Rawlings cottage. It sounded like a topic to avoid.

"Well, your home is really nice. You from around here?"

"Not really. We're from Douglasville. We've been down here ten years."

"Twelve." Alice chimed in.

"Ten, twelve... Took all that time getting it to where we like it."

"What'd you do in Douglasville?"

"Commercial real estate, but I had to give it up. Couldn't get the rent we wanted. Nobody has a good credit rating any more. We still have property up there we can't sell."

Ralph seemed pleasant enough, unless you were an armadillo.

"What about you, Brad? You're from Atlanta." It wasn't a question.

"Yup."

"What do you do up there?"

Simple question but for some reason it upset me. Most people are proud of what they do for a living. I was when I was a TV reporter. I loved my job. But I gave it up for Bettye. Now I didn't have Bettye or my job and I would probably never get in front of a TV camera again.

But it really surprised me was how Ralph's simple question brought this whole scenario into crystal clarity. I couldn't tell him much. I didn't want him asking questions and more questions.

Ralph gave me this look like, "What? It's a simple question, Brad. What's taking you so long?"

It also bothered me that he got my name wrong, even when I think he's thinking it. Just like he got Dr. Rawlings' name wrong.

I drew a deep breath and blurted it out, "I'm a freelance writer."

"A what?"

"Freelance writer. I write articles for the paper, magazines. Some broadcast copy, radio TV, ads and things."

"Like William Rawlings." Alice chimed in. I was beginning to like this skinny woman.

Ralph looked confused. "What, Bill? He's a... writer?" He said the word like a writer might be less loveable than an armadillo.

I smiled. "Dr. Rawlings is a novelist. He writes novels. Really good ones, too."

"You mean like books? Really?"

Alice folded her arms across her flat chest and looked at him.

"Ralph. We have several of his books inside. Don't you remember he signed them for us?"

"No, I don't remember that at all. I don't think I ever read any book Bill wrote."

"You haven't read a book in fifty years, Ralph." Alice said.

The morning sun gave Ralph's eyes a squint.

"You write for the Atlanta paper?" he asked.

"Sometimes."

"I thought you had to be a communist to write for that paper."

"It used to be that way. Now you can be a socialist or even a Buddhist."

"That's all it is up there. Socialism, racism, crime and traffic."

"Hasn't changed all that much."

He still had a puzzled look on his face and then the lights came on."

"Oh, I get it. Bill Rawlings has you down here to work on the place." Ralph smiled broadly.

Now I was puzzled. What was he trying to say?

"He doesn't let many people down here, give 'em a key and all."

That notebook up in the cottage suggested otherwise. Then it came to me. The discussion on my profession had given Ralph the notion that I didn't make much money, my otherwise bedraggled appearance notwithstanding. Naturally, a well-to-do friend might offer a struggling writer some work to help make ends meet.

Ralphie, old boy, you couldn't be more wrong. He didn't just get my name wrong, and it was to my advantage to let him continue thinking that. No more pesky questions. But one look at Alice and I saw she wasn't buying it. She kept her arms folded and eyed me with suspicion. But silently, like when she figured it out, then she might say something.

Ralph drew a deep breath like he was about to make a speech.

"Brad, I guess you could haul all that wood to the landfill but you don't have a trailer and it's twenty-five miles away. You can't burn it without a permit and you don't have a permit."

"What do you suggest?"

He nodded his head over his left shoulder, a vague gesture imparting neither destination nor direction.

"Stan, across the street. He's got a permit. Haul all the brush to his fire pit and stack the logs up by the woodpile he's got there. He'll burn it for you."

"Really? That's great." I wasn't sure I meant that, but it sounded good and kept the smile on Ralph's face.

"Say, Brad. Why don't you come over there this evening? We usually get a fire going around sunset and sit around solving the world's problems. Bring something to drink unless you like bourbon and diet cola."

I said, "My mother used to drink that but she wouldn't give me any."

Ralph got the joke, or at least he thought he did.

"Okay, Ralph. Thanks for the invite. I'll be happy to come. Now I guess I better get back to my side of the fence. Is there a gate?"

That took the smile off Ralph's face. Boy, this guy is touchy!

"Hell no there's no gate. You think I want to see what's going on over there?"

"I guess you don't." I said.

"You'll have to go back the way you came." He nodded toward the marsh. "And when you get down there, toss that armadillo into the marsh."

"What?"

"Yeah. The crabs will make quick work of it. Otherwise, the buzzards will be landing, shittin' all over my grass."

It ranked right up there with the most preposterous idea of all time, but Ralph looked serious.

Then I got it.

"Ralph, you Douglasville boys like to have fun with us Atlanta city-boys. But I didn't just fall off the turnip truck. The rule's the same all over."

"Rule? What rule?"

"Once you pull the trigger, the fun is over. You'll have to toss your own armadillo."

CHAPTER 5

"A Six-foot Alligator... at Least"

Gould's Landing, Townsend, Georgia
From the Journal of Brendan Macbean:

It was still early when I returned to the cottage.

I had no idea about the time and felt good about that. Early or late was for someone with an agenda. I gave Ralph the impression I was going to clean up Rawlings' yard, but I really didn't have to. Rawlings' yard was a mess. It was the least I could do to clean the place up a little.

I went inside and climbed the stairs.

My phone lay on the counter, deader than a doornail.

How could that be? It was on the car charger all the way down here.

Oh, I wasn't in a cellular reception zone. The phone pings incessantly to find a cell tower and with nothing in range, the phone just wears itself out looking for love. I didn't really need my phone, but just in case I plugged it into the charger.

I had time to get in a run before turning to any nonobligatory yardwork. Knowing nothing about the area, I could get lost, so I consulted the big map on the wall. Harris Neck Wildlife Refuge dominated the location. The refuge formed the north border of the Barbour River Yacht club. A half mile west of Rawlings' house Harris Neck Road swerved south and changed to Julienton Road. It was a curious five-way intersection with two service roads heading into the wildlife refuge and one, Gould's Landing Way dead-ended at the Barbour River Yacht Club.

The best way to not get lost was to return on the same road I ran out on. Thirty minutes out and twenty back and walk the rest of the way as a cool-down. Sounded simple, right?

What I know about myself is if I didn't get a move-on, I'd quickly talk myself out of running at all. So, I changed into my running duds and headed out the door.

No stopping at the bottom of the steps for me. I jogged toward the front gate, passed the Rottweiler sign and headed toward the entrance to Gould's Landing.

I glanced at Stan and Linda's place across the street, where I was supposed to put all the yard cleaning stuff. I had a brief glimpse of a standard ranch and then was immediately overwhelmed by a giant dog zooming past me, rocking my body by the wake of its passing.

No, it wasn't the long-dreaded Rottweiler attack. It was an altogether different kind of dog and maybe the largest dog I had ever seen. This giant canine galloped ahead of me, doing what seemed like fifty miles an hour, his furious paws kicking up clods of dirt and dust.

The encyclopedia in my brain suggested, "Irish Wolfhound" and reminded me the fastest dog in the world could only do about forty-five.

In seconds the wolfhound had a hundred-yard lead. Then he hit the brakes and twirled like a cat. In two giant strides he regained full speed headed straight toward me and...

The dog blasted past me again barely missing my right side. Again, I felt his air-turbulence, and I caught a ripe whiff of dog smell. I didn't have time to think about what it would feel like to collide anything that big going that fast. It would have been fatal. Broken bones at least.

Truly that dog loved to run. I heard the churn of dirt and gravel as he changed directions again. Maybe he was just showing off and needed something to chase.

The dog pulled alongside me, matched my speed, and gave me a look with his shaggy-dog face, as if to say, "Is that all you got, old man?"

In fact, I was probably running faster than usual due to the excitement. So, I ignored his taunt.

The dog was a magnificent animal, his shoulder as high as my waist, his long legs loping effortlessly. He was the color of coffee with cream, a shaggy, unkempt coat with endless burrs, twigs, bits of leaves and caked-on mud. Tears from the corner of his eyes and drool from his mouth streaked his head-fur a dark red. He wore no collar and I wondered how much a purebred Irish Wolfhound cost. It couldn't be cheap. So, who around here would own such an animal and leave it in such a neglected state?

Together, me and the dog ran on down Gould's Landing Way. After he proved he could outrun me, he chose to be my running buddy. I would have conceded the point, if asked.

Houses were sparse on this country road, but we did encounter a giant Largemouth Bass-on-a-post mailbox. I had seen this kind of mailbox before in my travels. In the country, they weren't all that rare. If this was your style, you better get your bass mailbox up before Willie across the road gets the idea. No point in starting a feud.

This particular household also had the more common mailbox-on-a-tall-pole labeled, "Air Mail" and to complete the yard-art trifecta, a sign nailed to a tree that said, "If you can read this, you're in range!" with a cartoon Yosemite Sam squinting down the barrel of a rifle.

The dog and I struggled to contain our laughter. This collection of artifacts left no doubt that we were passing the house of the neighborhood's wit. I hoped to meet him during my visit to see if he could live up to the hype.

A few minutes later the dog and I approached the entrance to Gould's Landing.

The big tree still stood in the middle of the road. The dirt road split around it like a snake swallowing a rat. The dog went right and I went left and we reformed at the brick columned gateway to Gould's Landing.

All manner of vegetation, vines, ferns, lichens, and mold covered the brick columns. The columns weren't old, just un-maintained and projected an image of neglect and decay.

Just past the entrance to Gould's Landing, I came to an intersection of five roads.

Harris Neck Road stretched off to the west. This was the road that brought me here last night.

It swerved to the left and became Julienton Road. Gould's Landing Way was behind me and another road to the northeast, a road that led to the boat landing, a public ramp maintained by the park. A sign next to the road said so… "Boat Ramp."

A sliding steel gate guarded the road north. The gate was open and a sign provided lots of reading material: "Harris Neck Wildlife Refuge – East Gate. Exit Only. No entrance. This gate will automatically close at dark." Below this sign was another sign, "All pets must be leashed."

I looked at the wolfhound, standing beside me. He stared at the sign, and I thought I saw his head move slightly left to right.

"What's a matter, dog? Too many big words?"

The dog turned to look at me and I swear he gave me a very human expression, like "Very funny."

The situation presented a problem. I intended to run in the refuge, but if the dog followed me, I'd be nailed by Ranger Rick for an unleashed pet. Violating federal laws did not fit into my new, low-profile life.

Well, that just couldn't be helped. I ran towards the road into the wildlife refuge.

As I passed the steel gate I glanced over my shoulder at the dog. He stood in the same spot, unmoving, watching me run away from him, the perfect picture of canine stoicism.

I never saw the dog again.

After passing through the sliding steel gate, the pavement ended, and the road narrowed to a single lane. Twin dirt tracks separated by a grassy strip wove through the forest. The road was flanked by large trees, more than just live oaks, hickory, sweetgum, and others I couldn't identify. Stout limbs crossed high over my head like the swords of an honor guard. A thick canopy of leaves blotted out much of the sun. What light came through cast slanting rays through the misty air and dappled the grass and road with yellow splotches of light.

Beautiful!

The temperature was warm enough to work up a slight sweat and a cool breeze felt refreshing.

The dirt track I ran on was littered with many footprints, hooves of deer and hog, paw prints, tiny hands and bird tracks. The waffle pattern of my Nikes obliterated them.

My feet pounded in rhythm with my heart and lungs. It felt good. I felt good and I could sense an oncoming rush of endorphins. The lovely forest enabled me to empty my head of all thoughts.

I can't describe it. I don't know how long it went on or how far I ran. I made no memories for a while, just blissful mindless running through the light-littered woods.

I wished that run could have lasted longer, but it didn't.

The trees thinned out, letting in more light through the canopy. Up ahead, I could see the edge of the forest giving way to grasslands. It wasn't like the grass of the marsh, but yellow-blonde, the kind you think about in Africa.

The road swerved to the left and rose in a slight incline. I saw that the road went across what looked like a dam or dike between two ponds.

The pond on the right was smaller, about an acre. A flock of ducks swam and dived in the murky water. I ran up and across the causeway.

The pond on the left was much larger, about the length of two football fields and nearly as wide.

What I saw in the larger pond stopped me in my track shoes.

Thousands of white birds, like the flock that flew over me this morning... this must have been their destination and the destination of many more flocks.

White birds everywhere, as far as I could see. They roosted in the trees that lined the pond, waded in the shallow water or perched on the pond's edge. The longer I stared at them, the more the preponderance of their numbers numbed my mind. I noticed they weren't all the same and not all of them were white. Egrets, both kinds with yellow beaks and the smaller ones with black beaks. I'm no expert but wading bird names flooded through my mind, struggling to identify them all... Curlews, Ibis and Spoonbills. Even a species I knew, Wood Storks, mostly gray with black bars on their wings. The proliferation of birds was stunning.

I should not have been surprised at what I saw. According to Rawlings' notebook, the wildlife refuge was a favored bird-watching destination, but nothing I knew about this place prepared me for this magnificent sight.

The birds took almost no notice of me, some of them no more than ten feet away. I received a few one-eye stares but little else.

And they were noisy. Not loud but chattering, burring, buzzing and squawking. With my feet rooted to the dirt road, I bird-watched, like a bird-watcher, a feeling of happiness rising in my chest. I don't know how many people witnessed this massive gathering of birds, but at this particular moment, I was the only one.

And I felt my familiar sadness coming. I knew it would. The dull ache was always preceded by a little undeserved euphoria.

Bettye would have loved this. It was the kind of scene we shared with each other. After her battle with breast cancer, we roamed Europe like honeymooners. We held hands on mountain tops, hugged on the Esplanade at Villa d'Este watching the sun go behind the hills over Lake Como. Always when the moment came, she would slip her hand around my waist and I would circle her shoulder with my arm. We'd hold each other and share the moment. In love, crazy love, unexplainable love.

Love is more of a constant than a variable. It sits somewhere between you and the other like a barrel of sugar. You dip in and scoop some out when you need it and it never gets low. And one day you come to expect that it will always be there, count on it being there and when you hit the bottom of the jar, notice it's not the same and wonder what changed.

You can't talk about it because what if the other person hadn't noticed and you have just hurt them by talking about it.

Humans are variables. We change.

For a while our honeymoon gave us daily miracles, like this gathering of white birds. Rescued from death, being with the man she loved, gallivanting all over Europe sharing the sights, the sounds, the scents and flavors of our love... it gave Bettye more than enough space, a solid foundation, the opportunity to find more to live for. The "us", the "we" allowed her to create and then launch her crusade, which, when she explained it to me, I wholly, enthusiastically approved of, supported, and for a while, gave it all my energy as well.

What I didn't realize was how her crusade would affect us. When she put on Joan of Arc's armor and took up Joan of Arc's sword, what I was left with was... Joan of Arc.

I remember sitting in a fancy hotel room in Bruges, while Bettye was downstairs in the ballroom addressing a hundred women and their families, all victims of the horrid disease of breast cancer, giving them the speech I had written for her... oh, she supplied the inspiration, the authenticity, she had been there, not me... I just supplied the pretty words and taught her how to give a speech, how to address a crowd... that was my shtick. That's what I was good at.

I sat in that fancy hotel room digging my fingernail into the fancy fabric of a fancy couch wondering why I wasn't down there with her, with that room full of devastated women and their husbands and children, watching Bettye deliver her message of hope and courage and urging them to fight for "one more day" or 'un jour de plus' to live for their children, their families, themselves, my own words delivered through Bettye's mouth, her own body devastated by her battle, her eyes streaming tears as if a terrific wind blew them from her. She galvanized the crowds, and I had to turn away. I hadn't been through what they had. Even with Bettye. We weren't even reunited until she had been through chemo and radiation and surgical mutilation to save her life. All that she faced alone, while I was ignorant of the whole ordeal, until finally, on death's threshold, she came to me and begged me to go with her to the clinic in Switzerland, to hold her hand while she died.

But Bettye didn't die. She lived and grew healthy again, but her beauty was gone and her youth. Gone.

But not her fire. And I didn't care. She was still Bettye, the passionate woman I fell in love with.

She joined a club I couldn't join. And paid dues I couldn't afford.

Digging my fingers into that fancy couch made homesick for my own couch, a decades old battle scared leather piece of essential comfort. I wanted my house, my home, my huddling place. I wanted the twenty-four seven hum of I-285, the gaggle of Atlanta, a Braves game, a hot dog with spicy mustard and the crack of the bat.

I packed my bag in a fit of impulse, wrote a note, "I'm going home. B." and caught the train to Brussels and a plane to Atlanta.

Eight months go by, ten… a year. Not a phone call, a letter, text or email.

Bettye had her mission and now I had a thousand white birds. Without her.

About the time my whining reached critical mass, a nearby Wood Stork turned toward me and asked, "Why so sad, city-boy? Ain't this what you came for?

"You left her, right? You made the choice. You should be happy.

"You're looking at these birds and you think, how beautiful! I wish I had someone to share this with. But you walked away from the love of your life to find yourself. You gave up your career for, your life's work and you couldn't stand the fire of someone who found her life's work, so you came here hoping nature could cure of your obvious, well-deserved melancholy."

The stork cocked his eye at me. "You had a woman. Twice. Spent precious months with her. Memories, beautiful memories. You're healthy with more than half your life ahead of you, while us birds would be lucky for couple more years before some predator grabs us."

He cocked his head the other way and turned and walk away with stately dignity. Then the stork stopped and turned for a final remark.

"Stop worrying about the past. Remember what Satchel Paige said."

My over-active imagination was giving me an Edgar Allan Poe moment, only it was a stork, not a raven.

But I noticed all the birds near me were edging away. I guess they finally realized they were too close to a top-of-the-food-chain predator. Egrets perching in the trees flapped to nearby branches, increasing their distance. The wading birds waded to deeper water.

Curious behavior. What did Satchel Paige say?

"Don't look back. Something might be gaining on you."

I turned in the direction from which I had come.

An alligator blocked my path. A six-foot alligator... at least.

CHAPTER 6

"Life Styles of the Rich and Framus"

Harris Neck National Wildlife Refuge, Townsend, Georgia
From the Journal of Brendan Macbean:

As a TV journalist, I traveled all over the South, many places where alligators thrived. Stories around campfires and cracker barrels gave me lots of information about alligators, or 'gators, as we call them. Apparently, no story is worth telling unless the gator is six feet long. At least.

A six-foot gator outweighs a man and is longer than most men. It's the minimum required to test your mettle, otherwise there' no point in messing with them. Believe me, there are more incidents of human's messing with gators than the other way around. Consequently, most gators, given the option, will steer away from us. But in the minds of some gators we're just a couple of chicken legs with a head.

Apparently, this was one of those, just a cold-blooded predator, a design Nature had not seen fit to change in over three hundred million years. Contrast that to us. Nature has been constantly fiddling with the human race since we climbed out of trees dragging our knuckles on the ground.

This big boy had just crawled out of the primeval ooze... the pond on the left side of the road, to catch the warm rays of the rising sun and encountered a hundred and fifty pounds of meat. What a treat! If I hadn't been warned by the stork, he might have seized the opportunity and dragged me kicking and screaming into the water, with no one around to come to my aid.

Okay, that may be a little dramatic. The stork's warning was just my over-active imagination, and I'll admit to a flair for the dramatic. But the dilemma was real. The alligator lay twenty feet away staring at me with cold black eyes, muscles tensed for an attack.

Alligator experts say that a gator can run faster than a man. So, the advice is to zig zag because they're not so nimble. The narrow road refuted that stratagem, but unlike with the dog, I wasn't about to concede this race. I had on running shorts and new Nike's.

And I had a twenty-foot head start.

And if a twenty-foot head start was an advantage, think what a thirty-foot head start would mean. Slowly I took a step back, keeping my eyes on the gator. He didn't move. Another step. A thought came to mind that I might be backing toward another gator, maybe even a seven-foot alligator. At least.

A quick glance over my shoulder indicated that the road was clear, but when I again looked at the gator, he had raised his head up and turned a little toward me.

It looked like imminent attack. Or it felt imminent.

Another step and another. Yes, my chances to escape had improved. I kept backing away. The gator never took his eyes off me nor mine on him.

Thirty feet turned into forty and forty into fifty. At that point I congratulated myself on staving off an alligator attack.

The gator, distant now, still sprawled across the road. My intention had been to return to the house by the same route, but it seemed like a bad idea. I did not know where this road lead or how long I would run before I found a familiar path.

Nature has no respect for the plans of man.

So, I ran away from the gator, into the unknown, away from the route that would have taken me back to the house. After a minute the road dead-ended in a "T" intersection, another road in both directions. A sign said the left took you to "Administration" and "West Entrance." I assumed that was the entrance to the wildlife refuge I passed on Harris Neck Road last night. From my recollection, that would put me at least two miles from the house and I couldn't tell how long this road ran until it took me there. The sign pointing to the right said, "Maintenance" and "Boat Ramp." According to the map the boat ramp was adjacent to the Barbour River Yacht Club, which was only a quarter mile from Rawlings' house.

I took the right.

Good choice. In minutes I passed the maintenance facility, just a locked shed with a sign that said, "Maintenance." A few minutes more and I arrived at a huge parking lot, about the size of a football field. A concrete ramp offered access to the Barbour River. The place was completely empty. I guess it wasn't boating season.

A thin line of trees bordered the south end of the parking lot, with a scrawny barb-wire fence precariously holding a rusty sign that said, "Private Property."

Obviously, folks didn't respect the sign or the fence. It looked like several large people had stomped the fence down to gain access to the "Private Property."

I respected neither sign nor fence and stepped over the barb-wire, shouldered my way through the trees and arrived at the Barbour River Yacht Club.

The rural nature of the area dashed my expectations of a fancy yacht club, but it turned out to be pretty nice anyway. On my left stood a small clubhouse with a nautical lifesaver hung on the wall stenciled with BRYC. On my right was a large warehouse-like building, presumably for boat storage. An obvious effort had been made to spare the trees. Several empty boat trailers were parked haphazardly among the pines along with a few pickups and cars.

A concrete drive circled under the boat lift. Stout wood poles held aloft a bridgework of steel beams that supported an electric boatlift. Even to my rookie eye, I could see the plan. You could back your boat trailer up to the lift, make the hookups and lift the boat off the trailer and run it down to the river. It wasn't hard to see the advantage of this arrangement over the boat ramp next door.

I walked to the front of the circular roundabout to gaze out at the marsh. The Barbour River flowed swiftly from right to left with the in-coming tide. Here the river was about one hundred feet wide and swung close to the land. It stretched to the southeast toward Barbour Island three miles away. A little down river a pair of herons worked a rapidly shrinking sandbar for a meal. The view was magnificent, the vast marsh lay as far in three directions as you could see, the crystal blue sky and the warming late morning sun above.

Something else caught my eye.

I looked down and saw a piece of paper pinned against my ankle by the breeze. I bent down and picked it up. It was a single page folded to fit in a pocket. Someone had run it over as lay on the concrete. A muddy tire print slashed across one side.

I unfolded the paper.

At the top of the page I saw "United States, Department of the Army" and "Fort Stewart, Georgia" and a zip code. The rest of the page was filled with alpha-numeric codes. I searched for something I read-able. Other than the words "Vendor" and "Approved" I saw little I could interpret. At the bottom were two pen-scrawls. Different. Unreadable.

And yesterday's date.

And the creepy feeling that I was poking my nose into someone else's business.

I felt a tingling... call it intuition or instinct... an inclination to let it go. Leave it. Drop the paper and let the wind skate it into the river.

The feeling was familiar. I often got it as a reporter. It was my job to mess in other people's business. My curiosity took me to stories others passed up and brought me fame and fortune... well, in a small way.

And then another feeling: the feeling I was being watched. Someone was staring at me.

I looked up and saw a man I had not seen before. It made my heart skip a beat.

Fifty feet away, sitting in a wooden chair on the porch of the yacht club clubhouse a man stared at me.

I walked in that direction.

The man watched me approach. He was dressed in the familiar uniform that Ralph had on this morning, worn tee shirt, cutoff shorts, a faded UGA baseball hat. His eyes were covered by a pair of those alien-eye sunglasses, so I couldn't really see them. Resting on the deck by his chair was a twelve pack of Bud Light, open at the top. Three crushed empties lay discarded on his left. He clutched number four in his right hand resting on the arm of the chair.

The man said, "I see you running here every day."

It seemed that this was my day to be assaulted by circumstances. Much like the paper in my hand, I could make no sense of what he just said, but the slight smirk on his lips revealed the truth.

Three empties on the deck and well into number four. And it wasn't yet eleven in the morning.

Okay, Macbean... don't be judgmental.

"I'm Brendan Macbean." I didn't offer to shake hands. Unlike Ralph, I didn't want to disarm him, since his most potent weapon seemed to be a Bud Light, and, as tight as he held that beer, he didn't look like the hand shaking kind.

He tilted the beer can at me and made his next pronouncement. "I'm Framus."

He took a swig and added, "Freddy."

For a moment I thought he had called me Freddy. Come on, Brendan. You're not going to let this early morning drunk outwit you. I took a deep breath.

"What are you Framus for... Freddy?"

He raised his beer can again. "I move the earth!"

He crushed can number four, dropped it on the pile and scooped up number five. It was such a graceful move I was momentarily overwhelmed.

I looked up at the sun climbing high in the late morning sky. "Looks like you're doing a great job."

The smirk dropped from his lips. His sunglasses made him hard to read.

Freddy shook his head. "Naw, not the planet Earth. Should have said, 'dirt.'"

"Dirt? Like you move dirt?"

"Yeah, I drive a big CAT up where they're building the new mall."

"There's a new mall?"

"Of course, there's a new mall. Up in Pooler." He shook his head. "You're not from around here."

"Nope. Atlanta."

He nodded like this confirmed all his suspicions about me.

"All that mess," he said.

"Yup. All that mess."

If you live somewhere in Georgia besides Atlanta, Atlanta is a mess. Hard to explain to out-of-state folks but it's typical rural versus urban culture.

"Anyway, a big CAT is an 'earthmover' isn't it?"

"Yep, it sure is."

"And to say, 'I move the dirt' isn't as impressive is it?"

He was smiling now.

"Nope."

At this point, beer five became history. Freddy grabbed beer six with the finesse of a blackjack dealer. He spent a few seconds becoming familiar with his new beer and then pointed his chin at me, maybe slightly in the direction of the piece of paper in my hand, as if inviting me to ask him about it.

I held the paper up slightly. "Is this yours?"

Freddy shook his head slightly. "Naw. I didn't lose any paperwork."

"Paperwork?"

"That's a shipping manifest from Fort Stewart…paperwork to get out the gate. Or in."

I waved it around. "I can't make heads or tails of it. It's all in code, seems like."

"Army does it that way. Couple years ago, I did some hauling for them. Twelve containers. Hauled them from Port Savannah to the main gate, one container at a time. Never knew what was in those containers, but an Army guy at the port gave me a page like that. Full of codes. Codes for what it was, where it was going, where it came from. Even I had a code. A code for me."

Freddy shook his head, like the Army having a code for him was somehow distasteful.

"Twelve containers? You did this all by yourself?"

"No, I had somebody with me… some…, ah, well a guy. They army always wants at least two guys in the truck. Don't know why. All he did was ride and smoke cigarettes… didn't say a damn word the whole time."

"So, this paper was to get you through security?"

"Yah, the supply officer at the port give me paperwork so I can get through the gate. The MP at the gate scans the little rectangle at the bottom and opens the gate. The sergeant at the loading dock takes the container off the truck and takes the paper. Then he hands me another just like it so I can get out the gate at the port."

"They won't let you leave without paperwork."

"Right. I gotta have an exit manifest to show the gate MP I'm not stealing something. Then I have to take this new page back to the port officer to get the next container. And after the last one, I still have to go back to the port to get paid. That's the way the army does it."

"So, someone loses his paperwork, he's in trouble."

"I don't know. Maybe he doesn't have to turn it in to get paid. I don't know."

"Hmmmm. So, can you tell what he's hauling from this?"

"Not unless you can read the codes. The Army has a scanner that reads it, but to the rest of us it's just jargon."

I felt like I had squeezed all the information out of Freddy Framus. I stuffed the paper in my pocket.

"Okay, Freddy, I have to get to the house. I'll see you around."

He raised his beer. I had lost count.

"Every day."

CHAPTER 7

"Trophy Wife"

Gould's Landing, near Harris Neck National Wildlife Refuge
From the Journal of Brendan Macbean

By the time I jogged back to the house, my stomach was singing, "Feed me" like Audrey Junior in Little Shop of Horrors.

Inspecting Rawlings' refrigerator revealed my poor planning in coming here. It was spotlessly empty except for Heineken and condiments.

And, miraculously, the half Five Guys hamburger I had thrown in there last night.

I needed groceries if I was going to spend time here.

I sat at the counter and ate the half-burger cold. I leafed through Rawlings' notebook while I munched.

The community of Shellman Bluff lay several miles south. It had a few restaurants and a "Clydes," described by Rawlings as a "generous" convenience store. The nearest grocery turned out to be the Piggly Wiggly in Eulonia, thirteen and a half miles away. Rawlings provided old fashioned directions to get to these destinations, noting that GPS technology "might be confused by the roads around here, and would likely get you lost or in the driveway of someone you really don't want to meet."

Thanks for the warning, Rawls.

The Eulonia and the Pig would have to wait until tomorrow. This afternoon I was determined to do some yardwork. It was the least I could do for my friend who sent me to this marvelous place.

Chainsaw operation was a guy-thing, even a city-boy like me. Rawlings provided everything: Stihl chainsaw, gloves, ears and eyes protection. He also had a nifty Kawasaki Mule, an ATV with a truck bed in the back. Rawls' notebook told me how to start everything but reading instructions... not a guy-thing.

Over the next three hours I cut and loaded about two tons of logs and brush. With the Mule, I hauled it all across the road to Stan's fire pit. The brush pile alone rose higher than my head, and I put it all near the ring of stones. During all this coming and going I saw no sign of mankind or beast.

As a workout, cutting wood and hauling brush exceeded just about anything I had ever done. My muscles sang like overtightened banjo strings and told me to stop. About four o'clock in the afternoon. I spent some time restoring Rawlings' chainsaw to white glove perfection before hanging it all up in the exact place it had come from.

I hosed most of the grime and sawdust off my body before climbing the stairs.

I was headed for Mrs. Rawlings fancy bathtub and nobody was going to stop me.

I eased myself into a full tub of very hot water, its slight sulfur odor diffused with a bar of exotic *L'Occitane Savon Extra-Doux* soap. I scrubbed every inch and then just lay there letting any dour residue seep out of me.

Ah! Mrs. Rawlings, you are woman after my own heart!

With growing affection for the Rawlings' place, I spent time restoring Mrs. R's tub to *"salle de bain chic"* perfection. Bettye would have been pleased, and that thought didn't even cause me a moment.

I made a cup of "blend" and curled up in a wicker chair on the cottage's deck intending to begin one of Rawlings' novels, "A Killing on Ring Jaw Bluff," but didn't even finish the back cover before the breeze off the marsh and the oscillating leaves put me to sleep.

I awoke to the sound of gruff, male voices and the scent of wood smoke tickling my nostrils.

Oh, yeah. Ralph had invited me to the neighborhood fire pit at Stan's across the street... to enjoy the fruits of my afternoon's work. I wanted to see that mound of brush I had piled up go up in flames. So, I loaded my red Igloo cooler with Heineken and ice, grabbed my backpack and headed out the door, remembering to turn on the outside lights to avoid a repeat of last night's dark disorientation.

Across the street I saw two men sitting at the fire pit with a large cooler between them. One of them was Ralph Freeman.

As I approached, Ralph told the other, "There he is. I wondered if he'd show up."

The giant pile of brush in the fire pit had burned to ash. I was disappointed to have missed it. Several logs had been thrown on the blaze and were blazing.

These two knew how to get a good fire going.

"Hey there, Brad." Ralph said cheerfully. "Stan, this here is Brad McCain or something like that. He's staying at Bill's place."

Both men had quart sized plastic cups in their hands. Ralph waved his at the other man.

"Brad, this here is Stan Hizeman."

Stan appeared to be somewhere between my age and Ralph's. He was a big barrel-chested man with a grizzled crew cut. His face seemed frozen in a scowl.

He nodded at me. "Like the football prize only not spelled the same." He returned his gaze to the fire.

"Nice to meet you, Stan. My name's really Brendan Macbean. Not Brad. Not McCain."

I took one of the empty lawn chairs to Ralph's right.

Ralph gave me a confused look.

"You're not Brad?"

"Nope. Brendan." I opened one of my Heinekens.

He seemed hurt. "Well, why didn't you say so?"

Stan said, "You old goat, you never get anything right."

Ralph said, "Anyway, when's your wife coming over?"

"Wife? I'm not married." Where did he get the idea I was married?

"Well, girlfriend, then."

"I don't have a girlfriend. I here by myself."

"Well, Macbean, that's disappointing."

Hmmm... I was supposed to provide entertainment?

I looked around. "Where's Alice?"

"Alice. She'll be out, but it won't help any. She's not much to look at. Had a vasectomy a couple of years ago... She's got no tits."

Stan shot him a look. "Mass. Not vas."

"Mass what?" Ralph asked.

"Mass as in mastectomy. Not vasectomy. Vasectomy is where they cut your balls off." Stan said dryly and took a pull on what was in his plastic cup. I assumed they had been at this drinking thing for a long time.

"They still do that? Cut your balls off?" He directed the question at me.

"Not exactly," I said.

Stan said, "That's what they should have done with you, you old goat. Instead of a frontal lobotomy. Then you wouldn't be staring at women's tits and getting your face slapped."

Ralph was unperturbed. "Well when's Linda coming out? She's got a nice rack." He turned to me. "You wait, Macbean. You'll see old Stan here has got him a real trophy wife. "

"A trophy wife, like winning the Hizeman Trophy?"

Stan said dryly, "We heard that one before."

"Well if you keep feeding me old straight lines, I'll keep tossing out old jokes."

A second later a woman came into the firelight. She was carrying something and set it on a picnic table behind us.

I guessed it was Linda, Stan's wife. She was indeed a beauty. Of course, it was hard to say in the gathering darkness, but the firelight reflecting off her face made her look young and pretty.

She strode across the fire circle straight toward me and defying convention held her hand out.

"Hi, I'm Linda Hizeman."

I stood like I was taught and shook her hand. She squeezed my hand like a man.

She had a beaming smile and, yes, she was pretty.

"I'm Brendan Macbean. Pleased to meet you."

She held onto my hand and gave me a penetrating look. "You are, really?"

"Yes. All my life, I guess."

"You're the guy on TV? On the TV news in Atlanta?"

I stammered a little. I had been more of a roving reporter than an anchorman. I received little attention off camera, in public and not many people recognized me.

Out of the corner of my eye, I saw Alice come into the circle of firelight, like a ghost. She sat in the chair to my right. Linda took a seat next to Stan.

"That's me. I used to be a TV reporter in Atlanta."

Alice said, "I thought you looked familiar."

Stan said, "What? You're some kind of celebrity?"

"No, not really. Just a TV reporter."

"But you quit?"

"Retired."

"You look a little young to retire. What, you're just sitting around doing nothing?"

"Doing a little freelance writing," I said.

Stan smirked. "That pay the bills?"

"Doesn't pay much, but when you retire, people find things for you to do. Mostly things that don't pay at all."

Stan nodded, like he understood.

Ralph said, "Well, what I want to know is what you have in that backpack you're always carrying around. Is that your 'man-purse' or something? Isn't that what you-all in Atlanta call it... a man purse?"

The man-purse comment rankled me. So, discarding my usual caution, I decided to show them what I had in the backpack.

I put my beer down, reached into the backpack and pulled out the Redhawk, taking care not to hold it by the grip, placing my right hand around the cylinder and frame. I didn't want to haul out the pistol looking 'combat ready.'

The Redhawk made a striking debut. Ralph, Stan, Linda and Alice all sat bolt upright in their lawn chairs like an electric tingle had blasted their asses. I didn't actually enjoy their reaction, except for maybe, Ralph's because Stan immediately went into a sort of mild combat mode of his own. He put his drink on top of the cooler and rested his hands on his thighs, intently staring at me with predatory eyes.

Very carefully, I opened the cylinder, hit the extractor button and ejected the cartridges, letting the bullets fall in my lap.

Strum, Ruger and Company made big revolvers, and this was one of their more beautiful examples. Polished stainless steel, redwood grips, seven-and-a-half-inch barrel made the Redhawk eye-candy for the gun lover.

With the empty cylinder still open, I handed it over, grip first to Ralph. He reached out with a shaky hand to take it. Ralph knew how to handle firearms, even unloaded ones and he inspected the cylinder, clicked it shut and took aim at the center of the roaring fire.

Ralph dry-fired it a few times. The Redhawk snickered like a racehorse, clickety-click, clickety-click, clickety-click, whispery, buttery, perfect mechanical efficiency.

"Wow," Ralph said, his voice softer than the crackling flames. "That's quite a trigger."

He looked toward Stan, but Stan shook his head, like he wasn't interested.

Ralph handed the Redhawk back, grip first.

"Forty-four magnum?"

"No. Forty-five Colt."

"Not as much kick, right?"

"I guess," I said.

"Why do you have that gun, Macbean?" Stan's voice carried a challenging tone. I had the distinct feeling he had his own gun close at hand. The feeling crept over me that I may have violated one of Stan's rules bring a loaded gun into his 'space'.

I may have waited too long to respond.

Ralph chimed in. "Stan's a detective. He'll get the story it of you."

That broke the tension a little. Even Stan smiled, or sort of smiled. I had been around lots of police. Some of them don't smile much.

"Well, if a truckload of crazed rednecks came barreling down the road, with shotguns and AK-47's, it wouldn't do me a whole lot of good if I left it at home."

I watched Stan relax a little. It occurred to me that the guy didn't like the kind of surprise I gave him bringing out the Redhawk. He took a deep breath, probably to calm the adrenalin.

"Okay, Macbean, why not a Glock. It weighs half as much and has three times the bullets."

"Sure, but the gun is largely symbolic. It gives you power even without pulling the trigger. It helps you avoid the feeling of helplessness when the bad guy shows up."

Stan thought about that for a minute. "Folks worry about that... running into a bad guy. Is that what happened, Macbean, a bad guy scared the crap out of you, and you went out and bought this hand-cannon?"

His challenging, condescending policeman's tone got under my skin.

"That's exactly what happened. A year ago, a guy stuck a gun in my face at a gas station. It was night and I was putting gas in the car and this guy came out of the shadows and pointed his gun about that far from my head." I held up my beer and my right hand about a foot and apart. "And yes, it scared the crap out of me."

Five silent people sat around the fire visualizing the scene in the dancing flames.

Stan took a long pull on his drink. "I hope you gave him your wallet."

"I still had the gas pump in my hand. He didn't ask for my money. He wanted the car."

"So, what happened?"

"I did something stupid." I set my beer down. "He was holding his gun horizontal like the gangs in the movies. I did my left arm like this." I set my left arm at an angle, fist in the air. "And swung it into his wrist. The gun flew out of his hand, fell to the ground. Then I pushed him. He fell on his back and must have hit the back of his head on the pavement because he didn't move. The police showed up and arrested the guy."

Stan shook his head. "Jesus! That was stupid, Macbean. The police sure got there quick."

"The clerk inside the store called them. It was right across the street from a precinct."

"Why didn't you get shot?" Ralph asked.

"The kid's gun wasn't loaded. He didn't even have a clip in it. He borrowed it from his brother and his brother stole it from a neighbor so both boys went to jail."

"Boys?" Stan asked.

"Nineteen years old and twenty."

A full two minutes of silence.

Stan was the first to speak. "Macbean, your story has more holes than a pound of Swiss cheese."

I felt another panic attack. Stan wasn't going to let up, and I didn't want to be interrogated. The story was the beginning of a twisted path to where my secrets lay hidden.

"Wait a minute, Stan. Ralph here claims his wife had a vasectomy and your wife won the Heisman Trophy. And you say my story is full of holes?"

That got them all laughing... but only for a moment.

Stan shot me a piercing look. "I thought you said you didn't have a girlfriend."

Ralph chimed in. "Watch out Macbean. He'll get a confession out of you."

"Yeah, I know. He's a detective." I looked back at Stan. "How'd you get me having a girlfriend out of all that?"

"When this happened, you weren't driving that 'command wagon' over there. No punk kid would go after that. It's obviously law enforcement."

"No, this was a year ago. I was in a different car then."

"So, what were you driving?"

I thought back to the beautiful new BMW 740i, midnight blue, new car smell, polished burl-wood dash, supple leather seats... Shelby Chadwick's car.

"BMW 740i." I said.

Stan threw the question to the group. "Have you ever heard a BMW owner refer to his car as 'the car' instead of 'my car'? You said it three times, Macbean... 'the car.'"

"It wasn't mine. The car belonged to... uh, somebody I worked with."

"They let you use their car?"

Stan had me on the ropes and was pummeling my midsection.

"Okay, I was having dinner with a colleague at work. We had just finished up a big project, working late and went to grab dinner."

"And this BMW owner let you drive his car?"

I took a deep breath. "No. It was a she."

Ralph was so excited he almost jumped out of his seat. "I knew Old Stan here would get you to talk."

"A guy wouldn't let you drive his BMW. A woman might. A woman colleague who wanted to allow you to feel dominant. Showing some consideration for your ego... your male ego. So this 'she' let you drive her car and she was sitting in the passenger seat when this attempted hijacking took place?

I nodded.

"Sounds like a date to me. Where did you go to dinner?"

I lost my will to resist. "Bacchanalia."

"What kind of place is that?" Stan asked.

Linda answered. "It's like the best restaurant in Atlanta. You never took me to a place like that." She pouted her pretty lips.

"Sounds like a date to me," Stan said. "So, you got one of those fancy, TV women, sitting in the passenger seat. She hands you the keys and says mimicking a Southern Belle, 'Take me somewhere fancy, honey.' And you're telling me this is not a date. Let's see, the gas filler door on a BMW is on the right, so you were standing on the right. The crook was staring through the windshield, down the bosom of this beautiful starlet and you knocked the gun out of his hand. Is that how it happened, Macbean?"

Somehow Stan's mocking tone had taken all the heroism out of the incident.

I nodded. "That's pretty much it, Stan. You got me." I held out my wrists like for him to put on handcuffs.

"Do we know this fancy TV woman?"

I sighed. "Yeah. Everybody knows her. It was Shelby Chadwick."

The derisive laughter that followed embarrassed and angered me. What the hell was so funny?

Still chuckling Linda managed to say, "Brendan, you don't look like a fifty-million dollar baseball player. Isn't that who she's dating these days?"

I had to set my beer down to fold my arms across my chest. "She was still in Atlanta then. We worked together."

I guess my mood was obvious. They all settled down.

Alice spoke in a quiet voice. "That girl interviewed the big crook who swindled all that money."

"Ray Suffield."

"Yeah," Ralph said. "He's in federal prison for a hundred years. She got that interview, and it was the biggest news story of the year."

Stan said, "Macbean, was that the big project you were celebrating? I mean, that was a big deal. Shelby Chadwick got the job on the network morning news right after that."

I took a deep breath. It had been me who did that interview, worked my ass off to get in to see the most hated man in America. I nailed that interview, got it on video and it was the most stunning achievement of my career. Only to have the network hand it over to Shelby. Their experts cut me out, reshot her asking the questions. Shelby went on national TV and everyone in America saw her interview Ray Suffield, and she got the fame and fortune.

And I got retirement.

"Yeah... that was her."

Stan gave me a long look. I could see the detective wheels spinning, but he let it go and stared at the fire.

Linda said, "Honey, why don't you stop grilling Mister Macbean and start grilling those burgers? I'm hungry."

I know I'm dense, but somehow I had plumb forgot my manners. I stood up.

"Well, folks, this has been fun. I'll get back to the house and let you-all get onto your supper."

Stan snarled, "Sit down, Macbean. You ain't going nowhere."

His voice was so commanding, I sat down like a guilty schoolboy.

Stan stood and pointed at me like the chief interrogator he was.

"You're going to eat one of these burgers and if it ain't the best damn thing you ever put in your mouth, I'll send Ralph over to finishing cleaning your yard."

"In that case, I'll stay and have a burger. If it's not too much trouble."

Linda said in a merry voice, "No trouble at all, Mister Macbean. We love celebrities."

"Please, Linda. Call me Brendan."

"Okay, Brendan." She fluttered her eyes at me and I was ready to hand her the Macbean trophy, except Stan was giving me another kind of look.

Stan cooked the burgers in a kind of wire basket held over a blazing hot fire. The giant burgers dripped fat and the fire hissed and flamed. It was entertaining to watch. Then he browned the buns on the same basket and served the burgers with creamy potato salad, sliced Vidalia

Onions and where he got home-grown tomatoes at this time of the year was a mystery.

It was marvelous. Delicious. The best thing I had ever put in my mouth, which meant I wouldn't have Ralph cleaning my yard. Disappointing.

Alice hardly ate at all, another sign of a breast cancer survivor. She sat silently and pushed a bird-size helping of potato salad around on her plate.

She looked up, at me with some fire in her eyes, a look I had seen many times before, the look of a survivor, of someone determined to live one more day.

"Brendan, you know that Shelby woman did another interview last week."

"She did?"

"She interviewed that French woman, the one that started that cancer support foundation, *Un Jour de Plus*."

Alice's Southern accent was slightly off with the French pronunciation.

I stopped chewing and sat silent. That was Bettye's foundation.

I swallowed and took a breath. "Bettye Le Boutillier."

Alice nodded. "That's her. Do you know her?"

"That magazine's Woman of the Year," I said. The evasion came easy to me.

Linda said, "I saw that. She was with that German doctor. My god, what a drop-dead gorgeous woman!"

I lowered my head. "I think she's Swiss. Doctor Birgit Bauerle. She and Madame Le Boutillier were named 'Women of the year.'"

I remembered the shock of seeing the cover of the magazine showing tall, beautiful Doctor Bauerle, looking like a Vogue model standing next to Bettye, looking like a skinny, grizzled, sad old woman. The disease had done that to her.

Stan said, "So you know this Swiss doctor, too? Geez, Macbean, you know everybody."

I lied, "I read the magazine, like fifty million other people."

I turned to Alice, "So Shelby interviewed them. Were they in Paris or Switzerland?"

She shook her head. "No, they were in New York, on that morning news program. Those three women were all crying and hugging. It was great!"

There were tears in Alice's eyes too, shining in the firelight.

Bettye had been in New York, a two-hour plane ride from Atlanta.

"Women of the Year was in December. I don't understand why Shelby interviewed them last week."

Alice answered the question. "Miss LeBooty is got a book coming out. She's touring the country. The book is the same name as her foundation, *Un Jour de Plus*." Alice's French pronunciation was a little better despite her mess-up of Bettye's surname.

"A book! That's great, but what about Dr. Bauerle?"

"Oh, she's going to put Dr. Friedkin's treatment into Sloan-Kettering and then Emory in Atlanta."

I knew all about Dr. Friedkin's treatment since I had accompanied Bettye to his clinic in Switzerland last year. Bettye was his first patient to survive. Afterward she became the Joan of Arc against breast cancer. The gorgeous Dr. Bauerle had been the clinic's director.

My head was spinning. Bettye was over here, and I was in South Podunk. But obviously she didn't want to see me, and I had walked out on her months ago… left without a word except for that brief note.

Alice said, "Dr. Friedkin's treatment is a miracle. He's saved about a hundred women last year. Miss Le Booty was the first. But his treatment came too late for me."

That snapped me out of my misery.

"Really." My voice must have carried a note of sympathy and compassion because Alice smiled and shook her head.

"No, I'm okay. I'm cancer free for over a year now. It's just I had to go through all that… surgery, chemo and radiation. What he does is different. Shrinks tumors without all that."

But I stopped listening after 'No, I'm okay and went spinning into my own chaotic reverie.'

I'm in South Podunk. And Bettye is over here.

CHAPTER 8

"Searching for Wi-Fi"

Gould's Landing, Townsend, Georgia
From the Journal of Brendan Macbean:

The party broke up after we ate. With nothing else to do, I turned in early and woke the next morning feeling as if bad dreams had chased me all night.

But sitting on the Rawlings' bench-swing again watching the sun come up over the marsh with a cup of the "blend" in my hand seemed to be the right antidote.

Antidote for... for what? For what ailed me, of course, and what ailed me had no cure.

Bettye.

When I heard she was in the country I was ready to jump in the Land Cruiser and cruise back to Atlanta just to huddle in my house until Bettye showed up... if she ever did.

But the dread of arriving home to an empty, cold, dark house and huddling there as an emotional prisoner made me shiver. In the light of a new day and a rising sun, that seemed pointless.

The sun cleared the horizon and cast an angry red glare over the tips of the marsh grass. Different day from yesterday which seemed like a month ago.

What was the saying? Red sky at morning, sailors take warning. Why hadn't this warning come sooner? Like a year ago when Bettye asked me to go to Switzerland? I had been weak and vulnerable, giddy with success. I had nailed the best interview of my life and had the most beautiful woman in the world fawning over me. Bettye was out of my life, then, like a drug addiction. You're never cured. You can only recover, but that's if you don't go there again.

The closer you are to the sea, the more vulnerable you are to the pull of the tides.

And sailors' warnings.

There was more water in the mud hole than the same time yesterday. A lot more. The tides don't seem to run on a twenty-four hour clock. The moon is on a twenty-seven day cycle, which divides into a rotation of twenty-four hours plus fifty minutes. The twenty-four hour clock is a government conspiracy going back to the Egyptians, but nature ignores the conspiracies of man.

Nothing today will be like yesterday and the moon will push and pull the ocean on its own schedule. The birds and the bees have no problem syncing up to it.

Me, not so much.

Everything looked the same, as yesterday, but the red sun promised a rough day for sailors.

I didn't want to go home and wait for Bettye. Maybe that felt like some sort of progress. I could stay here as long as I wanted. Rawlings would not mind that, in fact, I think he'd agree.

Nobody can find me here.

But to stay here, I needed groceries. And more important than food was my mission.

I needed to touch base with Daniel Conklin, my partner in crime. Daniel was "in the wind" hiding from the world, specifically gangsters and Federal agents.

He and I protected an ill-gotten fortune of somewhere between six and seven billion dollars.

Billions with a "B," money stolen by Conklin, from his ill-fated company, InCorps.

I met Conklin last year at the cancer clinic in Switzerland where Bettye had dragged me. We became friends, in part due to common cause. I knew immediately there was something special about him, something elusive. I figured it out, got all wrapped up in the swirl of gangsters and federal agents. I helped him escape a brutal kidnaping when they tried to torture the money out of him.

We had both been there to support the loves of our lives who had cancer. Daniel's Denise ultimately died.

Under the perfect logic of the grief-stricken, Conklin knew he must find a way to pay back the fortune he stole. Like the fool I was and still am, I agreed to help him. He disappeared and I became the visible half of a multi-billion-dollar syndicate. Both gangsters and the federal authorities wanted to get their hands on Daniel, so he had to stay "disappeared."

Neither of us were spies, but Conklin was very clever. He devised a way for us to communicate and avoid letting the federal agents, who surveilled my computer on a weekly basis, know where he was. Heck, I didn't know where he was, and I didn't want to know. From time to time we needed to make sure the other was okay. It was time for me to check in, and if he didn't hear from me, he might come roaring out of the shadows to save me, and thus endanger himself.

I walked back to the house, showered, shaved and put on the right clothes for a visit to the Piggy Wiggly in Eulonia, which turned out to be a polo shirt and jeans.

The Toyota Land Cruiser had been fitted with amazing communication equipment, including a built-in Wi-Fi hotspot and satellite phone connections, so this location's lack of cell phone coverage didn't prevent me from linking to the Internet. But almost as soon as I bought the Fire Chief's Command Vehicle, the feds hacked into it. Anytime I used the COM, an alarm went off in the US Justice Department and an agent started monitoring my computer.

It was safer to use someone else's Wi-Fi.

I always enjoyed firing up the Toyota. It was more like initiating a spaceship launch than starting a car. First, Toyota had replaced the standard car keys with something that was more like a TV remote. When I approached the car, the interior lights came on automatically. The car seat automatically moved to the proper position as soon as my butt hit the leather.

I hit the start button. Screens lit up in front of the steering wheel and center console. I took my laptop out of the backpack and plugged it into a docking station

Much like Siri or Alexa, voice commands activated most of the systems in the Land Cruiser. Mine had a sultry, Southern female voice, which I named, 'TLC'.

"TLC," I said.

"Yes, Boss."

I know I'm an imaginative sort, but it always sounded as if my TLC was a little too bothered to deal with my needs. Kind of sexy to think her day of lounging and tea sipping could be ruined by my needs.

"We are looking for Wi-Fi."

The screen showed a cream-colored SUV icon over the area map.

"I find no networks in our current location." TLC stated.

"TLC, I want to go to Shellman Bluff."

A few seconds passed. "Shellman Bluff, Georgia is eight point three miles away, by way of Harris Neck Road and Old Shellman Road. However there is no road in our location to Harris Neck Road."

"TLC, do you have a listing for 'Gould's Landing Way?'"

A few more seconds. "I have a listing but cannot locate, 'Gould's Landing Way.'"

I considered this. The road Rawlings' house was located on, Gould's Landing Way, had somehow escaped GPS mapping.

I could fix that. "TLC, keep searching for Wi-Fi."

I drove to the end of the driveway and turned right on Gould's Landing Way. The console screen still showed negative for wireless internet. I slowly drove into the yacht club, past Harold Unger's weekend house. No cars. Nobody home. Wi-Fi turned off.

I pulled up on the circular concrete pad under the boat lift. Freddy Framus was not guzzling beer at the clubhouse today, and the clubhouse had no Wi-Fi.

"TLC, I am now located at the eastern end of Gould's Landing Way."

"I have our location. Shall I update the GPS database?"

"No. Please track our path and update the path as Gould's Landing Way when I tell you."

"Okay, Boss."

I drove slowly to the entrance of Gould's Landing and stopped when I came to the intersection of Harris Neck Road and Julienton Road.

"TLC, this is the western end of Gould's Landing Way, where it intersects with Julienton Road and Harris Neck Road. Update the GPS database."

"Boss, I won't be able to update the GPS database until we have a connection to the internet. Do you want me to turn on the satellite phone?"

"Negative, TLC. Update it when we get a connection. There is no point letting the Feds know what I'm up to."

"I'll make the update when we get a connection, but your comment about the Feds means nothing to me, Boss."

I proceeded west on Harris Neck Road, encountering no houses except a burned-out house on the left that looked like it had been in that condition for a few years. Otherwise the land was all forest and provided little encouragement that I'd encounter Wi-Fi.

I drove a couple of miles before I encountered the first human being.

The coastal forest gave way to a section of marsh, which swept southward in a grand vista. A small creek flowed under the roadbed, presumably through some pipes since there was no formal bridge.

A man stood in water up to his knees, an old black man with white, close cropped hair. He crouched over a spot in the rising water holding some kind of net close to his chest. Curiously, next to him stood a Great White Egret, close enough to the man he easily could have thrown the net over the bird's head.

The pair stood motionless, fixed their gaze on a spot of the water. What they were hunting wasn't obvious to me.

I wanted to take a picture of this unusual sight but could think of no way to do it without intruding and disrupting. So I slowed to a crawl and inched by them.

Neither the man nor the bird paid the slightest attention to me.

As I slid past I remembered this fire-service command vehicle had no fewer than twelve high definition wide angle video cameras built into a strip of transparent, hardened glass ringing the perimeter of the roof line. All I had to do was ask TLC to turn them on.

Oh, well. Too late for that.

Less than a half mile further, I passed the west entrance to the Harris Neck Wildlife Refuge, and just past that a wide bridge across what I think was a creek connecting to the Julienton River.

A half-dozen fishing poles leaned against the bridge abutment next to a woman slumped in a lawn chair, her chin rested on her chest and her arms trailed the ground. The woman's straw hat was pulled low hiding the sun from her eyes. A battered cooler, another chair, empty, and a rusted, ancient pickup truck completed the scene.

The empty chair told me where the man fishing with the egret, a half mile behind me, had come from.

My phone lit up. Cellular phone service at last.

I could download email through my cell phone, but I knew the feds monitored my phone calls and probably my messages and downloads. I needed the anonymity of Wi-Fi.

A half mile further brought more signs of civilization: A small, whitewashed church, a fire station and a gated community named Belvedere.

But no Wi-Fi.

TLC, announced, "In two hundred feet, turn left on Youngman Road."

The name of the road summoned the song by the Village People.

"Turn left on Youngman road."

Youngman Road was just like Harris Neck Road with less to see beyond the forest and the marsh. I crossed another bridge with a several people fishing. Two of them waved and I waved back.

"Turn left on Old Shellman Road."

Old Shellman Road was just like Youngman Road, miles of forest, and few signs of civilization, fences, mailboxes, houses and finally a stop sign.

TLC said, "Continue straight on Sutherland Bluff Drive, then turn left."

With no traffic, I could sit there and study the map.

Ahead lay what GPS called "Shellman Bluff," which looked like a small grid of streets along the Broro River. According to Rawlings' notebook, Shellman Bluff was a "fish camp" kind of community. I had images of small structures made to house fisherman, probably the least demanding of our brethren. The map showed two restaurants, two marinas and a golf course. To my right lay the road to Eulonia, Shellman Bluff Road. The map showed several businesses.

On a whim, I put off searching the fish camp and headed right on Shellman Bluff Road.

"Recalculating," TLC's bored and bothered voice.

"TLC, cancel Shellman Bluff."

"Okay, boss."

As business districts go, it was modest, a couple of houses, a volunteer fire station, a coin operated car wash, a hair salon called, "Liza's Hair" and an absolute eyesore of a front yard junkyard, full of trash and the wasted debris of debased humanity, a total blot on what was otherwise a pretty little community.

Well, after passing the community eyesore, it turned lovely again, condos on the left and then a couple of holes of the golf course came up to the road and across the street was Clyde's, described by Rawlins as a "generous" convenience store. Generous it was, with no less than eight gas pumps. A gleaming white boat was getting refueled in one of them.

And I heard my computer announce there was Wi-Fi!

But so was the fire department. A big red ladder truck was parked in front of Clyde's, probably the on-duty crew getting their breakfast. Since I had acquired the Land Cruiser I have attracted the attention of the firefighting community, a gregarious bunch of guys prone to admiring other firefighters' equipment. I drove the fireman's fondest dream, a new, shiny fire command vehicle, and it was unthinkable I could sit in the parking lot of Clyde's, stealing their Wi-Fi without those boys in uniform swarming over me with warm attention and a thousand questions.

I drove on, seeking a quieter set-up.

Past Clyde's, the Shellman Bluff Business District petered out quickly. "Boating Sales and Service" looked like a bustling boat place but no Wi-Fi and then I was back to driving in the forest.

A series of small signs reminiscent of the old Burma Shave advertisements that used to dot the landscape in the last century boasted, "Georgia Wild Shrimp," "Fresh Crabs," "Local Oysters" and finally, "Seafood!" and before I could absorb all this information, "Dockside Seafood" whizzed by on my left.

But no Wi-Fi at Dockside.

Then I hit pay dirt.

Around a long bend in Shellman Bluff Road sat a place called "Zollers," a low rambling wood building that looked like it had been added on to during the years. A sign out front announced, "Slackwater Band Saturday 8PM" and "Trivia every Wednesday."

I made a guess that Zollers was a popular watering hole. Their Wi-Fi was saturating the airwaves, so I turned into the large, gravel parking lot.

There was a long deck built across most of the front of the building with a few tables and chairs and lights strung between the deck rail and the low roof. I nosed the Land Cruiser close to the edge of the deck in front of the door. A neon light "Open" sign hung in a window next to the door. The sign was off, the parking lot empty.

Perfect.

Even more perfect, "Zollers" Wi-Fi network had no password, saving me a five-minute hacking exercise. My email downloaded quickly.

I disconnected from Zoller's network.

I had received about ten legitimate emails from my bank, my dentist and my on-line investment broker and other usual sources. I had received nearly two hundred SPAM messages.

I copied all the SPAM messages to a micro-SD memory chip.

The trick here was to make it more difficult for the feds to decipher my communications. The US government had become adept at decrypting emails from fighting terrorism. Daniel Conklin had come up with our method of passing messages back and forth between him and myself. We knew they'd be scrutinizing my emails, so he came up with the process. Emails are essentially data producing words and pictures. Spam emails are the same only unwanted, often getting little attention. Of the two hundred spam emails I received, a few words of Conklin's message were contained in each. It would take a computer to pull out the relevant information and recompose the message. We hoped the feds would ignore the SPAM just like we do.

From the glovebox of the Toyota I took out an old LG tablet and inserted the micro SD memory chip. I powered up the tablet and carefully entered a sixteen-digit security code. The LG tablet was the link the feds hadn't spotted. If I entered a wrong number, the whole tablet erased itself. If I entered it correctly it automatically sifted through the SPAM messages to extract Conklin's message.

In a minute, his message appeared on the tablet's screen. It always gave me chills when I saw communication from this man who was a most-wanted fugitive.

"Hey, Boy Scout. This is Scoutmaster. I hear you have flown the coup. Hope you're relaxing on a beach somewhere with an umbrella drink. I'm chilling with a double espresso in the Marrakesh Market, planning my trip to Istanbul."

Conklin was nowhere near these places and for all I know he lived down the street from me in Atlanta. How else did he know I had left my house?

"I have included the two names you gave me into our help list. We will take care of them and hope their families rebound. I've also listed four more I think we can help."

By 'help' he meant 'save.' One of the ways we paid back was to seek out families devastated by cancer. Often a family's insurance and savings were exhausted in the process. When we found these situations, we stepped in, paid their medical bills and their mortgages and often other bills. This was done anonymously by a process known only to Conklin.

"Last but not least, HTO is a hot buy right now. They have just received patents on solar power electrolysis which should enable...."

Conklin went on trying to explain it to me, but he had me at 'hot buy' and since I have known him, he's been one hundred percent right when it comes to investments.

I read his note again and deleted it and all the spam emails that generated it. It was time to reply and my method was different. I don't know how Conklin generated SPAM that looked like SPAM and had the little digital clues that enabled the program on this LG tablet to piece together the message. What I did was type my reply and ran it through a program that generated an innocuous but encrypted message to Conklin. Then I pasted this into a chatroom entry. His software told me what to cut and paste and put in an internet chatroom and to which user of the chatroom to reply to.

I didn't understand how it worked, but Conklin was able to read the replies by some process on his end.

In thirty minutes from the time I had arrived in Zoller's parking lot, I finished checking in with Conklin. The feds would know I got on the internet and they'd figure out where and when. They would wonder why and parse every keystroke.

Best to give them a reason. I crafted an email to William Rawlings, my host who was out galivanting the West Coast on a book tour.

"Dear William, love your place. So quiet and serene. Wonder how you ever found it, but you are a 'miner for a heart of gold' and always have been. Thanks, as well for the complete coffee collection, especially that curious "blend" which I've found to be, when combined with your unique water source, the best I've ever tasted. Thanks again and hope you have a great tour. Best, Brendan."

I disconnected from Zoller's network.

Time to head to the Piggly Wiggly.

I sent out a telepathic message to Zoller, whoever he or she was, thanking him or her for the excellent Wi-Fi. When I stared at the front of the place, I noticed something was different.

The neon sign in the window had been turned on.

Zoller's was open.

CHAPTER 9

"The Prettiest Girl in Town"

Zoller's, Shellman Bluff, Georgia
From the Journal of Brendan Macbean:

I don't know what made me go in there.

Maybe all that spy mongering, decoding messages, deluding the feds... made me thirsty. Maybe someone inside saw me sitting out here and turned on the sign a little early as a kind of invitation.

I put away the tablet, got out and locked the Land Cruiser.

The deck stretched across the front of the building, a set of stairs on the right. I climbed the stairs with the direct sun in my eyes. The screen door made a nostalgic squeak when I opened it.

Inside the room felt dark and cool. My pupils opened revealing details. Tables and chairs to my right and along the front windows. An L-shaped bar with chrome legged stools, vinyl covered seats with car logos: Ford, Chevy, Buick, Pontiac... Toyota.

A bartender stood behind the bar... a woman...

And I realized with a shock and a thrill... somehow I had located the prettiest girl in town.

I don't know why it surprised me. My career as a TV journalist took me to hundreds of small towns and rural areas, pursuing stories for the evening news. Beautiful women abound and not just in the big cities.

She stood there watching me looking at her... expecting me to look at her.

Shoulder length red hair, sparkling with sunlight from the windows framing a perfectly symmetrical face, straight nose, wide-set dark blue eyes, a wide mouth, skin creamy and glowing with health. A wholesome face, beautiful in an intriguing way that wasn't immediately apparent, exotic, elusive... but for me, women are always a trove of mysteries.

She stood maybe five feet six or seven, perfectly proportioned, slim with feminine workout muscles, her torso wrapped in a sleeveless, red-checked blouse tied at the bottom revealing an inch of taut belly. At least two buttons opened at the top, a glimpse of tantalizing cleavage.

She followed me with her eyes as I approached the bar, smiling a confident smile, an in-control, smile. She was younger than me, a woman with a girlish expression on her face, the kinds of looks girls use when they experiment with maturity, but now applied by a woman who had mastered them. She was playing with me and had gotten away with playing with men all her life.

I didn't mind.

A small plastic name tag pinned over her left breast said, "Magill."

Automatically, my brain's smartass apparatus formed a perfect opening line.

"And everyone knew her as Nancy," I said.

A blunder. I saw it immediately. The smile vanished from her face and puzzlement filled her eyes. I knew better. I have a weird sense of humor and should have just said, "Hello" or something.

But a moment later her smile returned, an even bigger smile. Maybe she got it, an obscure lyric from the worst-ever Beatle song. Well, maybe, "Why Don't We Do It in the Road" was worse.

Her chest expanded. She was going to say something. I couldn't keep my eyes off her breasts as they lifted gracefully, and I despised myself for not better controlling my inner caveman.

She didn't mind. Apparently.

"That's only about the third most popular pickup line I've heard around here."

Warm, misty, throaty South Georgia, her voice a finely tuned mezzo-soprano. Her eyes whispered to me things I couldn't comprehend... more than welcoming and friendly.

I felt welcome. And friendly. I knew I was going to push my luck.

"Don't much care about popular. I just want the one that works."

Her smile widened to a grin showing perfect, white teeth, and she said, "I've always been a pushover for, 'Hi, honey, I'm home!'"

I laughed and surprised myself at how easy and carefree it was.

She reached a delicate hand across the bar. I took it... a thrill of warm flesh, my hand enclosed fine, thin bones and muscles, a woman's hand, made mine feel manly.

"I'm Lily."

I said, "Lily? Really?"

She held my hand longer than necessary, like she wouldn't let it go.

"Yes. Really."

"Well, I guess I'm Brendan."

"Brendan, you guess. Well, it's Brendan then, if that's your best guess." she said. "Do you call yourself, Dan?"

What? Oh, the Beatles' song. That song was way before her time, but I guess, everyone knows Beatles songs.

"No, just Brendan. Macbean."

"Brendan" she said, "Macbean. I'll bet you want a Heineken."

"Uh, sure. How did you know?"

"Brendan. Macbean." She said it again as two sentences. "Guy comes in here dressed in crisp polo shirt and clean blue jeans."

Like a girl, she rose up on her tiptoes, leaned over the bar, showing more cleavage. Innocently? Shamelessly? I don't know.

"And what are those, Brendan 'I guess' Macbean, Cole Haan loafers?"

I looked down at my shoes. I didn't know what they were. Bettye picked them out for me.

Lily hopped down, turned around, slid a door back and leaned over the cooler a long time as if selecting the right green bottle. She wore hip-hugging Capris pants the color of Supergirl's tights.

Nice.

Lily stood up, turned around and cocked her head. The lustrous hair swirled.

"You'll want a frosted glass with that, right?"

"Perfect," I said, hoping I wasn't grinning like an idiot.

Expertly she poured the beer into a frosty-white pilsner glass, letting the last drop drip, and set it down in front of me. Then she cozied up on the other side of the bar and gave me an intent look.

"Brendan Macbean. That name sounds like you'd be famous."

I thought about that. I had been semi-famous if you considered I was on the Atlanta TV news several nights a week. But I hadn't been on TV for a long time.

"I used to be on TV in Atlanta. The evening news... I did the roving reporter kind of thing."

"Television? Wow, that must be exciting."

"Well, it can be. Atlanta isn't like New York, but was fun."

"You said, 'used to be?'"

"I'm retired," I said and waited for the next question.

Lily looked concerned as if I said I had a serious ailment.

"You look too young to be retired."

"Oh, I still do some freelance work. Like stories for other reporters, write for magazines, and the newspaper. I keep busy."

Her eyes brightened. "Did you come here to do a story about Shellman Bluff?"

I thought about that.

"I might," I said. "I'm staying at a friend's place in Gould's Landing. He said it's a great place to unwind."

"Who is your friend?"

"William Rawlings. I'm staying over at..."

"The Doc?" Lily said. She clapped her hands like a child. "I love the Doc. He comes to see me every time he's in town. Nobody beats him at trivia."

I have to admit, her enthusiasm toward Rawlings made me jealous, but her job was to entertain men, make them feel welcome here so they could spend money. I could see Rawlings holding court at trivia.

While I was plotting my witty comeback, the room went dark suddenly like the sun hiding behind a cloud. Lily's expression went from happy to revulsion, then stark terror.

I looked to my left and saw a giant man blocking the front door. He was so big he filled the door and tall enough he needed to duck his head, and wide enough to have to turn a little to enter.

He took a heavy step forward and allowed a little light to stream around him.

He was the size of a NFL lineman, but no athlete. His sausage like arms were bigger than my legs, and they framed a barrel chest and a huge gut that hung over his waistband and stretched a tee-shirt that had at least four X's on the label. His shaved head gleamed like a tan bowling ball and hunkered over near-neckless shoulders.

And the guy was ugly too... and scowling like an angry swine. He had black eyebrows over his little pig eyes and a pronounced Fu Manchu mustache. His image consultant must have liked comic books.

He walked straight up to me, leaned in close and scowled. Scowling from a height was even more menacing that at eye level.

What the hell?

"This place is closed. Get. Out." Bad breath wafted over me. His voice squealed a little higher pitched than expected.

I didn't look away, but it wasn't easy. "No. It's not. The sign says, 'Open.'"

His mean face pouted in a child's nightmare expression. More comic book stuff.

"Closed for you, dude. Get out or I'll break your legs, your arms and kick in a few ribs. I might even pull your head off. Nearest hospital is an hour away."

"He'll really do it, too." That came from another voice and the giant's eyes registered irritation. I hadn't noticed, but two men had come in with the bully and stood behind him. Two much smaller guys, and they had been completely blocked by the big guy.

Three against one, but I bet the other two could be ignored. The big guy, who's breath I was breathing was one hundred and ten percent of the trouble.

I had trained at Taekwondo for several years. Master Kim had taught me well and I sparred in hundreds of bouts, but Kim had warned me that bar fights were different, as there was no reason to respect your opponent for any other reason than his strength, his quickness and his skill. This guy seemed strong and big. Master Kim had taught me that there were hundreds of ways to incapacitate such an opponent. The absolute best was to jab out an eye. The loss of an eye stopped the fight.

But getting in bar fights didn't fit my new low profile. Plus, I was scared shitless. The best thing to do was to accede to his demand and leave. But I had a stubborn streak and a bad temper.

"Okay, I'll go as soon as I finish my beer."

The guy actually looked at my Pilsner glass full of Heineken. With a sudden, sweeping of his left arm, he backhanded my beer sending it tumbling and the golden liquid swirling through the air. The glass crashed behind the bar.

I looked for Lily. She had disappeared.

I tried to go... I really did, but I had relaxed so much while flirting with Lily and had entwined my ankles around the footrest ring in the barstool. I actually had difficulty disengaging my Cole Haan loafer-shod feet and when I did, my lower legs tingled like I had disturbed their naptime.

The ugly giant frowned.

I finally stumbled off the barstool. I had to walk around the big guy, who wouldn't get out of my way. I made halting steps to the screen door and slid out into the bright sunlight.

I counted myself lucky. I had managed to get away without incident.

But I was shaking. And pissed.

A huge, black HumVee sat parked next to my Toyota, gleaming from a recent detailing. It must be the vehicle the three men had arrived in. I descended the stairs and paused near the front fender of my Land Cruiser. There were firefighting tools in the back of my vehicle. I had a notion of using bolt cutters to cut off the valve stems of all the tires on the fat guy's HumVee, but I couldn't do that to an innocent car. It wasn't the car's fault its owner was a pig.

But I did have a thought, and it didn't come from Master Kim.

I unlocked the Land Cruiser and opened the passenger side door. From the glove box I retrieved a remote controller. The Land Cruiser's upfitters had installed a six-ton power winch in the front and cleverly hidden it inside the Toyota's grillwork. I squatted down at the front bumper and opened a chrome door.

The remote was simple. Power, neutral, in and out. I pulled out the large steel hook and with it came a length of steel cable. Everything worked smoothly. I threaded the hook and cable through Zoller's deck rail and turned and climbed the stairs. Picking up the hook, I walked to the screen door, opened it and propped the door open with a chair.

Inside the dark blinded me for a couple of seconds. There was the ugly giant sitting at the same chair I had recently vacated. The other two men sat to his right. It looked like they had served themselves beers.

Lily was nowhere in sight.

One of the men said, "That guy... he's back."

I crossed the floor, pulling the cable with me. The big guy didn't even turn his head to look at me.

"You just made a big mistake," he said. "Now it'll be two months in the hospital."

With a shaking voice I said, "Well, someone has to teach you some manners. And I'm just the guy to do it." I tried to make my voice calm, but my heart was racing like freight train. "First, you're going to buy me a beer for the one you spilled, and then you are going to leave."

He turned his swine-like face to look me in the eye. I saw a trace of confusion, an expression of, "What's going on." I wasn't following the script. He was obviously used to bulling guys like me around."

He said in his weird, squeaky voice, "I ain't going nowhere."

I said, "Yes, you are."

Very quickly, I bent down and slammed the steel hook over the foot ring of his bar stool. He had also tangled his much bigger feet in the steel bars, just like I had earlier.

Perfect.

I hit the "IN" button on the remote and jumped out of the way. The six-ton winch took up the slack with amazing power and speed. The bar stool's feet rocketed off the floor toward the door like an exploding covey of quail. An enormous growl erupted from the stool's feet scraping on the floor. Three hundred and fifty pounds of bully lurched sideways. Falling, he smashed his face against the corner of the bar, and he hit the floor like a side of beef. Instantly the barstool slithered toward the door with the guy's feet still tangled in the foot ring. It wasn't smooth like a train but more in jerks and rushes as the friction of all that flesh gathered and jerked across the grimy vinyl. I saw that a leg of the barstool wasn't going to clear the door frame and I kicked savagely at it.

It just cleared the door, but the man didn't. There was just too much of him and he extruded himself through the door onto the bright sunlit deck like sausage through a meat grinder.

The man's tee-shirt had pulled itself up and over his head and shoulders, showing a bloated, gleaming white belly, now covered in serious abrasions, lacerations, bruises, contusions.

The guy was a mess.

I stopped the winch as it reached the deck rail. No point in messing up a perfectly good deck, other than the trail of blood and skin he had left in his wake.

Gee, I was beginning to feel sorry for the guy.

I bent down, unhooked the steel hook, hit the 'IN" button and saw the cable slither through the deck rail, across the ground and disappear into the grillwork of the Toyota.

Sirens blaring and lights flashing, no less than three police cruisers and a dark blue Chevy Tahoe screamed into Zoller's parking lot.

CHAPTER 10

"Deputy Leggo"

Zoller's, Shellman Bluff, Georgia
From the Journal of Brendan Macbean:

The police cruisers and the Tahoe all had "SHERIFF, McIntosh County" emblazoned across the doors in red-lined, silvery letters, "Emergency 911" and "Sheriff Lanny Boatwright" in somewhat smaller script. They pulled up and scattered across the gravel like kids' toys dropped from a box. Six policemen exited the cruisers in a training formation, not with weapons drawn but at the ready.

And from the Tahoe, a large, black policeman in a dark blue uniform stepped slowly out, put his hands on his hips and surveyed the situation.

I sort of anticipated what would happen next. I tried to remain calm, my hands visible and at ease.

Are you kidding me? Calm? There was three hundred and fifty pounds of bleeding fat man laying at my feet whom I had just whizbanged with a six-ton winch... Surely you could get arrested for that... and I'm supposed to remain calm?

I cleared my throat. "Sheriff, can you call for an ambulance? This man is seriously hurt and unconscious."

The large black policeman turned his head toward one of the others and barked an order. Then he turned his face toward me. He was calm. I wasn't.

"Sir, will you identify yourself?"

"Yes, I am Brendan Macbean."

The big deputy approached and climbed the stairs. On his left shirt pocket flap a name tag gave me another challenge. The small brass rectangle said, "LEGGO."

The short climb made him gasp for air. He also was a big man and in better shape than the fat slob laying on the deck. More like a linebacker than a lineman.

"Brendan, can I see some ID?"

I handed my driver's license to him. He held it between thumb and forefinger and took a picture with his cell phone. He turned it over, took a picture of the back and handed it back to me,

It's been a long time since I'd been pulled over. Cell phones had replaced clipboards, I guess.

Policemen were everywhere, in the parking lot, up on the deck bending over the unconscious man laying at my feet... two were on their knees trying to untangle the man's feet from the barstool.

I pointed. "Officer, I have a toolkit in my car. I think you'll have to unscrew the footrest."

Deputy Leggo looked at his men. They were attempting to roll the man over but were thwarted by his enormous bulk. One of them pulled his tee shirt down from his head but couldn't get enough of it free to hide the huge gut.

Leggo studied his face. One side was a massive bruise from temple to chin. Broken nose and cheekbone at a minimum, by my estimate. Blood seeped from his nose and mouth. Maybe a few loose teeth, too.

One of the policemen trying to untangle his feet said, "It's him. It's the Barn alright."

"Macbean," Leggo said. "Which of these vehicles are yours? The Land Cruiser or the Pimp-Limo?"

I pointed to the Toyota. "That's mine."

"Are you Fire Department?"

"No, sir."

"Why are you driving a Fire Service Command Vehicle?"

"Just lucky, I guess. I bought it from the Smyrna Fire Department. They had an extra one."

"Hmmm," Leggo said. "Smyrna, like up in Atlanta?"

I nodded.

Two of his men emerged from the front door of Zollers. One of them said, "Clear inside, Leggo." I guessed they had entered the restaurant from a back door and made sure there weren't criminals lurking. Foolishly I noticed I had left the front door propped open.

Leggo turned to me and said, "What happened here, Macbean?"

I took a moment to think.

"I was inside chatting it up with the lady bartender when this guy comes in and he tells me to leave. He says the place is closed and then he threatened to break my legs, arms and 'stove in a couple of ribs' as he put it. Oh, he also said he might pull my head off. Then he back-hands my beer across the bar."

"Your beer? Did you feel threatened?"

What a preposterous question!

"Officer, that man is three times bigger than me. Of course, I felt threatened."

Officer Leggo seemed unperturbed. "What did you do?"

"I left, but I was shaking so much I couldn't drive. So I'm standing by my car when I heard a commotion going on in the bar. It sounded like all hell was breaking loose and this guy comes flying out the door. I go up on the deck and you guys show up."

He looked at me long and hard enough to make me uncomfortable.

"That's it?" he said dryly.

"Yup." I folded my arms over my chest. Standard defensive posture.

"Macbean, we received a call about twenty minutes ago. Miss Magill, Lily, called us to report the arrival of a known felon, a guy we have more warrants on than anybody. Well, almost anybody."

"You mean there's an asshole around here worse than this guy?"

He chuckled at that. "Yeah, maybe. That's why we show up with the whole cavalry. Murder, attempted murder, armed robbery, extortion, assault..."

"Who is it?"

We both looked down at the mountain of white flesh, streaked red and blue with bruises and torn skin. It was hard to look at.

"This here is Keith Barnecki, a really bad actor. He's called 'Barn.'"

"Well that suits him although I could add a few more derogatory names. And you might as well add the charge of assaulting me to his list."

"Right, but we didn't come loaded for bear because of a bar fight."

"There wasn't any bar fight. At least as far as I was know. You should ask the other two guys."

"What other two guys?"

"Didn't you see two other guys inside?"

Leggo turned to one of the policemen who had just come from inside the bar.

"Hey, AB, did you see anyone else inside? A couple of guys?"

The officer shook his head. "No, just Lily. She locked herself in the office. We didn't see anyone else."

"So Macbean, what'd these two guys look like?"

"Hmmm... I didn't get much of a look at them. This guy got all my attention. They were like six feet, dark brown hair. Paunchy. One of them had some gray."

Officer Leggo gave me a smirk, like he didn't expect much from a witness.

"That's all you got?"

I folded my arms again.

"That's it."

The ambulance arrived. Most of the policemen had reached the standing around stage. Two of them still worked at getting the unconscious man's feet free of the bar stool. They had unbolted the foot ring and pulled the stool's legs and seat away. I guess they brought their own tool kit. But the man's massive legs and feet wouldn't fit through the steel ring even when detached.

The EMS crew were much more efficient. They backed the ambulance right up to the bottom of the steps, opened double rear doors and removed a gurney. They bounded up the steps in tandem and laid the folded gurney beside the stricken man.

They were also expert at moving large, inert bodies. Even so, they needed the help of several policemen to get "Barn" on the stretcher and everyone except me had to help hefting the gurney down the stairs and into the ambulance.

The ambulance roared off with lights blazing and siren blaring. Officer Leggo and I watched it zooming down Shellman Bluff Road.

Leggo's phone rang. He turned away from me to gain a smidgen of privacy.

"Yes sir, we got him. No, still out cold. The other guy's name is Macbean. You saw the license. Yes, I sent it directly to NCIC. No. He says he doesn't know. No. No, not really. Okay."

He switched off without saying goodbye.

Leggo turned toward me, his expression pained. I thought, this isn't going to be fun.

"Brendan, I wonder if you would like to ride down to Darien with me?"

"What for?"

"Sheriff Boatwright wants to talk to you."

I felt like asking the same question again, but a more important question came to mind.

"Am I under arrest?"

Officer Leggo backpedaled. "Oh, no sir. Sheriff just wants to talk to you. Mister 'Barn' has warrants out in at least five counties. There's going to be a lot of prosecuting coming up and we got to get all the details down. So, if you'd just come with me, we'd all be grateful."

"How about if I follow you in my car?"

He turned to look at my red and white machine gleaming in the noon sun.

"It'd be against procedure."

"I can't leave it here, Officer Leggo."

"If you don't mind, Brendan, I'll have AB bring it down. He'll be real nice with it."

"Nope. And you're not going to tow it either. That thing has Armageddon-level security. The wheels are locked up. You can't open it. You might blow it up with a couple of sticks of dynamite, but no, I'm not going to let one of your guys drive my car.

"But, Officer Leggo, I have a better idea."

Leggo frowned. "What's that?"

"Why don't you and I go in the Land Cruiser. I'll let you drive."

A huge grin spread across his face.

CHAPTER 11

"Feed me like a prisoner"

Darien, Georgia
From the Journal of Brendan Macbean:

TLC asked, "Boss, who's the big guy?"

Officer Leggo had just settled in behind the wheel.

"What's that?" he asked looking at me.

I felt uncomfortable sitting in the passenger seat. I didn't like the view or the lack of control.

"This vehicle has really cool technology. Most of the functions can be voice activated. There are computers on board with links to the internet, access to databases, cell data, GPS, you name it. The guys who put this Toyota together gave it a voice activated digital assistant, knowledge navigator and general all-around computerized go-getter. I went to a training course after buying this car and they told me I could personalize her, uh, it, anyway I wanted. I got to choose the voice, the personality and something they called 'adaptive interactive spontaneity.'"

Leggo thought for a second. "So it's like Siri... like on my phone?"

TLC chimed in. "I beg your pardon? That dull robot? Not even close."

"Uh, she's a little sensitive."

Leggo smiled. "Yeah, I get that."

"TLC, this is Deputy Sheriff Leggo."

"Hello, Deputy Sheriff Leggo," she said in her most sultry voice.

I was jealous.

"Deputy Leggo is going to drive us to Darien."

"I see that Darien, Georgia is about eighteen miles away. Deputy Sheriff Leggo, would you like directions?"

Leggo thought for a second. "I certainly do not need directions, but I you can totally tell me how to get there."

"Back off, Leggo. TLC is my girl."

"Boys, please!" TLC said mirthfully.

Leggo fumbled with the side of his seat.

I knew he needed more room for his linebacker body. I said, "Ask TLC to adjust it."

"Really?"

I nodded.

"TLC, could you take the seat back a little?"

The seat hummed. Leggo moved back.

"Like that, Deputy Sheriff Leggo?" TLC asked.

"A little more, please. And call me Leggo."

He was getting a little too chummy with my car.

"This feels good. Yeah," Deputy Leggo said with a sigh. "How do I start it?"

I pointed. "Red button there. Says, 'Start'."

He smiled, "Yeah. Oh wow, look at all the lights." I enjoyed his fascination watching all the displays light up. "This is like a jet plane."

My turn to say, "Yeah."

As he turned out onto Shellman Bluff Road, Leggo asked, "This thing have lights?"

"It's an EMS vehicle. It has lights like Times Square."

In a few seconds, his heavy foot had us up to seventy.

"And sirens?"

"A dozen different modes. TLC, show deputy Leggo our sirens on the display."

Leggo glanced briefly at the dashboard display.

"We're driving through small houses, churches and the like. No need to disturb the peaceful countryside, but when we hit I-95, I'm going 'French Connection' all the way to Darien."

We crossed another arm of the marsh over a bridge marked, "White Chimney River", and passed a large, boarded up facility enclosed in a weed choked chain link fence.

"Lockwood Marine," Leggo said. "Closed couple of years ago."

I nodded and we drove on, the big deputy pushing the Land Cruiser through the countryside not peacefully at all.

I counted three whitewashed churches and a smattering of small houses, all of it surrounded by pine forest.

I turned to Leggo. "I have to ask."

Without taking his eyes off the road he smiled. "About the name?"

"Yeah. What's with 'Leggo?'"

"My given name is Antonio Francisco Leggiero. My dad is Francisco Leggiero, the conductor. My adopted dad, that is. They adopted me when I was five days old. My real momma died of an overdose in the University Hospital in Charleston."

"Your dad's a conductor, like classical music?"

"Used to be. He's retired. Former Music Director of the Hilton Head Symphony. Anyway, my Italian parents are all I've ever known. Gave me a name my friends couldn't pronounce, especially when I started playing football."

I chimed in, "But everyone knows how to say, 'Leggo.'"

"Yup."

I had a zillion questions to ask him, but we had turned right and left and now were slowing to enter, 'Eulonia,' according to the sign.

"Now there's a name I don't know how to pronounce."

Leggo said something that sounded like, "You-loan-ya."

We passed the Piggy Wiggly grocery store and my stomach rumbled. I'd had nothing since that frozen waffle this morning.

He stopped the Toyota at a four-way intersection.

"What is that?" I pointed at a blinking red light suspended over the road.

"That's one of McIntosh County's two traffic lights."

He whipped the Toyota right and in a minute we were rocketing south on I-95 lights blazing and "French Connection" siren blaring. It felt like a Jason Bourne movie. The GPS display showed us accelerating past the double-digit threshold. I looked over at Leggo. He gripped the wheel with a calm exhilaration. The Land Cruiser remained steady, even quiet, the siren muted by the extraordinary sound-proofing engineered into its chassis.

The southbound traffic of I-95 parted like Moses himself was there with a whistle and the Land Cruiser roared and screamed by like a flaming eagle. It seemed only a minute until we slashed onto the Darien exit way too fast for my comfort level. I expected Leggo to bleed off some speed heading up the exit ramp, but he spun the wheel hard right at the top and we careened drunkenly to the left in a sharp right turn. I braced for a rollover, but all four wheels stayed on the ground, and we headed west without losing any speed at all. The few cars we encountered scattered like quail as the Land Cruiser straddled the centerline at over a hundred miles per hour.

And then massive deceleration squeezed the breath from my lungs as my body flung forward against the seat belt. We slid into another right. A big sign flashed,' the word "Sheriff" was the only one I caught.

We raced up a paved drive and slid gracefully into a parking space marked with a sign that said, "Reserved for the Officer of the Month."

And for a moment the only sound we heard was the smooth hum of the engine while the two of us quivered like horses after a race

I turned to Leggo and said, "Congratulations."

"What? For not killing us?"

I nodded toward the sign.

Leggo smiled, "I tell Lanny to give that to someone else, but he won't."

"Must be your driving," I said.

"Yeah, Macbean. What can I say? I love my job." His big hands fondled the leather wrapped steering wheel. "Nice ride."

"Yeah. I love it. Look Leggo, when we go in. I'm locking it up. I do not give permission for you to search my car. You won't be able to get in anyway without a jackhammer."

"I'll tell the guys to keep their distance, but this baby will draw a crowd. Can't help that."

The building that housed the McIntosh Sheriff's Department reminded me of a high school, a nice red façade and alternating red and tan bricks. Except for a high chain-link fence in the back of the building, you might have thought you were heading into school.

The lobby was so full of people there was nowhere to sit, but Leggo stalked straight toward a central booth marked, "Information."

A uniformed police officer sat behind a low frosted-glass wall. He looked up from reading a "People" magazine. Angelina Jolie pouted on the front cover.

"Leggo. Heard we got the Barn."

Leggo nodded. "Dave. We got him all right. He's on his way to the Brunswick Hospital."

Dave grinned. "You shoot him, Leggo?"

"Nope. He fell off his bar stool." Leggo shot me a glance. "Landed hard, I guess."

The "Information" officer looked me over. "Who's this?"

Leggo's smile vanished. "Somebody to talk to Lanny. Where is he?"

Dave said, "The Sheriff's on a call in his office." He gave us a squinty expression, like he had a big secret. "He closed his door."

"Come on, Macbean." Leggo headed toward a hallway on the left. He turned to say something to Dave. The "Information" guy had already returned to the magazine and I had an intuitive thought. That guy's never going to make detective.

"Tell Lanny, we're going to the conference room."

We walked through a large room, what most office workers know as a bullpen or cubical city, except there were no cubical walls, just a matrix of desks, all occupied with men and women, some in uniform and some not. I only saw one man in handcuffs, a sullen looking thirty-something with a bleary-eyed expression.

The conference room was like most I had seen. Large, rectangular table with a spider-like speaker phone in the center, enough chairs scattered around for about thirty people, big flat screen TV mounted high on the wall.

As boring as dust.

And to think I was watching a sunrise just this morning. Life can be a twisting-turning kind of thing.

Leggo ducked out and returned with, of all things, a can of Diet Dr. Pepper. He set the can in front of me and backed up a step.

"Thought you'd want something to drink." It was hard to look at his eager-puppy expression.

I shook my head. "What did I do to offend you, Deputy Leggo?"

"What?"

"It's after one o'clock and I haven't had anything to eat today except a stale Eggo, Leggo. And all you got is this can of chemicals? What'd you think, I was from Texas?"

My speech left him speechless.

"Where's the cafeteria? Why can't we wait in there?" Idly I picked up the TV remote and fiddled with it.

Leggo's look told me I had been too harsh.

"We don't have a cafeteria. We got a break room. It's got coffee," he offered hopefully. "We always have coffee."

I thought about the "blend" and I thought about police station coffee, made on a Bunn coffee maker about two hours ago and… suddenly the Diet Dr. Pepper seemed preferable.

"A breakroom? How do you feed the prisoners?"

"Prisoners? We don't keep too many. Maybe there's three or four. Anyway, there's a seafood place in town. They bring meals in for prisoners if we have any."

"That sounds good enough for me, Leggo. Feed me like a prisoner."

Uh oh. I could tell by the way his face sagged, he had more bad news.

"Prisoners don't get lunch until one. The restaurant… well, it's after their lunch crowd."

"Okay, Leggo. Not even a stale donut in the break room?"

"Macbean, you came through the bullpen. What chance would a donut have with that crowd?"

"Not much, I guess. Well, where's the sheriff? What's he got going that's such a big deal?"

I mashed the "on" button on the TV remote.

And we both saw what was more important. And it was a very big deal.

"Terrorist attack against Coast Guard?" That was CNN. I clicked to Fox News, MSNBC, HLN. They all covered same story with identical imaging, the same shocking video of a small Coast Guard boat with its cabin blown off.

And it happened just twenty miles away from where I sat.

CHAPTER 12

"Sheriff Boatwright"

Darien, Georgia
From the Journal of Brendan Macbean:

A good reporter's curiosity fuels his drive. Without it he can only transcribe other people's discoveries, which isn't journalism.

At the beginning of any story, there is just an event, something lovable, quaint, horrible, tragic, something big or small, possibly some congruence that no one else notices, but catches the reporter's eye and the tingle starts and this drives the reporter to find the story and get it out.

A good reporter must get the story out, will do anything, ask any question, take any risk, will get in people's faces, get thrown out on his or her ear, and will persist against censure and ridicule.

Just to get the story out.

A good reporter doesn't follow a leader, doesn't have an agenda, or a point to prove. Although he may follow the money because money is big motivator. Money, or a job or his bosses orders doesn't cloud a reporter's objectivity. He or she is glued to the facts.

And you must have the facts to get the story out. Not some or most of the facts. All the facts. A good reporter names names and takes the heat, is used to the heat and the hotter it gets the better the story. Good reporters face mobs, armies, guns, fire, storms, epidemics, risks his relationships, family, friends and definitely his career.

Lots of pain and little glamour. And there's not much money in it.

This wasn't my story. It was already breaking and somebody else was putting it out there. Reporters would be crawling all over this one.

I couldn't afford to get involved. I had to keep a low profile. I wasn't a reporter anymore. My shredded resume said so.

But something told me this was my story, and that no one else could do it. No one else could or would put all the pieces together. And I didn't even have any of the pieces.

I knew I was going to make a phone call and talk to the one person I swore I'd never talk to again... a man I despised who had threatened to destroy my life.

But I felt the tingle go down my spine, more seductive than a woman's touch.

Money motivates television, which is why it's prone to exaggeration. The TV reporters worked it as a big story. Right now, nobody knew much of anything, just the same facts and the same photo of the blown-up boat shown over and over again. I could imagine the endless speculation spewing from the babbling mouths of experts.

Idly, my fingers poked the screen of my iPhone trying to find a picture of one of these boats when it was new. What did an undamaged one look like?

The news coverage beat me to it.

"The Defender is an aluminum-hulled vessel, equipped with a rigid foam-filled flotation collar. The first generation of boats were built by SAFE Boats International of Bremerton, Washington, a manufacturer of government and law enforcement boats. The boat is powered by twin Honda outboards with a combined four hundred and fifty horsepower, a maximum speed of fifty miles per hour and a crew of four."

The promotional clip showed an orange and gunmetal colored boat proudly zooming through a moderate chop. It had a rectangular, centered cabin with forward slanting windows. A crewman stood in the bow manning a machine gun and another gunman in the stern. The boat bounced through the waves like an amusement park ride. Surely the machine gunner would have a problem aiming that gun, but it looked deadly and if I saw it coming at me, I would heave-to, immediately... or whatever they did on the high seas.

The damaged boat looked identical except for the blown off cabin and dark soot spread everywhere. The cabin hadn't been completely blown off, but the top half was nowhere to be seen, leaving jagged two-foot-high metal walls, a sad burned-out rectangle.

"Three Coast Guard sailors were killed when an explosion occurred aboard a Defender Class boat in the Georgia seaport of Brunswick. The boat was on a routine training mission when at approximately eleven forty-five this morning an explosion of unknown origin ripped the cabin of the boat apart, killing three crew members instantly. A fourth crewmember was rushed to a nearby hospital where he remains in intensive care, with life threating injuries.

"Pleasure boaters discovered the wreckage drifting off Fancy Bluff Creek and called nine one one. Another Coast Guard boat towed the stricken vessel to the nearby security terminal operated by the Georgia Port Authority."

Investigators from every cop organization, government security department would swarm over the wreckage and the chance a guy like me would get within a hundred yards of the scene was close to zero.

"Leggo, how far away is that?"

He was staring at the TV, his policeman's game-face on. "About twenty-five miles. Down I95."

I had the feeling that if I had said, 'Let's go!' at that moment he would have headed for my Toyota like a linebacker sacking a quarterback.

But something unexpected happened that changed everything.

Robert Redford entered the room carrying two large brown paper grocery bags.

It's amazing how a startling experience can empty your mind and fill it with spinning wheels.

I had met Mr. Redford many years ago in Atlanta at some black-tie function where he had given me a half-second smile. Once in Sundance, Utah, I saw several "Redfords" all at once. Promoters hired look-alikes to prowl the streets and taverns to give visitors a thrill. It's a little unnerving seeing four or five "Redfords" sitting at a table sharing a pitcher.

But here he was in the conference room of the McIntosh County Sheriff's Office hefting a couple of grocery bags. This was "Up Close and Personal."

Of course, it wasn't Redford. On closer inspection, it was just a man who looked like him, his age, maybe circa "The Horse Whisperer." I concluded that it was the sheriff, who's name had been painted on the police cruiser, "Lanny Boatwright."

I stood and held out my hand. He set the grocery bags on the conference table. The bags were expressing a delightful fried-food scent.

Sheriff Boatwright's handshake was gentle but not his stare, which was predatory.

"Brendan, I presume. Sorry to make you wait." His voice was a cultured Southern accent, not at all Redford-like, but crusty and world-worn. I had the feeling he didn't like me and had good reason to, I guess.

I nodded toward the television. "I guess you had more important things to do."

"Oh that? That's down in Glynn County. I've got nothing to do with it. Besides the Coast Guard has their own investigators, and so does the Georgia Port Authority, the Georgia Bureau of Investigation, the FBI, Homeland Security, NSA and I'm sure the Justice Department just put some guys on a plane."

He picked up the remote control and turned off the television.

The man was pissed about something, but I wasn't happy to be here either.

"Look, Sheriff, I'm spending my vacation time in your police station. At your request and not under arrest. I think I can find my way out."

Our eyes locked in that male-dominance thing that looks so silly if you're not involved. I was vaguely aware of Leggo standing behind me. He could easily make a move toward the door to cut me off if needed.

But the crystal blue Robert Redford eyes softened and out came a smile. I wasn't sure the tough-sheriff act wasn't just an act.

"Brendan, I'm forgetting my manners. You probably haven't had lunch." My eyes darted toward the grocery bags. Sheriff Boatwright pulled out three foam boxes and placed one in front me and slid one toward Leggo. Then he brought out a plastic gallon-jug of a brown liquid I was pretty sure was iced tea. That was followed by three foam cups full of ice.

I heard the foam box calling my name and promptly sat down.

"I had Slim bring us the fried shrimp lunch from B and J's over in Darien. That's sweet tea if you want it."

I did, infinitely more than the Diet Dr. Pepper. I slid the can over to Leggo who opened it and poured it over his ice.

The foam box contained six jumbo fried shrimp, a hushpuppy larger than a golf ball and a mound of coleslaw. Out of the bag came plastic tubs of cocktail and tartar sauce and some slim packets of tabasco sauce.

I was in Southern Fried Food Heaven. The shrimp were perfect, moist, crunchy, flavorful.

I ate. We ate.

I noticed I was nibbling down on the tail of the shrimp and my mother had taught me a gentleman does not to eat the tails of fried shrimp. But I don't think Mom ever had fried shrimp this good. Apparently, Sheriff Boatwright and Leggo had received different instruction from their mothers because the tails were ingested, and new shrimps eaten in a somewhat contiguous process.

And hushpuppies and slaw with a few drops of tabasco. It all disappeared.

Heavenly. Even the sweet tea was perfect. It was soul-filling food as real and Southern as heat and humidity.

What do three hungry men talk about when they're eating?

Well, not much really.

With abstraction, I noticed Leggo mixing Tabasco with his tartar sauce.

In my opinion his taste buds lined up with liking Diet Dr. Pepper. To each his own.

Finally, the sheriff pushed away his foam box, with little left in it that might be consumable. With obvious forbearance, he watched me finish my lunch.

When I had slowed to pushing around crumbs he said, "Brendan, before I came in here I was talking with the state attorney general."

The comment made little impression on me. The significance of talking to the state attorney general didn't penetrate my food-soddened brain.

Sheriff Boatwright's face went back to looking annoyed.

"It was the longest ten minutes of my life, Macbean."

I put down my fork.

"What?"

"The state attorney general... he chewed my ass out a straight ten minutes, called me a 'ignorant, red-necked hillbilly.' In fact those were his exact words. Then he accused me of running some 'Boss Hogg Dukes of Hazzard' speed trap and it wasn't going to fly up there in the capital'."

The fried shrimp lunch settled in my stomach like a bag of gravel.

I attempted to rescue myself from my predicament with my wit.

"You have a hill around here sheriff?"

Boatwright smiled, looking like he could survive an ass chewing as good as the next guy.

"The landfill, Macbean, about ten miles north. They pile the trash about two hundred feet high. It's a best place around here to see a bald eagle... or the worst.

"The attorney general said, 'Turn him loose. Give him a police escort.' Lunch was my idea."

"Who, me?"

"Yes, you, Macbean. I guess you have some sort of diplomatic immunity. The call came about fifteen minutes after Leggo entered your driver's license into the NCIC. I never intended to charge you with anything, despite the obvious evidence that you assaulted the guy. We're delighted to have Barnecki in custody. We've had warrants on him for two years and we couldn't find him. He's nearly the most wanted criminal within a hundred miles."

There was that word again, 'nearly' and I had to ask, again. "You mean there's a worse asshole running around in McIntosh?"

The sheriff winced at my vulgar choice of words.

"Oh, there's worse. There's always somebody smarter, meaner, willing to do worse things to people. There's a whole lot worse."

"I'll steer clear of all of them, Sheriff." But I wondered what kind of place I had wandered into.

"So why the special treatment, Macbean? How do you get to be above the law?"

I had my thoughts about that, but I wanted to avoid a complicated discussion.

"Sheriff, I don't think of myself as 'above the law.'"

The sheriff thought about that for a moment.

"Okay, Macbean, go ahead and confess your crimes. Leggo and I will listen." He slouched slightly in his chair and folded his arms.

I thought, Touché, sheriff. Funny.

Boatwright broke the silence. "My computer guy, Raju, looked you up. He says you're an award-winning TV reporter. And you had a best-selling book a while back."

"Let me bring Raju up to date. I'm retired. Any awards I got are ancient history."

"A little young to be retired, aren't you?"

I guess I'm going to get that comment until I finally get old for real.

"Sheriff, life is a twisty-turny thing. Let's just leave it that that's my business."

"Fair enough. Anyway, you have complete immunity in my county. From the State Attorney General's office and from me personally. That means I want to get you out of McIntosh as soon as possible. But before you go, tell me how does a guy..." He gave me a look over. "What are you? A hundred and fifty pounds?"

"Soaking wet."

"'How do you throw a three-hundred-and-fifty-pound bully out of a bar, smash in his face, dislocate his jaw and manage to cover him with cuts and bruises? Did I leave anything out?"

I only debated for a second. I might as well tell them.

"Sheriff, it was really quite easy. My Land Cruiser has a winch."

Out of the corner of my eye, I saw Leggo straighten up in his seat, as if his mind had been working on that very problem.

"A winch?"

"Yeah. In the front grillwork of the Toyota, they managed to hide a six-ton electric winch. It works on a remote control. Real simple controls, In, Out and Neutral. Fast or Slow.

"So, I walked back into the bar. Barn and I had some words, and I hooked the cable on the bar stool. The man had his ankles tangled in the footrest. I hit the 'In' button and the winch did the rest."

I felt their eyes on me as they pictured it in their minds.

"Just before you guys arrived, I unhooked the cable and rewound it back into the Land Cruiser. You pretty much know the rest."

"Wow, Macbean. I don't know what to say. That was pretty darned clever."

The three of us were silent for a minute. Finally Leggo said in his deep voice, "You hooked him, Mister Brendan. Hooked him good."

That brought out a little chuckle.

"Well, you're in the clear Macbean," Sheriff Boatwright said. "But I'd like to ask you a few questions."

"Sure Sheriff. All the questions you want but before I go, I'd like to ask a favor."

"What?"

"After your questions, Sheriff."

Sheriff Boatwright took out a piece of paper.

"Macbean, when my troops arrived at Zollers, they immediately covered all the entrances. There's two on the front and one in the back. Not one of my guys saw anyone else come out. You said two men came in with Barn."

I thought about it for a minute. "They must have ducked out the back. Before your men arrived. What's behind Zollers?"

"Just a neighborhood of small houses, lots of over-grown lots. It wouldn't be hard for somebody to slip away. But you said you saw them come in with Barnecki. What'd they look like?"

For a moment, I could not recall their faces. Just two guys standing behind the fat bully.

"Well, Sheriff, I think my focus was on Barn, not them."

"Close your eyes, Macbean," he said quietly. "How old were they?"

I closed my eyes and saw the two men standing behind the Barn.

"One of them was in his late forties. The other younger. The older guy had a goatee full of gray whiskers. The younger one, kind of a few days of scraggle."

"Hair color?"

"Dark. The younger guy had a hat on."

I opened my eyes. I had a picture.

"How tall?" The sheriff's voice was hypnotic

"About six feet, both of them."

"What else?"

"Sheriff, they had a resemblance, like cousins. Or just two guys who looked alike."

"Brothers, maybe?"

"Or just two guys who look alike. One of them had a funny voice."

"They spoke?"

"Well, after Barn threatened to pull my head off, one of them said, 'He'll do it, too' or something like that. His voice was funny."

"Funny how?"

"I'm not sure... like a puppy dog, eager to please."

Boatwright and Leggo looked at each other. I know how exasperating witnesses can be. I've interviewed thousands of them.

"Sheriff, one of them spoke when I came back in with the cable. He said, 'He's back. That guy's back' or something like that. Same voice."

"Same guy, maybe or two guys who might be kin speak the same?"

"No, Sheriff. It's like the older one was keeping his mouth shut."

"Not happy?"

I thought about that. No, that dude wasn't happy and the younger guy was jittery, nervous… talkative."

"Well, Macbean. We're getting a picture, here. How were they dressed?"

I thought about it. "Jeans. I didn't see their feet. The older guy had a short-sleeved shirt with a logo. Don't know what the logo was. Could have been Bass Pro Shops, for all I know. The one with the hat wore a golf shirt."

"We really want to find these two guys. They sound local. Leggo, you getting any vibes?"

Leggo was bent over a notebook, scribbling. He shook his head.

"Anything else?" the sheriff asked.

I closed my eyes.

"Sheriff! One of them had a bandaged ear!" I exclaimed, like I had seen Jesus.

Both cops straightened up.

"Really? Which one?"

"The one with the hat. The bandage on the top of his earlobe made his hat crooked like he couldn't fit it down on his head because of the bandage."

"The younger one, right?" and Sheriff Boatwright gave me a look like, why didn't you tell me this sooner?

"What?"

Boatwright took a deep breath. "Macbean, this is a multiple-choice question. How did the bandage look? Was it a thrown-on job like Aunt Martha did it in the kitchen with a cigarette dangling from her lips or professional, like done in an emergency room?"

I closed my eyes to get a better look at my recollection.

"Aunt Martha with the Marlboro in her mouth. Big thick wad of gauze and adhesive tape."

Sheriff Boatwright shrugged. There would be no local hospital records to check.

I tried to make him feel better. "Sheriff, there was a spot of blood seeping through. Must have been recent."

"Okay, Macbean. We'll look for these two hombres."

We sat in stillness for a minute, our thoughts swirling like the ceiling fan.

The sheriff said, "You said you needed a favor?"

CHAPTER 13

"Calling Bentley"

Darien, Georgia
From the Journal of Brendan Macbean:

In the middle of the conference room table sat a speakerphone with the name "Polycom" on it.

"Sheriff, I need to make a call. I'd like to use your phone in here."

Boatwright gave me a curious look. "You want to make a call?"

"Yes, and I want to use your speakerphone. That one." I pointed.

"It's not such a big favor, but why don't you use your own phone. You could make this call in the privacy of your car where it's probably quieter."

"I actually can't tell you, sheriff. I'd like you or your tech-person to set up the call..." I took a deep breath. "And leave the room."

The sheriff's curious expression turned to confusion.

"Who are you calling?"

"I'm calling the guy who called the state attorney general and ordered him to call you and ream you out about me."

Sheriff Boatwright winced at the word 'ream'. He looked at his hands as if they were guilty of something. Then his crystal blue eyes bored into mine.

"What they say is true, then. 'It' flows downhill."

"That's true, Sheriff, but you left out half of the word."

Sheriff Boatwright nodded. "I promised my wife I'd curtail my crude language."

"Very noble, Sheriff."

"What's going on, here, Macbean? Who is this guy?"

"Sheriff, the man's called Bentley, but it's not his real name. He works for the Federal Department of Justice. He's high-ranking and has been in his job through five administrations, practically untouchable. He runs the Federal Witness Protection program..."

"You're in WITSEC?"

"No. I'm a real person. The same your computer guy found on the internet... retired TV journalist. Born and raised in Atlanta, went to Georgia Southern."

Leggo chimed in, "Go Eagles!"

"Leggo, you went there?"

The big deputy snorted. "No. I went to Clemson. We played you when I was a senior. We expected a cakewalk, but you guys nearly killed us."

"GSU takes football seriously. But I was there a long time ago."

The sheriff tapped the table. "Brendan, why is this Bentley protecting you?"

I realized I couldn't explain anything to either of them. Or anyone. No one. My secrets, my isolation.

"I can't tell you, Sheriff. You're going to have to trust me. I want to use your phone because it can be encrypted. He won't talk on anything else."

The sheriff stared at the phone. "Our SPLOST dollars at work. The county manager bought those fancy things last year. I don't know what was wrong with the old one. That and new computers and lots of complicated equipment. They didn't ask me what I wanted.

"Leggo, you know how to work this thing?"

"Sure do, Sheriff."

Leggo had conjured a laptop and was banging away on it. He slid a piece of paper toward me.

"Brendan. Dial nine to get an outside line. The DOJ generates encryption codes with an algorithm every nine minutes. I wrote it there. When you reach your party, they'll give you a PIN number. They will tell you when to enter this number. Hit the pound key, then the PIN. They'll give you a countdown, then hit the green button. It'll light up while you're encrypted. Hang up when you're done."

While I absorbed this procedure, Sheriff Boatwright stood and laid a business card on the table. "Macbean, call me if you need to. Come on, Leggo. Let's give the man his privacy."

The two left the room and closed the door.

The room went cold.

I stared at the speakerphone for a second and dragged it over to me.

I went through the sequence Leggo had given me.

A dial tone... hit nine and another dial tone. I dialed from memory, etched deep by the eminence of the man I was about to talk to.

Bentley, director of the United States Department of Justice, Security and Operations, wielded the power of the federal government with impunity and indifference. I met him over a year ago and he took a liking to me, a dubious honor. The truth was he wanted something from me, something I could not let him have.

"Justice Department. How may I help you?" The voice was youthful, buoyant.

"This is Brendan Macbean. I need to talk to Bentley, please."

For several seconds my pounding heart seemed to be the only sound against the static.

"Write down this pin, please." The assistant recited a number.

"Whoa... that's..." I counted, "sixteen digits."

"Of course. Going encrypted in five, four, three, two, one, zero."

I made a note to tell Bentley not to hire millennials. I hit the green button and the noise changed to a soft silence, a buttery nothingness, not even a breath.

Then I heard a breath.

"So, you're getting into bar fights, now?" Bentley's voice blared out of the speaker phone, not loud but startling with its clarity. A year since

I had last spoke to him but my memory remained clear of that Jack Nicholson-like laconic accent.

I shivered and took a deep breath.

"Fight? I never touched the guy."

"So you said. Let's see... shattered facial bones on the right side, dislocated jaw. Hyper extended knees and ankles, both legs, cuts and bruises all over his forty-seven-acre body. And you stripped him naked? That's weird."

"He wasn't naked. His tee shirt was pulled over his head."

"It's still weird, Macbean. Remind me never to piss you off."

"Bentley, you're already pissing me off."

"I am? How so?"

"It's not enough you bug my home, hack my computer and tap my phone. Your unprecedented abuse of power messes up my life. You didn't need to call the state attorney general and have him read the riot act to the sheriff here."

I think I heard Bentley snort.

"Macbean, you never know what you're going to find in these rural areas. This sheriff... Boat-job? What kind of a name is that?"

"Boatwright. He's a great guy. He runs a first-class outfit."

"I can't have you getting into fights and getting thrown into some hick-town jail."

"Why not?"

"Yeah, right." Bentley's sneer came over the encrypted line. "You know why not. You travel with your own can of worms, and I can't let some small-time cop rubber hose you in a back room. No telling what you might say."

"Really? What am I going to say, Bentley?"

"Don't play coy with me, man. You're holding onto some powerful secrets, Macbean. It's eating your insides out. No relief for you until you give it up. You tell me your secrets and I'll go away. I'll leave you alone. You'll forget I ever existed. Won't that be nice? No more Bentley ruining your life."

"You want me to tell you where Daniel Conklin is."

"Ah-ha!" Bentley exclaimed. "A breakthrough. Was that really so hard?"

"Well, Bentley, I don't know. He disappeared right after his wife's funeral. I never saw him again and have not heard from him and have no knowledge where he might be."

Bentley sighed. "Same old tune and you really don't sing it very well."

"And all your surveillance, Bentley, hasn't resulted in a single clue."

"Listen, Macbean…" There was menace in his voice, now. Bentley had a slow, controllable anger… and the power of the US government behind him. "Things could get a lot worse. Up to now, I've been gentle, even patient."

"Okay, Bentley. I'm scared, now. I better tell you where he is."

For many moments he didn't respond. I could almost follow the evolution of his thoughts until he finally concluded he was being gamed.

"Well…"

I took a deep breath. "There's a lady in Ohio. Alicia Wentworth. Age fifty-six. Two daughters, three grandkids. Lives in Shaker Heights. Been married to her high school sweetheart for thirty years. She has breast cancer and has been fighting it for several years. Husband got laid-off from a job he's had for decades. They put their kids through college and have a mortgage…"

"Macbean, is there a point in our future?"

"Yeah, Bentley. There's a point. Mrs. Wentworth has been cancer free for a year. Her medical bills have been paid off. Her mortgage has been paid off and her husband starts a new job next week."

"Wonderful. I'm touched." Bentley's voice came across dry and resigned.

"The Wentworths went from financial disaster to where now they regained the so-called American Dream."

"Still waiting on the punch line, Macbean."

"That's where Daniel Conklin is."

"What? In Shaker Heights?"

"You're an idiot, Bentley. That's not where they live. You would send your goon squad in there, if I gave you real names and places. You want to hear another story?"

"No. I get it. You won't tell me where Conklin is, but you're suggesting that I leave him alone because he's doing some kind of hero work. You're trying to tell me that he's paying back for his horrible crimes by helping people. Very decent of him."

"And you want to kill the goose."

The sound of another heavy breath came over the phone.

"Don't want to kill him, just throw him in jail and get back the money"

"A month after he disappeared, St. Agatha's Clinic received a perpetual grant from an anonymous source run by a foundation in Zurich. Now they're treating hundreds of patients... savings women's lives. Isn't that what you wanted all along?"

Bentley's silence oozed like sweat.

"Johns Hopkins received fifteen million. Boston Biomedical, twenty million, Mayo Clinic, twenty-five, Emory University..."

"Okay, I get it, Macbean. You called me just to tell me I'm a real louse?"

My heart started pounding again. This is it.

"Bentley, you are a real louse, but you can be useful... somrtimes. I have a favor to ask you."

He blew out a heavy breath. "Let me get a firm grip on my wallet. Okay, what is this 'favor' and how much?"

"Like you carry a wallet, Bentley. This Coast Guard boat that blew up... I want in on the investigation."

Time passed. I knew better than to jabber on. Sales one-oh-one: he who speaks first loses.

"No way in hell. No way in bleeping hell."

"Gee, Bentley... I thought you'd say no."

"Macbean, no reporters allowed and if they were, you'd be the last I'd let in there. You are a meddler of the worst sort. You'd fowl up a poultry show."

"Clever metaphor."

"Every government agency that has initials is headed down there to investigate. FBI, CIA, NTSB, NSA, ATF and E…"

"Ah, 'E' for 'Explosives.'"

"Nobody's getting close to that boat. We're still in body armor and hazmat suits, making sure there's not another bomb. You go down there waving your press pass, you'll get stopped a mile away. If you're lucky they'll lock you up in an auditorium with the rest of the TV reporters and you'll get press briefings three times a day. Even the local police are backseat until we determine it's not terrorism."

"I certainly don't want to get locked up with all the other reporters. 'Sum of all fears' and besides there's too many 'Kellys'"

"Kellys?"

"Megyn, O'Donnell, Cobiella… all those Kelly's"

"What are you babbling about, Macbean?"

"Bentley, I don't want to go there. You already have a team down here. Besides all those government letters you gave me… you must have somebody gathering all the data. You have to have updates and keep on top of this, right?"

I didn't wait for him to answer. "I want to talk to the person you have giving you the three times a day briefing."

"I can't. It's all classified now."

"Give me a security clearance."

"I can't do that. You're not vetted."

"Yes, you can, Bentley."

"What's in it for me?"

"You need a meddler. You need a pest. I think outside the box. You government types always get in a box. You need an outsider's eyes."

This time his pause seemed infinite and loaded with possibilities.

"You won't like my terms, Macbean."

"What are they?"

"You'll be an investigator, not a reporter. You are sworn to secrecy. You report to me and only me. You go public with anything, leak any-thing… even talk in your sleep… you will go to jail."

"Okay."

"That was too easy. Are you playing me, Macbean?"

That's exactly what I was thinking. This was too easy. Maybe this is what Bentley had in mind all along.

"Macbean, as of this moment you have clearance to view information from this investigation and this incident, only. And related material, of course. I'll email the documents."

"Here's my email…"

"Geeze, Macbean. I already have your freaking email for god's sake."

"Uh, I guess you do. I'll sign…"

"You already signed. And the guy's name is Nick Carrillo. Here's his number. Before you call, give me thirty minutes to brief him."

"I'll warn you now, Macbean. He's a Millennial."

CHAPTER 14

"You Can't Roller Skate in a Buffalo Herd"

Between Darien and Eulonia, Georgia
From the Journal of Brendan Macbean:

As much as I enjoyed the lunch, I couldn't wait to get out of there.

By the time I climbed into the Toyota, I felt that familiar, tingling joy. I was back in the hunt, no longer sitting on the bench pretending to be a backup philanthropist.

The marvelous technology of the Land Cruiser sensed I wasn't the linebacker-sized Deputy Leggo. As I strapped in the motors whirred to return the seat to my favorite position.

For a moment I toyed with the idea of heading south on I-95, getting a hotel room in Brunswick where I'd have all the internet access and phones an investigator could want. The quiet, serene isolation in which I found myself this morning was no longer necessary. I didn't have to sneak around anymore. Obviously, the feds had found me.

Now I was a fed, but I decided I could do the same job in the serene setting of Rawlings' cottage just as well. I decided to skip the interstate and head into Darien. I could gas up and take the Coastal Highway, US

17, which paralleled the interstate. The travel speed would be slower, but I'd still get to Eulonia where the Piggly Wiggly awaited.

There was a Bi-Lo grocery straight across the intersection of Highways 251 and 17. Why not buy groceries at the Bi-Lo? Because the notion of shopping "the Pig in Eulonia" had hooked me. In Rawlings words, "If the Pig don't have it, you don't need it."

So, I turned left and headed for Eulonia. The GPS said it was ten miles away.

Highway 17, the Coastal Highway, listed as one of America's Scenic Highways... it had everything to recommend it but scenery. Trees and fields and more trees. The late afternoon sun flashed between the shadows trying to hypnotize me with its strobe effect, but I was too keyed up with my new mission. I glanced at the clock. Bentley told me to wait a half-hour to call his man, Nick Carrillo. Only half of that time had passed, but I couldn't wait. I-95 was still close, so I had a good cell signal. Ineeded to focus. I didn't want to call this Nick guy while driving.

I looked for a side road or a place to pull over, but the Coastal Highway closed up on me no convenient place to pull over. If I parked on the road shoulder, somebody, like a fireman or policeman might see me in my red firetruck and pull over to investigate or just to say, "Howdy!"

The pavement widened to three lanes. I approached a big building surrounded by a high chain-link fence. It reminded me of a federal prison lacking only loops of razor wire atop the fence.

Two police cars sat across the street from the gate. A yellow flashing light hung over the road with a sign that said, "Speed 35 MPH when flashing."

I slowed. Two yellow school busses came through the gate and turned south toward Darien.

A digital sign flashed, "Welcome to McIntosh Academy... Home of the Buccaneers."

Okay, not exactly a prison.

A few miles later I came to another enormous fenced in area. It looked to be a stockyard several football fields in size. The fence came up to the right of way with a dirt driveway guarded by a gate.

The place looked abandoned and empty... maybe a good place to pull off and make an undisturbed phone call.

I turned left and pulled my bumper up to the gate. Inside the fence sat a low barn and a shed. No vehicles except a rusted out short bus with the roof cut off with the battered interior left to the elements. Someone had crudely painted "Buffalo Wagon" on the side in rough lettering.

Buffalo Wagon?

Beyond the gate was a larger than life statue of a buffalo. A few mockingbirds had started a guano deposit on the back of the statue.

Next to the locked gate stood a tall sign, a single sheet of plywood that had contained some kind of message, but the wind and rain had long ago erased any writing.

I'm an investigative reporter. I can figure this story out.

Some guy thought a buffalo ranch in Georgia would be a great idea, just like out west. Decades ago TV mogul Ted Turner opened a bunch of restaurants called "Ted's Montana Grill" where you could get a buffalo steak and other Western fare. So, there must be a market for buffalo meat. Why not make a tourist attraction out of it? Build a western looking barn and cut the roof off an old school bus, dub it the "Buffalo Wagon" and give people rides among the herd, while playing Marty Robbins. And then the market for buffalo meat crashes and there's no market for buffalo chips. What are you going to do?

He's forced to sell his stock and close his doors. I say 'he' because it had to be a guy. No female would have dreamt this up.

The song, "Home on the Range" banged around in my head. What other songs have "buffalo" in the lyrics?" "Buffalo Girls" and "Shuffle off to Buffalo" came to mind. Is that it? Wait, Roger Miller wrote a song, "You Can't Roller Skate in a Buffalo Herd."

We hold these truths to be self-evident.

And having exhausted my entire catalog of buffalo songs, it was time to call Nick Carrillo.

My phone sat in its cradle facing me. I gave TLC the number Bentley had given me.

"New contact, Nick Carrillo. Call Nick Carrillo."

"Calling Nick Carrillo," she said in her sexy voice.

My call was answered immediately as if Carrillo was as eager as I was to talk. But instead of hearing a "hello" on my car's speakers, I heard chirp and saw a Facetime invitation on the phone's screen.

I accepted, and on the phone's screen, a face appeared. I adjusted the phone until my face appeared in the little square.

I had been warned that Nick Carrillo was a millennial, but I wondered if Bentley fully understood the term.

The face on the screen couldn't have been more than twelve years old. A bushy head of black hair, thick eyebrows of the same color over thick, Clark Kent glasses too big for his Tweenager face, the ghostly glow of the computer screen clouded both lenses.

Except for the hair, he looked just like me so many decades ago. The glasses had always been my trademark until a year ago when a Swiss eye surgeon worked miracles on me.

"Brendan!" A giant, toothy grin cleaved his face from ear to ear.

"Son is your father at home?" nearly escaped my lips, but I realized we were in the twenty-first century, and Bentley wouldn't have given me the number for the Brady Bunch house.

Instead I said, "You're Nick Carrillo?" Said it with barely concealed incredulity.

His face turned serious. "Of course, I am."

"Well, I guess I expected someone a little older," and wondered why I said that out loud.

Nick took a deep breath and reared back a little from his camera and keyboard.

"I'm older than I look," he said. "But, you, sir, are exactly what I expected."

"Me? I am?"

He smiled again. And looked a little older, but not much.

"Brendan, I've been reading your file the last three hours. I feel I know you."

"My file?"

"Yes, and it's a big file. Mr. B really likes you."

"Likes me? You mean like in an investigation?"

"No, sir. Mr. B's not investigating you. He's surveilling you."

"Well, I know that, but I don't know why."

Nick shook his head. "Me neither." I winced. "Mr. B keeps many secrets, but look, Brendan, I feel I need to credentialize myself."

"Credentialize?"

"Yeah. You obviously think I'm a kid, but I'm way older than I look."

"Okay. Look, uh, Nick, you don't need to, uh, credential yourself, if that's even a verb."

"Sure I do. I've been working for the Department of Justice for six years. I'm twenty-five years old and have a PhD in Economics from the University of Maryland. I get excellent job ratings. I..."

"Twenty-five? Jeez, Nick, I don't need all that. You are a little young looking, that's all."

He still looked miffed.

"So, Nick... when are you coming down?"

Nick's eyebrows shot above the rim of his glasses.

"I'm not coming down," he said, his voice climbing in pitch. "There's no point me being 'down' there. That's not what I do."

He emphasized the words 'down' and 'do.'

"Okay, Nick. What is it that you do?"

"I'm an analyst. Besides, I'd never get anything out of those guys."

I said nothing, trying to figure out why I wasn't getting anything either.

Nick took a big breath.

"Brendan, you think I'm a kid. I know I look like a kid. The agents going down there? Big guys, old guys, like you. FBI, NSA, Homeland Security, Coast Guard Shore Patrol, ATFE, all of them former jocks with degrees in Law Enforcement. They're going to slap me around like a hockey puck."

"Where are you now, kid?" I meant to use his name, but he was whining like a teenager. And the word, 'kid'... well, it just slipped out. But it didn't bother him, apparently.

"Mr. B told me about you. He said to keep you on a tight leash. Like I could do that. That you'd poke your nose in everything. He said you were obsessed with relevancy, but I'm not sure what he meant.

"Anyway, you don't need to know where I am now. It's not relevant."

I took a deep breath and let it out slowly.

"Nick, it's not relevant until it is."

Throughout the call, he had been fingering his keyboard in continuous motion. Well, I could do the same. The Land Cruiser's computer had been loaded with law enforcement software, among which was a program to look up addresses connected with phone numbers. Since I knew it wasn't the hall phone to the Brady's house, it must be a cell phone. I punched the phone number into the locate program.

An address in Silver Spring, Maryland. Near Washington, DC. Actually, an unincorporated part of Washington. I hit the locate button.

"Come on, TLC…" I mumbled. "Where is this little guy and his cell phone." The swirling icon spun for a while.

On the screen an address flashed.

Hinesville. Georgia. The software was sophisticated and immediately cross-referenced utilities. It was the Hinesville Water Department that gave him up. Since August of last year… hmmmm.

Google Earth showed it as a plain, brick ranch with a short driveway and a car that looked like a Nissan Altima sitting in the driveway.

"Brendan? Are you still with me?

"Yes, I am. Nick, does the address, thirty-two eighty-seven Sugar Pine Avenue mean anything to you? In Hinesville, Georgia? Looks like it's about thirty-five miles away."

With his thick glasses getting if anything thicker, the kid's astonishment was amusing, but he recovered.

"Okay, Mister Mac. Two can play that game." His hands fluttered over his keyboard. "Obviously you're not driving so I'm looking for a parked car. Near I-95, mile marker forty-eight. Oh my god!" Nick shouted. "I've want to go there!"

"Where?" I said.

"The Buffalo Ranch!"

Boy! That was quick. I had to be impressed.

"Okay, you found me," I said. "I'm here but the place is dead."

"Hey, Brendan. You have cameras on that Toyota of yours."

"You know about my car?"

"Uh, yes. File's up to date. Toyota Land Cruiser, donated by Marietta Toyota, upfitted y Fouts Borthers on Atlanta Road in Smyrna, Georgia. They made two of them and Smyrna Fire Department only needed one. Your friend on the police department put you on to it. You paid..."

"Okay, Nick. You got me. I don't know anything about your Altima."

"Mom and Dad gave it to me."

"Of course, they did."

He went on, squirming in his seat like a teenager.

"Your Fire Command vehicle has twelve HDTV cameras imbedded around the roof line. I want you to turn them on."

"Why? This place is dead. No Buf..." I looked out the window to confirm this and saw a herd of Buffalo not twenty feet away.

Black, wooly heads, muzzles glistening with mucus pressing against the fence. Dark glassy eyes staring at me... with expectation. I rolled down the window and animal stench wafted in. Hair, feces, buffalo sweat, dirt.

I rolled the window up.

"Okay, Nick. I don't know how to get the pictures to you."

"It's easy. I'll do it."

I watched in silent amazement and frustrating idleness while he opened the camera application. I could have asked TLC to do it, but I didn't want to talk about her to Nick. She had proven to be a fickle female with Leggo and here was a kid even cuter than him. Or me.

"Wow! Look at that!" he exclaimed.

I'm glad someone was having fun.

"Look, Brendan. Donkeys!"

Among dozens of massive black heads were two white ones, long, thin equine snouts also pressing against the fence. Ears perked forward toward me.

I said, "They weren't here when I drove up. I thought the place was empty."

"They think you're going to feed them."

Massive black and brown heads jostled against the wire. The pair of white donkeys dodged horns. One of the donkeys rolled his or her eyes and slashed teeth like castanets left and right. The buffaloes on either side gave way.

"What's with the donkeys?" I asked.

Nick was swift with Google. "Donkeys are protection against predators. I'm reading a livestock forum. Farmers having problems with coyotes. Cattle and I assume domesticated bison, with instincts muted by years of inbreeding allow coyotes to get too close before taking defensive action. Donkeys are very aggressive and will chase a coyote half a mile. They kill snakes too."

"Gee, Nick. Thanks. That's cool."

"Anytime!"

"I'm shutting the cameras off."

"Why?"

"A Coast Guard boat exploded this morning. Remember?'

"Okay," he said, his voice sinking like a wounded bird.

"Brendan, maybe we should start with the press release we're going to give to the media at six PM today."

"Okay, Nick. Let's hear it."

He took a deep breath. "At eleven twenty-six AM, an explosion occurred aboard US Coast Guard patrol boat 22365, killing three of the four crewmen. The boat was operating near the harbor of Brunswick, Georgia.

"The families of the deceased have been notified. They are Coast Guard sailors, Ronald Ortiz, Aaron Cobb, and Amir Hadad. The fourth crewman, Gerald Milton, was severally injured and has been taken to Brunswick Hospital where he remains in critical condition.

"The cockpit or cabin has been mostly destroyed by the explosion, killing Ortiz and Hadad instantly. Aaron Cobb's body had been thrown into the water by the blast, where it was recovered by boats responding to the emergency.

"The crew had been engaged in a routine training mission which began about thirty minutes before the explosion.

"At the time of the explosion, the boat was positioned midway between the Sydney Lanier Bridge and Saint Simons Island.

"Please remember this investigation is in its early stages. Several government agencies are working very hard to get more information to tell us exactly what happened. Until we analyze the information coming in, we won't be able to add much more to what we have told you."

While Nick read aloud in a nasally monotone, a computer-generated animation filled my laptop screen, showing a graphic rendering of a Defender Class Patrol Boat zooming under the easily recognized Sydney Lanier Bridge, heading east with the morning sun high on the horizon. They passed to the left of a giant ship on the same course, also sailing under the bridge. The ship and the bridge dwarfed much smaller the patrol boat.

The animation was excellently rendered. They had even provided an overhead drone perspective of the boat. The animation "flew" through the slanted cables of the bridge following the patrol boat far below. After this video tour-de-force, the drone-view closed with the boat. You could see a graphic man standing on the bow at some kind of gun. Inside the cabin were two men and another knelt in the stern behind the cabin.

The patrol boat turned north toward St. Simons.

A soundless, yellow flash bloomed on the boat. It appeared to come from inside the cabin and I immediately wondered if they had determined the location of the explosion or speculated on where the blast had occurred. The lack of noise made the scene spooky. The man at the bow was flung over the left side of the boat like a ski jumper. The front and sides of the cabin burst into pieces and the roof fluttered skyward like a gravity defying leaf. The two figures inside the cabin vanished and the one crouched in the stern fell backwards across twin outboards.

"I will take a few questions now."

My eyes drifted off the computer screen to the buffaloes lined up at the fence. One of them caught my eye and we stared at each other for a moment. The look of anticipation had disappeared from the bison's faces. They had finally concluded that I was not going to feed them. The bison backed away from the fence and walked desultorily toward the setting sun. The donkeys were the last to go, one of them curling his lips back from equine teeth, eyes rolling in donkey derision.

Nick's voice, "Sir?"

I took a breath. "If you insist on calling me, 'sir,' I'll keep calling you 'kid', kid."

He smiled. "I like you calling me, 'kid.'"

And I realized I like him calling me, 'sir.'

"Any witnesses?

"There's a guy on that big RORO ship, they passed going under the bridge."

"Row Row? What's row row?"

Nick's face broke into a grin. I guessed the kid really liked showing off.

"'Roll on. Roll off.'"

"You mean like cars?"

"Cars, trucks, trailers, tractors..."

"I get it. Roll them on and off. So, this ship brought cars into Brunswick?"

Nick looked at his screen. "Volvo Trucks. The big, eighteen-wheeler kind."

"And it shipped out empty?"

He glanced at his screen. "Nope. Shipped out full of trailers, the big, eighteen-wheeler kind. Great Dane, made right here in Statesboro, Georgia."

"Where's the ship headed?"

"Copenhagen. Denmark. Weird, huh?"

Facetime conversations had limits. I stared at him for a second, but he showed no abashment.

"Nick, you lead me to believe you were well educated."

"Huh?"

"Grunting is for cavemen. You said you had a Ph. D."

"Yes, in economics."

"We ship a boatload of Great Dane trailers to Denmark and all you can come up with is 'Weird, huh?'"

Nick said nothing.

"Nick, the English language is huge, complex and nuanced. A million years ago our ancestors grunted to communicate. We've evolved, I hope. I resist letting our dialectal de-evolve back to millennial-speak, because we humans will lose our complexity, our edge. I, for one, would like to know I'm talking to an evolved person. Do you think you can rise to that level? Just for a few more minutes? For this old guy you're talking to?"

Now abashment clearly showed in his face, even via Facetime.

He took a moment and said, "We ship Great Dane trailers to Denmark. Isn't that ironic?"

"Much better," I said.

"Satirical, peculiar, curious."

"Stop using your computer. I assume your vocabulary is quite large."

Defensively, he said, "Brendan, if I talk like you, nobody will pay any attention to me."

"None of your contemporaries, you mean. Speak to them anyway you want. Just to vouchsafe yourself as nuanced and complex."

"Wow, Mister Mac. 'Vouchsafe.' That's a word."

"So, what's this man's name, the one who saw the explosion?"

"Lars Thorenson. He's the ship's load manager. He was on deck at the time of the explosion. The FBI interviewed him by phone. I'll send you the transcript."

"Nick, go ahead and net it out for me."

"Okay. This guy Thorenson was watching his ship clear the bridge. Apparently when they go under structures like that they want to make sure they don't hit anything. Makes sense. He said he saw the patrol boat passing them and saw it headed toward St. Simons Island. But then he turned to look back at the bridge because their stern was still under it. While he faced away from the boat, he heard an explosion that he described as a short thunderclap and an echo, the sound of the explosion echoing off the bridge. He said he felt a wave of heat on the back of his neck and saw a flash of light reflecting off everything. When he turned around to look at the patrol boat, he said it was about four hundred meters away, dead in the water. A cloud of white smoke, which he said looked like fog was rising over the boat. He knew immediately the boat was destroyed, his words, and called his ship's bridge. The commander on the bridge called the Port Authority."

"That's it? Any other witnesses?"

"That's pretty much it. We had a few call-ins who gave us pretty much the same story, flash of light, echo and white cloud."

"Any other boats in the area?"

"No. Well, there was one large boat heading east. This was reported by the RORO ship bridge commander. He described it as a white, private cruiser at least twenty meters long headed east more than a kilometer away."

"Long way off," I said. "Anyone else see it?"

"No. No one else called."

No witnesses. In a very populated area. There must have been a thousand people who heard the blast and only a few looked to see what it was.

Ironic. Peculiar. Curious.

"So, Nick, what blew up? The fuel tank?"

"Nope. Fuel tank is undamaged and still full of gas."

"Did they have something like demolition charges onboard?"

Nick rattled his head like a dog. If he had big ears they would have flapped.

"Sir, if they had demo charges aboard, would we be conducting this massive investigation?"

I sighed. "No. We wouldn't."

"We don't know what blew up. These sailors weren't carrying anything that would explode."

"So, what...?"

"We don't know. An ATFE report is due at midnight. Then we might know something."

"ATFE..."

"Mr. B ordered the ATFE to release their findings by midnight."

"Really? Bentley orders the ATFE?"

"When Mr. B says, 'Frog!' you either jump or croak."

"Funny, Nick. So what kind of training exercise was it?"

"The Coast Guard Commander called it a Four Man PBJ."

"PBJ?"

"Yeah, it should have been called a PBG, but... poetic license, everyone calls it a PBJ."

"So what is it?"

"A Four Man Patrol, Blue Gun."

"Blue Gun? A training gun?"

"Ah, you know about a blue gun... like you use in firearms training."

"Non-firing replica. Blue color tells everybody it's non-firing."

"Right. In this drill is the sailors learn to deploy the gun while underway. The Defender Class boat has two gun mounts, one fore, one aft. They usually mount a M240B machinegun. With a four-man crew, they only mount one gun in the bow position. Ortiz and Hadad were in the cockpit, with Ortiz at the helm. Milton and Cobb have the task of mounting the gun in the bow. Ortiz probably steered the boat through the wake of the RORO ship to give the Defender some bounce. The sea was calm and he wanted Cobb and Milton to struggle... not make it too easy mounting the gun."

"Okay. Then what?"

"Well, they got the gun mounted. Milton made his way to the stern. Cobb stays with the blue gun in the bow."

"What do they do after they get the blue gun mounted?"

"Practice interdictions. Practice intercepting other boats."

"Is that why they use a blue gun instead of a real one?"

"Yup. The Coast Guard is allowed to interdict any craft for with or without cause. They can stop any vessel for a safety check, but with a blue gun it's supposed to make it not look so threatening. Usually they close within a hundred meters and then veer off. There's often lots of pleasure craft in these waters so most of time, and they don't want to scare anyone, blue gun notwithstanding. The guys just 'joy ride' around."

"Blue Gun Joy Ride," I said. "A four man PBJ."

"Yep… a favorite thing for Coast Guard sailors. The Defender is supposed to be a real hot boat. It's got twin Hondas on the back… fast and maneuverable."

"So they get the gun mounted, set off after some make-believe smugglers and the boat just blows up?"

"That's the way it looks."

"Nick. I'm looking at what you're displaying on my computer screen and not even asking how you guys got into it, taking over my screen without my permission."

"Mister Mac… I just thought it'd be easier."

"Forget it, Nick. I'm used to it. Government is not always knights in shining armor. I'm going to pull the plug on you guys someday, sue you for a zillion dollars and all that. I just want you to know. I never gave you permission to hack into my whole life and only tolerate it like I do the rats in the attic."

"Geeze, Mister Mac. You got rats in your attic?"

I took a deep breath… a reflex these days.

"Nick, I'm looking at the boat. It's sitting on the trailer in a warehouse somewhere. It's pretty sorry looking. That orange collar around the perimeter of the boat is mostly melted off forward of where the cabin used to be. The front of the cabin and most of both sides were blown away, including the roof. Have we recovered the pieces?"

"Not everything. They're still searching."

"Why did Milton go to the rear of the boat after they mounted the gun?"

"I don't know."

"Do they have a black box like airliners?"

"I don't think so, but I'll ask."

"They have radar. Do they record it? Was there any radio communication from the boat? Who else had access to the boat in the last few days?"

We both took deep breaths.

"Lots of people. Other crews use this boat. Contractors, mechanics. Civilians and military. We're still getting that list together but, since the explosion, nobody but investigators has gotten close to it." He looked up at the ceiling. "Except..."

"Except what?"

"They also use the Defender in public relations. They drag it to parades, put it on display. They let the public in... in fact, 22365 was at a boat show in Savannah last week."

"What?"

"Yeah, they took it up to Savannah to a boat show. Hundreds of people climbed on it and walked around it."

I muttered, "Hundreds of people..."

"Yes, sir. Hundreds." Nick said dramatically.

"Nick, are you familiar with Dynamite?"

The question caught him off guard a little. He cocked his head.

"I'm not familiar with it but I've heard of it."

"TNT? Semtex, C-4, you know, explosives?"

"What are you getting at, Mister Mac?"

"I did a piece for television a few years back. Up in Elberton, Georgia, our state's 'Granite City.' They mine granite and marble all over north Georgia. Drill holes in the rock and blow big chunks out of the mountain. So, I interviewed explosive experts. I'm not an expert but I know enough to write about it.

"All of these explosives leave a chemical signature. They explode and spread chemicals all over the surfaces of everything. Explosives are highly regulated, not being protected by the constitution and all. Manufacturers of this stuff put specific chemical tracers in their products so experts can determine where the stuff came from. Even foreign producers do this. These materials are difficult to obtain and easy to trace. For lots of reasons."

Nick thought about it for a few seconds. I could see the wheels turning behind his glasses.

"Nick, what are you thinking?"

"What you're getting at, sir is that is if the explosion was caused by a familiar explosive, ATFE would have told us what it was already. And probably where it came from."

"And?"

"I have a lot of work to do. It could have been anybody who planted the bomb."

"Nick, I think it's jumping the gun to call it a bomb or to assume it was deliberate, but if this boat was in a show last week, with hundreds of people climbing on it... and terrorists were involved, why didn't they blow it up then? As it was, the boat blew up where it was likely to do the least amount of damage and not hurt anyone except the crew."

"True that, Mister Mac!"

CHAPTER 15

"The Pig in Eulonia"

Eulonia, Georgia
From the Journal of Brendan Macbean:

By the time I ended the call with Nick the sun lowered to the line of trees to the west, burning puffy clouds with tinges of orange, which turned pink as I watched. I backed the Land Cruiser out onto Highway 17 and headed north toward Eulonia. The sunset kept trying to seduce me with flashes of changing color bouncing around in the Toyota's cockpit.

I growled at Mother Nature to give it up. My days of sunset watching were over.

Sad.

Had it not just been that morning when I watched the sunrise over the marsh while sipping Rawlings' marvelous 'Blend' and feeling my body relax with a distinct 'good vibe' feel? Where else in the world could I enjoy the sunrise over the Barbour River in the morning and the sunset over a buffalo ranch in the evening?

Rawlings' invitation had been a rare gift, a chance to get off the grid, away from the phone and the TV news, a golden opportunity to work on myself. But my resume says I'm an investigative reporter first and a substitute philanthropist second because there was no one else to take the job. Now that I had a chance at an investigation, my body felt alive, eager to be back on the job.

It felt right. It was right, wasn't it?

But I wondered if Bentley manipulated me into doing exactly what he wanted? What he wanted was to find Daniel Conklin and pull him back into the clutches of the Department of Justice. Bentley knew I communicated with Conklin, but he just couldn't figure out how. He had already bugged my house and my phone. The Land Cruiser was my last fortress of privacy. And I had just opened up the gates and practically invited them to invade.

Nick wanted to see the buffalo, like a kid at the zoo, so I turned on the cameras. He had seized control of both the onboard computer and my laptop. Now I pretty much had to keep the Land Cruiser's satellite communication line open, meaning that the feds could watch my every move.

Twelve cameras mounted on the rim of the roof. And I realized with a gulp that there were another four cameras mounted inside covering nearly every inch of the Land Cruiser's interior. Which meant they were probably watching me as I drove north on Highway 17.

I did a mental inventory of what they could see, what was on the Land Cruiser's computer and my laptop. Nothing that might lead them to Daniel Conklin. Every communication was encrypted and deleted immediately... hard drive wiped and scrubbed, like the security companies do.

I hope.

What could they see? If any federal agent was watching me, I intended to dull their wits with boredom.

I moved my right hand toward the console. I could almost hear the feds squawking.

"What's he doing? He moved his hand!"

"He's turning on some music."

"What? Sirius? Pandora?"

"Checking... Spotify."

"What's he playing?"

"He's playing... Oh, Jeez, Louise."

"What?"

"Rockwell... 'Somebody's Watching Me.'"

Long silence.

"Do you think he's on to us?"

I remembered the LG tablet in the glove compartment. I don't think the feds knew about it. All communication was done on the internet with my laptop. Both Bluetooth and Wi-Fi were turned off on the tablet. Data transfer to the laptop was through swapping a memory card which was erased afterward. The tablet only did one thing... the mysterious encryption of a message into one of my aunt's recipes. How Conklin decrypted it, I don't know. But if the feds saw me pulling out the LG, they might think, hey, what's this? And want a closer look.

I guess I better not send him any emails for a while. He wouldn't expect anything from me for three more days. By then, I'd figure something out.

Rounding a turn, I saw a blinking red light ahead. I eased off the throttle and glided to a stop at the only traffic light in McIntosh County, according to Leggo and Rawlings' notebook.

I saw no traffic, so I stayed where I was and looked around the evening heart of Eulonia.

Well, to my right was a weedy vacant lot strewn with last year's "vote for me" signs. To my left was a gas station-convenience store, that must have closed at dusk. Catty-cornered was a liquor store, open, brightly lit. Somebody walked out with booze in a bag and got into a pickup truck. Behind the liquor store was a restaurant, its parking lot full of cars.

My computer pinged and pinged again. I looked at the screen... Nick Carrillo sending me stuff. Millennials' streams of consciousness... one at a time, as he'd think of them. God forbid he'd put it in some kind of logical order.

I eased across the four-way intersection. Dry cleaners and something called the "Posh Pineapple." A self-serve ice machine and car wash, boat repair yard, hardware, auto parts... who ever said Eulonia didn't have what you needed? Another restaurant and finally, on the left the Piggly Wiggly.

The parking lot was dimly lit and practically empty, just a couple of cars parked in the shadows.

But the Pig was open, and I found the best parking spot, one space over from the wheelchair ramp. I grabbed my backpack and locked the Toyota. An automatic door slid open, and I grabbed a grocery cart. Somebody said, "Howdy!" and I looked up to see a guy grinning at me from behind a short glass partition in the little office at the front of the store. I waved, and he waved back.

Trapped by a row of cash registers, the lone clerk thumbed her cell phone and ignored me.

The Pig in Eulonia was nothing like the mega-grocery stores in At-lanta. I found it compact, clean, well-lit and completely adequate. They had great produce and a good beer selection. I loaded up on Heineken knowing I'd feel guilty mooching Rawlings' stock. I was overwhelmed by the variety of barbecue and hot sauces and totally disappointed by their coffee selection. Not a bag of whole-bean in sight, just common ground coffees.

I went through the store with a keen sense of urgency. I wanted to get back to Rawlings' cottage and begin reading some of the stuff Nick was sending. By the time I had wheeled the cart past the meats and diary sections, my grocery shopping neared completion.

Then everything changed.

I was halfway up the last isle when I saw a man. He seemed to be working behind one of those displays they put on the floor to highlight sale items. He was kneeling or squatting behind the display, eyes cast down, focused on his task.

He looked like the Marlboro man, the rugged, cowboy-looking guy from the ads, back in the day when they could advertise cigarettes. He wore no Stetson, his hair was grizzled black and white, his face the hand-some, chiseled-cut features with a western, brush-cut mustache.

Well, I couldn't wait to meet the Marlboro man, even if his celebrity status had faded about the time I was born. Capriciously, I thought, now the Marlboro Man has to find work in the Piggly Wiggly in Eulonia. Okay, not funny enough for prime time. It was just some dude who favored the look.

And then the dude looked at me. And I gulped and stopped.

Crystal blue eyes like from the bottom of a glacial pool... and colder than a grave digger's ass. He favored me with a two second blast from those eyes and turned away and began to glide toward the front of the store. I say glide, because he didn't stand up from his kneeling position. It was like he was kneeling on a skateboard or one of those carts auto mechanics lay on to slide under cars.

He moved awfully fast. When he came out from behind the display, I realized I was wrong again. He hadn't been kneeling. It looked as if his legs were a foot shorter than they should have been. Stunted, bandy, bowed, bent and misshaped, he bounded like a chimpanzee without knuckles dragging the floor.. But the guy was really good at walking that way.

I immediately felt sorry for him, but only for a moment.

Halfway to the Piggly Wiggly's front door he stopped, turned and gave me another look. Another blast from those nasty blue eyes. The left side of his lips curled into a sneer. His expression blazed contempt and challenge.

"You don't want a piece of me," he seemed to be saying. But he didn't actually say it. My instincts told me not to get too close. And my logical brain agreed. Actually, I found myself unable to move like my feet were glued to the floor.

Somehow my right hand had slipped into the open top of my backpack without me being aware. My fingers tightened around the rosewood grip of the Redhawk.

But the guy turned and scrambled past the cash register clerk and out the front door of the store leaving me to say, what?

I had lost my interest in grocery shopping. I urged my tingling feet to move.

When I got to the cash register, the clerk was trembling. We trembled together, but it was a sign she had seen him too and wasn't too happy about it.

I had to take my hand off the revolver to put my groceries on the conveyor belt, and it felt unsafe to do that.

The clerk had said something to me. She was a punky looking youth in her twenties. Sprayed pink hair, tattoos on both forearms, facial piercings. Lots of them. A name tag on her shirt said, "Jandi."

Odd name, but now I wish it had said, "Chuck Norris."

What had she said?

With shaking hands, she brandished a blue plastic card with a cartoon pig on it. I figured she asked me a perfunctory, "Do you have a 'Pig' card," or something like that, a Piggly Wiggly loyalty card.

I shook my head.

She scanned the card in her hand and proceeded to scan my groceries with no visible attempt at efficiency. But I didn't care. Her shaking hands told me that she had been as rattled by the gnome from hell as much as I had. Despite this she managed to get through the process and then for some unknown reason she stopped scanning.

I looked up. She had asked me another question and it had as much effect on me as blowing soap bubbles at a flock of geese. Her hand rested on the box of Heineken.

Oh, my birthdate. I told her, and she resumed scanning.

She finished scanning. It was all rote at this point. I slid my credit card and she handed me a long paper receipt.

As I pushed the loaded cart toward the door, I couldn't shake the feeling that I was walking into a bad situation. Dark outside. Dark parking lot. What could go wrong?

I stood before the automatic door. It slid open. I could hear the crickets and tree frogs chirping. I pushed the grocery cart outside.

The parking lot seemed empty except for my Land Cruiser parked ten feet away. Well-lit in places, yet plenty of deep shadows remained. Hiding places. Bugs clustered around the lights and bats swooped in and out of the gloom.

The store building had a rectangle jutting out of the front of the store like the top of a keystone. Twelve feet away from where I stood was a corner behind which he could be hiding, waiting. The wheelchair access ramp descended along the rectangle.

I pulled the Redhawk out of the backpack, its ample heft assured me it was loaded and ready.

With my left hand I guided the cart to the wheelchair ramp and gave a gentle push. The cart rolled steadily down the concrete ramp, onto the asphalt, past the corner and turned slightly toward the rear of the Toyota.

No fiends jumped out from the concealment around the corner. I was beginning to think I was alone out here. Still I crab-walked to my left, passing the front of the Land Cruiser's grill and turned the corner of the front passenger side bumper. I eased along the length of my car, keeping its mass between me and where I thought an ambusher might crouch.

Crouch? The guy in the store was so short, he didn't need to crouch. I derided myself for my paranoia but kept the Redhawk at ready. I made it to the rear of the Toyota and I saw no one crouching.

That I could see. Fifty feet away a giant live oak grew out of the asphalt. They had let it stand in the middle of the parking lot to provide welcome shade during the hot summer months.

No one lurked behind its massive trunk.

I checked Lurking off the checklist, right next to Crouching. That left only Skulking.

No one skulked, either.

My instincts told me I was alone. The gnome-fiend had fled. I thumbed the button on the key fob to open the Land Cruiser's rear gate and stowed my groceries. I climbed into the driver's seat, closed and locked the door and let out a big breath.

Bullet proof and unassailable... inside the Land Cruiser. Inside a fortress.

I pushed the start button. The Toyota hummed to life and lit up screens.

"TLC, I have a new contact."

"Yes, Boss. Who is your new contact?" Her voice purred as sweet as the Land Cruiser's engine.

"Sheriff Lanny Boatwright."

"Hmm, is that 'Sheriff' as in law enforcement or Omar?"

I wonder who programmed her sense of humor. I gave TLC the number and a command, "Call, Sheriff Boatwright."

"Calling, Sheriff Boatwright," she chirped.

He answered on the second ring. "Boatwright."

"Hi. Brendan Macbean."

"Macbean. What's up?

"Do you have an update on Barnecki?"

"I do. We have a detective down there trying to question him. He's awake and in restraints. Not happy, of course, and he's got an attorney who drove down from Savannah. The 'Barn' has clammed up."

"But he's okay?"

"Not at all. He's got a few years of felony trials in five counties to look forward to, followed by the rest of his days in prison. Not okay at all."

"I guess I meant his medical condition."

"Oh, he will recover, the doctors assure us. In fact, he's cleared to be transferred tomorrow to Grovetown."

"Grovetown?"

"It's Georgia's close-security prison hospital, near Augusta. The governor has provided us a squad of state troopers to make sure he doesn't slip away in route."

I knew I was beating around the bush a little.

"So, sheriff, a bad guy is off your streets."

"Right."

"Very nearly the most wanted criminal in the whole five county area, or something like that."

"Are you trying to say something, Macbean?"

"There's someone out there who is worse."

He waited.

"Let me describe him to you. About five feet two inches high. Normal from the waist up, but bandy, short legs like a chimp. Dark brown hair grizzled with gray. Handsome face, like the Marlboro Man in the old cigarette ads, complete with mustache. Cold blue eyes."

Sheriff Boatwright let out a long breath.

"Aw, Jesus."

"I won't tell your wife."

"What?"

"Your pledge to curtail profanity."

"Sometimes I'm weak."

"Aren't we all. So, Sheriff, who is this guy... the worst of the worst?"

"His name is Richard Lee Duggan. Around here he's called Ricky Lee if you're not afraid to say his name. Most people are."

"Just saying is name? Why?"

"Because he's a brutal son of a bitch, that's why. And mark me up for another infraction." His voice edged with anger, frustration, disappointment... and fear. "Macbean, where did you run into him?"

"At the Piggly Wiggly in Eulonia." I gave him the short version of the encounter, and he gave me a minute of thoughtful silence.

"And when you got to your car he was gone?"

"The parking lot is empty... I think."

"Where are you now?"

"Sitting in my car, still in the parking lot here at the Pig."

"I'm going to put you on hold for a second."

It was more than a second, but Sheriff Boatwright came back in less than two minutes.

"I'm calling out the troops. Macbean. Please wait where you are until my guys arrive. It should only be a few minutes. We'll give you an escort wherever you want to go, but my advice is to pack your bags and hightail it back to Atlanta. This guy is very dangerous."

"Sheriff, I'm safe in the Toyota. Bullet-proof glass and Fort Knox security. I don't need a police escort and I'm not going back to Atlanta... at least for a few days."

The sheriff thought about that and then launched into a soliloquy.

"I should have known he'd come back. The Barn comes with Ricky Lee. They're two-bit gangsters... drug dealers, smugglers and just plain total hoodlums. Barnecki came from somewhere up north. Ohio, Pennsylvania, but Ricky's home-grown. I served on the school board when he was at the Academy. An out-of-control punk kid, totally unmanageable. Got in a lot of fights. Punched kids, teachers, policemen... just too violent. He dropped out. Got work on a shrimp boat for a while and started smuggling. Real easy to do with miles of coastline like we have.

"Around here, Ricky Lee got a lot of support. He makes it worth people's while to help him. Hide him out or hide his stuff. He'd have the locals run his drugs, sell his contraband. Those poor folks would get caught and almost every one of them would hem and haw and finally point the finger at him. But by that time, he'd be long gone. He'd take off, disappear and leave the locals holding the bag.

"For years we've held a stack of warrants on both Ricky Lee and Barnecki. We organized a five-county sweep with the help of the state patrol, but Ricky Lee knew how to disappear. Nobody knew where they were. From time to time we'd hear about one of them popping up in Mobile or Little Rock or Nashville. Wherever we'd hear something, we'd call local law enforcement It never amounted to anything. The trail got cold, and we'd get comfortable with them being gone for good. Then somebody'd spot Barnecki in the Cypress Lounge... that's a bar in Darien. Or some other place. Usually not Zollers, where you ran into him. They know Lily works there. When Lily spotted him, she called it in and then she went and locked herself in the office."

Sheriff Boatwright seemed to get a cathartic release from this outpouring, but, in my mind I had already discredited the threat posed by this "Ricky Lee." Okay, he scared me in the grocery, but my adrenaline had subsided.

"Look, Brendan, you don't know what you're dealing with. He's back in town to run some kind of scheme, probably drugs. You got in the way and took down his partner, so Ricky Lee spotted your car at the Piggly Wiggly. Trust me when I tell you, he won't play fair. He's a bushwhacker. He'll come after you when you don't have that big Ruger in your hand."

"You know about that?" I asked. So much for concealed carry.

"The federal firearm registry tells us everything. It isn't hard to look up your concealed carry permit. If we asked, Ruger will send us full ballistic data on your gun. Nice of them. But seriously, Macbean, Ricky Lee is the king of the sucker punch. He'll jump you from behind. Break your legs, rough up your face, put you in a hospital room next to Barnecki. And if he feels mean enough, he'll kill you and dump you in the Atlantic."

"Is that multiple choice or all of the above."

"You can make all the jokes you want, but if you get hurt in my county, it will come back on me considering your special status with the state AG."

"Kind of sucks being sheriff. I'll be dead, and you'll be in hot water with the State AG?"

"Macbean, you have to take this seriously."

"I am taking it seriously...."

Whatever I was going to say was drowned out by the arrival of a horde of police cars, their flashing lights reflecting a carnival atmosphere against the front of the Piggy Wiggly.

"Sheriff, your troops have arrived."

One of the police cruisers pulled into the handicap parking spot to my left. A burly policeman exited the cruiser on the passenger side and flashed a powerful beam through the window of the land cruiser.

I winced and rolled down the window a few inches.

"Macbean?"

"Yes."

"We're escorting you to Gould's Landing. Please follow that car over there." He pointed to a cruiser edging out onto the highway. "Keep a distance of a hundred feet. The rest of us will follow you. When we arrive at the house, please stay in the car while we clear the place. We'll tell you when to get out."

The instructions seemed simple enough, but the many swirling blue and red lights were disorienting. I'm sure I nodded my head like a dumbass.

I rolled the window up.

"Sheriff, are you still there?" I asked.

"Yes, Macbean, I'm here. Please do what Officer Willoughby says. When they clear the place, you go and pack your stuff up and get the, uh, heck out of there. We'll provide an escort to the interstate. Head north and you'll be safe in your own home sometime after midnight."

With the sheriff still on the line, I backed up, turned and aimed at the police car nosing out onto Highway 17.

The cruiser took off like a jet.

I floored the accelerator.

We hit seventy before we crossed the bridge over the Sapelo River. Red and Blue lights from the police car ahead splashed off the trees, a psychedelic video game for maniacs.

"Sheriff, Ricky Lee won't get his chance. Your police escort is going to kill me. Tell your driver to slow down and turn off the roof lights. Folks are going to see us."

"You're a funny guy, Macbean."

"Yes, Sheriff."

"And as much as I enjoy jawing with you, I have massive responsibilities. Let my boys get you to the house. Then pack up and hightail it back to Atlanta. When you get there lock your doors, turn on the alarm and sleep cozy. We'll catch this bastard, and then you can come back someday for a nice visit."

"Sheriff, I'm not going back tonight."

Silence... the sheriff must have hung up.

CHAPTER 16

"Police Escort"

On the road from Eulonia to Gould's Landing
From the Journal of Brendan Macbean:

The cop in the car ahead switched off the phantasmagoric light show, just a pair of alternating rear taillights remained. The driver behind me did the same.

Much better. My impending seizure subsided.

The lead police car turned right on Pine Harbor Road and a few seconds later, hung a left on Shellman Bluff Road. I wasn't familiar with these byways, but they were clearly identified on my GPS. I had traveled them earlier in the day as a passenger with the frenetic Deputy Leggo at the wheel. As our convoy blasted down this rural road, I became convinced that the first criteria to become a deputy sheriff was a passion for NASCAR. My Land Cruiser had no problem keeping up, but, for my sensibilities, we were going a little fast on this rural road.

In a matter of minutes, we reached Youngman Road and made a careening turn to the left. We passed by the looming, empty buildings of the defunct Lockwood Marine. Soon all traces of civilization fell into the darkness behind us. It took a couple of seconds to get the echoes of YMCA, the song by the Village People out of my head, after which I noticed how rough the asphalt was on Youngman Road. Rough enough to penetrate the soundproofing of the Land Cruiser.

That didn't slow down the police car in front of me.

It occurred to me that Youngman Road would be the ideal place for this punk-ass Ricky Lee to stage an ambush. All he needed to do was park an old pickup truck across the road, blocking any vehicle trying to get through. The driver of the first police car wouldn't see it in time and plow into it broadside. I'd barely be able to stop before I plowed into the cruiser in front of me and the cop behind me would in turn, plow into me. That's how much faith I had in the sheriff's deputies' reaction time and driving ability.

Ricky Lee and his henchmen could be waiting in the woods flanking the road, ready to pour lead into the Toyota with illegal assault rifles. Heck, my car was painted like a target. How difficult would it be?

But I'd totally be incapacitated by the crash and the airbags. The tempered glass in the windows could withstand a full-clip fusillade from an AR style rifle, thirty rounds of 5.56 NATO traveling at three thousand feet per second, a full clip emptied in three seconds, probably fewer than half the rounds striking the glass, the glass cracking, hazing, splintering but holding. Ricky Lee yelling like a madman to get his guys to stop shooting since, ejecting brass, probably with his fingerprints on them, they were leaving evidence all over the place. But his guys have their bloodlust up. They empty their rifles and load another clip. Any of the deputies left alive might return a weak fire but it's all over before the shooting stops.

In the death-silence that follows, Ricky Lee gets a couple of guys to boost him up to the Land Cruiser's window. He peers in through the cracked glass, aided by a big flashlight. There I am, pinned by the airbag to the seat, bloodied and immovable.

"Put me down boys, He's done for," he says in his thick, South Georgia accent.

By the time my over-active imagination finished off this dismal fantasy, we reached the end of Youngman Road.

No ambush, nothing but quiet, empty country road.

Totally ignoring the stop sign, we nearly tipped over turning right onto Harris Neck Road, all three cars skidding, leaving rubber on the asphalt.

The Dukes of Hazzard couldn't have done better.

According to Rawlings' notebook, this area we sped through used to be the playground for the rich and famous.

A long time ago, post-Civil War reconstruction, vast tracts of land which used to be plantations became available to wealthy Northerners for bargain prices.

Before the Civil War, Belvedere, Springfield and Delta had been antebellum plantations, significant contributors to the South's economy. The fighting never touched this area like it did Atlanta. Bill Sherman's army passed fifty miles north. However, war impoverished the entire Confederacy and those who supported it found their farms and plantations broken up and falling into the hands of the winners.

In the latter part of the nineteenth century, Yankee robber barons bought into the land. Names like Gould and Reynolds and other famous Northerners used these acquisitions as "hunt" clubs, large tracts of land upon which they built and maintained mansions, with servants, caretakers and even mistresses. These ultimate "man caves" lured the new owners away from the hectic, Yankee-centric empire building. They'd sail their yachts or ride in private rail cars to Savannah and then make the arduous carriage ride from there to here, to fish, hunt and dally with kept women.

Railroads never touched McIntosh County, but a good road south from Savannah was always maintained. I can't imagine a carriage ride from there to here. It would take all day and perhaps more than a day.

This cultural anomaly didn't last. Surely these Yankees found fishing and hunting opportunities closer to home and the vicissitudes of kept-women-dallying might raise more than a few eyebrows and ultimately, questions like, is this trip necessary?

The hunt clubs fell out of use, sold to other interests, their servants and caretakers let go. History does not record what happens to kept women when their dallying days are done.

Nature was eager to reclaim those mansions, sending in armies of mold, mildew, termites and wood grubs, rats, mice, vermin and when the wood rotted, and the roof fell in, trees and brush took over and in time, all traces of the house were swallowed up like they were never there.

Today only historical markers show where these mansions used to be, their actual locations often in question and even the historical markers must be maintained since Nature is eager to reclaim them as well.

My police escort sped across the bridge near the west entrance to the Harris Neck Wildlife Refuge. Just this morning, I saw a woman of African descent sitting in a lawn chair on this bridge, fishing with no less than five fishing poles leaning against the concrete rail, an ancient foam cooler and an ancient pickup truck completing her kit.

This morning seemed like a lifetime ago.

And we passed the spot where the man of African descent and a Great White Egret shared a fishing spot in knee deep water so intent on what they were doing, they paid no attention to my drive-by.

According to the GPS we were running out of road, but the police car ahead of me showed no sign of slowing down. That hundred feet interval I was supposed to keep began to look like more of a guideline than a rule. My foot eased up on the accelerator and the hundred feet became two hundred. The police car behind me loomed closer in my rear-view mirror, apparently nobody told him about the hundred feet.

The pavement ended where Harris Neck Road ended. Gould's Landing Way swapped asphalt for dirt just before the narrow brick gateway, with a giant oak tree growing out of the middle of the road just past the entrance.

Well, maybe the tree wasn't a giant but big enough to wreck a car going sixty. The front cruiser hit the brakes, skidding his rear a little to the left. But they made it through. I held a more comfortable pace and passed the tree with ease, as did the police car behind me.

Once clear of the brick wall and oak tree chicane, the driver ahead of me immediately attempted to accelerate but his excess speed set up a bone-jarring, teeth-loosening, bumper-removing vibration which was sure to loosen any bolt on the car that wasn't torqued to spec.

My pace avoided any such discomfort. I glanced in my rear-view mirror but couldn't see if the policeman behind me held any concern for his dental work.

Gould's Landing Way was the end of our drive. The lead car turned precipitously into Rawlings' gate.

To my surprise I discovered that Rawlings' yard was already filled with police cars. Well, maybe not filled. Two police cruisers had arrived before us, parked helter-skelter in the yard with engines running and lights on. The policemen with flashlights prowled the grounds of Rawlings' cottage. My entourage joined them, left engines running and lights on... eight deputies looking for bad guys.

I felt safer by the minute and did what I was told. I remained in my car.

Two of the deputies walked by and opened the shed to my left. One of them found a light switch and turned on the shed lights. They emerged after a few minutes and left the lights on and the shed door open.

Rawlings' boat on its trailer was parked under an overhang on the north side of the shed. The two deputies removed the boat cover. Rawlings' boat was a small skiff-type boat... too small to hide a criminal but that's where the Boston Marathon Bombers had hidden out, so I guess you must look there.

No Ricky Lee.

I watched beams of white light snaking through the shadows. They even pointed their flashlight up the trunks of trees in case Ricky Leek had monkeyed into the treetops.

All other critters with any sense had fled the field.

Ricky Lee wasn't here.

A burly, barrel-chested policeman approached my window. Presumably it was deputy Willoughby, but I had not really seen his face back at the Piggly-Wiggly, and one burly, barrel-chested policeman looks the same as another.

He knuckled my window, and I rolled it down.

"Mister Brendan?"

"Yes?"

"If you'll give me the key to the house, we'll go in and clear it. Is there a security system?"

I shook my head and handed him the key. "No security system, officer."

I watched his burly, barrel-chested back head for the door. Three deputies accompanied him. They turned lights on and rummaged through the house and garage. I couldn't tell what they were doing to "clear" the house, since my vantage point wasn't the best.

There were three police cars parked in front of me and one behind, all with their engines running and their lights on. All I had to do was turn on the LED lights in the rim of the Land Cruiser's roof to create a "Close Encounters" moment. I saw four policemen, who were not engaged in clearing the house, standing around, chatting it up in a sort of Law Enforcement Fellowship group, two of them resting their butts against a police cruiser.

I was tired of staying in the car. I grabbed my backpack and got out of the Toyota.

The four policemen watched me approach. One of them lit up a cigarette.

"Officers," I said. "I thank you for keeping me safe."

They all nodded like they appreciated the comment but had heard it a lot.

Directed toward the smoker, I said, "Officer, would you like to hear my opinion on smoking?"

All these boys were just that, boys, men in their twenties. Certainly, if I had had children at their age, they could have been my sons. The three non-smokers looked eagerly at me as if the anti-smoking theme was one they shared and needed a little help with this lone transgressor among them.

"Well, here it is anyway. Make that your last smoke and give yourself a two thousand dollar a year raise."

No surprise, the toking cop showed no reaction. I don't think he got it, but the other three nodded their heads.

Okay, Macbean, change the subject.

"So, where do you think this Ricky Lee is hiding?"

The smoker took a long drag on his cigarette, dropped it and ground it into the dirt with his shiny black shoe.

"He ain't hiding, sir. He's long gone."

"Gone? Where's he gone?"

"We don't know. He's gone where he goes."

"How do we know?" I asked.

There was some hemming and hawing and shuffling of feet, the common body language of the uncertain. Then a sustainable babble ensued within our small Fellowship of Law Enforcement that sort of reminded me of a verbal game of "hot potato."

"We don't really know he's gone either."

"The Sheriff is going to search all his hangouts."

"Get with all the people who know him, his kin and such."

"They're going to all lie, for sure, every one of them."

"But they don't want to get in trouble, either."

I asked, "Well, I heard he hasn't been seen around here for two years."

"Yeah, two years ago, they had that thing at the Jelly Ball Plant."

"The what?"

"Jelly Balls. They're jellyfish. The boats go out and catch 'em and the plant in Darien dries and salts 'em."

"Jellyfish... what for?"

"The Chinese eat 'em."

One of the fellowship, cleared his throat. "I believe the correct term is, 'Asian.'"

"What happened at the Jelly Ball plant?"

"There was this nice kid, football player with Savannah State, moving up to Georgia for his last two years. He's working at the UGA Marine Extension in Darien and driving a forklift on the side at the jelly ball plant. He's loading pallets of jelly balls on the truck when these two guys come up, one "as big as a house and the other as small as a mouse.'"

"Sounds like Barn and Ricky Lee," I said.

"Yeah, well that's the way this guy described 'em. They walk in and spray-paint an "X" on one of the pallets. They're piled high with boxes of jelly balls and wrapped with plastic. The kid stops the forklift and asks them what the hell they're doing. Ricky Lee tells the kid to load the marked pallet last. The kid tells him to go fuck himself. He's a football player. He's used to busting three hundred pounders and he thinks he can punch-out the fat guy and throw the little guy in the river. Ricky Lee jumps up like a goat and grabs this kid off the forklift. Then they drive the forklift over him."

"Oh my god! Was he hurt?"

"Hurt bad. Broken ribs, lost an eye and they had to amputate left leg below the knee."

"Jesus."

"The guy was in the hospital for a couple of months, but he recovered, went on to UGA and finished his degree."

"But no football."

"Nope, no football."

"This Ricky Lee needs to go to jail."

"Yep."

"What happened to the shipment? Why did they want the marked pallet loaded last?"

"Well, somebody else finished loading the truck. But when it got to Brunswick, that marked pallet had been opened and five boxes taken off it. Maybe Ricky Lee had the driver stop somewhere and they took off what they wanted."

"I'll guess those boxes didn't contain jelly balls."

"Nope. Probably Fentanyl, hydrocodone, oxycodone."

"Five boxes? Is that a lot?"

"Yep. It's a shit-load."

"And he disappeared without a trace?"

"Until now. Probably made a delivery in a big city. Got paid and disappeared. Until he needed more money. Then he shows up with some new scheme, does his business and high-tailed it to make his delivery."

It was the smoker who delivered this narrative. He paused, took out his cigarettes and padded one out, though better of it and put the pack away.

Someone else chimed in. "We really don't know what he came back for."

"Drugs again?" I asked.

"It's likely. Easy to smuggle in. Easy to handle. There are hundreds of places to bring them in around here. Timing high tide if it's coming by boat. Got to find a quiet place. McIntosh County is famous for being quiet and isolated. Lots of places around here."

Our Law Enforcement Fellowship was broken up by the return of Willoughby. He arrived like an apparition, quiet and a little startling, like we weren't paying attention.

"I thought you were going to wait in your vehicle."

He turned and mumbled orders to the other policemen. They scrambled toward their cruisers.

The cruisers headed for the gate, raising clouds of dust, leaving the yard kind of empty by comparison.

In minutes, our police escort had shrunk by sixty percent.

When Willoughby had mentioned me staying in my car, I was on the verge of uttering sarcastic nonsense, but now I realized this man spent most of his day trying to get people to do what they were supposed to do. The McIntosh Sheriff's department had devoted precious resources trying to keep my sorry ass alive, with a dangerous criminal on the loose. Maybe I could be a little appreciative.

"Brendan, we've cleared the outside and inside the house. Deputy Cortland will stay with the Expo. I'll go in the house with you, so you can pack. The Sheriff has directed me to provide you and escort to the county line, which means I-95 at South Newport. I can follow you as far as the Midway exit if you want. Then we have to get back here."

I turned to look at Deputy Cortland, leaning against the Expo, a Ford Expedition, a burly barrel-chested SUV with "Sheriff" painted across the side of the vehicle... engine running, lights on.

"Deputy Willoughby, I'm going to stay here. I'm not going back to Atlanta tonight."

He gave me a thoughtful look, not critical, but more like he understood. I began to like this placid, by-the-book kind of gentlemen policeman, a young guy, maybe thirty, maybe thirty pounds overweight but with his over six-foot frame... a burly, barrel chested man, maybe Sheriff Boatwright's favorite deputy... well and Leggo, of course.

"Well, you know the risk."

I nodded. "Officer Willoughby, this Ricky Lee may be a badass around here, but if I go back home, I have to face Atlanta traffic.

"All that mess."

"Yup," I said.

"Mister Brendan, I'll get you a radio from the Expo. You can call me if you need help. We're going to be patrolling up and down Harris Neck all night. We can be here in two minutes."

"There's no need for that. My Toyota has command-center communications. I can call you on my cell phone and it can go out on the police band frequencies."

He handed me his card. "Call my cell, then."

"Officer Willoughby, there is one thing you can do for me."

"What's that? And call me Glen."

"Is that with one 'N' or two?"

"Sounds the same," he said stoically.

"I guess it does, but I may need to write you a check."

"All bribes must be in cash."

"Don't need to know how to spell it then, right?

We were both trying to keep a straight face, but I was older and more practiced. He broke into a grin and looked like a ten-year-old boy. A tall, burly, barrel-chested ten-year-old boy.

"Mister Macbean, what can I do for you?"

"I bought a pile of groceries at the Pig. Help me carry them upstairs."

The Land Cruiser sat with its engine running. And the lights on. I climbed in and moved it near the front door of the house, shut off the engine and turned off the lights.

We trudged upstairs, Willoughby carrying most of the groceries.

I started putting them away and Officer Glen or Glenn Willoughby nervously paced around, probably looking for ways bad guys could get in.

"Glen, relax. I'm in Fort Knox," I said.

He looked up startled, perhaps at the sound of his name. Maybe I should have said 'Glenn' with two 'n's.

"This house doesn't have a security alarm, but the Toyota does. The up-fitters put in a very high-tech perimeter alarm system. I can set it to detect anything within five to twenty meters... but I think ten meters is about right. Anything that comes into the perimeter, well it's sophisticated enough to tell if it's a man or a beast. If it's some kind of animal, the system blasts out ultra-sonic noise above the range of human hearing. If it's a man, you get a warning, something like, "Stop! Do not approach this vehicle. Police will be called." I gave my voice stern overtones.

Willoughby gave me a smirk. "And that stops them?"

"Well, it's really loud. Besides if the intruder does anything besides moving away, lights and sirens make like a carnival and it calls 911. Enough ruckus to wake the dead."

Willoughby looked skeptical. "You ever test this system?"

"Yes, actually I did. When I bought the Land Cruiser, I took a lot of training. The dealer insisted on it. He didn't want to turn me loose with all that technology and no instruction."

"Probably smart."

"Anyway, it works. When I set the alarm, that bastard can't get to the front door without setting off Armageddon."

"He could get a ladder and come up the deck." Willoughby waved an arm at the French doors on his right.

"Yes, he could get a helicopter and cut a hole in the roof, but which way is he likely to come in?"

"Most likely he'll come in through the door, but even more likely, he'll not come at all."

"You think he's gone?"

Willoughby nodded. "He's gone wherever he goes. He doesn't like getting caught, and there's a lot of heat out there."

My stomach had the next line... it began growling like a pit bull.

"Glen, I'm going to make a sandwich. Would you like one?"

He shook his head, but it was an automatic gesture, a first refusal. His eye had that lean and hungry look, like yon Cassius, from Shakespeare.

"I'm going to make you one anyway and one for your guy out there... uh, Cortland. If you don't take it, I'll know you're an idiot and I'll tell Sheriff Boatwright you're an idiot."

"He already knows. Macbean, I'd be grateful."

I commenced to making the best sandwich in the world, in my narrow-minded opinion. I lay out slices of Arnolds ryebread, slathered them with Duke's mayonnaise and Zatarain's mustard, then piled on slices of Swiss cheese and Gwaltney's Smoked turkey breast. I was lucky the Pig had these makings.

I put two of the sandwiches in one of the Piggly Wiggly's bags and added a bag of Utz's Barbeque Potato Chips, highly sophisticated food for a little old country store like the Pig in Eulonia, which had a BOGO on Utz brands.

It was time to say goodbye to my police escort. I handed Willoughby the sandwiches.

"Deputy Glen Willoughby, here, with my gratitude. I hope to see you again in better circumstances."

He nodded and headed down the stairs. I followed him. Exiting through the door, he turned toward the 'Expo,' the Ford Expedition police cruiser which was parked halfway between the house and the gate. Even with the exterior house lights on, Willoughby quickly faded into shadow, backlit by the Expo's headlights.

I watched the Expo execute a "K" turn and head out the gate.

I wondered if I'd ever see him again. It seemed as this drama unfolded, I was doomed to meet everyone in McIntosh County in a 'one and done' encounter.

I turned toward the Land Cruiser and opened the back gate again. I removed a thick electrical cord. The Toyota had a plug-in socket like a RV or camper, to keep all those electrical components powered up while in command-communication mode. I plugged the cord into an external socket on the house. The lights inside the Land Cruiser glowed a low blue haze indicating it had switched over from battery power to external power.

Back inside, I used my phone to activate the Toyota's perimeter security system and set the perimeter at ten meters.

Upstairs I sat down at the kitchen counter and opened my laptop. While munching my sandwich, I scanned my email. I had ten new email messages from Nick Carrillo. I skipped over them all looking for the ATFE's explosive report.

It wasn't there, but I had a message from Nick saying the report would be delayed until morning. So much for Bentley's frog power. I didn't have any interest in looking at autopsy photos. My body was telling me it was time to call it a night.

But not quite.

Something left undone nagged at me.

Next to me on the counter was a magazine, Garden and Gun, from September of last year. The cover was a gorgeous some-kind-of spaniel with wavy chocolate-colored fur and golden eyes. The dog looked smart enough to do math and was staring at the camera with a calm expression.

It wasn't the magazine.

Under the magazine was a single sheet of paper.

I had placed the sheet of paper under the magazine this morning to flatten it out. It was the paper I found yesterday drifting on the concrete ramp of the Barbour River Yacht Club. Local drunk, Freddy Framus had identified it as a shipping manifest from Fort Stewart, but all the information on the page was in code and unreadable to someone who didn't know what the codes meant. Perhaps meaningless anyway to someone who had no business poking into someone else's business.

I put the paper on the counter and photographed it with my phone. Four photos and turned it over and took two more photos of the back. Don't know why. It was blank.

I sent the photos to Nick Carrillo. Don't know why. I guess I just didn't like not knowing what was on the page. Nick worked on a project at Fort Stewart. He wouldn't tell me about his project, but he'd know how to decipher this page.

Amazingly, after I sent the photos, my mind relaxed. I finished my sandwich and glass of Heineken, took a shower and went to bed.

My head hit the pillow with wet hair, which meant my cowlick would be all over the place by morning.

The end of the longest day of my life.

Sleep came easily to me.

Tomorrow would change everything.

Again.

PART 2

Who, if I screamed, would hear me among the angels'
hierarchies? And even if one of them suddenly
pressed me against her heart, I would perish
in the embrace of her stronger existence.
For beauty is nothing but the onset of terror
which we are just able to bear and are overwhelmed
because it serenely disdains to destroy us.
Every angel is terrifying.
from First Elegy, Rainer Maria Rilke

CHAPTER 17

"The Best Day of My Life"

Gould's Landing, Townsend, Georgia
From the Journal of Brendan Macbean:

The best day of my life came as a total surprise, a gift out of the blue, which unraveled my carefully stacked plans like a cyclone might unwind a roll of toilet paper.

I had no input as to what the best day of my life might contain. Either my guardian angel designed the day with divine inspiration or a mysterious magic genie, who knew full well, if offered the traditional three wishes, I would have ordered up a ton of foolishness.

After a perfect night of sleep, my day began quietly. Lying in that most comfortable of beds, I eased slowly to consciousness feeling totally relaxed. Maybe I slept a little late but kept my eyes closed hoping to extend that wonderous sensation of languorous lassitude.

Light penetrated my eyelids, a sliver of a new day coming through the French doors.

I flicked an eyelid.

Red light parted the dusky gloom painting the room with a devil's palette.

Red light in morning, sailors' warning.

I am not a sailor. I had nothing on my agenda that might take me to sea.

But I found the red light compelling. Last night, due to circumstances beyond my control I had missed the sunset over the buffalo ranch. So I sat up, stretched and padded to the kitchen. I could get after those carefully stacked plans, but not until I watched the sun rise over the marsh.

The beer I had for dinner the night before clamored for release. But I needed to get the coffee going first. I used the last of the "blend" to make a full pot. My newly formed fellowship of law enforcement buddies might come to check on me. They would appreciate a cup of the best coffee in McIntosh County.

Despite the bladder clamoring, I made it to the bathroom in time. A glance in the mirror told me my prediction about the cowlick had come true. I looked like Johnny Rocket meets Leaf Blower. I fixed it as best I could with wet fingers and a hairbrush, hoping the only visitors I'd get today would be police officers who had worked night patrol.

With my Yeti filled with the blend, my Redhawk in the backpack, I turned off the Land Cruiser's alarm with my phone and descended the stairs. I opened the door cautiously and poked my head out. Movement to the left, I saw a police cruiser drive past the gate headed toward the yacht club.

My boys were still on patrol.

I turned toward the marsh. The beautiful colors of the dawn greeted me. Trees scattered the orange, red, pink and blue shafts of light through a morning mist. I reached the bench swing, brushed off a few twigs and leaves and sat down.

The eastern horizon was a dazzling sight. I counted seven giant columns of cumulus clouds climbing the sky like rising mountains, stacked scoops of ice cream melting into shapes and shades. The middle column blocked the sun, which scattered broad waves of sunlight in prism colors.

Red sky in morning.

It was magnificent. I had to show this to someone. I took several photos with my phone.

Movement to my left. Down at the yacht club dock I saw a patrol boat gliding on the Barbour River. The boat looked similar to the Defender Class boat, the one that blew up in Brunswick yesterday, but a smaller model. It cruised toward me and turned east to follow the river. Soon it was blocked by the marsh grass, the river being at half pool, all but the boat's masts and antennas remained visible above the grass. I watched it for a while and turned to look at the magnificent cloudscape on the horizon.

My phone buzzed. It was a text from Sheriff Boatwright. A lengthy text.

I read the first few lines and decided to save the remainder for later.

"Macbean, glad you're okay. One of my officers looked in on you at six-thirty this morning. Your place seemed undisturbed."

I shifted my eyes back to the dawn.

My phone buzzed again. This time it was a text from Nick Carrillo.

"Brendan! Where did you get this?!?!" he texted with an excess of punctuation.

Get what, I wondered. Oh, I had sent him photos of the Fort Stewart shipping manifest last night.

I texted him back, "I found it at the Barbour River Yacht Club a couple of days ago. Ponder it. We'll talk later."

I knew he'd look up 'ponder.' Always happy to expand someone's vocabulary.

"K" came back, millennial shorthand for 'Okay.'

I turned back to the dawn, but the moment had passed. As the sun rose, the whole scene shifted to a bright spring morning, the cool air making me shiver in my tee shirt. The majestic clouds headed east, away from me, growing smaller, losing their majesty.

Pesky phone.

I sat and sipped blend for a while and something told me my morning was over. Time to get to work.

I got about halfway to the house when a red pickup truck drove through the gate.

I immediately dropped to the ground. In the next second the Redhawk was out, and I held it in both hands, laying in the classic prone shooting position.

The red pickup stopped about twenty feet behind my Toyota. I remembered I had turned off the Land Cruiser's alarm. I wondered where my phone was. I had stuck it in the front pocket of the backpack, on the ground just an arm's length away.

The pickup was battered and old and red, small, a Madza or a Nissan, covered with dents and faded paint, the headlights glazed dusty yellow with age-scum.

The driver sat there, impossible to see through the unwashed, bug-splattered windshield. The engine clattered on making diffident sounds like a child testing a new drum set. In rural areas, you recognized folks by their trucks. I didn't recognize this truck, but I was the stranger here.

It seemed an odd way for this Ricky Lee to attack. Why a broken-down old pickup? Why not come charging in at full speed, with guns blazing?

And where were the police?

I thought of reaching for my phone and speed-dialing Willoughby, but that would mean taking my right hand off the Ruger. I felt fairly confident I could hit a human target at this distance, a little over twenty-five yards. I had won third place in the annual Calhoun Smashing Pumpkins Shootin' Jamboree, a fun even held around Thanksgiving in Calhoun, Georgia where contestants shoot at pumpkins left over from Halloween church sales. The hapless vegetables are set at random distances while strictly sober shooters blaze away with their prized firearms. Winners are decided by a panel of judges on a set of arbitrary rules. The local sheriff gives random sobriety tests, and safety is seriously stressed. Everybody has fun and the proceeds benefit the local food bank.

I held the gun steady with my finger in a safe position outside the trigger guard. Unless Ricky Lee came bolting out of that truck with a weapon, I didn't really want to shoot anyone.

The driver shut the truck's engine off. It didn't stop right away but clattered on for a couple of seconds as if unwilling to end the pitiful drum solo.

Then silence.

The truck rocked slightly, and the driver's side door opened. Or at least tried. A creaking hinge only allowed the door to swing about a foot. It stopped there, until a delicate, slippered foot came out, pushed the door, forcing it open further accompanied by a metal-tearing groan.

A delicate, slippered foot... like the ankle of a ballerina. The foot touched the ground followed by another one. I relaxed my grip on the Redhawk.

A tall child unlimbered out of the truck, stood gracefully and looked around. No, not a tall child... a medium tall woman.

The woman turned slightly and used her hip to push the truck's door shut. A sound-in-reverse... the groaning metal and creaking hinge.

She spotted me laying on the ground, cocked her head slightly and examined me as if I were an odd phenomenon.

I got to my knees and slipped the Redhawk into the backpack.

It was the woman from the bar, Zoller's. Lily, the bartender with whom I'd had a brief but pleasant conversation yesterday before that fat slob of a bully rudely interrupted.

Lily Magill. The beautiful Lily Magill.

It seemed a lifetime ago and impossible it was just yesterday.

I remembered. She captivated me, had me with the first smile.

What was she doing here?

She headed toward me, a joyful skip in her step.

She couldn't possibly be prettier than I remember, but she was. I had totally gotten her hair color wrong. It wasn't red red but more a deep brown with red highlights. No, it seemed to turn redder when she walked through the tree-scattered sunlight. I couldn't tell.

Her walk was like a ballet, like she weighed nothing at all, wouldn't even make footprints in the ground where she stepped. She glided, skipped and danced on the balls of her delicate feet, her slim hips swinging in a feminine gait, a prance like a racehorse wanting to run.

She wore Capris pants like yesterday, only white instead of blue, and a plain pale pink blouse. Her clothes fit her, clung to her wonderous, lovely feminine curvaceous body.

I didn't realize it, but I was walking toward her, slowly like a man in a trance, and we met in the middle of Rawlings forested yard. Lily moved straight into my personal space and slid her arms around me, pulled me to her and hugged me tightly.

The air whooshed out of my lungs. My arms encircled her, naturally, my hands chastely placed on the small of her back, a notion came to me to pull her hips into my hips but, having been raised right, not doing that. It wasn't the gentlemanly thing to do.

She buried her face in my neck and shoulder, moving her cheek against my trapezius muscle. I felt her chest against my chest, her breasts... a man reacts to a woman moving her breasts to touch him. Every square inch of a man's body is sensitized to know when a woman's breasts make contact instantly focusing all his attention to what it all might mean.

What did it all mean?

For seconds... longer seconds than I thought possible, she held me, and I held her.

Finally, she brought her head back and stared into my eyes.

Those eyes, blue of star sapphires with a pattern of gray, pupils contracted by the morning sunlight, dazzling, her untroubled gaze pulled me further into a mental haze. Her prettiness made her seem younger than she was, but fine lines around her eyes and mouth tattled on her, adding years of laughter and tears. A spray of pale freckles dotted her otherwise clear skin.

A wickedly mischievous grin formed on her lips and she said, "Is that a gun in your backpack, or are you just glad to see me?"

I laughed a hard laugh and it was just what I needed to dispel the unsummoned arousal making an appearance in my body. Instantly I became aware I was so poorly prepared for visitors, especially one like Lily. I had gone from sleeping in boxers to donning sweatpants, tee shirt and sneakers.

And my cowlick must have been flagging me as an idiot.

Lily had arrived totally put together, enough for a casual brunch at the Waverly.

She stepped back and gave me the once-over, got a look on her face, and closed into my personal space again. She started brushing me off with her strong hands. I looked down and saw that my tee shirt and sweatpants had picked up all kinds of sticks and leaves from lying on the forest floor. Maybe even a few scurrying insects.

She made quick work brushing it all off and stepped back again.

A single twig had fastened itself to the pink blouse right over her left breast. She noticed me staring at her chest and looked down. She saw the twig resting there.

She looked me in the eye and smiled, thrust her left breast toward me and gave me that dazzling, mischievous smile again, like saying, "If you think you have the nerve, go ahead."

Women will test you. I don't know why. They're trying to find out who and maybe what you are. Or maybe they know who you are and want you to prove it.

I took a deep breath and with the deftness of a surgeon, plucked the twig off her breast with the lightness and grace of a butterfly taking flight.

"Whew," I said. "That was a little scary."

She smiled deeply and lowered her eyes. Maybe I passed the test.

"Brendan. I wanted to thank you. In person." It was a Southern woman's voice, warm and musical.

"Thank me? What for?"

She dropped her smile, and her face grew cold, and I instantly knew I never wanted to face this woman's anger.

"For taking out that son of a bitch, asshole, piece of total shit that came into the bar yesterday."

I was about to say that it wasn't a big deal, but I knew it was.

"I should have just walked away," I said. "Getting into bar fights is not my thing." And now I was doing a poor job being humble about it, too.

She shook her head.

"What you did was smart and brave. He needed to be put away. Sheriff Lanny has been trying to get him for years. He's almost the worst son of a bitch on the planet."

"So the sheriff told me. That just means there's a worse one out there."

She smiled again. "There's always a worse one. Anyway, I also brought you breakfast... my way of saying thanks."

"Breakfast?"

Resting on the ground beside her was a plastic bag with the word, 'Clyde's' printed on it.

She picked up the bag. "Jolanda makes the best sausage egg and cheese biscuit in the world."

Her smile shrunk a little and I couldn't read her expression.

"I only brought two. They're big but there may not be enough for Mrs. Macbean."

Mrs. Macbean? Oh, testing me again.

"It's really nice of you to think of my mother, but she's not with us anymore. Long gone. Rest in peace."

Now she smirked. "I didn't mean your mother, smartass."

"There is no 'Mrs. Macbean'. I've never been married."

"That makes two of us." She turned her head around and looked over her shoulder at the French doors that formed the window to the bedroom I slept in last night. "You got a woman up there sleeping late?"

"Nope. I'm all alone."

She gave me a long, hard stare. "No girlfriend?"

"Nope."

She shook her head.

"Lily, if you're a coffee drinker, I can give you a cup of the finest coffee in McIntosh County."

The smile returned. "I am! I didn't bring coffee. Jolanda's coffee isn't that great, just her biscuits."

We headed toward the house. I let her climb the steps ahead of me, and it wasn't because I was raised right. We climbed the sixteen steps, her leading the way, and if I said I didn't watch her fanny, it'd be a total lie. I have never cottoned up to the term 'ass' to refer to a woman's buttocks, never liked buttocks either. In fact, the English language has never come up with any term that contains the poetry and magic of a woman's rear-end walking up a flight of stairs in white capris pants. And nothing in all of literature seemed adequate for this woman.

But I'm not going to lie about it.

At the top of the stairs Lily gave the place the once-over as I expected her to. I'm glad I tidied up a little.

In the kitchen I refilled my Yeti. Lily chose a large, green porcelain coffee mug from several that Rawlings kept hanging in a dish rack on the wall.

For some reason I thought of Bettye at that moment. She had always fancied up her morning coffee to a degree I thought excessive, with clotted cream and unrefined sugar. Clotted cream was her only nod to British cuisine, otherwise known as Devonshire Cream. From her perspective the French made better clotted cream than the British, of course. When in America, she had made-do with what we had available, heavy whipping cream, which, according to her was vastly inferior to either clotted cream or the heavy cream you could get in the little grocery on the corner near her flat in Paris. Rawlings had a big bag of the unrefined sugar, and like a robot, I had picked up a half pint of heavy whipping cream at the Piggy Wiggly yesterday. I drink my coffee black, a horrid, primitive, practice according to Bettye. Why I purchased the container of cream is a mystery to me. Maybe a nudge from my guardian angel or the magic genie, who knew what was coming and knew I needed to have it the refrigerator.

Lily set about doctoring up her coffee, opening the cream and spooning up a couple of teaspoons of the brownish sugar. She gave an eye to the dropleaf table.

"Lily," I said, and she looked at me. "Let's take your biscuits down to the water. Doctor Rawlings has a picnic table and a bench swing."

Her big smile warmed the room. And I knew I'd never get used to her smiling at me. I wanted another just like it.

We trudged down to the water's edge and chose the bench swing over the picnic table.

She sat daintily on the left side and I on the right. The gentle motion of the swing matched the wavelets on the rising water near our feet.

The breakfast she had chosen was near perfection. Foil wrapped biscuits filled with sausage and folded layers of scrambled egg and cheese. Packets of hot sauce, mustard, salt and pepper gave us choices.

Mustard? I squeezed a little on the biscuit top.

Jolanda gets my vote. As sausage, egg and cheese biscuits go this one surpassed anything the Silver Skillet on Fourteenth Street in Atlanta had to offer.

Lily ate a total of two and a half delicate bites and placed the remainder on the foil wrapper between us.

I had wolfed mine down in two and half massive-aggressive bites and eyed the remainder of hers.

"Go for it, big guy." She said in a husky voice that raised goosebumps on my arm.

I went for it.

We didn't talk much... just looked at the marsh. Lily obviously enjoyed the coffee without comment, taking long, unladylike slurps and holding the slurps in her mouth like she was at a wine tasting. Repeat as necessary.

It might have been a perfect breakfast, except for what happened next.

I heard footsteps and turned around and saw what was going to tarnish our perfect breakfast.

A police car had entered the gate and parked alongside Lily's truck. A long, lean deputy climbed out of the cruiser and started towards us.

He looked familiar. Not Leggo or Willoughby.

Cortland, the guy riding with Willoughby last night. The one with the lean and hungry look.

I stood up and faced him.

"Officer Cortland," I said.

He stopped about ten feet away.

"What's she doing here?" He pointed at Lily who had turned sideways on the bench swing and was looking at Cortland without a shred of welcome or joy on her face.

I was even less happy to see him. Looks like none of us were very happy.

"Why shouldn't she be here?"

"Don't you know, Macbean? She runs with that crowd. The guy we're hunting. She's his girlfriend."

I didn't look at Lily. "Officer Cortland, why are you here?"

He didn't have an answer to that question, obviously not expecting it either.

"No, Macbean...,"

I cut him off. "Call me Brendan. I don't know your first name."

"I'm here to check on you. I find you with a known accomplice of Ricky Lee's. I'm just not going to ignore that."

Now, I turned to look at Lily.

"Lily, do you know where Ricky Lee is?"

She smiled a thin angry smile.

"No. I haven't seen or heard from him in years. Nobody around here has seen him. You know, Corty, if I had any contact with him and didn't report it, I'd be in trouble."

"Macbean, here has seen him. Last night at the Pig."

Lily's eyes didn't waver. "How am I supposed to know that?"

"Well, I thought maybe he's told you. Everybody around here..."

I said, "Officer Cortland. Thank you for checking on me. Is there anything else we can do for you?"

He seemed to have no reply to that. He just stared at Lily. She looked back at him as if he were a fresh pile of swine excrement.

"Then I suggest you get back on patrol. Like go do your job."

I reached for my backpack. Cortland stiffened and put his hand on his pistol.

I pulled out my phone.

"I'll call the sheriff and tell him what a good job you're doing."

"You won't get a signal out here. Nobody does." Cortland said.

"Actually, I do, officer Cortland. My Land Cruiser has fancy communications. Goes direct to a satellite up there somewhere. I have four bars."

I started punching the screen of my phone.

Cortland coughed and said, "You don't have to call the sheriff."

He gave Lily a menacing look and turned back to his police car.

In a minute he drove out the gate.

I sat back on the bench swing.

Lily had turned to face the marsh, staring out at Barbour Island on the eastern horizon.

Neither of us said anything.

I heard her take a deep breath.

"I've lived here all my life, Brendan…"

I turned toward her. She kept her eyes on the eastern horizon.

"Lily, you don't have to…"

"Quiet, Brendan. I need to tell you something."

"No, you don't. I don't know anything about where you came from, what you did or what secrets you have. We all have secrets. I've already concluded that you're a good person."

She turned to look at me. Her eyes had that starry look like some do when they're about to cry. She scooted sideways, right up next to me and laid her head on my shoulder.

I let her. And I put my arm around her.

It felt good… really good. My hand closed around her forearm just below the elbow… a firm, thin elbow. She felt small, like a child, but I could feel the mass of her torso against my chest. Her hand fluttered like a butterfly and landed on the center of my chest, her dainty fingertips spread like a doctor trying to find my heartbeat.

My heart thudded along just fine, my breath coming and going, moving with the slight effort of her chest next to mine.

All the turmoil swirling around us, cops chasing robbers and cops with an agenda, why couldn't two people just have a moment of peace?

I took a deep breath, and it might have taken me two attempts. I was about to say something stupid. I knew it.

"Lily…"

She raised her head and looked at me. Her pretty face just inches from mine. My lips wanted her lips. What would that feel like?

It would be wonderful.

But that's not how I was raised.

She continued staring at me, so close I could feel the sun reflecting off her, almost see the blood racing in her arteries under that creamy skin.

Her perfect lips.

She backed away. A safety move. For both of us.

It's better to say something stupid than to do something stupid, isn't it?

She scuttled backwards to the safe part of the bench swing.

Not all the way. Just a safe distance.

It wasn't a rejection. It wasn't the right moment.

Not yet, anyway.

We both turned our eyes to the marsh, that blue and green expanse, miles of waving grass, sparkling water, fleeting clouds, birds crisscrossing the sky. Nature carried on oblivious to the turmoil of man, or in this case, Lily and me.

"I didn't know this place existed. I've driven down I-95 a dozen times," I said.

"Probably on your way to Saint Simons Island."

"Yes."

"Jekyll Island. Sea Island, Cumberland Island, Amelia Island, maybe Fernandina Beach?"

"Maybe," I said.

"They all have beaches you can drive to," Lily said.

"And here, you don't?"

"We have beaches. Blackbeard Island and Sapelo Island. But you have to go by boat. When you get there, you have miles of the finest beach anywhere and you'll be all by yourself."

"You can't drive to them."

She turned to look at me, gave me an ironic smile.

"Are you a boater, Brendan?"

"I've been on a boat," I said.

"A small boat?"

"The last time I was on a small boat, I nearly drowned."

She returned her eyes to the marsh and thought about what I said. Then she looked back at me and put her hand on my hand, resting on the bench between us.

"Brendan, if I promise you won't drown, would you care to try it again?"

"What, you mean go out on a boat?"

"Yes, exactly that. The Doc's boat. I'll drive."

"You. You can... uh, drive?"

The expression she gave me I've seen many times in my life. I don't know why, but it happens to me a lot. I say something stupid, something that's as obvious as a four-hundred-pound gorilla in the room and I don't see it.

"Brendan, honey..."

She called me 'honey' and I tasted honey on my tongue.

"Daddy ran the best shrimp boat out of Crescent, the 'Marvelous Mavis'. Mavis was momma's name. I used to go with him every chance I could. When he wasn't shrimping, daddy and I were prowling this marsh, in and out of all the creeks fishing for Reds, Trout, Flounder, Sheepshead, Sea Bass, even Tarpon now and then, only you don't eat Tarpon.

"Daddy had more boats than he did cars. Center consoles, Deep Vees, tri-hulls, little whalers... I love the ocean.

"Come on, Brendan. This will be fun!"

And she bounded off the swing like a catapult and was halfway to the house before I could react and follow her. We walked to the shed and under the overhang, to the concrete pad where Rawlings parked his boat.

I guess his boat was the part of his property I had paid the least attention to, figuring, this was one chapter in his notebook I'd skip. I had skimmed the section, "Green With Envy" which was obviously the name of the boat, moving on after the first paragraph. I guess if Rawl-ings trusted you enough to let you use his cottage, he didn't mind if you took the boat out, assuming you also took responsibility for it.

And yourself.

This became even more apparent when we rounded the corner and took our first close look at "Green With Envy."

I'm not a boat expert, but my first impression was that this boat had seen better days. Much better days.

I saw immediately how the boat got its name and why Rawlings didn't mind if you took it out, your boating skills notwithstanding.

When the boat was new, its hull might have been painted in an at-tractive teal-aqua color, which had faded into a blotched, uneven pale green, the color of whirled peas and lettuce leaves. The only new paint on the boat was a fancy-scripted "Green With Envy" emblazoned across the side, presumably both sides.

From above, the boat would show a rectangle about fourteen by four and a half feet, with a casting platform on the front and back, a bench seat in the rear with a driver's console handmade out of plywood on the right with a steering wheel, throttle lever and a couple of small gages. Except for the seat and the console, the interior surface was covered with old outdoor turf carpet, in green of course. A faded green, worn in places.

It had a look of homemade, handmade, do it yourself, a redneck restoration that might work but would win no beauty contests.

Sitting humbly on the transom was a Johnson outboard motor which I estimated came off the assembly line somewhere between my birthyear and Lily's.

I thought, we're going out in that?

"Wow! What a beauty!" she sang.

I walked around the boat and the only thing I could say for certain was that the name was indeed painted on the other side. I squatted down and looked under the boat, hoping I was exhibiting some sort of expertise.

The trailer had been painted over in white Rust-Oleum, but not soon enough. Rust spots bled through the white everywhere.

The two small tires weren't completely flat.

"Wow, Brendan. This is a Del Quay Dory! Look, a cathedral hull... good if we run into chop."

She had squatted next to me and we both gazed at spider webs and mud dauber nests coating the bottom of our vessel.

"Why's that?"

She stood up as if her knees didn't hurt.

"That's just boat talk, darling."

"Aye, aye, Captain Darling," I said.

Trading terms of endearment gave me a jolt, a breath of fresh air, a shot of adrenalin.

She turned toward the house. "Brendan, do you have a hitch on your Land Cruiser?"

I thought about that. "Uh, yes, but it's at the house."

"Well, let's go get it."

"No, Lily. The house in Atlanta. It's a big steel thing with a ball on the end?"

"Yeah, that's it."

"Well, it's sitting on a shelf in my garage. Sorry, I didn't think I'd be towing anything. It came with the car, but I removed it months ago."

"Brendan, you know Doc Rawlings. He drives that big old Mercedes sedan. He'd never tow anything with that. I can't tow it with my truck. Somebody stole my hitch last year."

"Stole your hitch?"

"We get a big crowd at Zollers when the band, Slackwater, plays. Somebody needed a hitch and took it. I don't use it. Got nothing to tow, anyway. Something goes missing off that truck all the time. It's like a junkyard on wheels."

"Lily, I know how he tows his boat. He's got a Mule."

She gave me a scornful look. "Seriously, he tows it with a mule?"

"Yep. A Kawasaki Mule."

A big smile spread across her face.

"Then we're in business!"

"You mean, you actually intend to go out in that boat?"

"You better believe it City-boy. And you're going with me."

Her excitement infected me. I decided to stifle my apprehensions. It seemed an obvious way to spend more time with her.

"What if it sinks when it hits the water?"

"It'll float."

"And if the motor won't crank?"

"You know Doc Rawlings better than I do. Does he have anything that doesn't run like a top? That Mercedes is older than I am and he spends more on it than he would buying a new one. I bet that old Johnson cranks right up."

She pointed to the house. "Brendan, go get the Mule. Make sure the pin is in the hitch. I'm going to give Greenie, here, the once over."

I did what I was told. I knew what pin she was talking about since I had removed the hitch off my Toyota. The Mule sat where I parked it and I found the hitch assembly on a shelf in the garage. Rocket science was not required to install it.

I drove the Mule to the shed and backed it up to the boat. Lily guided me with her hands, pointing left and right because backing up proved difficult and I needed a lot of instruction.

"Good!" she said. She bent over and did something. Then she got into the passenger seat in the Mule.

"What now?" I asked.

"Drive it to the house. We have get some things together."

She gave me verbal directions, sensing I hadn't much towing experience. We pulled the boat past her truck and alongside the Land Cruiser.

Lily held up her hands. They were streaked with black grease.

"Brendan, I spent too much on this outfit to go fishing in it. Let's see if Mrs. Rawlings has something upstairs I can wear."

I followed her upstairs intending to be more gallant this time. No such luck.

Lily headed straight for the bathroom, closed the door and exclaimed, "Wow!"

She noticed Mrs. Rawlings exquisite *décor de salle de bain.*

I used the time to make the bed and straighten up a little more.

Lily opened the bathroom door and exclaimed, "That's the most beautiful bathroom I've ever seen. I'd pay a hundred dollars to take a bath in there. The Doc must really love his wife!"

For some reason her comment made me chuckle. I stifled saying out loud what I'd pay a hundred for, but I couldn't help thinking how wonderful it would be to have Lily take a bath. In that bathroom.

She headed straight for the walk-in closet and began rummaging in the drawers. I leaned against the closet door and watched her, unsure what she was looking for. I was impressed with how neatly she went through the contents of those drawers. I had some misgivings about messing with the Rawlings' stuff, but he apparently trusted me with his cottage and his notebook seemed to give trusted guests carte blanche.

"Ah, that will work."

Lily stood up and held a pair of shorts against her hips. They were at least two sizes too big for her, well-washed, faded and threadbare. I wasn't sure they were ladies shorts but looked too small for Doctor Rawlings. Although Bettye had spent years trying to impart some fashion sense to me, it never took hold. I was certainly out of my league when it came to boating.

Lily pulled out a long-sleeved tee shirt that only looked one size too big for her. It too seemed to be well broken-in.

"I'll bet this is what Missus Doc puts on to go out on Green With."

"Lily, you wear that you'll be hanging on to your britches all day."

She gave me a huge smile. I got the impression that her dad kept a camera handy... Hey, Lily. Smile. And she would smile, and so she grew up becoming a smile machine and the world had become a happier place.

"Don't you go getting any ideas, Brendan. We know how to keep our britches on."

I felt my cheeks getting red and tried to fight it, but how do you do that?

"Brendan, my god! Are you blushing?" She dropped the shorts and tee shirt and came over and gave me a hug. Her arms around me felt like heaven.

"Hey, Brendan, let's see if I can find something for you."

"For me?"

She took a step back. She gave me a head to toe scan and looked like the happiest girl in the world.

What characteristic do I possess that makes women want to dress me up?

"Brendan, it's cool out there now, but this afternoon, we're going to get some sun. It'll be like it was spring, even if winter still has a week to go. Nothing like June or July but you may want to change to shorts."

"I didn't bring any. It's cold in Atlanta. Oh, I brought running shorts. I had hung them up on a hook and turned to look at them. They looked unpromising for a boating expedition.

"Hardly, Brendan." She knelt and reached in another drawer.

"Here." She handed me what looked like an even larger pair of shorts than what she had selected for herself. Same well-washed, broken-in, faded khaki cargo shorts.

They looked a little large for me.

"Well, we guys don't know much how to keep our britches on. Maybe you'all ladies could teach us something.

"Sure, baby. You just put 'em on. I'm going in there to change."

With that, she pirouetted out of the closet and disappeared around the corner.

It took me longer because I had to remove my running shoes. But I had just pulled the oversized shorts up when she came out of the bathroom.

She looked as adorable as a waif wearing cast-off clothes. She had conjured a wide-brimmed hat from Mrs. Rawlings wardrobe and had thrown on a long-sleeved shirt of some lightweight material, with lots of button-down pockets. A tiny marlin stitched on a pocket flap gave me a clue that it was a fishing shirt. The ensemble gave her a themed look like a magazine cover model... a beautiful waif... and all grown up in those oversized clothes.

She handed me a long-sleeved shirt like hers only larger. "You have to be careful with the sun, even this time of year. Do you have a hat, Brendan?"

I did. My faded GSU hat that I run in all the time. I fetched it.

"You're an Eagle? I picked you to be one of those Georgia Tech Smartasses."

I shrugged. "Eagles could out smartass Wramblin' Wrecks any day."

Lily was a take-charge kind of gal. We headed for the kitchen. She made a pair of sandwiches, probably better than what I made last night for the deputies. She cut up an apple and put it in a plastic bag.

We had a picnic.

I grabbed my backpack and followed her downstairs. In the garage we grabbed a five-gallon bucket and packed a cooler full of ice. Lily paused in front of a rack of fishing poles. She selected two.

I took a deep breath. "We're going fishing... not just boating."

She gave me a sympathetic look. "Brendan, I told you you're not going to drown."

I gave her my bravest smile.

"Just kidding, I have the utmost confidence in you, Captain."

This was the point where I became just a passenger. We loaded all our stuff in the boat and climbed into the Mule, with her driving.

She proved expert at that too. She drove out the gate and turned toward the yacht club.

"Lily, stop here for a second." She paused mule and looked at me. "I have to set the alarm."

I keyed the buttons on my phone arming the Land Cruiser's security system. With all the cops and robbers prowling the neighborhood, I couldn't leave the place vulnerable.

We drove the short distance to the yacht club. Lily pulled the trailer around the concrete circle and backed it under the boatlift with apparent ease.

We both got out, but all I did was stand around and watch, while she hooked up the lift-chains to an eyelet in the bow and two eyelets in the back. With a loud mechanical grinding, the lift hoisted the boat off the trailer as if it weighed nothing. Another button slid the boat toward the river and once over the water, Lily lowered *Green With Envy* gently down until floated.

The chains slackened, and with mixed feelings, I observed that the boat did not sink.

"Brendan, honey. Will you unhook the chains?"

"Sure," I said and then realized I had to step into the boat to do this.

I walked down the aluminum gangway to the quay alongside the boat, stuck a foot toward the green carpeted deck and felt the boat move under my weight. I retained my balance and with arms and hands outstretched, scrambled in a lubberly fashion toward the bow.

"That's right. Get the bow unhooked first," Lily said.

I got the heavy hook off the bow eyelet and headed to the stern. I was getting the hang of walking on this lightweight boat. Lily came down and tied ropes to the bow and stern. When I got the other two hooks free, she raised the lift chains over our heads and returned the hoist to the forward position.

She faced me. "Brendan, can I trust you not to fall in the river until I get back?"

"Where are you going?"

"I'm going to park the Mule and trailer, up there where it's out of the way. There's sunscreen in the picnic bag. I suggest you put some on."

She turned and walked back to the Mule.

I found the sunscreen and lathered up while standing with the boat gently rocking on the rising tide. Beside me the aluminum gangway squeaked and groaned as the rising water lifted it. A cool breeze brought the warm smell of the marsh to my nostrils.

I felt a happy pang of anticipation. Maybe I was growing a pair of sea legs.

I looked up to see Lily standing on the dock, looking at me and smiling.

"We're going to have fun, Brendan. I can feel it," she said like a kid going to Disney World.

"Let's get the motor down. Stand over there behind the seat." She pointed. "There's like a hand-hold on the back."

I felt around for it and found it.

"Now push that metal tab. There that's it. Lift a little."

I grasped that they didn't have motors with electric trim back in the day when this one was made. I pulled where my right hand was and found the metal tab with my left. I felt the weight of the motor but most of it rested on the point where it pivoted.

The motor lowered smoothly.

I stepped back.

"Now, Brendan, go squeeze the bulb."

"The bulb?"

"Yes, honey. See that black rubber hose coming out from under the seat. That's the gas line. The bulb pumps it to the engine."

"I got it!"

I kneeled on the green carpet and squeezed the bulb. A dozen slow squeezes and it firmed up.

"That's good, baby."

Lily turned the key on the console. The engine sputtered and groaned. She tried it again. It sighed like an old man getting up from his easy chair. More cranking, strangling, choking and moaning.

"Squeeze it again, Brendan."

I bent to do it again, my childish sense of humor creating instant lowball witticisms, straight out of "Travelling Riverside Blues" and Led Zepplin's, "Lemon Song". However I summoned enough adult restraint to not say them aloud.

"Oh, baby," Lily moaned seductively. "Nobody does it like you do."

Apparently, Lily, the bartender, a pro at flirting with men and sophomoric jokes, felt no such restraint.

She cranked the engine again.

Same noises, same sputtering.

Then the old Johnson caught, emitted a cloud of blue smoke and ran like a well-oiled contraption, as smooth as a sewing machine on a straight stitch… totally flattening my last misgiving. Looks like we were going out in the boat.

"Brendan, untie the bow line but don't cast off. Hold the loop around the cleat. Loosen it after I do the back."

I did what she said and felt the power of the tidal current trying to move the boat to the right. Lily loosened the stern line.

"Here we go!"

She put the boat in reverse and slowly backed out. I sat down next to her on the bench seat.

She turned the steering wheel slightly, and the stern of the boat moved with the current. The bow turned upstream, against the incoming tide.

Lily moved the throttle forward.

The boat surged ahead at a trot, past the floating dock. There were two "No Wake, Please!" signs which told me it was must be a serious issue.

Once past the floating dock, Lily increased the speed slightly. She took off her broad brimmed hat and stuffed it under the steering wheel.

"Brendan, I'm going to throttle up in a second. Do you want to stow your hat?"

I interpreted that to mean it was about to fly off as we increased speed.

I exercised wisdom, rare for me. I whipped off my GSU hat and handed it to her.

She moved the throttle smoothly forward.

The bow rose, and the stern dug into the water. In seconds we leveled, the hull lifted, and the ride smoothed out. The river turned east at this point. Lily weaved right and left gracefully crossed the river. The flying sensation increased.

I looked at her. She stood behind the console, a smile of joy and freedom framing her face, the wind whipping her flying hair, throwing sparks of color, red, auburn, gold. The wind-stream gathered the over-sized clothes around her body, molding against her legs, hips, belly and breasts.

It was the most beautiful image my sore eyes had ever beheld.

She swayed as she swerved the boat back and forth across the Barbour River. The river widened and we turned east.

Before us lay Barbour Island.

I could see the detail of the shore, docks, ramps and boats. The land looked like pure forest, but we were still a half mile away.

Lily slowed the boat as we approached. About two hundred yards from the island, she slowed Green With to a fast walk. The river widened even further and turned almost directly south.

The boat approached Barbour Island.

"Brendan, we're far enough out so we could go faster, but I like to cruise near the docks and see things."

"You're the captain, Captain," I said.

We pulled within a hundred feet of land and cruised along the shore-line of Barbour Island at a "no wake" pace. There were lots of docks with boats and a few glimpses of houses nestled among the trees.

"Who lives here?" I asked.

Lily made minor steering corrections as we water-trotted past docks and gleaming white boats, some hoisted out of the water on lifts, some rocked on gentle waves, tied to floating docks.

"Folks who really like getting away from it all. There's no road. You have to get here by boat. Oh, there's a grass airstrip behind all those trees. I guess you could fly in."

I thought about that.

"It looks peaceful," I said.

"It must be. No rednecks in loud trucks doing drive-bys," she said. "I've never set foot on the island. Never been invited to. It's a close community. I guess everybody gets along. If you make trouble, you get voted off the island."

A weak joke, but it poked a chuckle out of me.

"I guess you have to be a special breed to live here. You can't jump in the car to go get ice cream."

"Nope. Jump in the boat, cruise three miles to the so-called yacht club, park the boat, jump in the car and drive ten more miles to a gas station or fifteen to the Pig. You better learn to stock up for the long haul," Lily replied.

Barbour Island was not a big island, but at the end of the island's waterfront, I saw it had saved its best for last.

We cruised slowly past a magnificent two-masted sailboat. I didn't know if it was a yawl or a ketch, but the rear mast was shorter than the front. It looked to be seventy feet long with the mainmast soaring toward the sky. Meticulously maintained, it gleamed white with glittering metalwork, shiny, glistening woodwork. Every line looked new and taut, the sails folded along the booms, into neat sleeves. The sailboat seemed to move through the water even while moored to the dock. Lily pulled our boat even with the bow of the sailboat. She shifted the motor to idle. We drifted forward until the tidal current going the opposite direction cut our momentum.

We started to drift backwards, like reviewing the boat in the opposite direction.

"I love this boat," she said. "It's been moored here for a long time, but the owner keeps it in top condition. I know he takes it out, but I've never seen it running."

Her voice took on a peculiar, far away tone.

"You know what I'd do if I had this boat?"

"What would you do, Lily."

Putting her thoughts together took longer than I expected.

"I'd sail it to Monte Carlo, park it in the marina and sunbathe in a bikini until one of those rich princes made me his princess."

What she said seemed so unexpected, putting my thoughts together took longer than I expected.

I had an overwhelming urge to skip all that and make her my princess right there on Green With Envy. Of course, I could buy this boat or another one like it, hire a crew and we could sail off to Monte Carlo, park our boat at Quai Louis in Monaco because that's where the marina is. We could live on the boat and watch the Grand Prix every spring, go to the Cannes Film Festival and live like rock stars on vacation. And every day I'd get to see her smile, hear her merry laugh and fill my eyes with her beauty... and at that moment I wondered if that would be enough to sustain us. Would she stay beautiful after all the changes? After we had heard each other's stories, after knowing her history, her knowing mine. Would she forgive me, and could I forgive her?

I said nothing... don't know what a woman thinks when a guy says nothing, but at least at that point, a guy isn't responsible for what she thinks.

Or is he?

Lily put a hand on my shoulder. Her hand was hot, and the heat soaked through the fishing shirt and spread through my body.

"Brendan..."

"Yes, Lily?"

"Have you ever been there? To Monte Carlo?"

There it was, an invitation to share her wonderful fantasy. Her dream had just thrust itself through my brain like a seizure. She could actually have a chance to jump on board my version of her fantasy or, if I was wrong, laugh heartily at my folly.

And I wondered, not for the first time... what was wrong with me?

"Yes. I've been there a couple of times."

She took her hand off my shoulder. Maybe because my response had been lukewarm, unreadable, hesitant, unenthusiastic. I couldn't tell how I had said it or how she read it.

"What's it like?"

A second invitation. How many do you need?

The tide drifted us past the stern of the magnificent sailboat, the yawl or the ketch, but nothing was going to start, no motor would interrupt what I was going to say, she was giving me room to say what I could, no pressure, no demands.

Right. But she's not a guy and she's not infatuated with me.

Infatuated. Lovesick, obsessed, smitten, besotted. The words rolled through my brain like I had hit the synonym button on my computer. Unbidden, the synonym button kept going. Foolish, idiotic, unrealistic.

Needy.

The words of Joni Mitchell went through my head, from the song, "California."

"Will you take me as I am, strung out on another man..." Only in my case it was Bettye... another woman. A woman, who for many years had filled the emptiness in my chest which now was as hollow as an unfilled cauldron.

I took a deep breath.

"It's beautiful. Monte Carlo, Monaco, the marina. The whole coast there, they call it, *le Cote d'Azur,*" the French Rivera. It seems the sun never stops shining. The water is a blue like no other place. The people are happy and carefree."

I don't know why I said that. They're no more happy or carefree there than here or anywhere where people choose to be happy or carefree.

Lily stared ahead, watching the tide roll into the Barbour River.

She said, "I want to go... where people are happy and carefree."

"Yeah," I said. "... me too."

With that old Johnson gurgling behind us, we drifted away from the direction we had been going. The boat turned away... and we drifted.

Lily leaned toward me and nudged me in the shoulder, like to break my mood.

"Come on, Brendan. Let's make some of that 'happy and carefree' right here."

"Yeah, let's do that." I almost choked as I said that. I was ready to get down on my knees and propose to her. Despite my deep love for Bettye... I had never proposed to her.

Lily eased the boat into forward, and we cruised past the sailboat for the last time.

"Oh, dear," she said. "Here comes trouble."

Her eyes focused downriver, toward the south. There was the patrol boat I spotted earlier this morning, or one like it. Silver and yellow, similar to the defender class boat that had blown up yesterday. I had completely abandoned that investigation I was so eager to pursue yesterday.

Okay, I'm a flake, but I didn't understand why Lily thought it was trouble. The governor and sheriff instigated this massive manhunt, and the boat was ultimately there to protect us.

It seemed like as soon as the boat's crew spotted us, they pushed the throttle to flank speed and headed straight toward our tiny green boat.

It's funny how being on a boat makes you think in nautical terms whether you understand them or not. Where did I come up with, 'flank speed?'

Lily turned her head back and forth as if looking for a place to hide. Or run. But there was no way we were going to outrun the patrol boat which was already running faster than a torpedo.

She wasn't looking for a place to hide, as it turned out. She was assessing where we needed to be when the state marine patrol arrived. Away from the big sailboat where there would be no collisions.

Lily headed Green With Envy toward the middle of the river at idle speed.

The bigger boat looked like they would cut us in half. I grabbed for the console to find a handhold.

One hundred feet away the boat cut its speed, turned slightly and zoomed around us, continued about a hundred feet, turned sharply, like a pirouette, amazing for a boat of its size, and stopped in the middle of the river. We drifted toward them with the incoming tide.

There were four men on the state patrol boat. Three of them were suited up in body armor, life jackets and helmets, and holding assault rifles at the ready. One man sat inside a center cabin, the helmsman, I guess.

As we closed the distance with the patrol boat, the helmsman left the helm and came out of the cabin. He stood on the port side of the boat with his hands on his hips.

He wore no life jacket, no body armor and only a sidearm on his right hip. A pair of impenetrable sunglasses kept me from seeing his eyes, but the frown on his face told me this wasn't a friendly call.

He spoke in a deep, local Southern voice, "Lily Magill, what are you doing in Doc Rawlings' boat?"

Lily and I stood in Green With, watching the two boats coming together. The wake made by the patrol boats hit us and rocked our smaller boat nearly to the beam ends.

Nautical terms again. I struggled to stay on my feet. Our boat steadied.

"Corny, you caught me. I stole the Doc's boat and kidnapped Mister Brendan, here. His family will pay big money for his safe return."

"Really? How much we talkin'?"

Lily turned to look at me. She winked.

"Couple hundred thousand, at least. No... a million. Make that five million."

Lily had called this man, "Corny," like she knew him.

"All that money and you choose to steal this puny boat?"

"Puny! This is a Del Quay Dory... a fine boat and the Doc keeps this motor in great shape."

The man in the sunglasses turned to me.

"So, this is the mysterious Brendan Macbean. I got more emails and phone calls about you than when Prince William came to Savannah. What's all this fuss about, Macbean?"

A question that won't go away.

"I think the fuss is about a vicious criminal on the loose and a manhunt for him. It's not about me at all."

"I guess, Macbean, we owe you our gratitude for your role apprehending Barn Barnecki."

"I expect no gratitude. I was merely a witness. I suppose you read the report."

He rubbed his jaw.

"Sir," I said. "I'd like to know to whom I am speaking and why you stopped us."

He stopped rubbing his jaw for a second.

"I am Captain Reginald Cornelius of the Georgia's State Patrol, Criminal Interdiction Unit." He did a little bow and added, "At your service."

I cleared my throat. "Would you be so kind as to ask your troopers to stand down. Holding their automatic weapons at ready is not proper for a friendly talk."

"Sir, they've had extensive weapons training."

"Then tell them to train their weapons on the horizon... not on us."

"Boys," said Lily. "Dial down the testosterone a little."

Captain 'Corny' Cornelius removed his shades and smiled

"Gentlemen, keep watching for boats out there." He kept his eyes on me and waved his arm at the horizon.

"I believe you met Officer Willoughby last night."

I nodded.

"Well, he came to Doctor Rawlings' house this morning and saw Lily's truck parked there. And he noticed the boat was gone. He assumed you two were out on the boat. He asked me if I saw you to check on you. We have a pretty strong directive from the state AG to keep you safe."

I nodded. "We're as safe as anybody could be in Green With Envy."

"If Lily says it's a fine boat, then it's a fine boat," Captain Cornelius said. "I wonder, Macbean, if you realize how lucky you are."

His statement caught me unprepared. I wondered if he meant my having made several escapes from rough situations which seemed to be happening the last few days. Giant dogs, alligators, and of course, the two worst criminals within a hundred miles. Oh, add the pell-mell return to the cottage last night with a police escorto.

But something told me he wasn't talking about any of that. I looked at Lily and she was holding her mouth in a tight smile, a kind of unreadable expression. She and Captain Cornelius were looking at each other.

He meant I was lucky to be with Lily, and I sensed a speech was coming.

Captain Cornelius took a breath. Here it comes. I decided to endure as much of it as I could.

"Macbean, I've known Lily since she was a little baby. Her daddy, Robby Magill was my best friend. He and Mavis, her mother, raised her right. Lily is as beautiful inside as out. She has a heart of pure gold. Why, half the men in McIntosh County are in love with her."

Which begged the question, "What's wrong with the other half?"

He gave me a quick smile.

"Around here we have more than our share of fools, Macbean.

"You know how men are. Every guy who walks through Zoller's door wants Lily's attention. She's friendly, outgoing, quick with a smile and a cold beer. When a beautiful woman offers you a smile and a cold beer, well, it does something to you. Some guys want more than a smile and a beer. Lily sets limits. Some guys get out of hand. You know it's going to happen. But Zoller's is a peaceful place. Sheriff Boatwright makes sure about that. If you're rowdy, you get a ride down to Darien. Everybody knows that.

"Zoller's is peaceful... fun. Popular... all because of Lily."

Lily gave a sigh. I caught some of her vibe, beauty comes with a lifetime of guys making speeches. About her.

"Come on, Corny. We're losing the water."

"Where are you taking him, sweet girl?"

She smiled at the nickname, a fatherly nickname. But if I was his age, I'd wish I was twenty years younger.

"I thought we'd take a run up Blackbeard Creek."

"You going to the Cabretta Inlet?"

"We'll anchor at the dune and see the beach."

Captain Cornelius looked at the sun and water rushing at us.

"You got plenty of water."

When he said that, I knew more speech was coming. I was weary of it. Lily was weary of it.

"Look, Captain. You've probably noticed I'm an adult. It's a little late for the Dutch Uncle talk.

"You probably googled me after all those emails, and now you think you know me. But did you google Bertie and Bernie Macbean?" I didn't wait for his answer. "They're my parents, rest in peace. And they raised me right, I'd like to think."

"Yeah, Corny," she favored me with a smile. "Brendan's a total Boy Scout."

Captain Corny looked directly at Lily.

"Well, Macbean, if she says you're a boy scout, then you must be a boy scout."

He turned away from Lily and focused his steely eyes on me. I guess in his long career in law enforcement, he had developed a pretty good pair of steely eyes.

"We'd like to be on our way. You checked on us, and we're fine."

"Okay, you kids can be on your way. I'm headed up the Barbour and you-all are headed across the sound. If you need anything, give me a call. You can even get a good cell signal next to Sapelo Island."

Lily said, "And we have ship to shore radio."

She flicked the key and the old Johnson sputtered to life, noisy compared to the patrol boat's two Yamahas.

The boats drifted apart. Corny's crew found seats and the big engines roared to life. Captain Corny steered the boat like he was in a race and in a minute the patrol boat disappeared around the bend with only the boat's rooster tail visible above the marsh grass.

Lily hit the throttle, and we headed in the opposite direction.

The Barbour River swung to the left and we curved to follow it. The river widened, and ahead I could see a great expanse of water. The breeze stiffened.

Behold, the ocean.

I don't know why it came as a shock. I had known the Atlantic was there all along. The linear confines of the marsh had given me a sense of comfort which disappeared upon seeing the choppy water.

Storms, hurricanes, rouge waves, gale force winds, shipwreck from a thousand causes.

We headed straight for it.

The water broadened, no longer framed by a river's width, with land on the left and right only now seemed miles away.

The wind came at us off the Atlantic with new energy. River-sized wavelets grew into waves two feet deep. Green With Envy bucked through these waves like a horse with a grudge, leaping out of the water and slamming back. With each impact, sheets of spray flew out on both sides.

Lily gracefully managed this balance-challenge, her long legs moving like saplings in a breeze.

I managed to stay upright. My sea-legs improved with each pounding lurch.

"Hang on, Brendan!" Lily yelled and grabbed my arm like a square dancer in a do-see-do. She abruptly swung the wheel to the right and the boat skidded across the water like in a movie car chase. She moved the wheel to the left and we skidded back on course. I glanced to the left and saw something in the water that looked like a strange brown and gold and green inverted bowl with a head and flippers.

"Sea turtle," she yelled.

The creature's gentle eyes stared at me for a second and it was gone behind us.

"All kinds of life in the ocean," she said.

Exactly where we were headed.

My gaze fell on the distant land to our left. Lily said, "St. Catherine's Island."

"And over there?" I pointed to our right. There was a vast gap of endless ocean and a tree dominated landscape just visible on our right.

"That's Blackbeard and Sapelo Islands."

I didn't see two of anything. It looked like one long stretch of land. Lily had told Captain Cornelius that we were going to Blackbeard Creek, which I assumed was near Blackbeard Island.

Because we weren't headed in that direction, it dawned on me, we might be going around something.

"We're going around something, aren't we?"

Lily smiled, like a teacher at a bright pupil. She pointed at the GPS on the console. Like the one in my car, it showed a map and a tiny icon of the boat. She pinched a couple of her delicate fingers across the display and zoomed the image out. The GPS showed the broad Sapelo Sound framed by St. Catherine's, Blackbeard and Sapelo Island.

We were going around something.

"Brendan," Lily swept her arm in a wide flair. "There's a big shallow area over there. We have to go around it, even with the tide coming in. You come back here at low tide and you'll see a thousand wading birds walking around a big mud flat, looking for dinner."

Lily steered us south. The boat followed a wide arc until we were headed toward the twin islands of Blackbeard and Sapelo, which still looked like one stretch of trees.

The stiff Atlantic wind blew now from our left. The boat no longer bucked like an unbroken pony but wallowed corkscrew-like in the troughs between the waves. In the weird motion balance required flexibility in the knees, but I managed.

Blackbeard/Sapelo grew larger as we approached. At a distance of a few hundred yards, I saw a narrow beach backed by a sand dune. Could this be what Lily referred to as the dune?

Lily backed the throttle off. The reduced engine noise allowed her to talk.

"The old sailing ships used to stop here and unload their ballast. After crossing the Atlantic, the ships would dump the rocks they use for ballast and warp down the inter-coastal to Darien. Then they'd take on cargo to replace the ballast and sail back to England."

I understood about half of what she said.

"Cargo? Darien?"

"Mostly lumber, but cotton and rice, too. But now there's a huge artificial reef here from all those rocks they dumped. You don't want to run into it even at high tide. So, we're going to dog it a little 'til we get to the creek."

"Blackbeard Creek?"

She nodded.

And pointed.

Ahead I saw a tall telephone pole sticking out of the marsh. A sign on the pole said, "Blackbeard Island" and in smaller letters, "National Wildlife Refuge."

Lily powered up, brought our green boat up on plane and turned sharply to the left, entering this creek I hadn't noticed before. The creek was fairly wide and wound a snake-like path through the marsh. We slid through the curves like a wild carnival ride, zig-zagging, going straight and turning both left right, not slowing for any of it. I leaned my body into the sharp turns while Lily worked the steering wheel like a Formula One driver.

It was thrilling and quite a lot of fun. I cast a glance at Lily and she, too, was grinning. I was gaining respect for her boat driving skills. She was my only guide into this wilderness, and yes, it was just that. You could look in any direction and see nothing of civilization. And it didn't bother me. Faith more than recklessness... I knew in my heart she had mastered this wilderness and would bring us back safe.

It was then, while we were zooming through the marsh between Blackbeard and Sapelo Island, I became aware that I was experiencing the best day of my life, a day which required me to shed my misgivings, and despite the obstacles, everything seemed to be working out. I could easily ignore the factors and the path which had brought me here. Later I could examine the hows and the whys.

I was living in the 'now' like never before.

I even smiled at my mental caprice.

Lily glanced at me and said in a voice just loud enough to be heard over the old Johnson.

"What are you smiling about?"

I looked at her and loved her. I knew I did. She had come to me like an angel riding a golden sunbeam. It was the best day of my life and she had brought it to me wrapped to perfection in the gift of herself. How could I not accept it? How could I not love this beautiful young woman? Joy came from the knowledge and relief that my heart hadn't been so hardened and scarred as to make it impossible. It was like my trusted doctor, after a thorough examination had told me, Brendan, your heart's okay. You can love again.

I tried to dial it down before my cup boiled over and I sloshed out some of the preciousness of it. It couldn't be love I was feeling. It wouldn't last. It had to be temporary. It was just a perfect day, not a perfect forever.

I lowered the heat just in time. My cup didn't boil over.

Bettye. Memories of her flooded my mind at exactly the worst time.

Bettye had once been my guide to what I had thought was a happy life, and I had walked away from her.

What was it we had, I wondered. A perfect commitment to each other? But it hadn't been perfect. I had been full of obstacles. In our years together, we really only had a few months where we were really with each other. Now and then we had had perfect bliss, but life intervened and gave us plenty of reasons not to be together.

Her cancer changed everything. Aged her, changed her body, her mind. Like Jim Nightshade, she had taken a ride on the 'Something Wicked' carrousel and came out older and different.

She had seen death and survived.

She had decided to become the guide to a new sisterhood. Cancer victims. She could lead them to survival or to help them make accommodations with the inevitable. It became her mission, her passion, her crusade. How could I object to it? How could I compete?

One more day. One more day with your family, your loved ones. Fight for yourself and for them.

I had found myself unable to join the sisterhood and brotherhood. I was healthy. I had never been sick. Not like that.

I tried. I tried. I really tried.

I could make coffee for her and carry her luggage. I knew how to find the best pastries in whatever town we found ourselves, make hotel reservations and make sure we were on the train when it pulled out or the airplane when it lifted.

I didn't even know when enough was enough. I stayed too long. Until packing my bag and making a reservation for Atlanta felt like it was the only thing that could save me.

I had retreated again, to be alone.

When I left, we both told ourselves... it was for the best.

No tearful phone call, no long letter needed.

I was alone and Bettye on her crusade alone.

The wind streaked tears from the corner of my eyes straight into my ears.

"What's wrong, Brendan?"

Lily cut the engine. The boat's loss of momentum and the tidal current swirled Green With Envy around in the middle of Blackbeard Creek.

A stark contrast marked her two near-simultaneous questions to me. It seemed odd when you put them together. "What are you smiling about?" and "What's wrong, Brendan?"

Her concerned expression touched that needy place in my chest. I wiped a hand across my face. "I'm okay. Really. The wind made my eyes water."

The look on her face said my bluster didn't fool her at all. Her arm went around me, and she pulled me to her, close, tight. Her body felt hot, like my mother when I brought my childhood hurts to her, for her to heal. Band-Aids and hugs and her warmth.

"Okay Brendan. We're almost there."

She reached into the compartment under the steering wheel, pulled out her wide-brimmed hat and handed me my baseball cap.

"Here, before we get too much sun."

She kept the speed of the boat under a canter. We moved smoothly between the banks of the marsh. Rounding a bend to the right I could see a man-made structure along the Blackbeard side of the creek, a dock as it turned out.

We floated past the trees, I saw fragments of buildings on the shore.

"Ranger station," Lily said.

"I see something back in the trees... on shore."

"There's a house and a barn and a shed, I think. I've never been up there."

"A house. The ranger's live there?"

She shook her head. "I don't think they live there. Not regularly. They take care of the refuge. The whole island is a federal wildlife preserve. They come and go as needed. Nobody's there now."

"Really? How can you tell?"

"There's no boat."

She was right, the dock was empty. No boat.

"They have to get here by boat," I said.

"Yup. It's an island."

With Blackbeard Island blocking the wind, we glided past the ranger station. As soon as we passed the no wake zone, I thought Lily would power up, but she held the speed to a fast walk. We passed a tangle of large tree stumps lodged half out of the water and passed a high bluff with a cliff of packed earth topped by large trees on the brink of, themselves, collapsing into the water.

It was like we were on the African Queen.

The land surrendered to the marsh. The creek curved gently to the left and then through a series of S-curves. We maintained our moderate speed.

Curling right around a bend, we entered a large lagoon. I found it impossible to gauge the size of the lagoon. My senses were land-based where distances were short and based on scales common to urban areas. It must have been nearly a half mile long and a thousand feet across. Calm, blue water framed by the marsh of Sapelo Island on our right and the tall sand dune of Blackbeard Island. Blackbeard's dune tapered to a point ahead and through a gap, between the two islands, I could see an expanse of the Atlantic Ocean, dark blue water flecked with whitecaps.

That must be the gap Captain Corny mentioned. And the dune was the dune. The two destinations were adjacent.

And it was beautiful. I was in danger of overusing the word, but it was the best day of my life and what better word for that?

Lily circled the boat at a lazy pace, perfect for taking it all in. We idled near the gap to stare at the ocean for a moment. With timing more art than skill, she moved on at the right moment. We circled around, back to the dune and she pointed the bow directly at the narrow beach at the foot of the dune.

The bow of the boat touched the sand.

Lily went forward and took an anchor out of the compartment in the bow. She heaved it onto the beach and tied off the rope.

She turned around and examined my feet.

"Brendan, you may want to take off your shoes."

"I have winter feet, Lily."

"Sweetie, we all have winter feet, but bare and sandy is better than soggy shoes. We're going up the dune."

I didn't get that last bit and looked up. The dune towered over us, taller than a basketball goal.

Lily vaulted gracefully over the left gunnel.

"Oh, water's cold!" she said. "But you'll get used to it."

I wasn't so sure. The day was warm, but this water came all the way across the ocean.

I removed my shoes and socks and swung my bare legs over the gunnel.

The water stung like an icy hypodermic.

But I got used to it. After a few seconds, the warmth of the sun revived me. I reached into the boat and grabbed my backpack. My feet sunk into warm sand.

I looked up. Lily had climbed an alluvial chimney cut into the near-vertical face of the sand dune. She stood at the top holding our picnic bag over her shoulder with one hand on her hat to keep it from flying off her head in the stiff wind blowing off the Atlantic.

She stared at an ocean I couldn't see, but she looked so pretty standing there as if posed by an artist, the breeze flapping her oversized clothes, the smile on her face as if life itself was a breeze and she loved it.

I dropped the backpack and with my phone took two pictures. In the first photo she still gazed out at the ocean. In the second she looked down at me, the sunlight flashing through her blue eyes in a prismatic manner...looking at me with some expression I couldn't read but my libido could. I felt a heat not from the sun spread through my body and my muscles stretched spasmodically as if limbering up for action.

I loved her. It was as simple as that. I had no right to feel this way. I had no reason not to.

They say only fools fall in love, but wise men get no comfort from resisting it.

"Come on, Brendan. I think you're going to love this." And she disappeared over the top of the dune.

Climbing the sand dune turned out not to be difficult. There were places to put your feet and it wasn't as steep as I thought. At the top, I had to grab my hat as my head came out of the lee of the sand dune.

I did love it. Before me the Atlantic Ocean spread out in all it's late-winter energy. Dark blue everywhere flecked with vigorous whitecaps. Pale blue sky above quilted with fleecy clouds, a lonely, isolated beach with no one on it.

Except Lily and me.

Between the top of the dune and the edge of the ocean lay a hundred yards of sand. Halfway, Lily had dropped the picnic bag on the sand and was skipping toward the water like an eight-year-old on her birthday. Her long legs, wrapped in oversized cotton shorts, the brim of her hat bending backwards, her blouse rippling in the wind, baring patches of midriff.

I dropped my backpack on the picnic bag and headed after her. Her skittering feet hit the water, sending up spray which the wind blew back in my face. I ran and my feet and ankles hit the surf. She turned and flung a handful of salt water at me, which caught me full on the chest. I returned a bigger handful at her and we splashed each other until we were soaked and freezing and out of breath.

My hands reached for her, circled her waist and she turned. Our arms went each other in a full hug, bringing our chests together. Our bodies exchanged warmth that spread and tingled. She raised her head to look at me. The symmetry of her face, her smile, the sparkling blue-gray jewels of her eyes, her nose and cheekbones, perfect, exquisite, overwhelming.

I almost kissed her, the urge nearly irresistible but sensed kissing needed to wait. She turned and put her head against my shoulder. The floppy brimmed hat covered my mouth and nostrils with wind-frenzied suffocation. I caught her scent. And that of whatever laundry product the Rawlings used.

She tightened her arms around my back and spoke, her voice muffled in my wet fishing shirt.

"Well, City-boy with winter feet. You're standing ankle deep in the Atlantic Ocean and your clothes are soaking wet. You okay with that?"

"Well..." I drawled the word. "Sweetheart, I may have winter feet, but it's still too early for skinny dipping."

Lily laughed. It was a weak joke but laughing at my jokes gave me a perverse encouragement.

She pulled back gently. "Brendan, are you hungry?"

I took the question seriously. My body was filled with romantic adrenaline. All body functions except charm and lust were subdued. But my stomach gave me a practical nudge.

"Yeah, let's eat."

We sloshed out of the water onto sun-drenched sand. I felt solar heat coming through my winter feet. Lily didn't let go of my hand and firmly pulled me to where we had dropped the picnic bag and backpack.

Lily spread out a small blanket and used my backpack to hold down a corner. She sat lotus position on the right and I sat next to her, our hips touching. She handed me a sandwich and a bottle of water.

We stared at the ocean and ate sandwiches. Rather, I ate mine quickly, while Lily nibbled. I realized the sandwich was delicious. And then it was gone.

In the same span of time, Lily had eaten less than a quarter of hers. She noticed me eyeing her nearly uneaten sandwich.

"Here, Brendan. I've had enough."

"Are you sure, Lily. This is delicious. How did you do it?"

"Oh, just a little mayo and lemon juice. I sprinkled olive oil on the salad greens and some black pepper."

"Wow, the girl can cook!" I said.

"You better believe it, Winter Feet Boy," she said.

I felt a cooling breeze. The sun hid behind a cloud and chilled us.

I looked at her. Her lips had thinned to a line as she gazed out on the now-gray ocean. Her eyes darted at me and said, "Brendan, I have to tell you something."

She had tried to have this conversation earlier, but we had covered a lot of ground and water, since then. We were closer, easier with each other and unlike the kiss, maybe this had waited long enough.

"Okay, Lily. I want to hear you."

It took her a few minutes. Lily was easy at conversation with guys coming into her bar, but that's the façade, the lovely and lively bar girl semi-flirting with everyone, going home with no one, to no one. How that façade was built, where it came from, what it consisted of was deeply personal.

And hidden.

She faced the ocean, like it gave her strength. The wind tousled strands of hair that fell under her hat. Sunlight returned, reflected off the waves and played with the shadows on her face.

"I don't tell people this. Some, like Corny, who've known me all my life, know it. Lanny Boatwright... the sheriff. They were Daddy's best friends.

"Daddy ran the best shrimp boat on the coast. The 'Marvelous Mavis. Those three boys worked on shrimp boats since they could walk. It's what you do around here. Then Lanny and Corny both went into the Army and after that they became cops.

"Daddy loved shrimping. Worked on a boat for a while and bought his own.

"You don't make a lot of money shrimping. It's like farming... you have good years and bad.

"I guess to a lot of kids, their father is their hero. Daddy was mine. Strong, tall, handsome, capable, kind and generous. I always wanted him to love me, be happy with me. I couldn't stand it if he was angry with me or disappointed.

"He was my king, and I was his princess. I'd do anything to make him happy.

"When I was fifteen, Daddy died. Something on the boat fell on him. His crew got him to Brunswick hospital as fast as they could. The doctors worked on Daddy for hours, but they couldn't save him."

She slumped, her head down, tears dripped whipped by the warm wind off the Atlantic.

"I'm so sorry, Lily." What else could I say?

She looked up, gave me a brave smile, eyes sad and red.

"Gosh, Brendan. I'm thirty-seven years old. I've lived most of my life without Daddy."

Lily carefully dabbed her eyes on her sleeve trying not to smear her makeup.

She took a deep breath. "You'd think I'd get over it."

"Brendan, do you still have your mom and dad?"

I shook my head. "No, both gone, now."

"It's sad, but I still have Momma, if you could call it that. She's up in Hilton Head. She almost never comes down here anymore.

"After Daddy died, I guess I sort of went a little wild. Like rebellious, you know? Made Momma mad, worried her. I started running with the wrong crowd. Ricky Lee..."

I heard the name. It felt like a punch to my gut.

"He was older than me... dropped out of the Academy, but he still hung out there after school. Selling drugs, giving kids rides into Darien. He had fast cars and a gang of delinquents running around doing whatever he wanted. He wasn't afraid of anything. He threw parties with booze and drugs. Anybody could come and get high. Parents would get worried about their kids... call the cops and we'd get raided. Ricky Lee would be long gone. We'd hear the police coming and run off into the woods, straggle home red eyed, briar scratched and hair full of Beggar Lice.

"I wouldn't listen to Momma or Lanny or Corny. I knew Ricky Lee was no good. I knew he was bad.

"Just when the law was about to close in on him, he'd pull a disappearing act. Gone, nobody knew where he went. Gone for weeks and months. The whole community said good riddance. Then he'd sneak back into town. People would see him here and there, but not so the police could catch him. He had other kids selling his drugs now. They'd get in trouble and he'd skip out on them.

"I began to listen to Momma, Lanny and Corny. I straightened myself out and paid attention to my schoolwork. This wasn't the way Daddy raised, me and I didn't want to do harm to his memory.

"Daddy always called me his 'smart cookie'. He'd give me little puzzles to figure out and I'd figure them out. Now I was trying to get my life back together... just another rural teenager in trouble. Momma helped and so did Lanny and Corny, like they were my uncles.

"In any other town, you would have said my reputation was shot, but those towns have their snooty side and their poor side. You're either on the wrong side of the tracks or the right side. Well, McIntosh County isn't a town. Darien is the only town we have. Anyway, I didn't care. I had made my mind up to make my daddy's memory proud.

"I did my homework and got good grades. I didn't date and only had a little bit of high school social life. Momma took me to church and I actually sang in the choir. Do you believe that?"

She looked at me and smiled, a mild kind of smile full of remembrance and nostalgia. Anyway, I nodded. Of course, she could sing in the choir. Why not?

"Occasionally, Ricky Lee would be spotted but not long enough to get caught by the police. He sent some of his thugs to give me a message. He didn't like me straightening out my life. He kept sending his sorry messengers to tell me to run away... we could carry on like old times. All I had to do was skip out like he skipped out. He'd meet me somewhere and we'd run off.

"But I didn't want that. I was through with it. Whatever rebellion I had had after Daddy died was gone. I wanted a good life. I wanted more than anything to be my daddy's good girl, to make something of myself.

"When I saw one of his thugs coming at me, I call the Lanny. Lanny wasn't sheriff then. He was a deputy commissioner. He was also on the school board, the volunteer fire department and was working with the sheriff. Lanny would show up with a police car full of deputies and the thugs would run off. He and Corny protected me.

"Ricky Lee finally stopped sending his thugs after me. Nobody saw much if him. We all got the notion we'd seen the last of him.

"I actually graduated from the Academy with honors and was awarded a scholarship to SCAD."

"SCAD?"

"Savannah College of Arts and Design."

"Oh, I've heard of it," I said.

"I chose fashion design and loved it. I worked my fanny off and was on the dean's list six semesters in a row."

"Wow. Impressive."

"A photographer friend of mine took pictures of me. I liked doing that, too. Modeling. Fashion, clothes, getting all prettied up. He sent some of his photos up to this agency in New York City. I got invited to come up. Momma and I packed our bags and flew to New York.

"Wow! New York. Momma had been before when she was younger, but I'd never seen anyplace bigger than Atlanta. The agency offered me a contract and we did photo shoots. Momma and I stayed for three weeks. It was hard work. I must have modeled a thousand outfits. The photographers took thousands of pictures. I loved it. I know people think I'm beautiful. I don't know what else to call it. It's not something you can order out of a catalog. I didn't choose it and it's a little scary. Daddy always told me that what's inside a person was much more important. Whether they're kind, generous and loving. I hope I'm not conceited about it.

"The model management firm said I was just right for catalogs and magazines. More the 'girl next door type'... not tall enough for runway fashion, but still they offered me a big contract and I signed it. I wanted to finish my degree. I was just a few months away. Then, I was going to pack my bags and move to New York. Momma said she'd come up there with me just till I got settled.

"She had been seeing a new man, an attorney from Hilton Head. Things with them had moved along and they intended to get married. It looked like the last of the Magills were about to leave McIntosh County."

Lily paused her story, and I felt dread it wasn't going to end well. Something happened. Lily didn't become a model. She ended up tending bar in nowheresville.

"So, I came home to finish up at SCAD.

"And I got kidnapped. One afternoon after class, I was walking back to the apartment I shared with two other girls. A van pulls up and two guys grab me, hustle me into the side door.

"That's the last thing I remember. I woke up in a scabby room somewhere. I had been drugged. I don't know what they gave me or where I was. I didn't know how long I had been out."

"Oh, my god, Lily." Speechlessness wasn't a common thing for me. I was devastated and frightened by what had happened to her.

"And raped. While I was unconscious." Her head dropped and her hands came up, folded around her skull and wrenched the cloth of her hat.

"I didn't know how anyone could do something like that. I knew who it was...who could do something like that.

"Ricky Lee. I was alone in a room, in a bed, so strung out on some drug that I couldn't move. My body ached and my head. And my... " Lily took several rapid breaths, like sobs in reverse. Tears coursed down her cheeks and she made no attempt to salvage her makeup.

"My... down there."

She looked at me and I saw the young girl who had lost her father and then a little older, the sorrow of everything else that had been wrenched from her. I felt my heart beating, heavy like a clock winding down.

"It was Ricky Lee. I hadn't seen or heard from him in years. I had thought he'd moved on, stayed away from Shellman Bluff to avoid getting arrested. But he was waiting… planning this. He didn't want me to be free from him. He couldn't let me be…

"He came into the room. Said something like, 'Well, if it isn't the little princess. You forget about me, darling? You thought you could get away from me and have your goody-goody life. Well, darling, that ain't how it's gonna be. You're *my* little baby doll.'

"He came to the side of the bed and had a needle. He stuck it in my arm and I couldn't move. I didn't have the strength or will to stop him.

"That began the worst period of my life. I have been trying to deal with it ever since. I've been going to therapy trying to get the horror of it out of my head.

"When Momma realized I was missing, she called the police, but Ricky had taken me somewhere. We weren't anywhere around here. The police couldn't find me. Rumors went around that I had run off with Ricky Lee. I didn't find out until later that Sheriff Lanny and Corny kept trying to find me, but obviously, they were not successful.

"Ricky Lee gave me a daily dose until I was addicted. Until I begged him for the next hit. My body hurt and cramped and ached if I couldn't get it. Agony like you can't image. You don't understand, nobody does who hasn't been through it. You'll do anything, say anything, let anything be done to you to get the next hit.

"He didn't beat me anything like that. But I lost my appetite. I lost weight. He had to make me eat to stay alive. All I wanted was the drugs. And all I wanted was to not be on drugs… and get away… from Ricky Lee.

"Then he started using me. Daily humiliations, not like I wasn't already humiliated, but my whole life in a matter of weeks had become Ricky Lee and his van or some house we shacked up in.

"He took me everywhere and forced me to participate in drug deals. He said, 'Honey, you see that guy over there. Here, take this to him and he's gonna give you some money.' Then he'd give me a fentanyl tab or something like it and I'd go do it.

"Ricky began a new tactic.

"Opioid addicts go through a predictable cycle. When you take a hit your body rises pretty quick into the high. At that point you're oblivious to what happens in a normal day. Really you need to be isolated from things because you can't react to them. Phone rings, doorbell, somebody asks you a question. You don't give a flying shit about anything. You're in oblivion, feeling really good… and that's an understatement… that feeling… it's what you live for. When you come down, for a while you can function, you're okay… can carry on a conversation, get a few things done before the bad stuff starts.

"Sometimes, I'd beg him to let me go. I could call Momma. She'd come and get me, put me in a hospital to detox. Then a place where I could get clean. I wanted that. I wanted to get away. He didn't need me. He was just torturing me.

"He'd laugh at me and tell me I was dreaming. 'You're mine, babe. You're not going anywhere. You belong to me and you always will.'

"Most times I'd go into depression. I hated how I was living… the way I was kept. When I was, what's the word? Lucid. Functional. The time between the peaks. I wanted out. I wanted to be clean, get away from this awful existence.

"Then the pain would start, and I had to take something. A craving like you wouldn't believe… You've never had… unless you've been an addict. It's more than compelling… You feel like you're going to die if you don't get it. And when you do get it, you roll back away from the real world into the magnificence of the high.

"Some days Ricky'd ask me, 'Hey, babe? Can you drive?' And we'd go sell some drugs.

"I'd take the wheel of whatever old car we had. Barnecki riding shotgun and Ricky Lee in the back. We'd hit I-95 south and drive a while. At the time I didn't know where we were, but soon I figured out we were in South Carolina. We pulled off somewhere and parked at a convenience store. Ricky Lee told me to park in the handicap spot near the front door. Soon some scruffy looking dude walks up. I roll the window down and he hands me a roll of bills. Ricky, from the back, hands me a brown-bag and I hand it to the guy.

"Five minutes later we'd get back on the road again. Sometimes we'd get off and take other highways. We'd go places. I didn't know where we went. Sometimes Columbia, Augusta. We went to Atlanta, stayed in a hotel. Ricky and Barn would go out for a long time.

"I know. It was a great time for me to try an escape. But Ricky had one of his guys watch me. He told me if I wasn't here when he got back, he'd go after Momma and her new husband, my stepdad. And he'd do it too. I've seen it with my own eyes. What he does to people.

"He told me, 'Babe, your momma done forgot about you. She married rich old Max Samson and moved to Hilton Head.'"

I said, "Max Samson? The attorney on TV?"

"They met when he came down for some fishing and golf. Momma ran the gift shop in Eulonia. They dated. He was always nice to me, but distant. He wasn't my daddy, but Momma liked him. I got kidnapped before they got married. But hearing this made me realized some time had passed Momma had moved on... after losing her daughter, I guess."

I just nodded.

"Ricky showed me a video on his phone. It was Momma going to the Whole Foods store on Victory Drive. What was Ricky doing taking videos of my mother? He said, 'See this, babe? You try to run out on me, and I go after your momma. You want what happened to you to happen to her? I'll shoot her up with stuff and let Barn have her. You know he likes it rough. You want that to happen to your momma?'

"I shook my head. 'Well, babe, you better be here when I get back.' Then he and Barn would head off somewhere.

"I waited for days for Ricky and Barn in the hotel room. One day someone shoved a USA Today under the door. I picked it up and read the date. That's when I realized I had been kidnapped and two years had gone by. Two years of my life destroyed, gone up like puff of smoke. My life was gone, whatever I hoped for vanished. I didn't even know it. My whole sense of who I was had vanished with it. Whatever I wanted... gone. Family, friends... gone.

"All destroyed. All flushed down the commode. I was as good as dead. I might as well have been dead.

"I sat on the bed and cried. Until I needed to take some drugs. Ricky left me a supply and I kept it in the room safe. Daily doses. I thought about taking it all at once and ending my suffering, but I didn't. I wouldn't. Somehow, I hoped this nightmare would end. I just didn't know how. Or when.

"We drove all over the place. Sometimes I knew where we were and sometimes I didn't.

"Ricky Lee let me handout the packets to his customers while he watched from the back seat. I don't know how long this went on.

"I did it because I had to. Withdrawal was scary, like choking. You didn't know if you were ever getting the drug again, especially with a guy like Ricky Lee running your life. Sometimes he'd let it go so long I was screaming in pain and then give me the fix I needed like he was doing me a big favor."

"Then one day, we headed south. I think we were in Columbia, but I couldn't be sure. We drove to where I-26 hits I-95 and headed toward Savannah."

I sat and listened to Lily's story. The Atlantic Ocean had become stormy and angry. 'Red sky in morning...' It matched my mood. I sensed she was coming to the last chapter. Overhead, the clouds fleeted, occasionally covering us in shadow. We had moved closer together, our hips and shoulders touching. Without knowing it I had moved my right arm around her. Between us was a constant warmth, untouched by the vagaries of the sun and wind. The waves crept away from us, increasing the distance from where we sat. I guessed the tide was rolling out.

The world moves on and all the foolishness of man can't stop it.

"I knew we were going somewhere to sell drugs 'cause Ricky told me to dress in what he called 'the outfit.' The outfit was a tight-fitting tee shirt with no bra and a pair of pink hot pants. With all the weight I'd lost, I didn't have much of an ass, but the boobs were still perky.

"Ricky and Barn would get drunk from time to time but they didn't use any drugs. They knew a lot of the people we sold to didn't give a hoot about a pretty girl, but what Ricky wanted was for me to get all the attention.

"I was feeling the dull aches and pains that come before withdrawal. I knew I had about an hour before the bad symptoms arrived.

"We crossed the bridge into Georgia. I thought we might be heading for Savannah, but we passed both exits. We passed Richmond Hill, too. Maybe we were headed for McIntosh County, but Ricky told me to get off at Midway. We turned right, drove to Highway 17. Then we turned into the parking lot of a strip mall that had a liquor store. As usual, I parked in the handicap parking space, right by the front door. It was a hot day, so we kept the engine running and the windows up.

"In a few minutes a guy wanders up and I lower the window. We didn't say a word. He just held out a wad of money, which I passed back to Ricky. He counted it and gave me a bag which I handed to the guy.

"The guy walked off. A few minutes later, another guy came up and we did the same thing. It was unusual that we did more than a couple at any stop, but Ricky sat quiet in the back, not telling us we were going anywhere.

"Then an old, white pickup pulled up. Faded paint, dulled. Dents, rust spots, duct tape on a window, maybe a headlight missing... you get the picture.

"A woman got out of the truck and walked toward the car. Shuffled might be a better word. She was hunched over, dressed kind of rough, like a poor farmer... dirty jeans that were too big for her, tee shirt and a grimy baseball cap. She was clutching herself like she had abdominal pain... like I was beginning to feel myself.

"She wore dark glasses and her lips were pulled back, wrinkled skin... I thought she was someone's grandma, gray hair streaked blonde, where you could see her hair.

"She held out a wad of bills and said, 'Tell R...' and stopped herself before she said his name. 'Tell him, I'm a couple hundred short. My kid was sick and I don't have health insurance.'

"Ricky growled from the back seat, 'Why she's got a kid? Maybe if she didn't have a kid, costing her so much damn money... Is that what she wants?'

"I didn't need to repeat it. She heard him. 'I'll get it for next week. I'll be sure I have it with next week...'

"Ricky barked, 'Add a couple hundred. Tell her that's the interest on a week.'

"She didn't say anything to that. Just looked about as sad as an old woman could look. Despairing, that's how she looked even through her sunglasses. I handed her the bag of stuff she needed, but she didn't turn away. 'Wait. I know you,' she said, looking at me. She took off her glasses, maybe to get a better look. Something about her eyes. I didn't look at her...looked straight ahead through the car's windshield.

"I said, 'No you don't. You don't know me.' But I did. It was Nancy Lou Brannon. She went to the Academy with me. She and I were cheerleaders together, on the Homecoming Court. She used to be a pretty little thing, all blond and blue-eyed. I took my sunglasses off and turned to look at her. The skin of her face looked old, wrinkled and tight against her cheekbones. Her eyes weren't sparkling blue anymore, but gummy and sad and glistening with tears. She looked at me as if to say, why are you doing this? And the accusation broke my heart. We were a pair of human tragedies, the real walking dead with our lives wrecked and a monster pulling our strings. In those seconds I took a long look at what I was and what my life was worth.

"And I was helping the monster.

"I saw that she saw the same thing in me that I saw in her.

"She said, 'No, I don't know you. Not anymore. The girl I used to know is gone.'

"She turned and went back to her truck. We sat there for a few minutes. My tears dried up. I could no longer cry for myself or for Nancy Lou. I was the walking dead, and at that moment, I wished I was dead.

"But Ricky Lee spoke from the back seat. 'Lily, I want you to get out of the car.' I took a deep breath. I had to do what he said. I got out of the car. Through the window, Ricky said, 'Go up to the door of the liquor store. I want you to check something out.'

"I got out of the car, into the bright summer sunshine. I stood before the door to the liquor store. I heard Ricky ask, 'Lily, what's that over the door?' I looked. 'Looks like a security camera,' I said. 'Is it working?' he asked? 'How the hell do I know?' I shot back at him.

"At that moment the door opened, and this big guy came out of the store. He was mad and said something like, 'What the hell you people doing outside my store? You get the hell out of here before I call the cops.' Ricky came out of the car like a charging bull. He slammed the guy upside the head with a big pistol he always has with him. The guy fell like a poleaxed beef and lays on the ground not moving. Ricky kicked him a couple of times.

"Ricky opened the liquor store door and walks in. 'Come on, Lily,' he says. We go inside. A woman screams, maybe the guy's wife. Ricky points the gun at her and says, 'Okay, bitch. Shut up and you won't get hurt. Open up that cash drawer.' He waves the gun at her and she opens up the cash register. Ricky hands me the gun. 'If she moves, shoot her in the head.' I can't point a gun at someone, so I just hold it somewhere else where nobody's in the way. Ricky takes all the money and stuffs it in one of the store's bags. He hands me the bag and takes the gun. He walks over to the woman and sticks the gun against her head. 'Get down on the floor.' He has to say it again. She flops on the floor sobbing, crying. I'm crying, 'Don't... don't.' Ricky smiles at me and says, 'Lily, go grab a bottle of Wild Turkey... the hundred proof, you know the good stuff.' There's a stack of boxes with a display with a bunch of bottles. I grab one. We walk out the door.

"He says, 'Get in the back. I'm driving.' I get in the back holding the bottle of Wild Turkey and the bag of money. There's a fix kit on the seat. Ricky must have left it for me. I drop everything on the floor and go for the fix. I'm hurting really bad by now.

"Ricky drove out of the parking lot, but I have no idea where he's going. I'm hitting up and the whole drug rush comes at me like a freight train. It's too much. Ricky must have gotten the dosage wrong, I'm heading into oblivion and I'm scared and elated at the same time. It's like going to heaven where everything is going to be right. I'm finally free… I know how people feel when they feel it, believe in it… free at last, the nightmare is over."

Lily had her arms around me and her head on my shoulder. She wept, deep, even sobs like the slow beat of a muted drum. I tried to hold her. I want to comfort her, but what comfort could I offer against what she endured. If I had heard this story before I ran into him in the Piggly Wiggly, I felt I could have emptied my gun into the filthy son of a bitch. And the world would have given me a medal for it.

Lily straightened up and wiped her eyes on her sleeve. She shook her head as if to clear it, and I thought, it's not over. The nightmare continues.

"I woke up in the hospital. Momma's standing over me, her eyes red from crying. 'Oh, my baby! She's awake. Look everybody.' Something like that. I felt worse than if I had come back from the dead. My chest hurt. Everything hurt. Even the voice of my precious momma hurt my ears.

"I saw the room was full of people. Momma and her new husband, Max. A couple of policemen. A nurse came in the room.

"I wrists were manacled. So were my legs. I was restrained. My chest pain came from a too-tight strap around my ribs.

"It took a while, but I gradually found out what had happened since I passed out in the back of Ricky's car.

"The doctor came in and told me I had almost died from the overdose. I was in the Liberty County Regional Medical Center. They took me there because Savannah was too far. I had been minutes away from dying.

"And he told me I was six weeks pregnant. Mamma gripped my hand when the doctor said it.

"Then the Liberty County assistant prosecutor came in and told me I was under arrest. Armed Robbery. Aggravated assault. Possession. Distribution. They had me on camera selling drugs out of the car, holding a gun on the poor woman in the liquor store. The guy Ricky pistol-whipped had a concussion and broken ribs and I was standing right in front of the security camera when he did it."

I said, "Sounds like the bastard set the whole thing up. Wasn't enough to ruin your life. He stole your life away from you and set you up. And a baby?"

Lily placed a warm hand on my arm. "Brendan, she's beautiful. Little Maggie isn't little any more but she's tall and straight and as beautiful as a girl could be."

She lowered her head and sobbed some more. I didn't know how to comfort her. I never felt so helpless. I tightened my arm around her and couldn't think of a single thing to say or do that could help.

"Because I was pregnant, they couldn't detox me until I had delivered. Too much strain on the baby. I was actually under medical care for seven months while little Maggie grew in my belly.

"Then she was taken away from me and I went to prison.

"It was part of my plea deal. Maybe Momma marrying the biggest TV lawyer in the South wasn't so bad, but I lost my baby even before she was born. I couldn't be her momma.

"My plea deal worked out with the Liberty County prosecutor and five or six other counties and states where we went during my crime spree. Max and his criminal defense attorney cited a ton of mitigating factors, all of which pointed out that I wasn't a willing participant.

"I had to give up my baby and there's a restraining order against me going just about anywhere outside of McIntosh County. I have to get permission to make a monthly visit to my parole officer in Richmond Hill and my therapist in Savannah. If I don't get back to McIntosh in four hours, I go back to prison.

"My baby... Momma and Max adopted her. I have a restraining order preventing me from going to Hilton Head and Max won't let Momma bring her to me. I've written letters, made phone calls, but he thinks I'm bad for her and sometimes I think so too. But my baby's eleven years old. She's going to be a teenager soon. When will the day come when I get to be a momma? When can I get free of this, so I can meet my baby? What do I have to do to get Max to let me see my child?"

Lily shrugged herself out of my embrace. It was a cold gesture, not so much against me but against the world, a world that had dropped this cluster-bomb of tragedy on her. Everything I knew about Lily now had to be viewed in light of her circumstances, where the world of natural beauty surrounding us was nothing against the misery in her heart.

And I could do nothing. I was totally ignorant of adoption laws or custody. I knew nothing about what rights Lily might have and apparently, the biggest TV lawyer in the South must be a powerful force in any legal contest.

This bastard, Ricky Lee had fixed her good. Taken away the life she made after getting away from him. And when she got pregnant, he got rid of her and the baby and devised a perfect way to ruin her life. And make it permanent.

Lily wiped her eyes and looked at me with incredible intensity.

"Look, Brendan. I know you. You're a first-class do-gooder, Mr. Superhero slash boy scout, and you think you can right wrongs and all that stand-up guy stuff... investigative reporter. I looked you up on the internet. I'm not telling you this so that you go running off trying to fix things. I don't want you to do that. You have to promise me you won't do that."

"Lily, I..."

She placed gentle fingers on my lips.

"No, baby. Don't say it. Don't do it. I'll tell you why. The bastard's still out there. Barnecki's in custody and that's good, but Ricky is a hundred times worse than that fat, stupid lout. And a whole lot smarter. My baby Maggie is safe now. I don't want Ricky Lee going after her. I don't want to give Ricky a reason to hurt me more than he already has. And I don't want you to get hurt. Don't tell me you can take care of yourself. You can't stop a bullet and you can't hide from a sneak attack. That's what Ricky Lee does. He waits until your guard's down and jumps you out of the dark. You'll get no warning, and he doesn't care who he hurts or how much."

I have to admit, at that moment my brain was boiling overtime with everything I could do to right her wrongs... everything from attorneys to hit men. I couldn't imagine this punk Ricky Lee would last long if I put Zinsser on his trail. The former Israeli security service operative, who now worked for Conklin, was deadlier than a bag of cobras and stealthier than a mosquito. If put him on the hunt, Zinsser could locate Ricky Lee and erase him before he could utter a WTF. But I knew it was a nuclear option, and it wasn't in me to push that button.

Instead, I reached for her hand and held it in both of mine.

"Lily, you are abused, I mean, really, awful abuse, terrible and tragic. I know you'll always be struggling to deal with it. I promise you I'm not going to do anything except be your friend…, if I you'll let me."

Lily stood up and pulled me up. She faced me with her arms around my lower back. Her eyes were red-rimmed with crying. "Brendan, my love… you are a really good person. I can't believe it… I just dumped on you all of my sorry-assed baggage and you still want to be my friend."

She laid her head on my shoulder and hugged me tight.

"I do, Lily," I said, "but if you think of anything I can do, just ask. Okay?"

Lily broke away, gathered up the blanket and the picnic bag. "Bren, we got to high-tail it out of here. I've been running my mouth and not paying attention to the tides."

She turned and ran up the sand dune. I grabbed my backpack and followed.

We both stopped at the top of the dune and viewed the dismal state of our boat, Green With Envy. The tide had gone out leaving it completely out of the water. Its cathedral hull canted lazily in the mud. The nearest water's edge was officially ten feet away.

"Uh-oh," I said.

Lily looked at me and smiled. Why was she smiling?

"Come on, Bren. We got to get our boat in the water."

She skittered down the sand chimney to the lagoon side of the dune. I skittered after her, wondering how we were going to save the boat.

Lily took charge. She stepped boldly into the mud and threw the picnic bag over the bow.

The anchor was caked with sand, so I rinsed in off in the cool salt water before placing it on the green carpeting which had given our boat its name.

"Okay, Brendan, push!"

We both put our shoulders into the flat bow of the boat and grunted, our feet sinking and scrambling into the sandy mud.

The boat moved maybe an inch.

"Puuussshhh!" She growled like sled dog.

We pushed. The boat moved a foot. Then another foot. Gaining momentum, we gave it maximum effort and, like it was on rollers, slid gracefully into the shining blue water.

"Brendan, grab the line!"

She pointed to the rope used to tie the boat to the dock. The boat glided into the lagoon. I grabbed the line and pulled the bow toward us.

Lily hopped on the bow. I followed pushing the boat back into the lagoon.

We both had muddy feet and ankles. Lily sat on the bow dangling her legs into the water. I did the same, kicking and swirling our feet and calves in the cool water.

"Don't want to get the Doc's boat dirty."

"No Ma'am," I said. My sort of clean, wet and cold feet hit the green carpet.

I didn't have to be told to lower the engine and squeeze the bulb.

Lily said, "Don't start it yet. I want to catch some bait."

Bait? We need bait?

Lily retrieved a big net from the compartment in the bow. The boat had swung in a half circle so that the bow pointed toward Sapelo Island.

She shook the net out and stepped up on the bow platform. Lily coiled her body, twisting her left shoulder and torso back. She flung the net with a frisbee-throwing motion. The net flew out, expanding to an imperfect circle about ten feet in diameter. Somewhere I had seen someone throw a cast-net before, another skill Lily was good at.

She waited, holding onto a thin rope, while we both watched the wide circle of ripples left behind where net entered the water. She waited about ten seconds and started hauling on the rope. Watching the rope snake toward the water, I could tell there was some weight in it. Her hand over hand hauling became labored, and when the tip of the net broke the surface, I heard her exclaim, "Oh, my god!"

I thought to go help her haul in whatever was in the net, but Lily easily handled the job. She slung the whole net over the gunnel into the boat and it sprawled wet and flopping on the bottom of the boat.

Wet, flopping, wiggling, squirming. The net was full of sea creatures, large and small, most of what I recognized was shrimp.

All I could say was, "Wow... and wow. Lily, you call this bait?"

She gave me a look like I was denser than tungsten. Instead of answering me, she bent down and began sorting through the aquatic menagerie. Reaching into the writhing mass, she extracted what looked like a bouquet of flipping shrimp. She lay them out on the green carpet. Their bodies were at least seven inches long, with even longer antennae. They wriggled, flipped and rearranged themselves. Daintily she picked the four giant shrimp up and put them into the cooler.

"For later, sweetheart."

Okay... I was thrilled there was going to be a 'later.'

She reached in the net and pulled out a handful of considerably smaller shrimp and put them in a bucket of seawater.

"That must be the bait, right?" I said.

"That's right, baby."

Then she lifted the net, opened it up from the bottom and allowed the entire remaining sea creatures to fall back into the lagoon, to resume their aquatic life, lucky not be chosen as bait or 'later.'

A few stragglers fell out on the bottom, squirmed and wriggled. We crouched down, chased them around and gently dropped them over the side.

"Okay, Brendan, start her up."

The motor barked into life like it was ready to go.

"Give us a fast-idle speed and follow the line back, Brendan." Lily pointed to the GPS. The screen map showed a black line, presumably the path we traced coming in.

It looked like she expected me to take the helm. I gently nudged the throttle to a nautical trot. The boat was easy to steer. I kept the little GPS boat icon on the black line as we glided back the way we had come on Blackbeard Creek.

As we approached the first bend in the creek, a feeling came over me and I turned around and looked back at the lagoon we were about to leave. It looked different, of course, because it held considerably less water, but still absolutely lovely.

"What is it, Brendan?" Lily asked placing a hand on my arm.

I faced forward, the direction we were traveling. I didn't know how to answer.

"I'm not sure. A feeling, I might never come back here. This place is unique... unlike anything I've ever seen before. It feels kind of sad I'll never come back here."

"Why wouldn't you come back here?"

But I knew gloomy reflections didn't come in ones... they came in chains of one after another. Except for my home in Atlanta and perhaps, Bettye's place in Paris, there weren't too many places I had ever returned to. My life had been a connect-the-dots-reality, making a weird single-dimensional diagram, a zig zag across the state, the country, the globe, which seemed like aimless wanderings. I'd seen many, meaningful and wonderful places... places Bettye and I loved and pledged to return to but never seemed to actually do so when there were so many places we hadn't yet seen. And I had let her call the shots, while I paid the price by never standing my ground long enough to grow roots.

So, what was I left with? This moment, this woman who had become a prisoner of her own device, as the song lyrics go... Lily was like me, and we are all a prisoner of some kind. Only some prisons are worse than others. I had never known one like hers.

So many lives ruined because of one complete insensate villain.

I reminded myself that most villians were completely uncaring about their victims' feelings and the disaster they caused, but Ricky Lee was worse than that. He seemed to enjoy destroying lives. He had done it to

Lily. He had done it to the UGA football player. He had done it to many anonymous drug adicts.

Yes, he was worse than the Barn... maybe worse than anyone.

At that moment, I knew I was going to break my promise to Lily. When this was over... and I had to define what 'this' was... the investigation of the Coast Guard boat... when it was over, I was going to hunt down Ricky Lee and settle some scores.

But Lily stood beside me waiting on an answer. She had asked me a simple question.

I said, "I don't know. Just a feeling."

We let it go at that. I kept the boat traveling on the GPS line.

The view had changed. With the receding tide, the water lever in Blackbird Creek had lowered several feet, exposing banks of mud topped with marsh grass. It was like cruising through a shallow valley... walls of mud topped by the marsh grass.

But still beautiful in a less dramatic way. We now hid from everything except the wide blue sky above.

We turned a sharp right in the creek and the marsh on our right narrowed to a high bluff, a feature of Blackbeard Island we had passed before. In the distance, around a wide curve in the creek was the ranger station dock.

Lily put a hand on my arm. "Brendan, let's slow down here.

I did that.

"Put it in neutral and cut the engine."

I did that.

"Some people call this place Little Racoon Bluff," she said. The big one is over there on Sapelo Island." She pointed across the marsh.

"Just some people?" I asked.

"Yes, some call it the bluff past the Ranger Station."

I gave the bluff a quick scan and saw just a high dirt bank topped with pines and oak trees.

"Lily, I don't see any racoons."

"Well, if you did, I'd grab that gun of yours and shoot the bastard."

"A cute little racoon?"

She turned to me. Her benevolent, 'I love all creatures' expression, had been replaced by one of animal cruelty. "Disgusting creatures. Raiding trash cans, bird feeders. Getting muddy footprints all over your boat. And worse yet... they like to take a dump on your dock. Like they don't have the whole wilderness to do their business. They have to do it on your dock."

While I thought about that, she stepped forward and took out one of the fishing poles that had been stored in a rack along the right side of the boat.

"Wow! Doc Rawlings must really like fishing," she said.

"He does?" I asked.

"He's provided us some first-class equipment!"

I could not tell the difference, so I said, "Nothing but the best for us, I guess."

"Right!" Lily reached into the bucket and grabbed one of the shrimps she had saved as 'bait.'

"Sorry little guy. This ain't your lucky day."

Then she looked at me. "Brendan, how are you with a spinning rod?"

Well, many years ago I had used one on the only fishing trip I had ever been on, so I guess I wasn't a total rookie.

"About like I am with a tennis racquet."

"You play tennis?" she asked.

"No, but I think I can explain how it works."

"Here, city-boy. Let's see what you got."

She handed me the rod.

The spinning rod was as tall as a basketball player, light and lively. I was no expert, but it felt great in my hand. I held the fishing line with my index finger and folded over the stainless-steel bail on the reel.

"Over there, Brendan. As close to the water's edge as you can." Lily pointed. It wasn't a long distance, not even fifty feet. I got the heft of the rod, the line and the weight of the rig and made a gentle cast. The float, hook and shrimp curved through the air and plopped down at the exact spot where Lily had pointed.

I looked at her expecting one of her brilliant smiles, but instead her face was all seriousness, her eyes predatory.

She didn't even glance at me, but said, "I know you like looking at me, city-boy, but you better watch your float."

I tore my eyes away from her and put them on the hot pink float.

Immediately, something pulled the float under.

I was so shocked, I forgot to set the hook, jerk the rod or whatever you do when a fish takes the bait.

Apparently, it was okay with Lily. "That's good, Brendan. Steady pressure... no need to pull hard."

"Somebody needs to tell that to the fish," I said gasping. My heart raced and I frantically cranked the reel, but still the monster fish pulled out line like I had hooked on to a submarine. The rod quivered and jerked like a live cobra. Every jerk, flap and pull the fish made in its frantic effort to escape vibrated through the fishing line and felt like a hand-buzzer. I made progress only by lowering the rot tip and reeling in a couple feet of line. Eventually I felt the flapping, squirming fish become less frantic.

I saw the orange float beneath the surface of the murky water. When the fish saw the boat, it made a last-ditch effort to escape, but I slowly reeled it in.

Out of the corner of my eye, I saw Lily had conjured a dip-net, presumably from the inventory in the boat's bow compartment. She stood watching the line and the float zip around in the water. A flash of silver as the fish turned side-up and dove for the umpteenth time. I cranked the reel with a steady hand.

Lily thrust the net and brought up a flapping fish. She lay the net and fish on the bottom of the boat.

Okay, it wasn't the salt-water monster I had thought, but Lily liked it.

"Wow! What a beautiful trout!" she said.

Lily expertly removed the hook from the fish's mouth and held it up to a ruler sticker on the side of the boat.

"A little over twenty inches. Great fish, Brendan."

She turned around and saw that I had my phone out and was holding it up for a picture.

She struck a pose, an ideal fishing magazine cover.

Lily opened up the cooler, dropped in my fish and closed the lid. The trout made a few more flips and settled down.

"For later?" I asked.

Lily bent over the left side of the boat and rinsed the fishiness off her hands. She stood up, wiping her hands on her shorts. She gave me an ironic smile.

"Brendan, McIntosh may be the poorest county in Georgia, but one thing we can be proud of... we can offer our visitors the finest seafood on the entire coast. I'd like to cook dinner for you tonight if you'll let me."

I'm sure I smiled like a kid at Christmas, like I had been handed the second of three wishes, I hadn't even wished for.

"Lily, of course I'll let you. Just let me know what I can do to help."

"Well, Mr. World Traveler, I'll let you pick out the wine." She secured the hook on the rod and placed it in the rack on the side of the boat. She dumped our 'bait' back into the water.

"We better get on back to the dock while the creek still has water."

I took my position behind the wheel. A flick of the key started the old Johnson.

Lily said, "Keep it at no-wake speed until we get past the ranger station. Then we can open it up some."

Green With Envy glided on Blackbird Creek toward the ranger station dock. As we approached, I noticed a furry animal resting on the fixed portion of the dock, looking down at us as we motored past... a racoon. Lily didn't reach into my backpack for the Redhawk, but she did make a pistol with her hand, aimed and snapped her thumb down. The racoon didn't even flinch.

Two white headed pelicans, perched on the adjacent "No-Wake, Please" sign, watched the drive-by shooting with typical avian stoicism. Their golden eyes followed us with nary a thought of taking flight.

I pushed the throttle forward. The little green boat came up on plane and we whizzed out on the waters of Blackbird Creek.

In seconds the first obstacle came upon us. Exposed by the low water, a mound of mud guarded a small creek on the right. I hugged the left bank of Blackbird Creek. According to the depth finder, we had just enough water to slide by.

A sharp turn to the right by a tangle of fallen tree trunks on the left... I whipped the wheel sharply and we banked like an airplane racing around a pylon. I kept the boat icon on the black line, but it took both hands. The speed of the boat, the narrow creek and looming mud banks came at us from one side and then the other.

I glanced at Lily, saw her smiling into the wind. It wasn't just me who was having fun.

After several minutes of this thrilling ride, the water widened. I realized we reached the end of the creek. The broad expanse of Sapelo Sound stretched out before us. We zoomed past the wildlife management sign. The black line of the GPS took us close the beach at the north end of Blackbeard Island, squeezing between the pile of ballast rocks Lily had told me about. The low tide exposed the rocks which looked like myriad of barnacle encrusted shapes covered by shallow water.

I pushed the throttle forward. Green With Envy zoomed ahead in the light chop, bouncing from wave to wave, keeping on Lily's GPS line, a shallow curve that headed first toward the southern tip of Saint Catherine's Island and gradually more westerly to the mouth of the Barbour River. As we approached the Barbour River, I saw to our left the vast shallow area Lily had pointed out. It extended nearly a half-mile, a big, dull mud bank exposed by the low tide. Thousands of wading birds of all colors and sizes browsed the mud for their supper.

The Barbour River was wider than Blackbeard Creek, but still, I felt comfortable throttling back a little.

As we approached the Monaco-worthy sailboat, Lily leaned in and shouted over the noise of the Johnson, "Stay to the left. We can go fast as long as we don't get too close to those docks."

I made a wide left turn and saw in the distance, Mister Unger's unusual house and to the right of it, the Barbour River Yacht Club.

A right and a left and another right and left, and the yacht club dock was straight in front of us. I kept to the left as the river had narrowed and was guarded on the right by a hundred feet of oyster reef, now exposed by the low tide.

Throttling back to idle, I made a pretty good landing at the yacht club, bringing Green With Envy gently against the floating dock. Lily jumped out and tied the bow and stern lines with expected aptitude. I shut off the motor and lifted it up.

Before we trudged all out gear up the steep ramp to load it in the Kawasaki Mule, I stood on the dock and looked out at the Barbour River. The miles of marsh grass waved its stony indifference at me. Like the feeling I had when we left the lagoon behind Blackbird Island, I had a melancholy moment, a feeling that the river and the boat were paths to a fantasy I'd never return to again. Like catching the fish, it was a one and done experience. It had never been on my lifetime agenda, and only the most extraordinary, serendipitous encounter with this amazing woman, who had taken a liking to me had made it happen.

I didn't know what else to feel, but the astonishing awareness of the moment surprised me, as I had been completely unaware of my linear journey through life. I had always been more of a foreword thinker, always dreaming of tomorrow instead of enjoying the moment. Now I had had an entire day of staying in the moment and knowing most of it was behind me, this moment wasn't particularly enjoyable.

I turned and saw Lily halfway up the aluminum ramp, arms loaded with fishing poles and the big cloth picnic bag. She turned and smiled at me, the golden light of the descending sun behind her gave her hair a glow, casting her face in a slight shadow. She was beautiful in any light and the smile of pure happiness she shone upon me warmed my body like a heat lamp.

The descending sun... my perfect day would not last forever. Like everything in my past, the roads I had traveled and the people I shared them with... the sun had set on them and the glaring light of new day would bring harsh realities and new hurdles to leap.

I had to stay in the moment and... I realized that a new moment was about to be revealed. The mysterious genie had granted two wishes and these things came in threes, didn't they?

I took a deep breath. It was time to pick up the cooler and see what 'later' had in store for me.

We left the boat tied up at the dock, and I drove the Mule back to Rawlings' cottage, remembering to stop at the gate and turn off the Land Cruiser's alarm.

We silently went about our chores like we knew what we were doing. Lily washed the fishing rods with the hose, and I went inside to pick out the wine.

Doc Rawlings had quite a selection of wine in the garage beneath his cottage. Rows and shelves of bottles arranged in appropriate categories... the years I spent with Bettye provided me more than a casual acquaintance with a sommelier's responsibilities.

Deciding to splurge, I selected a bottle of Perrier-Jouet Gran Brut and an unknown Sauvignon Blanc from New Zealand. I took both bottles upstairs and put them in the freezer.

Downstairs, I took a shower and donned jeans and a long-sleeved knit Henley, clean socks and my Cole Haan loafers. Lily had me pegged as a fancy boy and I was dressing for a date... at least as well as I could under the circumstances.

My prep for the date then compelled me to ice down the champagne. Rawlings had a lovely hand-painted crystal ice bucket which seemed too elegant for the place, but when at the cottage, use what you have at the cottage.

I took the bucket out to the deck and set it on the wicker table. I found some cushions in the closet for the wicker love seat, hopefully appropriately named.

I sat down and waited for Lily.

I heard the water pipes buzzing indicating she also was cleaning up.

While marveling at the thick tree canopy, I saw movement. I turned and witnessed a police cruiser go by the gate. It continued toward the yacht club.

Still on patrol, I guess.

I sat waiting for Lily. The temperature dropped slightly as the sun set behind me. It was still warm enough, but I was glad I wore a long-sleeved shirt.

I sensed her approach. Lily appeared at the sliding glass door, paused a moment and slid it open.

In the last of day's sun, she glowed with elegance as she emerged through the French door, dressed in the same outfit as this morning, having added a light sweater. She looked fresh and crisp, lustrous hair fanning out framing her perfect face. I felt very lucky. She stopped and took in the deck, surrounding forest, the fading light and slowly shifting shadows. Her eyes stopped on the ice bucket, champagne, and flutes.

"Ooh La La!"

She crossed the deck with dancing steps, leaned in, kissed my cheek and took a seat beside me. Actually a significant portion of her right thigh landed on my leg, but she managed to twist onto the cushion with some saving grace.

She laughed, merrily, "Sorry, love. Didn't mean to sit on you."

"Lily, you just missed me." I didn't care if she landed squarely in my lap.

I pulled out the bottle of Perrier-Jouet and began tearing off the foil.

"Oh my god, Brendan! Do you know how much that costs?"

"Un, well, actually, I do. Don't worry, Lily. We deserve it... we're celebrating."

"Okay, congratulations then, Brendan. It may be the most expensive thing I've ever had."

I felt some irony. Did she know it was the best day of my life?

Over the years, I had developed a special way to open champagne. Bettye didn't entirely approve, but it was fun, and she often accepted some of my rustic ways, me being American and all.

After removing the foil and wire muselet, I used my thumbnail gently to nudge the cork out of the neck. Once it started moving, the compressed gas in the bottle gradually forced it out.

The cork moved.

Pop! The cork flew with force straight up, ricocheted off an overhead tree limb, banged against the siding of Rawlings' cottage and came to rest somewhere on the deck.

"Ooh, I love that sound," Lily exclaimed.

"So, do I."

I slowly filled two flutes and handed Lily one. She held it up to the last light of the day, pink and orange hued shafts that filtered through the trees. Her flute glowed and sparkled like a living jewel.

"How pretty," she said.

I watched her, hoping she wouldn't grow self-conscious with my attention. She did not appear to. My eyes feasted on her face like they couldn't get enough. The unreality of it gave me glow that pushed away the shadows.

We both took a sip. It tasted like a miracle.

Lily liked it too. "Oh, wow!" she said in a low voice. "I'll let you pick the wine all the time."

She took another sip. A more serious expression crossed her face. Her eyebrows leveled. Her mouth came down from a smile. She turned and looked at me as if she had something unpleasant to say, something that concerned her.

"Brendan, I have to ask you a question."

"What? Lily, you can ask me anything."

"Okay, Brendan, how is it that you're single? You told me this morning that there's no girlfriend, no wife. You're a fine man, honorable, a gentleman. You're good looking and funny. And, I hope you don't take offence at this, but you don't seem be able to resist a woman's charms. There's millions of gals out there who would think you're perfect. Tell me why there's no ring on your finger."

I pretended to give the question some thought. The truth was I was a little embarrassed and nervous about answering.

"Lily, I'm not even trying to resist your charms, and no one has called me good looking since I was in kindergarten."

"Brendan, you're probably not the best judge of that. Gals have different standards. You're a catch. If you stay here a few more days, there's going to be a line out in front of the house."

I chuckled at that.

"I knew as soon as you walked into Zoller's yesterday. Nice guy from the big city. I guessed Atlanta. Money."

"Money?"

"Yes, money. More than most guys around here. You and I both know it. The Doc has money and you're the Doc's friend."

I refilled our glasses.

"So, Brendan, you're a mystery to me and I want to know more about you."

I took a deep breath and thought about how much to tell. Just the highlights, I guess.

"I did have someone. She was the love of my life," I said it, and it hurt.

Lily said nothing. She sat next to me, touching me with her shoulder and hip, sipping champagne holding the stem in her left hand like a delicate flower.

"I met Bettye many years ago and we fell in love."

"Bettye?" Lily asked, mispronouncing her name.

"Like Betty with an 'e' at the end. Bettye LeBoutillier," I said, giving my best French pronunciation. "Accent the third syllable."

"Beautiful name."

"Bettye's a beautiful woman. Parisian… even more French than French. She was as rooted to Paris as I was to Atlanta, but for years we carried on the perfect long-distance relationship. I'd spend a month there and she'd come over here. When we were separated, she'd call me nearly every day and I'd call her. When together we traveled a lot… it was like a honeymoon. We were so close, so compatible, despite the differences. It was impossible for us to see what was coming."

"What happened?" Lily asked.

"I guess we got to the stage where we needed some kind of commitment. We never talked about it, but when everything is going so well, you sort of need to step in in fix it. I know she wanted me to move to Paris, but I could never carry on my career there. I could barely speak even a few words of French and my pronunciation was horrible. In Atlanta I did a lot of folksy, human interest stories. French TV does little of that, but you would need to be an expert in French culture to make it work.

"I mildly suggested she could move to Atlanta. She was head of languages at a prestigious private school. She could easily get a high paying job in Atlanta, but she wouldn't hear of it. She said, 'You can't even get decent bread here', but it wasn't the bread.

"Our times apart became longer and the same with the daily phone calls. A month went by and she didn't call, so I called her. She said she couldn't talk, and she'd call later. Sometimes she would. I did not know what she was thinking, but I was afraid what she'd say, like maybe she wanted to call it off.

"Worrying about it was almost as bad, but I was too scared to call her and maybe Bettye felt the same. The weeks turned into months and before you know it, two years went by without a call, email, letter. Nothing."

"Oh, my god, Brendan. How could you deal with that?"

"I just sucked it up and focused on my career."

"Brendan, that's just like you... shove all that pain to one side and get on with life."

"Well, what else can you do?"

"That's not the end of the story, is it?"

"No, it's not. My career was heating up. I was getting major stories, award-winning stuff. Then I get a message from Bettye. She said, 'Brendan, I need to see you. It's important."

"She was in Atlanta and wanted to meet at a place that used to be our favorite café. I had to go, but for some reason, I didn't get the message in time to call her back. I barely had the time to jump in the car and go, but I didn't want to miss seeing her.

"When I got to the restaurant, I didn't see her. There were a few customers..." I paused and swallowed, "and a really old lady sitting alone."

"Oh, my god..." Lily gasped.

"It was Bettye. She looked eighty years old, shrunken and wrinkled. Her beautiful auburn hair was gone... short grizzled gray. She was all skin and bones. Her lovely face, ancient and worn. So weak she couldn't hold her head up.

"She looked up, saw me and started crying. I ran to her, put my arms around her. We hugged for a long time."

"Brendan..." Lily's voice cracked. "What...?"

"She had been fighting breast cancer for those two years. I didn't have a clue what she went through. It had spread... metastasized. She had been through every kind of treatment medical science could give her. The cancer had won, and she told me that she had been given less than a couple of months to live. She barely had the strength to make this trip.

"The reason she made the trip to Atlanta was to see me. She told me that I had always been the love of her life, that she never stopped loving me but when she found out she had cancer and that it had spread before even being diagnosed, she didn't feel that she could drag me through her battle and she had decided to go it alone.

"Now that she had accepted her death sentence, she had one last thing to do. She was going to a clinic in Switzerland where they had an experimental treatment. They couldn't cure her, but they could make her feel better.

I turned to look at Lily. My eyes were filled with tears. Hers were too.

"She wanted to spend her last few days with me. She wanted me to fly to Switzerland to be with her."

"Oh, god, Brendan... You went didn't you."

"Of course, I went. What else could I do? That afternoon, I was on the plane sitting next to this scrawny old woman, a cancer-wracked version of the one I used to love. I didn't even think about it. Packed my bag, locked my house and didn't even call work to tell them I wouldn't be coming in tomorrow.

"This clinic was supposed to make her comfortable and feel a little better while her life wound down, but that's not what happened. Like a miracle, what they did, killed all her tumors, killed the cancer and Bettye lived!"

"Brendan, how wonderful!"

"It was wonderful... a miracle. Bettye survived cancer and got healthy again. But cancer had taken its toll on her body. Her breasts were gone, and she never did reconstruction. She never regained her voluptuous body and her beautiful auburn hair came back in grizzled and gray. But the most beautiful thing about her had always been her eyes. Bright and gray-green and full of emotion. Her eyes were in this old woman's body.

"But I loved her and to me it didn't matter.

"We were in love again and we went back to her place in Paris like newlyweds. We traveled to our favorite spots and some new ones.

"We took the train to Nice on the French Riviera. Bettye wanted to visit this prestigious cancer clinic there, and she met with women who were going through the same battle. She lifted up their spirits, encouraging them to fight for their lives, to live another day.

"It was amazing what Bettye did for their morale. It all went so well until one of the women said to her, *'Quel plaisir d'avoir votre fils avec vous!'* I don't speak French all that well, but I saw the look on Bettye's face. 'votre fils' means 'your son.' Bettye did not say a word until we got back to our hotel room. Then she lay on the bed and cried for an hour. And then she got up and raged around the room. I thought she was going to hurt herself she was so angry.

"But she got over it, or at least I thought she got over it."

Lily shook her head like she understood... understood that Bettye did not get over it.

"From that point, our travels focused on the visits to cancer clinics. Bettye carried her message of hope and courage, to fight for one more day, *'un jour de plus'* as they say, or an extra day. I helped her craft her message and her story to be more effective."

Lily said, "Of course you did, you're a pro."

"Bettye received invitations to come to hospitals and treatment centers. A big French TV network wanted to interview her. I supported her every step on this journey. Around Europe, she was known as the Joan of Arc in the battle against cancer. She even appeared on the cover of one of those French magazines, dressed as Joan of Arc in a suit of armor, '*La Jeanne d'Arc dans la lutte des femmes contre le cancer*' the headline read.

"Bettye was inspired to start a foundation, called it, Un Jour de Plus, after her main theme. She hired a manager and a secretary. She received a huge donation from an anonymous donor and many other donations, invitations."

I did not mention, nor did I tell Bettye, the donation had come from Conklin and me.

"Her foundation continued to grow."

Lily asked, "Brendan, where were you in all this?"

"I guess I got out of the way of it all. Bettye and I as a couple were overwhelmed by how important her mission was. In the scheme of things, we, as a couple, didn't matter.

"And something else. Bettye had nearly died from cancer. She could relate to women fighting this battle. I hadn't faced it. I couldn't know what it was like. It was easy for her to dismiss my perspective as irrelevant. I had to hang back and let her go to the front. I guess I got a little depressed. I was losing her, and I didn't matter. Bettye was the celebrity. Nobody called me her son anymore. I was hardly noticed at all.

"The day came. We were in Bruges at a fancy hotel. Just about every hotel guest was there to hear her speak. Before she left the room, she came to me. 'Would you please stay in the room? I don't want anything to interfere with our program.'

"I said something sarcastic, 'Well, Bettye, this is a pet-friendly hotel, I'm sure there's a kennel I can crawl in.'

"She stared at me and said, 'Sometimes I wonder why you are here at all.' And she left the room.

"I sat on the bed for ten minutes. Finally, I packed my bag and took the train to Paris. I waited at Orly for the next plane to Atlanta. My phone didn't ring. Still hasn't."

"Did you leave her a note or something?"

"My note said, 'I've gone home.'"

"My, god, Brendan. How long ago was that?"

I thought for a moment. "More than a year."

I took a deep breath and let it out. It had been painful to talk about it.

"So, Lily, you see. There's no woman. No girlfriend. I'm as free as a..."

Lily raised her glass in the darkness. We both had a sip of champagne remaining.

"A couple of free birds. Here is to us."

We drained our glasses.

"Except, Lily... you're not free."

She gave me a wide-eyed, dry-eyed look.

"And, Brendan, you're still bleeding."

The treefrog symphony began tuning up. For a long time, we sat in the darkness.

Lily patted my knee, a kind of maternal gesture. "I think those treefrogs are telling us to go inside and cook dinner."

"Let's go."

We rose. Lily took the glasses and I the ice bucket. Inside, I set the empty champagne bottle on the counter and pulled the bottle of Sauvignon Blanc out of the freezer.

Lily said, "Brendan, can I have some of that? For cooking."

"Sure, but is it for cooking or the cook?"

It was a twist off cap. I poured some in a wine glass and handed it to her. She gave me a smile and said, "Strictly for cooking. If you're trying to get me drunk, I like your chances."

Her humor was a little forced and the natural flow of talking to each other had become stilted. I had an uneasy feeling that something had put her off.

She went into the kitchen and got to work. I watched her as she moved about the small space with efficiency and speed. She quickly had a small pan of rice boiling and a large skillet heating up. She placed a small amount of oil in the pan. From the refrigerator, she retrieved two nice trout fillets and four giant shrimp, pealed and deveined. She lightly floured the fillets and placed them in the frying pan.

Although fascinated watching this pretty woman cooking with such efficacy, I tore myself away to set the table. By the time I had finished, Lily had the shrimp sautéing next to the fillets.

When these were done, she placed the trout and shrimp on a platter and put them in the oven to keep warm.

A few ounces of wine and juice from a lemon went into the frying pan to deglaze and reduce. After a minute, she dumped the rice into the pan and stirred. Lily's hands flew so fast I wasn't sure what she did next.

She looked at me watching her and grinned, almost embarrassed to be seen cooking.

That smile put me at ease. Whatever had been bothering her, I guess she was over it.

Out came the platter. She arranged the fillets, shrimp and rice in an attractive array and sprinkled on some parsley flakes.

"Check this out, Brendan." She showed me the platter.

"Wow! That looks magnificent!"

It was. And I was famished. The trout was tender, crisp and delicately seasoned. The shrimp, meaty and fresh. I had to cut them with a knife, and they had been cooked to perfection.

"Wow, Lily! What did you season the trout with? It's delicious."

"Really... thanks. Oh, Doc Rawlings had some House Autry in his cabinet. It's always been one of my favorites. It's an old Southern breading. I just barely dust the fish and cook in light oil You don't need to cook Seatrout in heavy oil. But I'm super-happy you like it. This is my version of 'dirty rice' the way Momma used to cook it. Just whatever you have in the pan."

My plate was clean. Lily had barely eaten half a shrimp and a few bites of the trout, but she folded her napkin and rested her hands under the table.

Her body-language baffled me for a moment.

"Lily…"

She lifted her face slightly, her mouth set in a tiny smile more enigmatic than the Mona Lisa.

"Yes, Brendan."

The easy badinage of the day had vanished. Her reply invited nothing. The ball was in my court.

"I'll do these later," referring to the dinner dishes. "Let's go over there."

I led the way to the loveseat, and we sat, our knees nearly touching.

For a while neither of us said anything. Lily took a breath like she was going to speak. Instead, she dropped her eyes and spied the guitar case sitting on the floor next to the wall.

"Brendan, is this your guitar?"

"Me? No, I guess it's Rawlings'."

"Do you think he'd mind if I looked at it?"

I considered this. I knew a few musicians. Some of them were fanatic about their instruments and William Rawlings was the kind of person who could be one of them.

"I guess it's okay if you're careful."

Lily reached down and unsnapped the buckles. She lifted the lid. Although I'm no expert, it seemed to me the case contained a very high-quality guitar. Lily carefully lifted it out. Like it was a living thing, the guitar let out an ambient hum, a slight protest at being disturbed.

"Wow, it's as light as a feather," Lily said. "The Doc must be really picky about *this* guitar."

Beautiful, light-brown woods, polished to a high gleam, the guitar's headstock had the word, 'Taylor' inlaid in iridescent abalone.

Lily's fingers tickled the neck and stings. The guitar made exquisite sounds. She fiddled with the tuning keys, made more notes. It seemed her fingers had more than a casual familiarity with the instrument. She played some chords, The music summoned goosebumps on my arms.

Lily picked and strummed and the sound was wholly satisfying. She began to hum along with the guitar.

More goosebumps.

She sang, slowly, softly.

> *"Now, I've heard there was a secret chord*
> *That David played, and it pleased the Lord*
> *But you don't really care for music, do you?*
> *It goes like this, the fourth, the fifth*
> *The minor fall, the major lift*
> *The baffled king composing hallelujah*
> *Hallelujah*
> *Hallelujah*
> *Hallelujah*
> *Hallelujah..."*

I knew the song. Everyone who ever watched the talent shows on TV knew Leonard Cohen's Hallelujah. Lily's voice was a whispery contralto, not good enough to be a singer, but her voice rang true and the very existence of it made it delicate and other-worldly. She kept her eyes lowered on her hands and fingers as if she was self-conscious about singing for me... singing to me... the last 'hallelujah' her voice raised in timber in a way that wrenched my heart, so much tragedy and suffering, like a victim in a Kafka story, the inevitable, innocent wounded sufferer...

Lily's eyes came up to meet mine, a strong expression on her face, no longer a victim but a victor... in command, challenging...

> *"Your faith was strong but you needed proof*
> *You saw her bathing on the roof*
> *Her beauty and the moonlight overthrew you*
> *She tied you to a kitchen chair*
> *She broke your throne, and she cut your hair*
> *And from your lips she drew the hallelujah*
> *Hallelujah*

Hallelujah
Hallelujah
Hallelujah...."

The last word rang out, and she held it to the limit of her lungs and she never took her eyes off mine. She broke eye contact, turned and lowered the guitar to its case. The instrument made a muted strum that hung in the air while the rest of the world went silent.

Lily's eyes came back to mine, blazing, tear filled. Steel chains held me motionless as if paralyzed, as if the spinal tap tapped my will, my thoughts. Her lips parted like she might sing another 'hallelujah', and if I was a mind-reader I could identify what was in her head.

Seconds passed and an impossible tractor-beam pulled me toward her, and this was it... the genie's final wish, a wish I could not have dreamed of, but had I had this dream, I wouldn't have believed I deserved anything so fine as this, so wonderful, so miraculous... so essential...

As her lips.

Her eyes closed in surrender just before our mouths touched and it was the slowest of collisions, the compression of bits of our flesh, gentle, soft and full and warm and scented. The touch of another, our flesh with so many millions of nerve ends you could feel the nerve ends of the other and feel their thoughts only you can't read the calculus of another's thoughts so it only registers as chaos.

And our lips became the total of us, warmth, taste, reaching with hands and arms compressing two into one.

And our lips, her lips.

And we pull apart. Just an inch but that small space creates in us a tremendous hunger. For that again, the same. More.

We came together again. Not quite so gentle. Open mouthed. Her tongue on mine. Darting, searching, the touch, hot and liquid, we made a seal so nothing could escape, our nostrils exchanging frantic breath.

Oh, forever.

My head spung like a carnival ride. Dizzying, intoxicating.

Stop.

It took me seconds to realize...

Lily pushed me... gently, like a ballet dancer whose foot you just stepped on.

Something hurt her. She pulled her face away from mine. Her eyes clouded over. Tears rolled down her cheek, but I was too close and the tornado in my head took longer to die.

"Huh?" In such moments, I'm the master of articulation.

"Oh, oh. Uh," was all she could say. Her cheeks were flushed, and I could almost feel the blood pulsing in her arteries.

She pushed further away from me.

"Oh, god. Oh god," she whispered.

"What, Lily. What?"

"Oh, Brendan, I can't. I can't"

Her face became a terrible mask... sudden sadness beyond words.

I reached around her, but her body stiffened. Her arm straightened and she put a hand on my breastbone.

"Stop. Please, stop," she said sobbing. Her head dropped and I could feel her hot tears falling on my pants.

"Okay, okay."

Breathing in and out she raised both fists as if she were going to hit me.

"Stop. Oh, please stop."

I moved backward on the couch, as far as I could away from her, but it was a small couch. I watched her heavy breathing subside. Each breath shorter, a slow return to normal.

What was normal about this?

"Oh, Brendan, give me a minute."

"Okay. Okay." I tried to sound uh, normal. Calm, but I was not calm.

Lily took another, very deep breath and held it. She let it out, slowly.

"Oh, Brendan, I need something."

"What, Lily? Anything!" and I meant it.

"Stop, Brendan. Stop. Being. So fucking nice. I can't take it anymore. You're too goddamn nice. Stop, please."

Okay, but now I don't know what to do. How can I stop being nice? I said nothing, a coldness forming somewhere below my heart.

Lily turned her head to the side and kept her eyes on the floor, away from me. I wasn't sure if she was mad at me or not. For kissing her? What guy in his right mind would not kiss her?

"Brendan, I need you to promise me. You have to stop. And I need a tremendous favor."

Nothing coming out of her mouth made any sense.

"What promise?" My voice had an edge to it.

Lily shook her head. Back and forth, like trying to dislodge something awful perched on her skull. She cast a sidelong glance at me. I caught a single, sorrowful eye looking at me for a fraction of a second.

"My therapist says, when you understand the source of your pain, it gives you control of it. Sometimes that doesn't work."

I said nothing.

"The most hurtful thing one person can do to another is to take away their power of self-determination." It sounded like therapist talk. "When you can't decide for yourself what is going to be done to you, and the other person just does it to you. Like rape. Like drugs.

"You don't know what I'm talking about. It's just an abstract to you. It's the words you hear in therapy. It's like a bunch of bullies get you in the shower and hold you down and punch and stick you and slap you with towels. You might try to fight back but they're too powerful and you can't do anything to stop it and they just dehumanize you. You're humiliated and you're angry and you want to do something to get back at them.

"Only, Brendan, what happened to me was a million times worse. Rape. Some guy sticks his penis into you against your will. Sometimes you don't even know about it. Sometimes he holds you down or threatens you with something worse if you don't let him and now you're complicit in the act. You decided you don't want to die or get your bones broken so you hold still and don't fight back. You get raped and the one thing you want to give to the man you love is taken away from you and ruined and it's not really yours to give anymore. After that happens to you, you wish you had let him kill you or break your bones. Or whatever.

"My body... it's not even mine anymore. And I can't get it back. Having a normal life is gone because you're now the worst kind of victim. Society doesn't protect you. Society protects the rapist... the brute. Your rights were taken away and your chance to have a man love you is gone.

"What can you do, Brendan?" Her words came out in wretched sobs, torturing me. I wanted to put my hands over my ears. I said nothing. I didn't know what to say. It was like Bettye's cancer. It had never happened to me. How could I know?

"And then it gets worse. The man who rapes you keeps you and turns you into a drug addict. And then he has so little regard for your humanity, that he lets other thugs rape you. Rape you when you're awake. Rape you when you're unconscious. You become a bang body for the worst men in the world... mindless thugs, brutal animals. Worse than animals. An animal wouldn't do it to you.

"You, your self-worth means nothing. It's gone like it was never there. And drugs are thrown at you and you take them and you become complicit in turning yourself into even a lower piece of human scum than the people who do this to you.

"Brendan," and she looks at me. Her eyes are red and dry and the pain in them is like acid. My heart is afraid to beat. My lungs won't take air.

"Brendan, how do you feel when this happens to you?"

I said nothing.

"You lose the ability to feel. I can't feel anything. I try to feel something and I'm scared to... to let myself feel anything.

"Eventually, even my value as a sex toy went to zero. I became no fun because I lost my ability to feel. Drugs took me away and having some sicko stick his dick in my hoo-haw meant nothing. It didn't even happen to me. I was lower than a corpse. You might as well go fuck a bowl of Jello.

"I heard them say, 'She ain't no fun. I'd rather do a crack whore.'

"Nobody wanted me anymore. I didn't want me, either. And Ricky never gave me enough Oxy or Fentanyl to kill myself. But I was able to kill a part of myself. That part. That part down there is dead. My therapist said I killed it. To survive...

"A decade of therapy hasn't brought it back. I thought I could, Brendan. I tried.

She looked at me, obviously holding herself under ridged control.

"When you walked through the door at Zollers, I thought this time it might be different. I saw a nice-looking guy...a gentleman. We talked and I felt something...sparks. I thought, maybe. I had hope, you might make a difference.

"It didn't. I gave it all I had, Brendan, but I'm just not there. I can't promise you I'll ever be there. I'm a wicked, awful person for leading you on. For pulling me into my prison. How can you forgive me?"

My answer was immediate, like I knew the right things to say.

"Of course, Lily, I don't need to forgive you. You've done nothing that needs forgiving."

She looked at me a long, uncomfortable second, the unfathomable stare of a predatory bird, a savagery in her head that I could not believe or understand.

Lily spoke a chilling whisper, "Yeah, baby, but I might."

A moment of furious ringing in my ears. It passed.

She inhaled sharply, "Brendan, promise me you'll give me a chance. I feel like we might have a chance. But I have to control this. You have to let me decide when it will be all right. Can you do that?"

"Yes, Lily. I promise you. Nothing until you say it's all right."

And my brain went around inside my brainpan, like a carrousel spun out of control. What did I just say? Innocent words full of ignorance and unworldly meaning. You know just the right things to say… but what did I just say?

A promise is a promise. Dad used to say that. A man keeps his word.

"And Brendan, I need a tremendous favor."

"What?" I was running out of things to say.

"You need to find a way for me to stay here tonight."

The genie granted my final and most profound desire. And inside my head I heard him chuckle.

"Of course, Lily. You can stay here." The chuckle turned into a short, hard laugh, like I had just sealed the deal.

"The McIntosh police are out patrolling, especially Cortland. I'll bet he's driven by here a dozen times today, getting madder each time he sees my truck still here. If I head home, he'll pull me over and arrest me. I've been drinking… half a bottle of champagne and some more wine with dinner.

"I'll go to jail," Lily said. She sat up straight and folded her hands in her lap, suddenly acting like a kid… with no resources, needing a grownup to make her safe.

"Of course, you can stay here," I said. "That big chair over there folds out to make a bed. I'll sleep out here and you can have the bedroom."

I said it and I meant it. But at that moment, I had no idea, no inkling of the complicated plan the genie had in store for us.

"Brendan, you are the best. So kind… wonderful. How could I be this lucky to have met you?"

My mind spun like the gears of a poorly made clock. The simple solution was to drive her home myself, but apparently neither one of us wanted that.

What were we thinking? I had just taken a vow of chastity, sort of. Of the Seven Deadly Sins, only one remained uncommitted.

We sat there in silence for what seemed like a long time, but probably wasn't more than a minute.

I stood. "I'll get the sheets."

And I went off to do that. Lily still sat on the loveseat when I returned.

She looked up at me. "You really don't mind, Brendan?"

I mustered as much bluster as a buster could muster.

"No problem, Lily. I'll be fine." I sounded unconvincing.

When I removed the chair's cushion, I saw we had a problem.

"Lily, we have a problem. There's no mattress. The frame is there but the mattress is missing. Rawlings says it's where he lets the grandkids sleep, but the mattress is gone."

The two of us attempted to solve the puzzle by staring at the empty frame.

Lily said, "The solution is obvious." She stood up and took my hand in both of hers. She nodded toward the bedroom. "It's a big enough bed. Mister and Missus Rawlings sleep in there, so there must be enough room for two."

Although I instantly accepted her idea as rational and pragmatic, I pretended I had a moment's hesitation.

"Are you sure, Lily?"

"Sure, I'm sure. You don't snore, do you?"

"Maybe a little," I said.

"Well, I'll make no promises about me."

She put her arms around me, and I did the same. We hugged and the tension of a few minutes ago seemed to have vanished.

Lily said with her mouth against my chest, "I have your word and a promise is a promise." She brought her gray eyes level with mine.

"Lily, that's what my dad used to say."

She smiled. "Your momma and daddy raised you right. You belong in the Gentleman's Hall of Fame... if they have such a thing."

"A woman's heart is like the ocean. Warm and caring... the origin of all life. Or angry and deadly, the scariest thing on earth. Okay, Lily, this is how it's going to work. You go and take advantage of

Mrs. Rawlings super fancy bathtub, while I take care of the dinner dishes."

"I'll help you with those."

"Naw, you're the best chef within a hundred miles and certainly the prettiest. Let the help do the dishes."

"Okay, then. That tub is calling me. I'll leave a hundred-dollar bill in the soap dish."

And she headed for the bathroom.

In the kitchen, I put the leftovers in the fridge along with the remainder of the wine and tackled the dishes. I heard water running and Lily humming a tune that seemed familiar. Memory gave me the singer's name... Darius Rucker and then the title, 'Wagon Wheel.' Idly I thought someone else had recorded the song before, but that's about as far as Name that Tune got with me.

Lily sang, "And I gotta get a move on before the sun, I hear my baby calling my name and I know that she's the only one, and if I die in Raleigh at least I will die free..."

I finished up and wiped the counter and table. The water in the bathroom stopped and I heard a diminutive splash and a long sigh.

Ah, I thought, that must feel good. Moisture laden air scented with L'Occitane... Lily left the door open a few inches and the bathroom air wafted throughout the rest of the cottage. The scent came to me...

Temptation... but a promise is a promise, and I averted my eyes as I passed the door.

But I did not avert my imagination.

I gave serious thought to changing my normal sleeping attire, boxers and tee shirt, an outfit that offered little in the way of a barrier. Sleeping in the same bed with Lily might prompt some serious complications.

I began humming the Beatles, 'Norwegian Wood,' a song which popped into my head totally unbidden. The magic genie was piling on.

Due to lack of reasonable alternatives, I ended up donning my boxers and a tee shirt, but it was a clean tee shirt.

Then I stood between the bed and the ajar bathroom door feeling uncertain about what to do next. I waited for some inspiration. Get into bed... take the left side furthest from the bathroom.

Lily's voice came through the slightly open door, reverberating slightly as voices from the bathroom do.

"Brendan, honey. Are you out there?"

"Uh, yes, Lily. I'm out here."

A swirl of water.

"Brendan..." a long pause... "Why don't you come in here and see with your own eyes what you've been fantasizing about all day."

A human's ability to comprehend speech is largely based on experience and expectation. Because it was unexpected, I didn't immediately understand what Lily had said, and it took a long time to for that comprehension to arrive.

"Brendan, did you hear me?"

"Yes, Lily." I paused a second. "I think it's a bad idea."

A playful giggle and another splash. "I can assure you, honey... it's the best idea I've had all day."

My heart stopped. I stepped forward... just to get it going again. I opened the door just wide enough to slip through and then closed it to keep the room warm. It may have been my last rational thought, but by that time I had changed from a mindful, sensitive man to a just a man. The reins on my moral fiber loosely slipped through numbed fingers.

She lay there in the tub, relaxed and beautiful, glamorously resting her arms on the edges of the tub, legs below the water slightly bent, breasts, half in the water and half out, her nipples gloriously pink and round and... perfect, protruding slightly from those complex and wonderful curves.

The bathwater hid little, her long dancer's legs rested at angles, knees breaking the surface like little round islands. Her hair was pinned up in a 'Helen of Troy' style, luxurious red-brown tresses piled on top, tantalizing curls dangling beside each delicate ear, framing her fragile neck. Lily saw me looking at her and turned her head back and forth slowly to give me a better look.

I froze like a statue. I don't know who else in the last thirty-seven years got to see this and frankly, I didn't care.

The exhibition of her nakedness was personal and intimate. And arousing. In fact, that part had commenced, and I feared my boxers might prove inadequate. But Lily's interest was on my eyes, as if she was more keenly interested in what was happening behind my forehead.

I took a couple of shuffle-steps toward the tub and sat down on the marble edge, just inches away from her. Closer to her now... it magnified the wonder of looking at her. I felt my heart trembling, my breaths short and shaky.

Lily smiled confidently, dimples showing a little that my being there looking at her... amused her.

I viewed her beautiful body, stared at it, really. She didn't care.

Her smile deepened and she sat up a little and reached her right hand toward me. I took it, wet, warm and soft, and I stood. With her left hand in mine she rose as gracefully as a dancer. Balancing between my hand and her other hand on the wall, Lily elegantly stepped out of the tub onto a plush area rug.

She turned toward a towel hanging on a hook on the wall, but I reached for it ahead of her.

The towel was thick, soft, warm and expensive.

She stood in the center of the room on that white rug, her dainty feet sinking into its nap. I draped the towel around her shoulders and began to dry her, lightly pressing the towel to her neck and shoulders.

In that fancy bathroom, drying her naked body proved to be a fantasy like nothing I could imagine. She seemed to like it too. Her eyes glowed with pleasure as they followed my hands.

I moved the towel down her left arm. She held her arms out from her body to accommodate me.

I dried the left arm and moved to the right.

Then her chest. I patted her taught pectorals and moved the towel around her breasts, her breasts like flowers to a butterfly. And I dried them like a lover would dry them, slowly, intimately. I moved the towel down her ribs, drying both sides at a time, wrapping it behind her to dry her back and then moving it like a fleecy belt down to her buttocks and hips.

I knelt to dry her legs. Lily spread her feet a few inches apart and I wrapped the towel gently around her left leg, the thigh, the calf and shin, her ankle and arched foot. Beginning at the bottom I moved in reverse up the right leg, calf, thigh, and hip.

I stood and dropped the towel, my face inches from hers. Her eyes looked at me unblinking, maybe a little challenging.

I reached behind her and placed my hands gently on her buttocks, firm and muscular with the right amount of curve.

I moved against her, pulling her into me. I felt my blood surging from my core to every corner of my body.

Her breath drew in sharply... and another, a shuddering breath. Lily's eyes widened, suddenly darting like an animal.

A firecracker went off in my head, slamming shut a door that should never have been opened.

I pulled my hands away, but my body bucked the storm, my mind whirling, looking for loopholes.

There were no loopholes. A promise is a promise.

For a long moment I looked into her unfathomable eyes. The surge of my blood retreated slowly leaving my muscles quivering with adrenalin... and an unfathomable emotion...anger.

My brain did little thinking, so I opened my mouth to say something stupid,

"You're not dead down there," I said, my voice harsh and throaty.

Lily's mouth parted slightly, the corners of her lips descended. She raised a hand to her forehead, touching fingertips to her temple.

She spoke, a soft, dry whisper, "No, my love. I'm dead up here."

As if her words opened a valve, Lily's eyes filled with tears. They streamed down her cheek like there was no stopping them. I backed up a step, my mouth hanging like a fool, an electric numbness spreading through my legs.

Another stumbling step backwards, I had to escape from the sorrow in her eyes.

She stood there, her hand at her temple, her body slumped. She wrapped her arms around herself, hiding her nakedness.

Another step. I slid through the bathroom door and closed it.

The latch clicked. With the door between us I could finally breathe.

In the darkened room I moved to the other side of the bed and slid between the sheets, stiff, tense, robotic... no relaxation, no comfort.

I lay there for a long time, a petrifying corpse. I heard the clicking off of the bathroom light and the room became profoundly dark, like it had been on my first night here in Rawlings' cottage. I rolled onto my left side facing away from the bathroom and lay there as stiff as a fallen tree.

The door opened, filling the room with humidity and the scent of fancy French soap.

She took a long time to come to bed, her thoughts while she stood there a total mystery. I heard her feet tread across the floor. She paused next to the bed, a short pause for maybe final thoughts.

Then Lily pulled back the cover and I felt the pressure of her body sliding between the sheets.

She had been right about the bed... large enough to leave enormous gap between us.

Lily crabbed over and spooned the length of her body against me. Her feet cupped under my feet. Her knees pressed against the back of my knees. Her thighs, hips and belly against me. Her breasts pressed against my shoulder blades. She slowly snaked her right arm around my chest and pulled to her tightly.

I moved my hand over her delicate hand, clasped it and pressed it against my stomach. I felt her fingernails against my skin, but I didn't roll over and try to hold her.

I left things the way they were.

A promise is a promise.

Her last gift was to plant a kiss at the base of my neck. The kiss burned like her lips were a brand heated to a level that would hurt but not wound. The heat remained, the stimulation of nerve-ends, of something that made me wonder if it was a kiss at all.

Suddenly all the hints of the day rolled into my brain and reconfirmed the love I felt for her earlier in the day. I knew I loved her. She wasn't perfect. I wasn't either, but at least I could give her my kind of love, flawed and needy.

Like love was going to save us... when it never had before.

A minute later, I heard her breathing, a dry whistle, deep, even, rhythmic... just below a snore. I loved the sound of it, like a child asleep, innocent and trusting.

The other thing she could not promise me.

Outside the tree frog symphony finished their last encore. The overcast parted and what little moon there was cast a diffident light, some of which entered through the window.

I knew the best day of my life ended there. Neither my guardian angel nor the magic genie asked me to fill out a survey. If they had, I would have pressed the "No Thanks" button.

PART 3

Perhaps all the dragons in our lives are princesses who are only waiting to see us act, just once, with beauty and courage. Perhaps everything that frightens us is, in its deepest essence, something helpless that wants our love.
Rainer Maria Rilke

CHAPTER 18

"The Worst Day of My Life – 6:00AM"

Gould's Landing, Townsend, Georgia
From the Journal of Brendan Macbean:

Naturally, the worst day of my life followed the best, and neither my guardian angel nor the magic genie stepped up to take the blame. Furthermore, my worst day resulted entirely from my own choices and as expected, I ordered up a ton of foolishness.

No sleeping late for me, I awoke in the now familiar pitch blackness. My memory of yesterday unraveled like some haywire yo-yo... the day, the woman, emotions like a tsunami.

Instantly I knew Lily was gone. My subconscious reported that she had just vacated the bed, gathered her belongings, and slipped out the door.

I had the impulse to jump up and chase after her, to apologize and ask her to stay, the first order of foolishness... the idea that more talk could save and heal us, drag us back from the abyss we tottered near. I knew an obsequious apology could work wonders, but if Lily knew the words that could unlock that magic, she had left with them unsaid.

Her abrupt departure left an emptiness that I felt as acutely as an organ donor. Something vital had been removed and a cavity reamined that might take years to fill.

I heard her at the bottom of the steps clicking shut the cottage door quietly as if not to wake me. I immediately thought to turn off the Land Cruiser's alarm before she set it off but remembered in our haste and turmoil of last night, I had forgotten to turn it on.

I heard the metal screech of her truck's door followed by the clattering engine. The crunch of tires on dirt and the noise diminished.

She was gone.

I turned over and lay on my back. I felt nearly as tired as I did when I fell asleep.

What now?

Well, I found myself in painfully familiar territory.

I knew what I was going to do about it. I rolled over and caught her scent where thousands of her skin cells had rubbed off on the sheets.

Thanks for the reminder.

I headed to the kitchen. All the blend was gone so I splurged and opened a new brand, something organic, something from Bolivia in a foil covered bag decorated with what I guessed was the Bolivian flag. The coffee grinder ground it with enthusiasm and in minutes, the maker was making.

My laptop delivered a deluge of communication from Nick Carrillo. Sometime early yesterday Nick had opened a one-sided Facebook chat with me that after a half dozen unrequited messages, he had concluded with, "Okay, Brendan, you're taking the day off with this lady. Mr. B says it's okay."

"You better believe it, kid," I said to my computer screen.

Nick had sent me dozens of emails with dozens of attachments. It was a deluge of information. I scanned through the list several times and finally concluded that the report I really wanted wasn't there.

So, I called him. Not a telephone call. I Skyped him. What the heck, it wasn't even dawn yet, but I wasn't going to let Nick Carrillo sleep late on the worst day of my life.

He answered immediately.

"Brendan... you're back!"

"Yeah, kid... I was never gone."

"Wow! That sounds like a quote. Somebody famous say that?"

I was getting used to his lack of eloquence, PhD, notwithstanding.

"No, Nick... although it's close to something LL Cool J said."

"Who?"

"LL Cool J... he's a rapper or I guess they call it Hip-hop these days."

"I don't know him," Nick said.

"I'm not surprised. He's older than I am."

"Wow!" Nick exclaimed, artlessly. His fingers clattered over his keyboard and I knew he was searching on 'LL Cool J'.

"Wow," he said again. "'Don't call it a comeback... I been here for years.'"

"Something like that," I said.

Nick said, "I guess if Miss Lily offered to take me to Blackbeard Island, I'd drop everything and go."

"So how do know Lily?"

"Well, she has a Facebook page... like everyone else, I guess."

"Yeah, okay. Nick, I see you sent me lots of information."

"Uh, yeah. Never can have too much, right?"

"Look, kid... for the love of all that's holy, you sent me the maintenance manual for Honda outboard engines... and the University of Georgia's, 'Mariculture of the Golden Isles?'"

He dropped his eyes. "Overload, I guess. Too much, maybe?"

"I'll never read most of it. It'd take months."

Now he looked like his feelings were hurt.

I tried to be more gentle. "Nick, where's the explosives report? Didn't Bentley set a deadline for two nights ago?"

"He did, but we didn't get it. They issued a brief, instead... a two-pager."

"So, who jumped and who croaked?"

Nick didn't answer. I guess I pushed him a little hard.

"Okay, Nick. Just asking... what's going on with the explosives report?"

"Well, it's just that they didn't find anything."

"Didn't find anything? That doesn't make any sense."

"They found lots of residue, but it was all from the boat. Nothing foreign. Like something just exploded for sure, but we can't tell what it was."

I sat there for a half-minute.

"Nick, are you telling me that dozens of analysists combed over that boat and they found nothing?"

"Well, not exactly. You know from one of your articles... you did that thing on granite... how they blast rocks..."

"I remember," I said.

"Explosions make heat and pressure. And the pressure blows stuff around, like debris and shrapnel, right?"

I nodded.

"This explosion blew off the front of the boat's cabin and the roof, right? And the heat from the explosion melted the hard foam collar around the boat's gunnels and killed the three sailors.

"Well, they scraped stuff off of every square inch of what's left of the boat and they didn't find any explosive material."

"What? That's impossible," I said.

Nick shook his head. "I know, right? They didn't find any TNT, Semtex, C4, Dynamite... none of that stuff."

"Then what blew up the boat and killed those sailors?"

"We can't say, Brendan."

I felt my brain hitting a wall.

Nick chattered on as if trying to fill the silence. "The lead investigator, the FBI guy gave a press conference yesterday afternoon. It was televised. You should watch it."

"But, Nick, they didn't find anything. No fingers to point. Why brief the press?"

He didn't respond. I gave it a couple more seconds.

"Nick, you federal guys are playing a dangerous game."

"What do you mean?" His dark eyebrows come together.

"When you give a press conference and don't give any facts... well they're reporters. Reporters must report something. I can't imagine the headlines this morning. What is it, terrorists or aliens from outer space?"

Nick gave his laptop camera a sheepish grin. "Yeah... both. The press is running a little crazy."

"It's their job to sensationalize. What did you think would happen?"

Nick made no reply. He angled his head so his glasses caught whatever lighting was overhead, hiding his expression behind a glassy sheen.

"Yeah, we should have expected it, but Brendan, Mister B thinks you're different."

"What? What's that supposed to mean?"

"I briefed Mister B a half hour ago. He told me to suggest that you watch the press conference and read the two-pager and then call me back."

I couldn't think of anything to say for several moments, but when I did it wasn't nice.

"Hey, kid... do you like being Bentley's little hand puppet? Because I don't."

"What do you mean?"

"Bentley is making you do all the jumping and croaking. He's a master manipulator. He can't just tell me what he wants. He's got to get you to deliver his hints, like he expects me to 'be different.'"

"Well, Mister B is my boss, Brendan. I do what he tells me."

"And he told you to tell me to watch the video and read the two-pager. And then call you back, right."

"Right. Will you do that?"

"Sure, why not? You've given me nothing else. I take a day off and the whole investigation comes to a screeching halt. So maybe I'll start with the maintenance manuals for those outboards. Hondas, right?"

"Very funny, Brendan."

"No, you guys... you and Bentley are the funny ones. I know what he wants. Tell your boss I'll call back as soon as I come up with the answer to his riddle."

CHAPTER 19

"The Worst Day of My Life – 7:00AM"

Gould's Landing, Townsend, Georgia
From the Journal of Brendan Macbean:

The press conference seemed a waste of time. A stiff FBI type stood at a generic lectern in front of a red, white and blue background, all of it tedious, subliminal, and manipulative. He read a generic statement honoring all servicemen and women who risk their lives to protect America, honoring our great country and the freedoms we enjoy... and on and on. I'm not against honoring our people or the country, but like the rest of the reporters in the audience, I wanted data. The FBI investigator added nothing more than what Nick had revealed to me and by the end of the press conference, concluded, "Despite hundreds of man-hours of analysis, at this time, we're in no better position to declare the source of the explosion."

He added, somewhat cheerily that the investigation was on-going and that was supposed to give us hope that one day we, they might know something.

Then surprisingly, he yielded to a few questions, which delivered the only substance of the press conference. Like I said, reporters want information, not mollycoddling, and what the FBI had staged so far was TV viewer pablum.

A bland diet makes us restless.

Here are the questions and answers somewhat paraphrased:

Reporter: "Were you able to determine the size of the explosion and its exact location?"

FBI: "Yes, we were. Please consult your evidentiary brief." (Note; the evidentiary brief, given to all attendees of the press conference, was a somewhat puffed up version of the ATFE's two-pager. Nick had sent the document to me as an attachment.) "The force of the explosion was roughly equivalent to five to seven kilos of TNT. It was powerful enough to blow off the front of the patrol boat's cabin. The exact location was near the front of the cabin, roughly at the center of the cabin's windshield."

(Note; the FBI uses terms like 'exact location' and then fuzzies it up with 'near' and

'roughly.' The ATFE two-pager, which was not handed out to the press, gave the location as 'roughly' 927.6 millimeters, from the right side of the windshield, or, as it turned out, the exact center of the center post of the windshield which was an aluminum strip 33 millimeters wide, which divided the windshield into two plexiglass rectangles... not a fraction of millimeter off the center of the boat.)

Reporter: "Does the explosion's force and location suggest an origin or maybe a type of ordinance that might have been used?" (Note: a great question! Kudos to that reporter. I scanned

the video to see if I knew him. I didn't.)

FBI: "Due to the information available, we're not in a position to say what the origin of the explosion is. To do so would be speculation and right now all possibilities are being considered."

(Note: At this point I began to suspect that the FBI was not being honest. Something wasn't right and I hoped to figure out what it was. Unfortunately, the assembled reporters had other ideas. The next question swerved away from the nature of the explosion.)

Reporter: "European news agencies are reporting an unnamed terrorist organization claiming responsibility for the attack. Can you confirm their involvement?"

FBI: "We are aware of the report. We thoroughly investigate every claim. We do not think this claim is credible. Although, we're not in a position to say what caused the explosion, all of our intelligence assures us that there is currently no real threat of any similar attack from any known terrorist organization."

The reporters erupted with questions, but the FBI investigator held up his hand and said, "That's all the time we have. We'll announce the next press briefing on the website that's listed in the handout."

He turned, left the lectern, and disappeared. The shouting reporters fell silent.

I closed the video's web page.

Whenever I think I'm being lied to, I deploy a reporter's trick. I take the factual statements and reverse them. Something always rings false when you do this, and I seem to know it when I hear it.

It didn't take long to figure out which of these 'facts' was a lie. And it didn't take an hour to figure out what was going on and why. But I didn't call back Nick immediately. I did a little research first, about twenty minutes of Googling, and I think I had a pretty good working theory.

The Skype computer-circle whirled, and Nick's youthful face came up on my computer.

"Mister Mac is back and he'll get us all on track!" he rapped with enthusiasm. I'm sure he used the interim to research LL Cool J and now was parroting him to appear, well, cool, but his rapping was pitiful and a long way from cool.

"Get serious, kid. We're in trouble."

Nick's expression fell. "Yes, sir."

"If I can figure this out in thirty minutes... well there's reporters out there smarter than me and who probably pulled all-nighters."

Nick said nothing. His eyes darted around like a thief in interrogation.

"Bentley set me up in this investigation and gave me a security clearance so I can't say anything, I can't actually go to the news desk with this, but lots of reporters are free to report what they want. Your boss wanted me to see the video, which I would have watched anyway, and you played along with him."

Nick looked at his keyboard.

"Nick, we're in trouble. Bentley knows that this story is going to blow up. And when it does the focus shifts and points straight at our wonderful Federal Government. Instead of answering a few questions you'll be fending off hundreds of questions. The press will smell coverup and, well, we're in trouble.

"Nick, are you listening? Bentley wanted me to assess his exposure, and I'm telling you... you have about thirty-six hours."

Nick raised his eyes. "Okay, Brendan. Tell me what you think is going on."

I took a deep breath.

"The feds are lying to us. It won't take those reporters long to realize that."

Nick gave a tiny smile. "What makes you think we're lying?"

"You know exactly what caused the explosion. You never said you didn't. You and that FBI guy kept saying, 'We can't say' or 'We're not in a position to say...' It's straight out of a whitewash scrip, a badly written whitewash scrip. You think you're going to fool the press for long?

"Look up TWA Flight 800, 1996. FBI uses the same language. Coverup. Government conspiracy to defraud the public.

"This explosion was caused by a military weapon," I said calmly, like an expert. "Our military weapon... something very powerful and very accurate. Highly classified, maybe even experimental. It was fired deliberately at the Coast Guard boat, blew it up and killed our guys. It did exactly what it was supposed to do."

Nick remained silent, his expression quizzical like he was studying an archaic text.

"You Federals didn't redact the ATFE's two-pager... you rewrote it, bloated it and removed key information. The two-pager gave the power of the explosion in precise numbers... with fractions. The so-called evidentiary brief used the word 'about'.

"When they demolished the Georgia Dome in Atlanta, this giant stadium collapsed straight down in the center of a major city with no collateral damage. Those engineers knew exactly how much explosive power they needed and where to locate it. The ATFE analysts surely have this level of expertise.

"Whatever blew up the Coast Guard boat landed within a millimeter of where it was aimed. Are you familiar with Target Acquisition Systems?"

"I am," Nick said.

"TAS is vital to military weapons. It can find targets, evaluate, match data, and make sure the weapon gets where it's going. Hellfire missiles, Tomahawks, rockets. They acquire, analyze and provide ballistic guidance to projectiles. They hit the target."

"Wow! Mister Mac, the military hardware expert." Nick tainted his speech with a little sarcasm.

"I'm no expert, but I saw a presentation on the Hellfire missile at the Redstone Arsenal in Huntsville, Alabama a few years ago. The Department of Defense analyzes everything that can be a potential target... tanks, ships, artillery, buildings, bridges... everything. They match the weapon with the target and figure out how to get the explosive charge, whatever it is to the most effective part of the target. You place the explosion in the most effective place... where it will do the most damage. Whoever blew up the boat did it with confidence it would do the job.

"I don't know who did it or why... or how they got their hands on this weapon. I know we didn't do it."

Nick didn't move. The kid wasn't a good poker player, but is silence told me he was grinding what I said over in his mind.

"Nick, any terrorist who got his dirty hands on twenty pounds of TNT could have caused so much more damage, so many more victims. This Defender Class boat was at a boat show last weekend up in Savannah. Hundreds of kids, aunts and uncles and everybody crawling all over it. Why didn't they blow it up then? Bigger disaster, more publicity. Why not a softer target? Why not shut down the Port of Brunswick or the J. Torras causeway and strand twenty thousand people on St. Simonds Island. Why not the Sidney Lanier Bridge..."

"Because it wasn't terrorists?" Nick ventured.

"Exactly. I don't know how difficult it is for a terrorist to obtain twenty pounds of TNT. I hope it's not too easy."

"Here in this country, it's not, really," Nick said.

"Twenty pounds of TNT is like the explosive charge of a six-inch gun. Artillery... a field piece or something mounted in a destroyer, right? Any of that around?"

"Nope. No destroyers or any military assets in range.

"Right. Why would we do it to ourselves? Four of our finest, highly trained Guardsmen, and a valuable boat?"

"Keep going, Brendan. You're on a roll."

"The Coast Guard protects our coasts and waterways from pirates, smugglers, drug runners. Whoever attacked the boat had a reason. It was a brash, bold and maybe even stupid, but for whatever reason, they couldn't risk getting stopped and searched. And they took a chance they'd get away with it.

"The guy on the RORO ship mentioned a big, white boat. Do we know anything about that?"

"Brendan, there are hundreds of big white boats in the area. It's St. Simons Island, a very crowded place for pleasure boating. Private jets, too. It's a rich man's playground."

"Doctors, lawyers, corporate execs?"

His dark eyebrows came together.

"All those, yeah."

"Drug runners, smugglers, cartels?"

"I guess them too."

"Thing is, Nick, you can't tell one from the other."

"No, of course not. Criminals keep a low profile in public. Nobody knows who they are. They try to blend in, look like everyone else."

"Right, Nick. They look like everyone else… same with their boat… but I think the Swede said 'white, twenty meter' boat? How many of those in St. Simonds?"

"He was a Dane not a Swede. And I don't know."

"Find out. Also find out how many big boats fueled up locally, maybe that morning. Maybe they paid with credit cards and you might get a registration number."

"Cool! This is just like real police work!"

"Well, suppose you, the crook, are cruising around St. Simons with something on board you absolutely aren't supposed to have, and here comes the US Coast Guard. You absolutely can't be stopped and searched, so, you tell your helmsman to get the heck out of Dodge. Make some wake.

"Your guy turns around and sees the Defender steaming straight at you and he says, 'You can't outrun them, boss. She can do fifteen, twenty knots more than we can. And she can call in helicopters and the whole, damn US Navy if she wants to.'

"So, what do you do? One of your guys is tinkering with this new gadget, and he says, 'Hey, boss! I think I can make this problem go away. You want me to do that?'

"You don't spend a lot of time thinking about it. The Defender's closing the gap, so you say, 'Yeah, make it go away.'

"Your whole crew steps to the back of the boat to watch. The weapons guy looks at the TAS screen. It centers the Defender in a red box and the readout shows course and speed. Whatever this thing is, it must be incredibly easy to use because he had figured it out in less than a day.

"The box around the Defender goes green and he pushes the button on whatever it is.

"Two seconds later the Defender goes boom.

"The problem has gone away, but it takes seconds for them to realize what's going to happen now. Not just helicopters and the whole damn US Navy, killing US servicemen is an act of war. The whole country is going to come after them.

"If it were me, I'd head toward the big, wide ocean as fast as I could before someone figures out where the boom came from."

"Wow, Brendan. Where did you get all this?"

I shook my head. Staring at Nick's face on a computer screen, well, it makes you do things like shake your head when there's no one in the room.

"I'm making up a scenario based on eliminating what's unlikely. Nick. I'm really just winging it here, but I'll tell you this... reporters speculate like crazy when they have nothing else, like facts and evidence. Reporting and police work are not the same. It may seem impossible that someone would fire a military grade weapon at a Coast Guard boat, but obviously it's not. Some reporter is going to speculate just like I did and put his or her theory out, might even call it a 'likely scenario' just to watch what you do, and see what you say in response. You feds are horrible liars and pretty soon, everyone is going to think it's true.

"A storm is coming, Nick. You better do something fast."

Nick thought for a moment.

"Well, Brendan, I guess I better tell you what's going on."

CHAPTER 20

"The Worst Day of My Life – 9:00AM"

Gould's Landing, Townsend, Georgia
From the Journal of Brendan Macbean:

Nick turned his head to one side like he was looking for something he had written down. "Brendan, have you ever heard of LOXAM?"

"Roxanne?" I asked, "Like, 'You don't have to put on the red light.'"

He snapped back to his computer screen.

"What?"

"'Roxanne,' by the Police."

"What police?"

"The Police, a rock band. You know, Sting. The Seventies?"

"Before my time, Brendan. Not 'Roxanne' but LOXAM. It's an acronym for Liquid Oxygen Assisted Munitions."

"Never heard of it."

"New technology. The DOD has been investigating it for quite a while. The idea is to get more bang per pound over traditional combustive materials. Combustive explosives have the oxygen and fuel combined. All that energy is released as the chemical bonds are broken.

"Boom!" Nick said zooming his face into his computer camera.

I actually jumped back.

"Brendan, you probably already know some about explosives from your experience with the rock quarries. They use a lot of dynamite and TNT."

"Yup," I said.

"Well, one of our defense contractors experimented with liquid oxygen and chemical propellants, the caloric compounds used in formulating explosives... sorry, I'm getting technical."

"That's okay, kid, I can handle it. It's me you're talking to, not your buddies."

"Uh, okay, Mister Mac. Oxygen is universal in all combustion. Liquid oxygen is its most concentrated form, but it's difficult to store since it boils at minus one hundred eighty degrees centigrade. Our contractor experimented with LOX and a little bit of Thermite powder and got a big explosion, bigger than an equivalent mass of TNT or dynamite."

"Thermite?" I asked.

"Pyrotechnical powder. Used in incendiary weapons. There are lots of different compounds, mostly powdered metal. Thermite makes lots of heat and light. With liquid oxygen it also produces a spectacular pressure wave."

"Bigger than dynamite?"

"Ounce for ounce. But LOX is difficult to store. Especially in smaller containers. Cryogenic containers store liquid gases. Big containers are more efficient. We wanted a small weapon, light weight. In combat, weight is everything. The thing must be carried, and easy to store without a lot of extra stuff. So, the contractor came up with a tiny cryogenic container that could fit into a beer can."

"A beer can? You'd seriously freeze your lips off if you opened the wrong can."

"Very funny... but think about it... we make millions of aluminum cans a day... beer, soft drinks. We have this seriously powerful weapon, but you don't have to invent a new container. It fits in a cheap little beer can. Well, it's a little different but essentially the same size, sixty-six-millimeter diameter aluminum tube, a small cryogenic container of liquid oxygen, a detonator and a small amount of a special compound. This beer can weighs less than a can of beer. You can throw it or put it on a drone, you know one of those multi-rotor drones, or drop a hundred of them in a combat zone."

"Combat zone? Nick, have we used this in the field?"

Nick's eyes darted away. "Uh, yes. Under tight controls. Syria and Afghanistan. Just a few specially trained units. All hush-hush. This weapon is very classified."

"Not anymore, kid. Everybody's going to know about it."

"You might be right. At first, we used them against the enemy. They like to hide in buildings, bunkers and caves. We put them on rotor-drones. Fly right into the caves, around walls, through windows...

"Bam!" Nick yelled.

"Nick, you like saying that. I don't. I get the idea."

"Sorry. The enemy didn't know what hit them. And then they got smart. They started rigging nets across the openings to caves and kept the windows closed.

"So now we have to use two drones. One to take out the barrier and another to blow up the room. Or cave.

"But drones are expensive... cost thousands each. And lots of drone technology comes from Asian manufacturers. All this to carry a warhead that's costing us twenty dollars."

"What, it only costs twenty dollars? What do they call this thing?" I asked.

"Soldiers like to give them nicknames, but the official designator is XL-66. The soldiers call them Route 66, like in, 'Let's send them down Route 66,' like in 'Get your kicks on Route 66.'"

I said. "That's an old song, Nick. But if the soldiers are giving them nicknames, the word must be out about this weapon."

"We monitor a lot of chatter on the terrorist networks. The enemy can't go investigate a battlefield to determine what we used on them, so they get on the Internet to see if anyone else knows what it is. Because we have tight controls on where it's used, there really isn't a lot of information and hopefully we're keeping our secrets. But that didn't stop the chatter and speculation. The terrorists gave this weapon a nickname. They call it 'The Cleaner.'"

"Because it doesn't leave any residue. Oxygen... everything is consumed... canister, mechanism, whatever... all burned up."

"Right, Brendan. And it burns everything laying around. Cans of gas, food supplies, stores. An oxygen-enriched environment... everything burns."

"That's a nasty piece of business."

"Yes, it is nasty. We quickly discovered that drones, besides being expensive, were vulnerable. Anyone with a shotgun could take one out. A barricade can stop a drone, and you need an operator. Drones are good for special situations, but ultimately, we wanted a cheap, lightweight, and accurate weapon.

"So, the contractor added another beer can, only this beer can is a small rocket with directional capability. Launch out of a tube with compressed air so you don't have to deal with rocket-burn at the launch point. The rocket ignites in mid-air, solid fuel propellent with about a thirty second burn. That gives it a practical five-kilometer range. Now it's called the XLR-66, with a new nickname, 'The Cleaner.' They mated it with target acquisition software, and uh, I guess you don't like me saying, 'bam' to emphasize things, well, we have a new weapon."

"You said, software, not system."

"Right. The new target acquisition software is really an app. I can run it on my smartphone, a tablet or laptop. It can work with any high definition camera. The better the camera the better it works, but even a cell phone is good enough. TAS can identify an object, its range, direction, motion... all of that, and it has a database of targets, like trucks, buildings, planes, oil rigs, groups of people and so forth and can recommend the best place to put the warhead for maximum effectiveness, and how many warheads you need to take out a specific target."

"My god, Nick. This takes nasty to a new level."

"Yes, sir. The enemy doesn't know what hit them.

"So, all the terrorist networks continue to ask if anyone knows what this is. Have they seen one, and so on. They put out a bounty, a reward...

bring us one of these whatever it is, and we'll give you a hundred thousand dollars. No takers so it grows to a million. No one can get one. They're under total security, but now our leaders are worried someone will find out where they are and figure out a way to steal one.

"Terrorists won't have the capacity to replicate it, but if it gets into the hands of somebody like the Chinese or the Russians, they could do it pretty easily. And seriously, the Chinese and Russians use terrorist all the time to spy and hack the United States.

"So, our leaders decide to pull all the XLR-66 units from the field. The classified field test is done. The order goes out to recall all the units, back to the factory for evaluation. They recall the four units tested in the Syrian theater. They all came back no problem.

"Eight units were deployed in Afghanistan. Eight units were pulled from the field and waiting at the airport in Kandahar to be shipped back to the manufacturer.

"The terrorists raised the reward to five million, and that's when we lose one."

Nick paused somewhat dramatically to let it sink in.

Maybe Nick didn't think it was sinking in properly, so he started to list the sum of our greatest fears.

"You called it nasty, Brendan. Well, now they have one, actually the whole thing, rockets, warheads and launcher. If they can hack into the Department of Defense cloud, they can download the TAS software and make the unit fully functional." Nick swallowed hard and added, "And who can't hack into that?"

He continued, "The twelve units deployed for field testing in Afghanistan were labeled A through L. All of them came back to Kandahar. Unit L had been deployed in Forward Operational Base Geronimo in the Nawa-I-Barakzayi District in Southern Afghanistan.

"The whole thing fits into a container about the size of carry-on suitcase, a launcher that could fire off six at once, plus twelve beer can sized rockets, twelve beer can size warheads. As soon as you stack them together, just like stacking a couple of beer cans, they become operational.

Add the TAS and a camera and you're in business, all of it linked and controlled with Bluetooth connections.

"Some of the units came into the Kandahar staging center empty… no more rockets. Unit L returned with two unfired rockets and warheads. But when they loaded the plane in Kandahar, they only had eleven units. Unit L was missing. In that tightly secured space, someone had figured out a way to steal one of the XLR-66's."

I thought about it and asked, "When did we learn this?"

Nick's eyes fell to his keyboard. He looked like a dog about to be reprimanded.

"About an hour after the Coast Guard boat blew up."

Instead of delivering the expected chastisement, I said, "This Unit L disappears in Afghanistan. How did it get to Saint Simons Island?"

"We have no clue," Nick said.

"By way of Fort Stewart?"

"No, definitely not. None of the XLR-66's were sent to Fort Stewart. They all went straight from the factory where to the field, in Unit L's case, Afghanistan. We could never field test them here in our own country and hope to keep the weapon a secret."

"Nick, do you realize how preposterous that statement sounds?"

"Yeah, I guess it does."

"Nick, it's outrageous that we field test this secret weapon, under tight security and all someone has to do to get their hands on one is offer a pile of money."

"Yeah, it makes us look pretty bad, doesn't it?"

"And whoever has it killed three of our guys. I guess that's why they wanted it. To give us a taste of our own medicine."

"Mission accomplished," Nick said.

"Well, Nick, I hope our brilliant leaders realize a few things."

"What things?"

"We have serious breaches in security if persons unknown can steal a secret weapon out from under our noses in a tightly secured area in the most major battlefield, we're in at the moment.

"Second, they can transport this secret weapon half-way around the world and use it on us in one of the most peaceful places on earth. Why didn't they march it out to FOB Geronimo and blow up a truck or something?"

"Good question, Brendan."

"It's obvious to me that they didn't get their hands on it in Afghanistan. They got it here. Why take the risk? That means you have security breaches here and there. You have no idea how it got into this country, once it left your control. It certainly did not go through customs in somebody's suitcase."

"Highly unlikely," Nick said. "Smuggling and diplomatic pouch are the current theories."

"Diplomatic pouch, my ass!" I said. "No country would risk that. Are you investigating how it left Kandahar... Afghanistan?"

"Yes, we are. We got nothing. No idea."

"What else is missing?"

"What?"

I sighed. "Nick, if you came home from the laundromat and your TV was missing, would you look to see if something else was gone?"

"Uh, sure... I see your point. Yes, there's a taskforce working on that."

"I'm so relieved. You and I don't have to do everything. Just figure out who stole this thing, who has it, who used it and how they got it. Not all that daunting, is it?"

"Brendan, are you being sarcastic?"

"Yes, Nick, I am. Glad you're familiar with the concept. Well, it looks like there's only one thing in our favor."

"There is? What's that?"

"Whoever has it... They're out of ammo. You said Until L came back to the staging area with two unfired rockets. I would think whoever's paying the reward wants some live rockets and warheads. That's what they stole it for... to see what it is and how to counter it. But the thieves shot their wad and don't have any rockets left. All they have is a suitcase and a launcher. The TAS software... if anyone can hack into the DOD database, well, they're not paying five million dollars for that.

"So why did they fire off both rockets? Why not save one?"

"I know why," Nick said eagerly. "The TAS database recommends two XLR-66 rockets to take out a Defender. One warhead only gives you thirty-five percent chance of success, while two raises it to one hundred and fifteen percent."

"Two rockets. All of the witnesses thought they heard an echo. What they heard was two explosions very close together."

"Right, Brendan. The first rocket is timed to blow out the windshield. The XLR-66 is much more effective in a closed in space. So the second rocket flies through the hole where the windshield was and, now inside... blows up the cockpit, the console where all the boat's electronics are... and of course the two guys inside, Ortiz and Haddad... but they were probably already... uh, gone from the first explosion. Everything inside goes, uh, except the rear wall."

A reminder of the horrible and sudden death of those poor sailors silenced us both. Unexpected and instantaneous death. Obliteration. Annihilation. The thesaurus in my head rolled on like a juggernaut. Devising a better, more efficient way to kill people seemed antithetical to our country's current, professed morality and our place in the world community.

It had come back to bite us in our well-deserved ass.

"Uh, Brendan, I have to go."

"What's up, Nick?"

"Uh, Milton. He's waking up. They're going to interrogate him."

It took me a moment to remember who Milton was. The Coast Guard sailor who survived the explosion, who lay injured and in a coma in the hospital in Brunswick.

"Yeah, I guess I should have said, he woke up. The doctors have been working on him all morning."

"Nick, you said interrogate, not interview him"

"Yeah, Brendan. He's still a suspect. The MPs and FBI each have an investigator who will interrogate him."

"A suspect? You think Milton had something to do with the explosion?"

"No, of course not. I know what happened."

I thought for a second. "Obviously you haven't briefed the FBI on XLR-66. Not the Coast Guard, either."

"Why would we tell them?"

"To keep them from spinning their wheels... wasting time following the wrong investigative trail."

"The FBI leaks stuff all the time, but they have the lead in this investigation, so we have to let them, uh, lead. The Coast Guard's investigator is only allowed to be in the room as a curtesy. I'd be surprised if he even gets to ask a question. He's a Lieutenant Commander with lots of uniform candy. Milton will be impressed."

"Until he realizes he's a suspect. He'll clam up or ask this Lieutenant Commander for representation," I said.

"Yes, he could. Anyway, this is Mister B's call. He told me to observe as a protocol witness."

"Protocol witness? You're supposed to see that procedure is followed?"

"Right. Anyway, got to go. I don't have much time to get it up on my screen."

"Can you patch me in?"

"Sorry, Brendan. Invitation only. Don't waste your time. I'll call you later if there's anything interesting. Maybe I can get the transcript for you."

And with that, he signed off and my Skype window closed.

CHAPTER 21

"The Worst Day of My Life – 10:00AM"

Gould's Landing, Townsend, Georgia
From the Journal of Brendan Macbean:

Nick's abrupt departure left me with a lot of questions.

I wondered why our government chose not to brief their chief investigator on the XLR-66. This covert weapon was bursting at the seams to get outed, and the feds had done a poor job trying to cover it up.

The Department of Defense knew about it. The Army knew about it. They had deployed the weapon in the field, under covert circumstances, but those deployments had to involve hundreds of soldiers, special training, security arrangements... just to keep it a secret. Anyone who had had contact with this nasty little beer-can rocket and just happened to watch yesterday's press conference, must have let out a long "Hmmmmm."

It smelled like a Bentley scheme. Nick called him, 'Mister B, but I knew him longer than Nick. Bentley always had a hidden agenda and enough power to hold sway over the Department of Defense and lots of other agencies. He wasn't quite ready to 'out' the XLR-66, and I wasn't sure why.

To admit a classified, experimental weapon destroyed the Coast Guard boat and was in the hands of America's enemies would be more than a career changer for dozens of federal employees.

Another reason was Bentley wanted to see what information Milton would give where he might be considered a suspect. Even as we pondered these mysteries, Bentley had teams of federals working on effective coverup scenarios.

Nick Carrillo had sent me a huge amount of information… and kept sending. My inbox burned red-hot with new emails. I scanned it to see if he sent me anything on the four Guardsmens' service records. I found an email with the subject, "Ortiz, Cobb, Hadhad and Milton, service record summary" I opened the email's attachment.

As it turned out, Gerald Milton was the youngest of the four sailors, just out of school waiting on his promotion from E2 to E3. Graduated from Akron University, he went immediately into the Coast Guard. In other words, no combat experience. Little hope he'd have the background to shed much light on the explosion, but he might tell us about circumstances leading up to the explosion.

If he remembered.

One of the emails Nick had sent me referenced the piece of paper I found at the yacht club, my first morning here. Freddy Framus, the binging beer drinker, had identified it as paperwork from Fort Stewart. The page had been covered in unreadable codes. Out of curiosity, I had photographed it and sent it to Nick, asking if he could decipher it.

Yesterday morning, I had responded to his text somewhat tersely and gone off on an all-day adventure with Lily.

Remembering yesterday gave me a pang of melancholy.

Well, Nick had sent me an email deciphering the Fort Stewart shipping manifest.

"Brendan, I hardly know where to start. It's totally just Army paperwork… permission to take a load off the base. A contractor picks up a shipment at the recycling center. This paper authorizes them to take the shipment out. But I don't expect you'll be satisfied with that, so I'll give you the whole thing.

"To begin with, the top third of the page lists a string of DOD general orders from earliest and most prominent and of the highest authority to the most current and relevant.

"The first is an executive order 12873 by Commander in Chief, W. J. Clinton, the forty-second president, Federal Acquisition, Recycling, and Waste Prevention, requiring all federal agencies, departments and organizations to recycle all materials and providing for the separation of waste and refuse from that of recyclable materials. In other words, a presidential order to recycle. The order spreads to all branches of government, including the military. What follows are the implementation orders issued by the Department of Defense and Departments of the Army, descending through the chain of command to Fort Steward itself, its base commander and the unit within the base that has the responsibility of recycling these materials.

"The second area deals with the materials that specifically make up the shipment that left the base four days ago according to the date, or last Sunday."

That was my first night at Rawlings' cottage.

Nick's email continued.

"In 2002, the Defense Department issued a general order effecting all branches of American Military. The order was called, Operation Clean Battlefield and effected all troops in combat, specifically to clean up all areas and battlefields where combat had occurred, of all materials deployed by US troops or such forces opposed to US troops. In other words, our soldiers were to remove from the battlefield any and all material and equipment used in combat, to 'clean up' the battlefield. This meant no equipment was to be left on the field of operation regardless of how damaged it was or how unimportant it may be regarded. In the memos I've read, clean meant clean. In battle lots of stuff carried by our soldiers and the enemy gets damaged or left behind. In the heat of battle, guys drop their rifles, belts, backpacks, anything they're carrying. Sometimes by accident, sometimes in panic. Under this order, our soldiers were required to return and retrieve this stuff, even gather stuff left behind by the enemy.

"Clean the battlefield. Pick up spent brass, weapons, blown up vehicles, pieces and parts, glass, metal, everything.

"This was dangerous duty. In the kind of war we were conducting, stuff left behind could be used by the enemy. Even disabled vehicles, like wrecks. The enemy planted explosives in wrecks and blew them up when our soldiers came back. Drop a near-empty clip of ammo, those bullets were going to be fired at you. I don't know. I've never been in combat. I don't know what goes on. But the order was out... clean up the field. Nothing left behind.

"It's a lot of stuff, apparently. Brendan, I'm doing the research here, so you don't have to. I don't want you worrying about this insignificant piece of paper. You need to be focused on the Coast Guard boat, not some piece of paper you found. Anyway, that's my excuse for this OCD email.

"This stuff is collected at a great deal of risk to our troops, who apparently don't like this duty. It gets assigned to soldiers who were in trouble with their superiors. Apparently going back into a combat zone to collect junk isn't very popular, so they'd do the clean up immediately after the shooting stops.

"They collect the junk and ship it back to the States. That's right, they'd take care to make sure there were no IUD's in it and bin it up and load it into C-130's and fly that stuff out of the country. Here I'm going to reduce some of the detail I'm reporting... there's a lot of complication about shipping stuff back from a combat zone. More when it's Afghanistan. All you have to do is look at a map to see how difficult it is to fly out of that country. We have to find a destination within twenty-five hundred miles, the useful range of a C-130. We fly to Romania and Pakistan for the first hop and then many hops after that until a shipment reaches the US. It's a logistical nightmare and this operation is costing us billions.

"But I digress. So, once these shipments reach the US, they are sent to three OCB stations, depending on how the shipments enter the country. A lot of it ends up in Fort Stewart where they've been sifting through this battle-junk for fifteen years or more.

"So, where does your piece of paper come in? At the OCB center on the base here, they sort through the junk shipped from our combat zones. Most of it is junk and, other than to screen it for explosives... I guess they x-ray it and use bomb sniffing dogs... I don't know what else, the OCB operation here separates the stuff into piles, plastic, glass and metal. The plastic and glass go into the Army's recycling program. The metal is sold to a local vendor. The local outfit comes in here and hauls it off and that's what this paper is all about.

"Fort Stewart granted a contract to a local metal recycling contractor, Coastal Recycling, based in Midway, Georgia, about fifteen miles from the fort. They tell them when to come in and get a load and Coastal Recycling sends a truck.

"So, the unit inside Fort Steward that arranges this is commanded by a Captain Robert Coleman, but the like a lot of units in the army, it's run by a Master Sergeant, Richard Skinner, a twenty-plus year career noncom. On the bottom of the page, that's his code and his signature. This authorizes Coastal Recycling to take out a load of metal scrap.

"Now what is interesting is that at the end of last year, the Provost Marshall issued new regulations that any load over ten tons has to be out the gate before eighteen hundred hours... that's six o'clock PM. The reason they did this was last year there was a lot of supply shrinkage going on. It takes a lot of supplies to run Fort Stewart and someone was stealing it. Some of the stuff specifically sent to the army base was showing up places it should not be, even weapons and military hardware. The MP's thought somebody was smuggling it out in big trucks. Lots of eighteen wheelers going in and out of Fort Stewart. So, the Provost Marshal changed the regs to make sure the big trucks were going out in daylight. Somehow, the recycling unit arranged to pick up this load of metal scrap after ten PM, so instead of backing the exit gate up with this big truck blocking the road, the MP's at the gate inspected the load and cleared it, despite the Provost Marshal's order. That code under Sergeant Skinner's is a MP Corporal and his scrawl... probably the guard at the gate when Coastal Recycling's truck went out.

"You can see if the army tries to put all this information on paper without using codes, it'd be pages and pages. It's confusing, but it's how the army does things.

"Anyway, I know it's a big email for what appears to be no big deal. A civilian truck came into Fort Stewart and hauled off a load of scrap.

"No big deal. Right?"

The end of Nick's email did nothing to slow down the speculation in my head.

'No big deal, right?' Well, a load a scrap isn't a big deal, I guess. The Army recycles scrap metal including battlefield wreckage. They have a contractor to buy it. It helps the local economy. Everybody's happy. Truck comes in, loads up and drives off.

No big deal, right?

Except they didn't haul their load to Midway, Georgia, where this Coastal Recycling outfit is located. They drove to the Barbour River Yacht Club, a stone's throw from where I spent that Sunday night. Right here, where I sat staring at my computer screen.

No big deal, right?

Except when you google map Fort Stewart to Midway, Georgia, and then from the fort to the Barbour River Yacht Club, you're driving many miles out of your way. Double that if your final destination is Midway.

On the darkest, blackest night of the year.

I heard them. I remember that. A big truck creeping down a lonely dirt road with the headlights off.

No big deal. Of course, the logical explanation made itself apparent, even last Sunday night. One of the people in the truck lived on Barbour Island and wanted to be dropped off at the Yacht Club so they could take a boat to the island.

On the darkest, blackest night of the year.

After the boat had departed, I remember hearing the truck start up and leave the yacht club, and there was so little to make of that that I drifted back to sleep and didn't even blink until morning.

Now it seemed exactly like a big deal.

I wonder what it was like guiding a boat on that zig-zag river with no lights. Or for that matter, driving a huge truck in Gould's Landing on the same night.

And then I remember the tingle. The next day I had finished my morning run at the yacht club and the wind blew the piece of paper against my ankle. I picked it up and had a weird feeling.

An instinct. How many times had I felt that tingling... over what seemed like nothing and still something in my brain wouldn't let me let it go? Sometimes it turned out to be nothing... no big deal. But sometimes it turned out to be some of the biggest stories of my career.

Nick had prepared this OCD email in the hopes that by clearing the air, he'd free me up to focus on the Coast Guard boat investigation. But Nick didn't have the personal experience that connected me to the incident.

And as far as the Coast Guard boat explosion, the next logical step was to interview the lone survivor. And I wasn't invited. I had to wait until the FBI and MP's interrogated him and then they might let me read the transcript!

I thought about this for all of five seconds.

And I decided I was going to follow my instincts to see where it led me.

Fortunately, the Georgia Secretary of State provides a great deal of information on registered corporations. I went to the database and looked up this Coastal Recycling. The LLC was first registered two years ago, about the time Nick said they were awarded the Fort Stewart contract.

How convenient.

Coastal Recycling listed three principals, President, Merle Cuthbert Senior, Vice President, Merle Cuthbert II and Donald Cuthbert, Secretary.

It seemed none of them lived on Barbour Island, but maybe, like Rawlings, they had a weekend cottage.

Merle Senior apparently lived where he worked. His address matched the one for Coastal Recycling. Merle Junior lived in nearby Richmond Hill as did Donald, who I guessed was his brother. I googled

Junior's address and Zillow told me he purchased the home two years ago for five hundred and fifty thousand. Not to be outdone, brother Donald purchased his home in the same neighborhood for six hundred and fifty thousand. A fancy, gated community... the fastest growing neighborhood in Bryan County, so said Zillow... fountains, tennis courts, marinas, swimming pools and a mansion-like clubhouse.

The Cuthbert boys must have come into some money.

Two years ago. My tingle wasn't going anywhere.

They say, to understand someone, you must walk a mile in their moccasins. Well, how about driving their route?

CHAPTER 20 - "THE WORST DAY OF MY LIFE – 10:30AM"

Gould's Landing, Townsend, Georgia
From the Journal of Brendan Macbean

I shaved and showered, setting a personal-best time for getting ready, throwing on my ubiquitous white polo shirt and khaki pants, and Cole Haan loafers. A glance in the mirror told me I looked like Jake, from State Farm.

I said to my reflection, "What are you wearing, Jake from State Farm?"

"Uh, khakis."

A cornerstone of my career had been to cultivate a non-threatening appearance, and since Bettye wasn't around to provide wardrobe mandates, or gentle suggestions like Lily had yesterday, I fell back into my habit of wearing the same thing every day.

Polo shirt, khakis, Cole Haan loafers. Bettye had called it my uniform. Well, it would have to do. All my beautiful clothes from Neiman Marcus, Nordstrom's, Savile Row were divided between my closet in Atlanta and Bettye's flat in Paris.

For stalking Coastal Recycling, khakis and polo shirts would have to do.

I made a quick sandwich nowhere near as good as what Lily had made me yesterday, filled my Yeti Rambler with ice and water, grabbed my computer, phone and backpack and headed down the stairs.

Outside, the marsh hailed me with a cool breeze, bringing salt tang to my nostrils, reminding me of my perfect day with Lily. Twenty-four hours ago, we were cruising Blackbeard Creek, in pursuit of the best day of my life. It wasn't, of course. Our perfect day crashed after her bath, what followed, and me knowing I needed to apologize for something.

I knew I had lost her... how could we ever repair the chasm that had opened up between us? I stood there facing the marsh, flat-footed between the cottage and the Toyota and my heart feeling like it beat in a vacuum.

I took a deep breath, for no reason but to fill the space.

It was over and maybe there never was anything there, but my desperation kept me reaching for some kind of lifesaver. Another deep breath and I felt like I could move. I stumbled around the front of the Land Cruiser and climbed into the driver's side door.

All the rich familiarity of the Toyota's interior surrounded me. I pressed the start button and watched the Land Cruiser come alive, dashboard, lights, smooth running engine. Slowly circling the turnaround, I drove down Rawlings' driveway, took a right and sidled toward the yacht club.

With the windows open I listened for the crunch of tires on the dirt road, unsure of how this would gain me insight on Sunday night's incident. What I heard Sunday night had been a much bigger truck and much darker night. Broad daylight made it altogether different, but like a neophyte magician trying new chants from an arcane tome, I followed the formula as close as I could.

I crept past Unger's spaceship-like house and entered the yacht club. I turned onto the circular concrete pad and stopped the Toyota on the spot where I had found the piece of paper. I turn off the engine and got out.

I looked around and took in the vast marsh to the east. Green with Envy, still tied up at the dock, rocked gently with the rhythm of the Barbour River. I turned again and saw the forested land to the west, the boat warehouse, trailer and truck parking lot.

I tried to imagine how those men had functioned in near total darkness. They could see nothing but whatever was up close and somehow had to watch out for sand bars and such.

Of course, I had no idea of the state of the tide or how familiar these guys were with the Barbour River, but maybe it could be done.

I looked down at my feet. That's where I found the paper. Somehow the truck's driver had put the folded paper in his pocket and when standing here, lost it. And then the truck had driven over the lost paper and imprinted a dirty tire track on the back.

What did the guys do then? The first and most obvious guess was that they or he drove back down the dirt road to Harris Neck Road and on to Midway. Their destination had to be Coastal Recycling. My GPS would tell me which way they went.

It seemed the yacht club had yielded up about as much insight as it could, so I climbed back into the Land Cruiser.

GPS or not, there was only one way out of here. I followed the dirt road to the entrance of Gould's Landing. The Land Cruiser's tires made a smooth transition from dirt to the smooth paving of Harris Neck Road. With the address of Coastal Recycling loaded in the GPS, I headed west to Highway Seventeen, the Coastal Highway.

When I approached Interstate 95, the GPS threw me a curve. I had expected to be routed north to the Midway exit, but instead the purple line said to stay on Highway Seventeen.

I followed the GPS, passing through the quiet village of Riceboro and the entrance to International Paper, the ingress for several eighteen-wheelers. I saw a line of the same waiting to get out. Miles of forest-bordered highway brought me to the red-light intersection with Highway 84. The onslaught of traffic let me know I was sort of back in civilization.

The GPS told me to turn right.

Within a mile, the GPS warned me of another right turn, onto Cuthbert Road. I looked for the road and failed at first to see it. No sign announced the location of Coastal Recycling headquarters, just a gap in the line of trees revealing a barely visible single lane unpaved road.

I turned right.

It was a good road as single lane roads go. A new load of gravel made the Land Cruiser's tires pop, but otherwise it was a straight half mile through the pines. I wasn't sure what I'd do if one of Coastal Recycling's trucks came out. There was nowhere to turn around.

The road widened to a gigantic clearing dominated by a high, chain-linked fence. The fence was at least ten feet high and new. Shiny razor wire topped the fence, intimidating enough for a minimum-security prison and big enough to enclose a football field. This end had a sliding gate large enough for a big truck to pass through.

The gate was closed.

I heard a huge amount of noise coming from within the compound, the sound of a demolition derby, growling engines and the crash of steel, a racket loud enough to penetrate the soundproofed interior of the Toyota.

Recycling must be a raucous business.

Inside the chain-link fence, I saw a house, a small brick ranch from the Sixties. On the right of the house, in a carport, sat a truck only a few years younger than the house. Both the house and the truck looked to be in pretty good shape. The house had a new roof, fresh paint on the window trim and soffits, the truck restored to Barrett-Jackson excellence.

Recycling must be a prosperous business.

I brought the Land Cruiser to a halt just short of the fence. One of my famous instincts made me turn on the forward-facing video cameras built into the Land Cruiser's roofline.

Just a feeling... nothing more. I had no plan and sat waiting for the gate to open. No sign identified the place as Coastal Recycling, but four signs conveyed four very explicit messages.

"Private Property."

"Keep Out."

"No Trespassing."

"This Area Under Video Surveillance."

I saw no fewer than five security cameras, and probably there was more I couldn't see.

Expensive, state of the art cameras.

I was being watched and they probably weren't going to open the gate.

I glanced to my left and saw a callbox mounted on a post under a small, protective overhang. Above the call box another camera was mounted. I lowered the driver's side window and extended my hand.

I paused before pressing the callbox button, unsure what I was going to say.

Before I could press the button, the callbox squawked and a gravelly voice said, "It's about time you got here. The sprinkler system's been installed for over a week."

I understood the confusing statement. The gravelly voiced man saw me in a fire department command vehicle. That newly installed sprinkler systems needed inspection by the local fire department.

I guess.

So, I said, "Well, I'm here now."

"Hey, you're not Bill!" Gravel voice followed with a two-report cough.

"No, I'm Brendan."

"Brenda who? Where's Bill?"

"I don't know where Bill is. The boss asked me to come out and do this. So, here I am. If you want to wait for Bill, fine with me."

I started raising the window.

"Hold on. I guess it don't matter. The sooner we get it done the sooner I get my insurance rebate."

Silence for a minute.

"Well, are you going to open the gate?" I asked.

"Hell no, I ain't going to open the gate. Leave your truck there and come in through the people gate. It's right in front of you."

Just to the left of the sliding gate was a people-sized gate. It looked as substantial as the rest of the fence.

"Okay. Let me grab a tape measure."

"I'll hit the unlock when you get to the fence. Make sure you close it behind you," the gravely-voiced guy said.

I went around back of the Toyota and retrieved a tape measure. Just as I arrived at the fence, the people door unlocked with a large click. I made sure it latched behind me.

The house was raised on a concrete block foundation, A large handicap ramp connected the front porch to the carport. Before I could knock on the front door, the gravely voice shouted, "Don't knock. Come on in. I can't get to the door."

That might be something Bill already knew about.

The front door opened into a small living room, completely lacking any living room furniture. The room seemed to be furnished as an office with an old, gray metal desk heavily cluttered with stacks of paper. An ashtray with a smoking butt balanced on the edge topped the shortest stack.

A man in a wheelchair sat facing the far wall which held a large flat-screen television, which was actively showing Family Feud, with a grinning Steve Harvey. The man had muted the sound, thankfully.

The room was a complete mess. I noticed the entire floor of the room held office storage boxes of full of paper, some stacked four high. Some had lids on them. Some did not. Typed pages of various kinds of paperwork lay scattered everywhere. A drunken office party with dirty dancing could not have produced more disarray.

Apparently, the celebration was over.

The man turned his head from the TV to give me the once over.

He was probably in his seventies and had not aged particularly well. Permanent sunburn, heavily wrinkled skin, and the poor guy was in a wheelchair. He picked up the cigarette and took a deep drag. His exhale launched a smoky cloud over the desk.

"Ain't seen you here before," he coughed.

"There's always a first time. What do you-all do out here."

The cigarette glowed from another toke.

"Coastal Recycling... we recycle." He gave me a look, like I was the only knife in the drawer that needed sharpening. "You know... metals? Mostly steel, some copper and aluminum."

"Where does it come from?" I asked.

"Salvage, construction sites, for rebar, junk cars, the landfill..." he paused. "Some of it comes from Fort Stewart."

"Fort Stewart?"

"Yeah, we buy a lot of steel from the Army."

"What do you do with it?"

"We clean it up, compact it and..."

The racket coming from behind the house compelled us to raise our voices nearly to shouting. A particularly loud crash halted Old Man Cuthbert in mid-sentence.

"We load it into our compactor and, uh, we make blocks of steel."

"Somebody buys it?"

"An outfit down in Brunswick. But we ain't sold 'em much lately. Our compactor is broke. Donnie said he can fix it, but he ain't gotten around to it."

"Your compactor's broke? What's all that racket, then?"

Old Man Cuthbert turned his head toward the back of the house.

"The boys are unloading the steel. We got a big load from the Army last Sunday. They got to get the empty bins back to the Fort for the next load."

Sunday, I thought. That's when I heard the truck, but this is Thursday. They weren't in much of a hurry apparently.

Old Man Cuthbert stared at me for an uncomfortable few seconds.

"Your name's really Brenda?"

"Brendan."

"Well, look, Brandon, I got things to do, so why don't you get on with it."

"Yeah, well, Mister Cuthbert, where's this sprinkler system, I'm supposed to look at?"

He gave me an unfathomable look, smiled slightly and raised his eyes to the ceiling over my head.

I looked where he was looking. Above me was a high-tech looking ceiling sprinkler, newly installed. Over Old Man Cuthbert's head was another.

I looked down at him and smiled. Might as well grin like a fool since that's how I felt.

He let me off the hook and reached across the desk with a piece of paper in his hand. The page held a drawing, the floorplan of the house and the location of the sprinklers for each room clearly marked.

"Thanks, Mister Cuthbert. This'll help."

He turned back to Family Feud and unmuted the TV. The sound returned loud enough to overcome the racket from the back yard. I commenced measuring the locations of the room's sprinklers, an exercise in theatrics since I really could not care less about their new system.

While Old Man Cuthbert watched TV, I puttered around and made my way out of the front room, into the dining room, another room devoid of furniture but stacked with more boxed paperwork. I guessed if you bought steel from the Army, it came with a lot of documentation,

I concluded the entire house was a mess but didn't really care. I made way to the back door, sloshing through scattered forms and printouts. I passed the kitchen... dirt everywhere and dirty dishes in the sink and on the stove.

Where was Mrs. Cuthbert? Nowhere did I see evidence of a woman's hand in attempting to stem the tide of clutter. I thought Old Man Cuthbert lived here and guessed somewhere down the hall he slept in a messy bedroom. I didn't have the courage to look in the bathroom, even if it was part of my plan, which it wasn't.

I wanted to see what was going on behind the house.

A door near the kitchen lead to a small mudroom. I opened the back door and was met by a blast of sound. I stepped onto a typical Southern screened porch.

It took me a full minute to understand what I saw.

A rather new JCB front loader, an earthmover with a steel bucket on the front, loaded scrap steel from a pile the size of a VW Beetle. I had done a story on the JCB plant in Pooler, Georgia, a few years ago. JCB, a British company manufactured heavy equipment similar to American Caterpillar.

The JCB loader was expensive, one which Freddy Framus would have been proud to operate. The man driving this JCB wore a yellow hardhat and seemed to know what he was doing.

But my eyes were numbed by the massive pile of scrap at the back of the compound. The huge pile spanned the width of the fence and in places, exceeded the height of the fence. I could not see how far back it went. Where the giant scrap heap piled up against the fence it bowed out the stout steel poles.

And it stunk of rust and decay. Old man Cuthbert said they cleaned the scrap. They must be cutting corners.

But I recognized a photo-op when I see one and got out my phone. I never had good results filming through screen, so I eased the screen door open and held out my phone. I thumbed "video" and hit the red button.

The operator of the JCB loader wheeled the earthmover around with a pile of scrap in the bucket and headed for the nearest edge of the mountain of steel. Raising the bucket as high as it would go, he dumped the scrap on the top. The cascade of scrap complained about this rude treatment with an eruption of bangs, pops and screeches.

To my right, Coastal Recycling's metal compactor lay idle... itself a giant piece of machinery, it sat inert, rusty and broken with weeds growing out of its moving parts.

How could they form the scrap into big blocks without it? The answer was, they could not. Coastal Recycling was not recycling. They were stockpiling... and running out of room.

A forklift approached from the right carrying a very large, dumpster-sized metal container. The container had the number 'three' pained on the side.

The hard-hatted forklift operator set the container down and backed up slightly, disengaging the forklift's forks. Then gently, he brought the forklift forward, pushing the forks into the side of the container, tilting it. He continued until the container toppled over on its side.

It sounded like a car wreck... demolition derby... engines and collisions.

The forklift repeated the maneuver, toppling it again until the container was upside down. Then he engaged the forks into slots along the container's sides and lifted it. Scrap poured out of the top of the bin, now pointed groundward. Higher and higher he lifted the bin while tons of scrap fell accompanied by a symphony of ear-shredding noise.

The forklift operator turned and carted the container away, while the JCB operator came forward to devour the pile of scrap from bin number three.

Old Man Cuthbert had mentioned the "boys", so I guessed these two guys driving the heavy equipment were Merle Junior and Donald Cuthbert. I didn't know which was which, but unless "Donald" turned out to be a concert violinist, I don't see how he could escape being called, Donnie. Merle on the other hand, was the oldest son of Old man Cuthbert, Merle Senior. He'd probably be called Merle Junior or just Junior.

The forklift driver returned with bin number four, the number pained on the side like before. The process to upend the container was the same but somehow, when fell on its side, it made a quieter sound. Maybe my hearing was ruined by the continuous din, but this time the crash was muted.

The forklift engaged number four and turned it upside down.

A door popped open on the side.

This was different. A long dark rectangle appeared, the full width of the container.

I expected to see the steel scrap exposed but what I saw was dark, shadowy... nothing.

The forklift operator idled his machine and climbed down from his lofty perch. The man's movements appeared painful, slow, and careful. His body was thick with middle age, too little athletic exercise, too much work and meals on the go.

This one must be Merle, Junior, the older brother.

He walked to the side of the container where the door had popped open. Carefully he closed the metal door, returning it to its original position. The opening in the side of the bin seemed to disappear.

The JCB operator, having disposed of the scrap from number three, took a moment. He removed his hardhat and threw his head back and took a long drink from a bottle of water. The JCB driver looked thinner, younger, but somehow aimed for the same physical destiny as his brother.

Donnie.

Donnie Cuthbert pulled his dark hair back before putting his hardhat back on. I noticed something white on the side of his head. I zoomed the video to get a closer look.

It appeared to be a piece of gauze held by adhesive tape, a bandage.

The dirty yellow hardhat went on, casting his face in shadow.

The forklift's engine growled and bin number four levitated off the ground. The scrap poured out of it, clattering to the ground.

But it was different. The amount of scrap was smaller, not even half as much as container number three.

Merle Junior backed the forklift up carrying away bin number four, now empty. Donnie moved the JCB forward to move the pile of scrap. The much smaller pile of scrap.

I stopped the video and closed the screen door.

I had to take a closer look at bin number four. Moving through the back door, the mud room, the filthy kitchen, dining room to the messy front room heading for the front door, like a man in a hurry.

Old Man Cuthbert muted the television. "Hey! You get everything?"

"Pretty sure I did," I said and turned toward the door.

"Hey! You get that report to the insurance company. Bill has all the forms."

I negatively reacted to 'Hey' and another 'hey.' I turned back to Old Man Cuthbert desperately trying to stifle the words forming in my head.

I was not successful.

"Look, *Mister* Cuthbert..." I pointed at all the paper strewn about the room. "If I write what I should to the insurance company, they'd cancel your policy. You got enough fuel here to burn the whole of Liberty county. Every room of this house. And you're sitting under a sprinkler, chain smoking. Your system must be turned off so you could chain-smoke. You want an insurance rebate? What insurance agent in his right mind would give you a rebate?"

Old Man Cuthbert unmuted the TV and reached his fist across the desk, giving me the finger.

It turned out not quite to be the Parthian Shot I had intended.

Outside, I made a beeline to the people door in the chain-link fence. It buzzed at my approach, unlocking. Instead of exiting, I wadded up the paper with the sprinkler diagram and stuck it in the gate's locking mechanism and carefully closed the door, hoping that it would stay unlocked while I checked out container number four.

I knew I didn't have much time before Old Man Cuthbert tore his eyes away from Family Feud, checked his security cameras and saw me still inside the compound. I ran around the end of the house and saw a large flatbed truck parked there. Scattered around the truck were the empty scrap bins, four of them numbered one through four. One container remained on the flatbed and presumably, Merle Junior had taken number five to the dumping area.

All the containers looked the same. My tape measure showed they were all four feet by four feet by six feet long. The interior measured forty-six inches deep.

All but number four. For number for, the depth measured only twenty-five inches deep. And there it stood top open to the sky in a bizarre compound in the middle of the Georgia pines, its secrets exposed to the world.

False bottom. Secret compartment. Hidden door.

I squatted down on the side of number four and looked for the door I had seen when Merle Junior had overturned the bin.

It wasn't there. The side looked as seamless as the rest of the bin. I checked all four sides, thinking I had it wrong but could not find the hidden door. Back at the first side I got down on all four s and practically stuck my nose against the steel to get a closeup.

It was there, the seam so fine it was nearly undetectable. I had no idea how to open it, but it was there, spanning the width of the side of the container. I took several pictures from several angles hoping the light would catch it right.

Someone had gone to a lot of trouble to make number four.

Their scheme was nearly perfect.

I rose on unsteady legs and hightailed it to the people gate. Luckily my wad of paper had kept it from locking. I swung the gate open, climbed into the Land Cruiser and drove out of there like a hellhound was on my trail.

CHAPTER 22

"The Worst Day of My Life – 2:00 PM"

The Kroger in Richmond Hill, Georgia
From the Journal of Brendan Macbean:

"So, Brendan, what's the big emergency?"

I waited a long time for Nick Carrillo to finally Skype me that afternoon. After my panicked departure from the Coastal Recycling compound, I calmed down and searched for the nearest Starbucks. There were two, one in Hinesville and the other in Richmond Hill, Georgia, apparently inside a Kroger grocery store. I headed for that one despite it being a few miles further. My instincts told me that Hinesville, which was near Fort Stewart might be flocked with Army personnel and I'm not sure why that bothered me. I wanted a crowded place where I wouldn't draw attention to myself and the awful, newly discovered secrets I held.

My instincts proved wrong. The Kroger in Richmond hill was booming and thoroughly infested with the Army. Men and women in fatigues, some toting soldiers' kids swarmed the giant grocery store.

I found the Starbucks and ordered a Grande Pikes Peak. They had provided a few tables and, of course, free Wi-Fi.

I set up my laptop on a table and skyped Nick to call me. About the time my Grande was cool enough to sip, his youthful face blossomed on my screen.

"Brendan, where are you?"

The question surprised me a little.

"Nick, I thought you knew where I was at all times."

"Hmmm… let's see." His fingers flew over the keyboard.

"The last transmission on the Land Cruiser was from…" He rattled off map coordinates. "That looks like Ford Avenue in Richmond Hill. Um, the Kroger. But you're not in your Toyota, are you?"

"No, Kid. I'm in the Starbucks inside the Kroger."

"You're sitting. Kroger has tables?"

"Yup and I have a nice Grande Pikes Peak cooling beside me."

"Wait a minute! You're not on the Starbucks' Wi-Fi are you?"

"No, I think it's the Kroger Wi-Fi."

"But it's unsecured," Nick moaned.

I hadn't thought of that. Nobody could hack into the Land Cruiser's communication, but unsecured Wi-Fi in a public place was pretty much an open book.

Nick said, "Brendan, are you familiar with CANDI?"

I was. CANDI stood for 'Cloak and Dagger Interface' and was a popular freeware encryption program, supposedly from a couple of independent hackers in Switzerland. In fact, Daniel Conklin had suggested CANDI last year and then he decided against it because he found out it was a secret, conspiratorial plant devised by our own National Security Agency. CANDI was developed in a US government computer lab as malware disguised as freeware encryption software. Once you installed it on your computer, they had you and everything you were ever going to read, write, say or do on your computer was pretty much an open book. To the US government.

"Yeah, Nick, I know CANDI. It's toxic. I would sooner get leprosy."

"No, Brendan. It's good stuff and totally harmless. Let's see. Oh, you have the install files downloaded. You just never installed it. Here, I'll do it."

"Nick, don't..."

But it was too late. My mouse cursor moved wildly on its own. I watch helplessly while Nick Carrillo dug deeper into my precious computer.

"Wow, Brendan... your version is a year old."

A download ensued.

In minutes, CANDI was loading, and I was clicking 'agree' to everything and I didn't have to lift a finger.

Note to self... this laptop was going to Goodwill.

The CANDI install window asked if I wanted to run my Skype session with CANDI and of course I said sure, why not?

CANDI asked me to enter the encryption key and I didn't even have to do that since Nick was doing everything for me.

Skype went dark and then Nick came back with a youthful smile on his face.

"There, now, Isn't that better?"

I sighed. "I guess. So, what happened with your interrogation of that poor kid in the hospital?"

Nick lowered his eyes. "Oh, well... you were right, Brendan."

"I was?"

"Yeah, Milton's mom and dad were there. They pretty much shutdown the interrogation angle. Milton's dad is JAG, a commander in the Navy. His mom is a head nurse at a hospital in Jacksonville."

"My guess, they're both tough as nails," I said.

"Yes. The dad got in the FBI agent's face. Told him if he wanted to interview his son, they had to do it on his terms. It got a little tense but guess who won."

"The parents."

"Yup. Anyway, Seaman Milton had little to tell us we didn't already know. They were on a training exercise, practicing intercepts. They passed over the RoRo ship's wake, mounted the blue gun. Cobb stayed with the gun while Milton went to the stern doing 'latches and hatches.'"

"Latches and Hatches?"

"That's what Milton called it, slang for stowing gear and closing hatches."

"Okay."

"He said he felt Ortiz alter the defender's course but didn't know why. He didn't know anything about the explosions. Didn't even know they happened. Everything is a blank until he woke up in the hospital. His doctors expect him to make a full recovery."

"That's great news."

"So, Brendan, why the urgency?"

I took a deep breath. "Nick, while you were busy interrogating Milton, I made a bunch of discoveries. As a matter of fact, I think I know why Bentley sent you down here. Do you remember you told me it was top secret?"

The look on Nick's face was priceless... total non-comprehension at first, then a dawn of understanding and finally a smile.

"Okay, Nick... what's so funny?"

"Mister B said you'd figure it out."

"He did?"

"Yeah, he said, don't tell him... it will drive him crazy. It did, didn't it... drove you crazy, Brendan?"

"Well, maybe a little."

"So, what do you think my secret mission is?"

"Leaks, theft, inventory loss, perhaps even contraband. Fort Stewart is leaking stuff. Stuff that should not be getting into the hands of the wrong people. Bentley sent his prized genius down here to investigate. How is this stuff getting out? Fort Stewart is supposed to be a highly secured place. Somebody figured out a way to sneak stuff out and now I know how they're doing it."

Nick took a deep breath. "It started with parts."

"Parts?"

"Yeah, firearms dealers alerted us, I mean the ATF&E, that there were military gun parts available on the market. Some of these dealers keep an eye on the secondary firearms markets. Because they want to keep their licenses, they alert us when something weird pops up.

"Illegal stuff?"

"Yes, and other stuff started showing up on these black and gray markets, war material, like explosives, detonators, grenades, mortar rounds and RPG's. And then money and drugs."

"Money? Drugs?"

"Big blocks of cash and drugs and equipment and material. The logistics around this stuff pointed at Fort Stewart as the source. Mister B sent me down here to investigate."

"What did you find?"

"Nothing. It was a total fail. We even set up special inventory with tracking devices hoping somebody'd steal it and it would lead us to the criminals."

"And it didn't work?"

"Nope. The stuff is still sitting there. Nobody has touched it."

"So, you set up a trap and nobody sprung it?"

"That's the way it looks."

"Maybe the stuff wasn't coming from Fort Stewart inventory."

Nick seemed to think about that for a moment. "Then where is it coming from?"

"Nick, with all due respect, you got too close to it. I'm sure you're a supply-chain expert. They told you somebody's stealing stuff out of Fort Stewart, and you set up the perfect trap to catch the rat. But the rat's doing something else entirely and your trap didn't work."

Even on my computer screen, Nick looked a little hopeless and lost.

"Nick, you're too young, not cynical or suspicious enough."

He smiled, "And you, Mister Mac, are a suspicious, old cynic."

"You better believe it, kid. Now let me show you whose doing it and how they're doing it. I sent you a couple of videos and some photos."

His hands flew over his keyboard. I could see his eyes rolling over his computer screen. His lips moved while he read.

"Private Property."

"Keep Out."

"No Trespassing."

"This Area Under Video Surveillance."

"Wow, Brendan. Where is this?"

"Nick, this is Coastal Recycling, but do you see a sign that says, 'Coastal Recycling'?"

"Looks like the front of a prison. I hear talking. Are you talking to someone?"

"Yeah, there's a squawk box and somebody started talking to me. He thought I was from the fire department. If you look closely, there's a house inside the fence, about fifty feet back."

Nick squinted at his screen.

"Okay, I can see it. I zoomed the screen some. It's not easy to see. The fence is too reflective."

"It's a new fence. It contains an area about the size of a football field. How much do you think that costs?"

"I have no idea," Nick said. "Hey, there you go. Are you going in there?"

Nick had seen me in the video walking from the Toyota to the people gate.

"That's me. They let me in. They thought I was the fire inspector. They had just installed a sprinkler system in the house and was awaiting an inspection from the fire department. I played along and they let me in."

"Well, you look the part... all white shirt and khakis pants and arriving in a red and white Land Cruiser. Totally false pretenses, Brendan."

"Would I do that?"

I took Nick through my findings... a contractor buying scrap metal for the purposes of recycling but stockpiling the scrap instead of selling it. No other means of income. Spending money on security, fences, video surveillance, expensive JCP loader and forklift. Compactor not working, not fixing it. I took him all the way up to the unloading of container number four.

"Watch this, Nick. Only half as much scrap comes out of number four as the other one."

"Yeah, why?"

"Container number four has a false bottom. See that door in the side flapping open?" I paused the video and waved my mouse pointer over it. "That's where they put the contraband. That's where they put the XLR-66 kit."

Nick looked startled. "The XLR? These guys stole it?"

"No, they smuggled it. Think about this. The XLR disappears while awaiting shipping from Afghanistan. A shipment of battlefield scrap arrives at Fort Stewart about the same time. It would make sense if the people who offered the five million dollars got a direct shipment of the XLR, but security is too tight. So, somebody over in Afghanistan buried the XLR inside the scrap and shipped it. This shipment goes straight to Fort Stewart from a trusted source. It doesn't go through customs... no x-ray, no bomb sniffing dogs. A bomb sniffing dog would go into sensory overload. This stuff comes from the battlefield. Everything smells like a bomb."

Nick's eyes widened.

"Nick, if you hadn't interpreted that shipping manifest, I would never have found this out."

"And I told you it was no big deal, Brendan."

"My instincts told me otherwise. I'm a suspicious old cynic."

Nick smiled at that. "Hooray for that!"

"Here's some more. Watch this."

I advanced the video until the part where the JCB operator took off his yellow hard hat.

"See that white thing on his head?" I zoomed the video.

"Yes. What's that?"

"It's a bandage. His ear is bandaged."

"What about it?"

"You remember the bar fight I got into Tuesday morning? The police apprehended this guy, Keith Barnecki, considered to be nearly the worst badass in a hundred miles."

"Yeah, I remember. I read the police report."

"So, I told the sheriff that two guys came into the bar with Barnecki. When the fight started, they must have slipped out the back because the police didn't see anyone else. The Sheriff asked me to describe the two guys, but I didn't remember much except one of them had a bandage on his ear."

Nick's hands froze over his keyboard. "These are the two guys? The Cuthbert boys?"

"Donnie and Merle Cuthbert. I think Donnie is the JCB operator and Merle ran the forklift. These guys are in cahoots with Barnecki, a known associate of Ricky Duggan, *the* worst badass within a hundred miles."

"Oh my god! Brendan, you got the whole package!"

Nick's enthusiasm annoyed me, a little. "Slow down, kid. It's not the whole package by a long shot. All we have are the Cuthbert boys and I don't think they're very serious criminals.

"Somebody inside Fort Stewart is key here. Somebody over in Afghanistan should also be on your most wanted list. I would look for a local connection... someone from around here. Maybe the Fort Steward guy and the Afghanistan guy served together, one or both of them came from around here. Start with Fort Stewart. You mentioned two guys, a Captain Coleman and Sergeant Skinner. Maybe one of them. You have all Fort Stewart's personnel records. We're looking for a guy working in the recycling project with local connections who possibly served in Afghanistan. When you hook up with that combination... that's where we focus."

"Okay, Brendan, I'm searching now. Might take a while," Nick said.

"We have to hurry on this, Nick, or we lose our advantage."

"Okay, okay."

"When you find this guy, very quietly you bring him in for a meeting and you don't let him out. Ever. Backtrack his finances and look for the windfall showing up about two years ago."

"Two years?"

"Two years ago, the Cuthbert family filed a corporation license, Coastal Recycling, LLC. Then the two boys, Merle Junior and Danny bought half-million-dollar homes in a ritzy neighborhood in Richmond Hill, not far from where I sit right now. Old Man Cuthbert got his truck restored to Barrett Jackson elegance. Like I said, they aren't serious criminals but I think before they broke bad they probably operated some kind of family business that wasn't too successful. I doubt the Cuthberts know the true nature of what they're smuggling, but they have to be getting nervous. We don't want to make a move on them just yet."

"Why not?" Nick asked.

"Because we lose our advantage if we do. All we have is the small guys. I personally want to nab this Ricky Lee. He's the worst of the worst. He hurts people and ruins their lives. Folks around here protect him because he tosses them a little money, but he needs to be caught and punished.

"And we don't have the guys who fired the XLR-66 at the Coastguard boat and killed three of our beloved servicemen. Here's how it played out, the Afghanistan guy called the Fort Stewart guy and told him about the five million reward for one of these whatever it was weapons. And the Afghanistan guy says, 'I think I can get one into our next shipment.' So the Fort Stewart guys calls Ricky Lee and tells him about it and they sneak it into container number four. It goes out the gate to the Barbour River Yacht Club where Ricky Lee and the Barn load it onto a boat and ride it out to Ricky Lee's cartel connection, probably cruising around in that white twenty meter boat the Swedish guy on the RoRo ship saw."

"He was Norwegian."

"Whatever. Saint Simons Island is a millionaires' playground and these cartel guys are hanging out enjoying the good life until they can make the connection to the terrorists and get their five million dollar payoff. Then the Coastguard comes after them and they panic and shoot off the last two rockets in their kit.

"Now the cartel guys may have gotten away but they have damaged goods. The terrorists wanted the complete package, They want to study it, figure out what it is and develop countermeasures. Now all they have is the launcher."

"Not exactly, Brendan. They have the weapon's software and targets database. That's worth millions."

"Maybe they don't know that. Yet. The cartel guys are trying to sell damaged goods and that gives us an advantage. Supposed instead of an empty launcher, they had a full XLR-66 weapon with a full twelve pack of rockets? That puts them back in business."

"I hope they never get that."

"I say we hand one over to them. Discretely, of course."

"Bentley would never go for that," Nick said. "This is a top-secret weapon. Highly secured. You understand we go to a lot of trouble to make sure it doesn't fall into the wrong hands."

"Nick, this is our advantage. Besides, the United States of America is a very clever and highly paranoid organization, and this weapon depends a lot on technology. It's got a computer chip inside and software and communication. I bet the DoD has a backdoor routine to turn this beer-can rocket into a dud. If it does fall into the wrong hands, some dude in a bunker can clack a keyboard and turn the damn thing off."

Nick looked skeptical, and I was totally shooting in the dark here. If they had that capability, why didn't they turn the XLR off when it slipped out of their control?

"Brendan, I'll have to check on that," Nick said.

"Check on it quick, Nick. We don't have much time."

Nick's expression changed as he noticed something on his computer screen. I should have expected that he was multi-tasking like all young people do these days. The only thing I had on my computer was the Skype session with Nick.

"Hey, it looks like Sargent Skinner's our guy. About the same age as this Ricky Lee, went to McIntosh Academy and into the army right after high school. Deployments in Iraq and Afghanistan, non-combat roles... he's been at 'The Stew' for a couple of years."

"Call Bentley. He'll know what to do. This has to be done quickly and very quietly. If this guy gets any inkling we're after him, he'll bolt.

"Does he live on the fort?"

"No, his residence is in Hinesville. He's got a wife and four kids listed as beneficiaries."

"Ouch!" I said.

"What's a matter, Brendan? You okay?"

"Yeah, it's just rough, him having a family and all."

"But he's breaking the law," Nick said. "Treason, actually."

Skinner's family, an Army family, had gotten used to a regular school and dad coming home at night. The whole thing chilled me. Dad is not coming home. Not tonight. Probably not until his kids are married and his grandkids are in high school.

"Nick, you call Bentley. Give him your update. Tell him the plan. He'll jump on this because he's a smart guy. You have to get this sergeant to make a call to Ricky Lee with this new deal. He'll do it because he's facing capital charges for treason. Ricky Lee has to call his cartel connection and we have to be ready to capture some dangerous criminals."

"I'm on it, Brendan!"

"Oh, Nick. One more thing. When Skinner makes the call, tell him to tell Ricky Lee the price has gone up to twenty million."

CHAPTER 23

"The Worst Day of My Life – 4:00PM"

Richmond Hill, Georgia
From the Journal of Brendan Macbean:

The paranoia that drove my panicked flight from the Coastal Recycling compound earlier this afternoon was gone. I walked confidently out of the Kroger in Richmond Hill, my only fear came from dodging hectic shoppers vying for the best parking spots.

I felt pride having solved a mystery the experts found impossible, although I had to give considerable credit for being in the right place at the right time, and my mysterious instincts that compelled me to micro focus on that piece of paper I found. It all led to the unraveling of Coastal Recycling's secrets and their connection with arch criminal Ricky Lee.

I knew my limitations. I was no sting operator. Bentley could mastermind the rest. He was the best when it came to Machiavellian schemes.

And with that I felt a great sense of relief and accomplishment.

As I walked to my Toyota, parades of yellow school busses streamed by in both directions on Ford Avenue. To my right a matching yellow sun descended, casting beams through fleecy white clouds, but in front of me, on the southern horizon a buffet of dark and stormy clouds loomed casting doubt on tonight's forecast.

My Land Cruiser was a sorry mess, having born the indignity of dirt and gravel roads. While others were scheming to catch criminals, I decided to indulge in what I considered a pleasant way to spend the rest of the afternoon.

I climbed into the Land Cruiser, pressed the start button and watched the lights come on.

I activated the voice command button.

"TLC?" I said.

There was more than a second delay and then a quiet "Hmmm..." and a deep sigh, and a murmuring voice, whispery with sleep said, "Yes, boss."

"TLC, did I wake you?"

"Mmmmm... Well, boss, you haven't talked to me in two days..." Sounds of a heavy breath. "What's a girl supposed to do?"

"TLC, you're beginning to sound like a real girl."

An indignant sniff, "Really, boss? With boobs, butt and bellybutton? Is that what you want?"

The conversation seemed to call for a little sarcasm. "And while we're at it, blonde hair and baggage... lots of baggage."

TLC was prepared. "If we had a date, you would wait while I got ready? Patiently or impatiently?"

"Impatiently, I'm afraid."

"And parade me in front of all your friends like some sort of conquistador's trophy?"

"Wouldn't that be nice?" I said.

She was silent for a few seconds. I could almost hear the electrons churning. "Well, boss... that's certainly not the apology I expected."

"Okay, TLC. I'm sorry."

But she wasn't finished. "You drive over a hundred miles and don't even say, 'Hi'."

"I'm sorry. Hi, TLC. I've missed you."

Another sniff, like hurt feelings on the mend... for now.

"I've missed you too, boss. You're all I have, you know."

The Land Cruiser's AI interface adapted to experience and interaction with humans, uh... me. I wondered, did I make her this needy?

"TLC, is there an auto parts store nearby?"

She came back with, "There's an Auto Zone and an Advanced Auto Parts, both about a mile from here. Do we need auto parts?"

"More like, 'supplies.' I'm going to give you a bath."

"Oh, goodie!" TLC said with an excited giggle.

She took me a back way because there was an issue with making a left turn on Highway 17, but Auto Zone came first and they had what I needed, car detailing supplies.

"TLC, now I need a self-serve car wash."

"Okay, boss. There's a place called, 'Car a la Mode' just south on Highway 17."

"A la Mode? Sounds like whipped cream."

"Ooh la la!" TLC said.

Car a la Mode turned out to be what I expected, a series of car-sized walled booths equipped with high pressure water hoses and an ATM-like pay-panel. The place was empty. No one seemed interested in washing their cars except me. I parked in the center of one of the stalls.

My cell phone trilled with an incoming text from Nick.

"We got Skinner! Sent MP's to recycling center. We're 'interviewing' him."

Text messaging leaves out a lot of detail, but I got the gist. I thought for a moment and decided not to respond.

My phone buzzed again.

"It's him! He's giving it up. Twenty years in prison is better than life."

The statement made my heart heavy, again the vision of Skinner's fatherless family at the dinner table, his wife left with four kids to raise. Well, it had been Skinner's choice. I didn't know if he fully considered the consequences. He saw a chance to grab some money and knew it was illegal, but treason?

But I totally immersed myself into cleaning my car. Hosing off the grime felt therapeutic. The hose blew out soap like whipped cream all over the shiny red, gold and white paint. Rinse and repeat and wipe down the beaded water with soft cloths. Spray the fenders and doors with liquid wax and buff to a shine. When the exterior sparkled like jewels, it was time to vacuum the interior.

When I opened the driver's door to clean the interior, I saw my phone had several more texts from Nick. I settled into the driver's seat to read his texts.

His texts were like going through a bowl of fortune cookies. Each snippet of information revealed more of the story.

"Captain Coleman is in the clear. Had no idea Skinner was smuggling. I guess it's easier for a sergeant to keep secrets from a captain than the other way around. We'll talk later."

"We found a duffle bag in the recycling center stuffed with hundred-dollar bills and a dozen cell phones. Burners. Call you later."

"He's giving up his contact in Afghan. A guy he served with a couple of years ago. Call me."

"The Cuthberts are just drivers. Their only contacts are him and Ricky Lee. They don't even know what they're carrying, just pick it up and deliver."

I thought, more lives ruined. And I thought of the sloppy way they ran their part of the operation. They were the weakest link in the chain... and the link snapped.

"Mister B is super proud of you, Brendan. He said you'd figure it out. You're the mostest meddler and the snoopiest snoop. Call me later."

Somehow, Bentley's high praise failed to gratify me. It reminded me of my days as a basketball player. Lacking height, speed and ball handling, all I was good at was getting in the way, so my coaches only put me in for defensive situations. The opposition crumbled trying to get around my slow-moving clumsiness.

It worked. Sometimes, but I got a lot of skinned knees and elbows, and sneaker prints from getting stepped on.

I loved basketball.

"Mister B loves your idea of using the XLR to lure out the cartel and this Ricky Lee. You're a genius again. He's putting a brand new, still in the shrink-wrap XLR field unit on the G4 tomorrow. We need to talk."

I guessed that the G4 referred to a Gulfstream, a high-class business jet manufactured at nearby Gulfstream Aerospace. Our wonderful federal government was their biggest customer.

The sting was set in motion. Bentley would lure out of hiding, the criminals who had murdered Coast Gardsmen. Our enemies would suffer the defeat of a thousand details. They'd be lured into a trap and surrounded by the forces of the United States of America, land, sea, and air, agents dressed in virtual ghillie suits made to blend into the natural background of wherever the meet took place.

Bentley would take the lot of them into custody, isolate them in an unknown location, subject them to persuasive interrogation until, one by one, they would recant and divulge and blabber the threads of their hierarchy, their leaders, contacts and associates, who would all go on Interpol and ally intelligence lists, be hunted down, captured and themselves interrogated...

An explosion blasted near my left ear. I lurched out of my seat and felt the top of my head hit the ceiling.

Okay, I was a little high-strung at the moment. I realized it wasn't an explosion, just somebody banging their knuckle on my window. I had been so deep into my dreadful reverie; the knuckling had startled me.

I turned and saw a very fit young man dressed in Army fatigues in the new digital camo pattern. I rolled down the window.

"Good afternoon sir," the young soldier said. "You sure have a beautiful truck."

"Uh, thanks," I said.

"It shines up pretty good, doesn't it, sir?"

"Yes, it does. Thanks again." I saw an embroidered patch bearing black bars sewn into the middle of his chest, with 'B. Meyers' on a strip on his right breast

"Uh, Captain, Meyers, I appreciate..."

"Sir! You looked to have completed detailing your car in an exemplary manner."

"Captain?"

"Sir, there are twenty cars out here waiting for a wash station to open up."

Then it hit me. The crowd had come in while I was dallying with my texts from Nick.

"Sorry, Captain, I was checking my phone."

"Sir! Yes sir!"

I thought he was going to salute, but he cracked a friendly smile.

"I'm moving out, captain," I said.

"Yes sir. Have a nice day, sir!"

"You too and thank you for your service..."

He was gone.

I pulled out of my stall. The Richmond Hill Car Club had indeed descended upon Car a la Mode. They waited in orderly lines waiting for a wash station. From the occupied stalls water and spray flew like above Niagara Falls.

I turned right onto Highway 17. Ahead was Interstate 95. Instead of heading south on the interstate, I kept to the right on Highway 17, passing under the overpass, passing fast food restaurants, gas stations and the usual, close to the interstate businesses.

The Coastal Highway passed from suburbia to empty, grassy meadows and tall pine forests. My eyes took it all in, my brain, numbed with thinking. A spur highway, looking itself like a broad interstate swerved off to the right toward Hinesville and Fort Stewart, the better to feed the giant defense machine.

I'll bet the Cuthbert brothers never took that road.

I soon arrived at the intersection of highway 84, with Fort Stewart to the right and Coastal Recycling to the left.

I paused at the red light, noting the rush hour traffic, modest for this neck of the woods. My phone buzzed with a new text message from Nick.

"Skinner's calling Ricky Lee! The sting is on!"

Good, I thought. Best of luck, guys.

I drove on through the intersection and thought of Lily.

Yesterday… the best day of my life. Lily had shared her day with me, shown me the beauty of her world… and her own beauty. She had barred her soul to me, her heart. And so had I, bared our wounds to each other, the things we couldn't fix on our own, our empty spaces that needed filling.

I had peered into her beauty, the prettiest girl in town, a woman sought by every man who laid eyes on her. All her flaws were internal, and she suffered in a fearful world made by the monster, Ricky Lee.

The gentleman's code says after a date you were supposed to call the woman and tell her you had a great time, a polite, non-committal way to say you're interested. These days, such genteel ways had been replaced by new forms of social interaction, but I was an old-fashioned guy, raised in a previous generation's ways. I wanted to see Lily again. I felt a spark between us, more than just neediness. I could help her even if we weren't going to be more than friends.

And she could help me.

And it would be wonderful just to see her smile and hear her voice.

I didn't have her phone number, didn't know where she lived. Didn't know dink about her, really. Just that she worked at Zoller's. Probably was working tonight, after her day off and all. I could go to Zoller's and see her in her element, a bar, guys checking her out, her flirting with them, keeping them at a comfortable distance.

Why not?

I would stand in the back of the room and do nothing to get between her and her fans. Just hope for a private moment, however brief, just a look and maybe a smile and some encouragement.

I was a total mess. My 'Jake from State Farm' look had been sullied by the car wash. Even a glance in the fading sunlight told me that a considerable amount of grime from the car had settled on my clothes. The best plan was to return to the cottage, shower, change and head to Zoller's. It was trivia night, or they were having a band… I couldn't remember which.

I crossed under the I-95 overpass at exit sixty-seven, over the South Newport River and turned left on Harris Neck Road. The gathering clouds combined with the sinking sun made for a gloomy drive. A fat raindrop plopped on my windshield.

All the way down Harris Neck Road, I felt a tingle of excitement about walking into Zoller's and seeing Lily. I reached the end of the road, passed through the brick gateway into Gould's Landing. When I reached Rawlings' place, I noticed for the first time that he had a mailbox. Of course, he had a mailbox, but even in the last light of day I could see it was stuffed to overflowing, with the door hanging open and excess mail sticking out.

I drove through the gate, parked the Land Cruiser and thought, wow, how come I never thought about a mailbox? I guessed the neighbors didn't empty it out for Rawlings when he had a guest.

Another dollop of rain splattered on my windshield.

I decided I'd better go get the mail before the rain turned it into paper mâché.

It was a long walk and it annoyed me. I heard not felt, the rain begin, the drops hitting the leaves, a kind of velvet splatter in surround-sound.

Yes, the mailbox was full and stuffed to overflowing. It was difficult to dislodge all of it. A giant wad of mail had been stuffed into the mailbox. It was a bewildering pile... at least five copies of the Darien News, with headlines like a world war had ended: "THE 'BARN' APPREHENDED!", followed by subtitles, "Ricky Lee Sought in Massive Man Hunt! And smaller super-subtitles, "Witnesses Report Sightings, but Ricky Lee escapes another dragnet."

I pulled out so many junk mail catalogs, I thought it might be the holidays. And if my eyesight wasn't playing tricks on me in the post sunset gloom, Stan and Linda Hizeman and Ralph and Alice Freeman's utility bills were stuffed in with Rawlings' mail. I looked across the street and saw that Stan and Linda had their own mailbox.

I thought it odd that the lazy mail carrier had stuffed all the neighborhood mail into Rawlings' mailbox.

The rain increased. I gathered all of the mail in an awkward two-handed bearhug and started back to the house.

The raindrops pelted me on the top of my head. I decided to dump all the mail inside and sort it out tomorrow.

The rain quickened and so did my pace, a sort of head down trot-canter.

I made it about halfway when something hit me in the back, a hard, smashing blow, like a linebacker sacking the quarterback.

An unprotected quarterback.

My arms went out, flinging my cargo of mail into the darkness and rain. I belly-flopped to the ground, landing on my torso and face, the air whooshing out of my lungs, the wet dirt, sticks and bits of leaves working into my mouth.

For seconds I couldn't breathe, my mind racing with "What?"

A heavy weight dropped onto my back, immobilizing me. The recent breath I had drawn whooshed out in a gust scattering dirt and mud and leaves.

"Don't talk. Don't move." A deep, Southern voice, a local Georgia drawl, laconic and close to my right ear. I could feel his breath, hot against the cold spattering rain. A metal thing pressed hard into the right side of my skull, just above my ear.

I didn't move. I didn't talk.

"Don't talk and don't move," he repeated. "You feel that?" Whatever the metal thing was he pushed it further into my head.

I felt it. It hurt, but I didn't know how to respond to his question. Instinct demanded I move and talk, but I didn't.

"That's the barrel of an AR-15 rifle, sometimes called an M-16. That's actually the flash suppressor on the end of the barrel you're feeling. It shoots the standard five point five six millimeter NATO round, but I've loaded hollow points. They're tiny little bullets hardly bigger than a popgun, but with a big casing full of powder behind it. Muzzle energy is over half a ton and it'll pop your skull like a hammer on an egg and splatter your brains over a ten-foot circle.

"So, don't move and don't talk. I'll do all the talking and your answers will be limited to the affirmative. Now nod your head to show me you understand. I can see in the dark better than most."

It took me a second to realize I needed to respond. I nodded my head twice, scraping my left cheek against the wet ground.

"That's good, Mister Brendan Macbean. I'm glad you understand. It would be a huge inconvenience for you to die right now. I spent five minutes on Google and concluded you're too much of a big-ass celebrity. Your demise would bring a shitload of unwanted attention down here in little old McIntosh County. It'd mess just about everything up. My contact in the sheriff's office said the state attorney general called and gave old Boatwright a shitload of grief for hauling you in. Who the heck are you to upset state attorney general?

"Blowing your head off is bad idea, but I can't let you keep poking your nose in everything. Like we need a big city reporter down here.

"And you got Lily all wound up."

I involuntarily winced.

"Macbean. I told you not to move. Wasn't that the sweetest piece of ass you ever had? She'd make any man lose his head."

"Every once and a while some dude comes into town. Got more money than sense and there's Lily looking like gazelle in a pig farm, pretty, graceful... even funny. If a guy has any moxie, she'll latch onto him, spread those pretty legs of hers and fuck his brains out if he has any.

"I'm sure she's told you her fantasy, hasn't she? She needs some handsome prince to take her away from all this and put her on a yacht somewheres... isn't that how it goes? She needs help to get out of her legal problems and get her kid back.

"Did she float that one by you, Macbean? Don't answer, that's rhetorical. I'm sure she did. Well, I'm not about to let that happen. Before I came here, I went and paid Lily a little visit. I had to tune her up a little.

"Hold still, you fool!" The deep voice spat out the words, "She won't be spreading her legs for long time. Maybe never. Not after what I done to her.

"She knows better even if you don't. She ain't free to go getting her problems fixed. Her kid ain't free and no prince is gonna come and save her. You ain't gonna do it. You see, Lily comes with me. And you don't want me."

The rain lessened. The background noise subsided to a whisper.

"So, Mister Macbean from Atlanta, Georgia, in a few minutes this is going to be all over for you. You're gonna get up and walk away unharmed." He shoved the barrel of the gun again, a wince of pain above and behind my right ear.

"I know where you live, a nice place in Vinings, a ritzy part of Atlanta, where the rich people live. Your neighborhood, Vinings Traditions, a gated community. Zillow loves the place. Doctors, lawyers, chiropractors. Probably an Indian chief, who the fuck knows?

"The couple that live across the street from you, Billy and Bobbie Blanchard. He's retired, she still helps out at the hospital. Nice people, your friends. I'm gonna burn down their house. It'll burn to the ground because your gate's gonna get stuck. It'll take the firemen about thirty minutes to get in. We got a kind of incendiary accelerator that will make the place go up like an oil-well fire. By the time the firemen get there, won't be much left. Hope that nice old couple get out.

"And you'll know, Macbean... this one is on you. Because you were stupid and tried to be a hero. But you're not a hero, just a shit-head snoop who got into something he should have left alone.

"You can prevent all this human suffering... you gotta do three simple things.

"First you got to leave McIntosh County and never come back. I'll give you twenty minutes to pack your bag and hit the road. Don't stop to clean up the Doc's cottage. Just hit the fucking road. And don't come back.

"Second, you're gonna keep your mouth shut about this place. Nobody cares about what you found out with all your snooping. You clam up about your trip. Talking is like rolling balls downhill. I'll find about it and burn down the house across the street. All I got to do is make a phone call and the place goes up like a volcano.

"Third and last, you forget about Lily. For you, she don't exist anymore... and now that I tuned her up a little, she'll never gonna be like she was. Her prettiness, her beauty, well that was mine and I took it away, just like everything else she ever had. You had your day with the prettiest girl in town, but that was yesterday. That's over. She ain't never gonna look like that anymore. Lily's still mine and I'm gonna keep her... for... ever.

"So you forget Lily. You don't call, text or send an email, card, letter... nothing. Any contact from you whatsoever, to her, her mom or that lawyer, Samson, and I burn your neighbor's house down.

"You got this, Macbean? Three simple steps. You leave and never come back. You don't ever talk about this place and Lily is out of your world forever. Now is the time to man up and save your life. My finger's beginning to cramp on this trigger and the easy thing to do is to blow your brains out but I don't want all the fallout from that.

"You got your marching orders. Now's the time to nod your head."

A heartbeat and I nodded.

"That's good. You got twenty minutes."

CHAPTER 24

"The Worst Day of My Life – 7:00PM"

Gould's Landing
From the Journal of Brendan Macbean:

I wasted precious seconds face down in the dirt, not sure he was gone, thinking as long as I didn't move, he wouldn't pull the trigger. Then I realized his two knees weren't boring into my kidneys and the gun barrel wasn't poking into my head.

He was gone. And I had twenty minutes... less than twenty minutes, now.

The rain stopped, leaving only heavy drops popping off leaves. I managed to get to an awkward hands and knees position and then to my feet. feeling like my whole body was asleep.

I staggered toward my Toyota and the house, unlocked the front door and climbed up the stairs. Every motion, every movement minimalized to get it done. I grabbed my duffle bag and stuffed what clothes were laying around. I looked around for what was left.

The bathroom still held my toiletries. I swept them off the counter and into the duffle.

It didn't take long, but it took too long. With the urgency of a madman, I prowled Rawling's tiny cottage. It all went against my grain…how I'd been raised…dirty sheets on the bed. Dirty towels on the bathroom floor, dirty dishes in the sink, leftovers and perishable food in the refrigerator.

At least I turned off all the lights.

Downstairs, outside, I locked the door and bounded into the Land Cruiser. As I drove through Rawling's gate I remembered I hadn't switched off the hot water heater. I'll have to make some arrangements later, but now I was hell-bent urgent to cross the county line.

I guessed I had about ten minutes. Or eleven. Or nine. And about ten miles to go.

I flew the Toyota over the bumpy graveled Gould's Landing Way, not slowing to go around the tree in the middle of the road and through the brick gateway and onto the much smoother and paved Harris Neck Road. Accelerating to nearly eighty miles per hour I only slowed at the curve around the wildlife refuge.

I barely stopped at the intersection of Highway Seventeen, burned past the Smallest Church in America, and flashed across the bridge over the South Newport River, the northern boundary of McIntosh. I slowed and looked at the clock.

I either made the deadline by a full minute or ran a minute over. I just didn't know which it was.

Foolish thinking on my part. Ricky Lee would do what he wanted and my obsession with the clock was just pure foolishness.

I approached the intersection of I-95, the glare of streetlights pushed away the darkness. Highway Seventeen grew from two lanes into four and then into five. Citgo, El Cheapo, BP and Shell and a McDonalds.

I pulled against the curb of the entrance lane the McDonalds. I wasn't hungry and didn't need gas. I put the Toyota in park and leaned back in my seat. I just knew a bout of the shakes was coming. Adrenaline, like a bad injection of the wrong drug, a sour taste in my mouth a sheen of sweat

The Willies... Heebie Jeebies, churning stomach, and the unwelcome feeling of being royally pissed. In a few minutes, the Shakes, Willies and Heebie Jeebies passed.

Just being pissed remained.

To hell with Ricky Lee. I wasn't powerless and I needed to take care of my neighbors.

"TLC, call Connie Garza."

"Calling Connie Garza," she replied.

"Hi, Brendan! You coming home? Where are you?"

Connie and Jose took care of things at the house when I was gone. Heck, they took care of things when I was there, too... cleaned the house, yard work, anything in the realm of maintenance, like "Hey, Mister Brendan, you need to clean out those gutters." Or, "Your furnace filters need changed. I can fix that sticky lock on the back door." Jose could fix anything. He retired from the Marines and now worked part time at Dobbins Air Force Base. He and Connie took care of several houses in my neighborhood and I suspected that they shacked up in my place when I traveled. But when I came back, the place was always spotless and every blade of grass, perfect.

But her first question put me in a dilemma. I had my doubts about whether I was going home like Ricky Lee told me. He said to get out of McIntosh County. That was clear but he didn't actually say I had to go home.

I wasn't ready to go home. I still had a job to do.

"Mister Brendan...?"

"Yes, Connie. I'm here. No, I'm not coming home for a few days. I'm still here in South Georgia. Maybe by Sunday. I'll call you."

"Okay. Just let me know. I'll get the sheets changed and fresh towels."

"Connie, do you clean the house across the street?"

"Brendan, I'm looking across the street right now. There's three houses there. Which one do you mean?"

I guess that proves my point about Connie and Jose hanging out at my house while I was away. I didn't care.

"Billy and Bobbie's place. Right across the street."

"Oh, yeah. I do their house too. I do a lot of folks' houses. Why, what's up?"

I had to think of something. I sure didn't want Connie going over there and getting Billy and Bobbie all worked up.

"Oh, somebody called the HOA and said there was a strange car parked in front of their house."

I could almost hear the wheels turning on Connie's head.

"Strange car? I guess it was parked in front of your house too, Brendan."

"Yeah, I guess it was. They didn't leave a description of the car."

"Well, Billy and Bobbie are gone on a trip. They're not home, anyway. They went to, uh, the Bahamas. No, not that. Barbados. Not there either. Someplace that has a triangle..."

"Bermuda?" I offered.

"Yeah, that's it. Bermuda. They rented a house on a lake. Not going to be home until, uh the seventeenth. I got to get in there and change the sheets and put out fresh towels and all that.

"Jose has a strange car," she offered. "But nobody's seen it. He parks our van inside your garage and closes the door. Besides everybody knows our van."

"He's not getting oil on my garage floor, is he?"

"No, Brendan. You think Jose would let his car leak oil on your floor?"

"No, I guess not. But if you see anything strange, just call it in."

"Okay, will do. You coming home Sunday?"

"Maybe. I'll call you."

"Okay, Brendan. Bye." Connie hung up.

I sat and watched the river of traffic crossing the I-95 overpass, just ahead of where I parked.

Billy and Bobbie safe in Bermuda swung the momentum needle a little toward the good guys. I thought about what else I could do.

I put the Land Cruiser into drive and headed for I-95.

Now my biggest fear was for Lily. Ricky Lee said he had already done something horrible to her but had forbidden me to do anything about it. Until we put an end to his freedom, he was free to destroy people's lives.

I desperately wanted to call Sheriff Boatwright, to find out how she was. Certainly they had gotten her to a hospital, but that was forbidden to me as well.

As I merged into the northbound traffic on the interstate, my cell-phone rang. TLC announced, "Lanny Boatwright calling."

"Accept," I said, and then, "Sheriff."

"Macbean... where are you?"

I thought, everyone asks me that. I guess I'm not that predictable.

"On the interstate, headed north. Uh..." My headlights lit up a small green sign. "Looks like mile marker seventy or thereabouts."

"Going home, I hope."

It rankled me that he wanted me to go home and put another obstacle in my path to asking about Lily.

"Sheriff, I'm heading in that direction," I said.

"Good. For all of us. You need to go home."

I took a deep breath. "How is Lily?"

His voice narrowed to a clipped tone.

"You know about Lily?"

"Yes. Ricky Lee paid me a visit too. He told me he..."

My heart sank. What was I holding out hope for? Ricky Lee was a monster.

"She's bad, Macbean. Worse than I've never seen. We should have known. I thought Ricky Lee was gone. We should have protected her. We didn't. I don't know..."

"Sheriff, where is Lily?"

"Oh, no, Macbean. You're not going anywhere near... you stay away from her, you hear me? You want him to kill her?"

"No, of course not. I, uh just..."

"Go home, Macbean. Lily doesn't want to see you, and the rest of us... we don't need you here." Sheriff Boatwright choked again. "It's bad... really bad."

He hung up.

I drove on in the dark, people passing me on both sides, like I was somebody's grandpa in moping along in a fast lane.

It was frustrating. Both sides of the law had kicked me out of McIntosh County. Maybe I should go home, but the thought of being three hundred miles away when all this was going down would leave me even more frustrated.

Patience, I cautioned myself, and drove on.

At the intersection of I-95 and I-16, I turned east toward Savannah instead of heading for Macon. Interstate Sixteen east dumps you out in the center of Savannah's Historic District, where I drove a zigzag route down Liberty, Randolph and General McIntosh Streets to the Marriott Savannah Riverfront Hotel and pulled into the well-lit Valet Lane.

A man in Marriott livery approached. He opened the door for me and made a bow.

"Good evening, Sir. Are you staying with us tonight?"

Upon returning to an upright position, the valet gave me the onceover that was uncompromisingly askance. Of course, I knew the reason. I had lain in the dirt in the rain while a madman ground his knees into my back and shoved a gun into my head.

"I clean up pretty good," I said.

"Sir, it looks like you and your car could both use a little pampering."

"We could indeed. Do you have a nice safe spot to put her? Where she won't pick up hangar rash?"

He thought for a second, maybe unfamiliar with the term.

"I have just the place. If we don't get too busy there won't be another car within ten feet."

He gave the Land Cruiser a critical examination.

"And, sir, you will let us give her a wash, vac and shine."

My Land Cruiser was a sorry mess... after all the work I did cleaning her up.

I reached into my pocket and pulled out cash, peeled off a couple of twenties, thought about it and pulled off a few more.

"No, sir. That's not necessary. We'll bill it to your room."

"No, son, it's for you. I appreciate you taking care of her."

I grabbed my duffel and backpack and after a moment, reached in the glove box to get my super-secret LG tablet. I wasn't sure I needed it, but it would be a hassle to get it if I did.

I headed for the front desk, where the desk clerk gave me an equally skeptical look.

"Sir, how can I help?" she said with an audible sniff.

I looked around the grand lobby. The place was practically deserted. I handed her my Bonvoy loyalty card. "I'd like a nice room on the river, please."

We bantered over the room rate, but they were having a quiet night, so she gave me a king for half price and upgraded me to a mini suite. A bellman loaded my meager luggage onto a wheeled cart and showed me my palatial quarters. He opened the curtains, and I peeled off a few more twenties.

I was prepared to be dazzled but the view. It was spectacular with the city of Savannah all lit up on both sides of the river.

I was anything but dazzled by my reflection in the mirror. It recalled the lyrics of Queen's We Will Rock You, "You got mud on your face, a big disgrace, kicking your can all over the place."

I had mud everywhere, clothes and face along with leaves, bits of sticks and other debris of the forest floor. No telling how much of it fell off during my headlong flight out of McIntosh County. I carefully peeled it all off and stuffed it into a Marriott laundry bag. While I was at it, I filled another bag with the rest of my clothes and thoroughly scrubbed my tired body in a very long and hot shower. A Marriott staffer came and collected the laundry bah and promised to have it back first thing in the morning. I said, "Fine, cause your robe is all I got till then."

An hour later, I stood at the huge, panoramic window, gazing out at the Savannah River below me. A room service meal lay destroyed on the kitchenette table behind me, two empty Heinekens laying down like fallen soldiers.

Savannah was beautiful at night, the lights across the river at the convention center, to my right about a mile down river a container ship lay at anchor, lit up like someone's lawn at Christmas.

My phone chimed. It was Nick Carrillo texting me, "Can you talk?"

"Is it urgent?" Me back at him.

"Uh, maybe it could wait," accompanied by an undecipherable emoji.

"8 AM, okay? It's been a long day."

"K," and I knew what that meant.

With the lights out I lay on a fluffy bed almost as good as Rawlings cottage.

The worst day of my life was over, thank God. It couldn't get any worse, but I knew absolutes like that exist only in theory.

CHAPTER 25

"The Worst Day of My Life – Unknown AM"

Savannah Marriott Riverfront
From the Journal of Brendan Macbean:

From a deep slumber, something woke me. My fuzzy thinking suggested it wasn't a person. That somebody would have had to scale over a hundred feet of brick and concrete and find a way to get through the locked and bolted sliding glass door. Or they'd have to batter down the double-locked steel door with the little steel tuning fork safety-thingy flipped over.

That's a lot of work to get an out-of-work, has-been TV journalist.

The disturbance was just a gentle vibration, like the room buzzed with a subtle energy from an unknown source.

Unknown but hauntingly familiar...

My memory cranked like a rusty tractor.

Years ago, Bettye and I boarded a cruise ship in Piraeus, Greece. The ship wasn't due to sail until well after midnight, so like the rest of the passengers we ate, drank and partied and climbed to the top deck to watch the sun go down over the island of Salamis. I think that was the name.

Later, we turned in well-fed and over-served, as happy as loving couple could be, but sometime in the night, I awoke when they started the engines. I have no idea what powers a ship seven hundred feet long. Something powerful… and I felt it as I lay there. Separated by at least ten decks, the engines weren't loud but spread a subtle vibration I could feel. Maybe some people wouldn't feel it, but I did, because even in my sleep, the engines spoke of adventure.

Our stateroom was lit only by the lights of the terminal building, but I saw Bettye at the sliding glass door that lead to our balcony. She was naked and looked beautiful standing there in the near-darkness with faint harbor lights reflecting off her skin. This was years before cancer had ravaged her body. The sight of her drew me out of bed. I stood behind her encircling her with my arms. She arched her head back and her lustrous hair tickled the stubble on my chin.

We opened the glass door and walked out on the balcony as a slight acceleration warped the ship away from the wharf. We stood at the railing and watched the terminal building recede.

In the dark, the cruise ship pirouetted sedately, the bow circling counterclockwise until we pointed in a southerly direction. A bright half-moon swung into view, its light scattering lunar pearls across the Aegean Sea. As our speed increased, the ship's waterline sung a burbling warble. The breeze blew across our nakedness, chasing us back inside where we slipped our chilled flesh beneath the sheets and cuddled closely for warmth.

I don't remember if we made love, but Bettye and I were wonderful together and, thinking our future unlimited, we seldom considered such a time as an opportunity lost.

Until they were all lost…, I guess.

But this night's vibration didn't come from the hotel, which, as far as I knew, wasn't moving.

I managed to get a single eyelid open, kind of like a submariner raising the periscope.

Dark room, a horizontal shaft of light coming under the door into the hotel's hallway and faint light leaking around the heavy curtains drawn over the room's sliding glass door, leading to my room's crescent-shaped balcony.

And this faint light was moving.

The mystery drew me out of bed. I padded over to the balcony door on bare feet and spread the curtains wide.

Mystery solved.

In the Savannah River, a giant container ship glided past, looking as big as a city. Those engines had to be too far away for me feel them. It must have been the solid shockwave of air displaced by the passing of the huge ship that I felt.

Such a sight might be familiar to Savannah residents, but to me it was new and impressive. Thousands of containers heading somewhere... Europe, South America... maybe around the Horn to India or China.

I wished the sailors a safe passage and the investors a big return.

And returned to the bed.

By myself, of course.

PART 4

Out of infinite longings rise, finite deeds like weak fountains, falling back just in time and trembling. And yet, what otherwise remains silent, our happy energies, show themselves in these dancing tears. Rainer Maria Rilke

CHAPTER 26

"What Just Happened?"

8:00AM - Savannah Marriott Riverfront
From the Journal of Brendan Macbean:

"Brendan! Oh my God! What just happened? Are you all right? Where are you?"

His vocal bursts came out of the screen in a somewhat chaotic order like an auto-loading grenade-thrower.

After my encounter with the container ship, I had finished an uneventful night's sleep by bouncing wide awake at six AM. I made in-room Keurig coffee, fired up my computer, sent Nick an email report on Ricky Lee's rampage. Then I ordered a room-service breakfast and waited for pings, rings and knocks at the door.

I didn't have to wait long.

"Nick, I'm fine. Ricky Lee went berserk. He beat up Lily. Put her in the hospital and then attacked me. I had to leave the area. I'm at the Marriott in Savanah.

"Savannah! You're in Savannah... The Marriott? On their WIFI? You got CANDI running?"

"Yes, Nick. Of course."

"Okay, okay, okay..."

"Nick, take it easy. Ricky Lee wasn't the only one who wanted me out of McIntosh County. Sheriff Boatwright called me to make sure I was heading out of town."

"What? Did he know Ricky Lee attacked you?"

"No, I don't think he did. He was angry with me because Ricky Lee went after Lily. She's like a daughter to him. He thinks I'm a troublemaker and caused the attack on Lily. He wanted me gone. He warned me to stay away from her. He didn't even tell me what hospital she was taken to."

Nick clicked on his keyboard.

"I know where they took Lily. She's in the hospital in Brunswick... the same place where Milton is."

"Brunswick!" I said. "And I'm in Savannah."

"You can't visit her anyway. She's under total guard...two deputies and two state troopers."

"So *now* we're protecting her, but when we thought it was safe, we didn't. Criminals like Ricky Lee attack when you least expect it."

"He beat her up pretty bad," Nick said.

I saw his eyes sliding back and forth.

"Nick, what are you reading?"

"Uh, the police report. Uh, and the hospital EMR."

His dark eyes traveled right to left rapidly, and I wondered if he could read two reports at once.

"How bad is it?" I wasn't sure I wanted him to answer that question.

"It's bad. No broken bones, mostly bruises. Initial EMS diagnosis was broken ribs but they're bruised not broken. Facial bruising and swelling. Split skin, lots of facial stitches. Dislocated right shoulder. Right knee hyperextended. You don't want to see these pictures."

"No, I don't."

My heart felt sick. Lily brutally attacked by a monster. I could do nothing. I did nothing.

"Her mom's there," Nick said.

"Her mom?"

"Staying in the room with her. She won't let anyone in but the doctors and nurses."

A cloud of confused thought washed over me. Her mom was protecting her. Her family... Lily has a family and of course they would rush to her aid as did Sheriff Lanny and Captain Corny. She had friends and family. There was no place for me. If I showed up, it would be confusion and animosity. I was the catalyst for this disaster. How would her mom feel if I showed up?

Maybe Sheriff Lanny was right. There was no place for me in her world.

Nick let me have a moment. He must have sensed me having some feelings for her.

"Okay, Nick. We have to nail this bastard. How's our operation going?"

He brightened. "Wow, Brendan, things are happening!"

"What's happening?"

"The XLR field unit arrived in the wee hours. It's over at Fort Stewart's recycling center. Sergeant Skinner is fully cooperating. Everybody, including Mister Bentley, loves your idea of twenty million dollars. Apparently Ricky Lee is a total swine when it comes to money.

"The Cuthbert brothers are dropping off the truck at the recycling center sometime this morning. Then, according to Skinner, they head over to the Exchange and have lunch, brunch or whatever. When Skinner finishes loading the containers with scrap metal, then he calls them, and they come get the truck and drive it to wherever. Of course, our XLR unit is hidden inside container number four."

"Do we know where they're going to meet up with Ricky Lee?"

Nick shrugged. "Nope. Skinner said, once it leaves the fort, he doesn't have a clue where it goes. But don't worry. We can track this XLR unit anywhere in the world."

"Even inside a steel container?"

"Yep. We were even going to track the truck," Nick said.

"Why, if we can track through the XLR?"

"Well, after Ricky Lee gets the XLR, we want to find the Cuthbert brothers, like if they make a break for it in the truck."

"I've seen the truck, Nick. Not a good getaway vehicle."

"We don't have to bug the truck, Brendan. Skinner told me Ricky Lee bugged the truck months ago, with GPS tracking and even sound in the cab so he can listen to the brothers talking. State of the art unit. We have the frequency and all that. Their tech is now talking to us.

"We'll wait for the Cuthberts to show up, get the XLR loaded and send them on their way. They meet up with Ricky Lee and hand it off. Then we track the XLR while Ricky Lee takes it to the cartel. It's those guys we really want. They killed our Gardsmen."

"What about the terrorists, the ones who'll buy it from the cartel?" I asked.

"That's Mister Bentley's call. It's his thing. He'll decide. Oh, for sure we'll round up the Cuthbert brothers and put Ricky Lee away. Win-win for the good guys."

"I hope it all works," I said.

"Mister B says to thank you for all your work. He thinks you've done good work. So take a rest, get a massage. Enjoy the Marriott. I'll keep you updated."

I thought, they don't want me in McIntosh County either. Bentley also wants me out of the way.

"Nick, do me a favor. I'm kind of hunkering down here, but I may go someplace nice for lunch and walk the Riverwalk today. I haven't done that in a while. Send me texts so I don't have to take my computer."

"Right, Mister Mac! I'll do that. You have a good time in Savannah."

"I will," I lied.

An hour later, dressed in my newly laundered 'Jake, from State Farm' outfit, I headed out the Marriott's front door, leaving the rest of my clothes, both my phone and computer up in the room. I felt naked leaving them behind, but I wanted a little freedom to move around without Nick and Bentley knowing where I was all the time.

I did take the super-secret LG tablet.

I had a nifty app on my phone called 'Echotext' that could send any texts I received to a remote device, through either the cell network or the Internet. The old LG tablet might come in handy.

I waved a twenty-dollar bill and immediately got the doorman's attention. I said, "I want my Uber driver to pull up here, not down there, where I have to walk a hundred yards, okay?"

Like most doormen, he was adept at taking money without lengthy speeches.

"Yes, sir!"

Almost immediately a shining crystal blue Mercedes GLS SUV pulled to a stop at the doorman's outstretched 'Halt!' signal. The doorman opened the door and I got in.

The Mercedes was an extremely fine car with smooth leather and a bright new-car smell. An info card on the headrest identified my driver as 'Aaron Babcock.'

But before I could comment on it, he turned around and beamed at me.

"Brendan Macbean! Sir, it's an honor to have you in my car, sir."

I wasn't sure how to respond. Despite my days as an Atlanta TV celebrity, it always surprised me when somebody recognized me in public. Or maybe he greeted all his customers this way. The difference between Uber and a taxi is that everybody knows who everybody is before the first encounter.

"Well, thanks..., uh mister Babcock."

"Sir, I went to Georgia Tech. You were my favorite TV newscaster. I tried to catch the news every night. I loved your stories. You were great."

His use of the past tense made me a little sad. I guess my career really was over.

"I hardly recognized you. You look, ah... different."

"My last girlfriend gave me a makeover... hair treatments and eye surgery. It's new for me too and I'm still getting used to it myself."

He laughed and said, "So we're going to the bank on Abercorn near Stephenson?"

"Right. And can I ask you to wait? I'll just be in there a couple of minutes."

He looked at me in the rear-view mirror. "You're not going to rob the bank, are you?"

"Not today. Just getting some money... that's all."

"Okay. The setup's all wrong. That parking lot is a mess. You could get blocked in, easy."

"You sound like a true 'Ramblin' Wreck.'"

"Go Jackets!" he said. "Mr. Macbean, I can wait for you, but give me your next stop so I can put it in my computer."

I gave him the address.

"Spanish Moss Motors. You're buying a car today?"

"That's the plan."

Savannah is considerably more compact than Atlanta. Our drive to the bank took just ten minutes. It took less even less time to get the money, and I didn't have to rob the place.

The trip to Spanish Moss Motors took even less time. It was just around the corner on Eisenhower Drive. Spanish Moss Motors seemed to be a multi-generational family business that now found itself surrounded by urban progress. It had a small ranch house, trees, and a yard full of inventory hemmed in on all sides by big re-tail.

My Uber driver, Aaron waved goodbye. I turned and saw an attractive woman approaching from the house in the center of the lot.

I headed her way and we met in the middle with a handshake.

"You must be Mister Macbean," she said in a musical Savannah-style voice... the kind that makes you want to respond, "Yes, Ma'am."

This time I wasn't surprised to be recognized. I had called earlier and told her what I wanted. Told her I intended to donate it to Goodwill and to get the paperwork ready. She had told me they often donated cars and trucks to Goodwill and was familiar with the process.

"Well, when a customer tells me what he wants, I try very hard to give it to him. Mister Macbean, do you want to see the truck or go sign the papers?"

"Let's go sign the papers."

Twenty minutes later we emerged from the yellow house. Someone had parked my newly purchased 2004 Chevrolet Silverado, Crew Cab pickup truck in front of the house. It gleamed with recent detailing. Dark gray silver metallic paint, once the color of new motor oil, now faded by the years and nearly two laps of the odometer. A white decal on the tailgate announced its origin, "Ne-Smith Chevorlet, Buick, GMC, Jesup, Georgia." Beneath the tailgate a trailer hitch stuck out with just the right amount of rust.

"Perfect," I said.

"Fully broken in... it's ageless," the woman said.

I smiled. "It shouldn't be too hard finding Goodwill. It's on Eisenhower I think."

She gave me a curious look. Then she grabbed my arm and pulled me in close to her. Our bodies gently collided. Dark blue eyes swallowed me for a second, and I thought she was going to plant a kiss on my lips. But instead, she nodded in the direction she wanted me to look.

There it was... right across the street... Now I could see it, no longer obscured by a large tree... a huge building, as big as a Walmart with giant red letters spelling out 'Goodwill.'

"It's a good thing it's not foggy this morning," she said. "You'd never find the place,"

Her remark caught us both funny and we shared a laugh.

With the keys and paperwork, I climbed into the driver's seat. The truck began telling me the differences between it and my Land Cruiser. The controls a nostalgic mixture of old and new, the smell, a subdued mix of stale humanity and air freshener. Foot on the brake I turned the key. The engine, a big Chevy V-8 cranked, caught, and hummed with power. obviously the truck was still up to the task. To back up I had to use mirrors and crane my neck, just like the old days.

Perfect.

I waited on the light at Abercorn hoping nobody at Spanish Moss Motors saw me heading away from Goodwill. I fully intended to deliver the truck to them tomorrow but today I had another mission.

The LG Tablet chirped. Nick giving me an update, "The Cuthberts arrived with the truck. Skinner is loading. We're on track."

It was a long traffic light. I almost replied to Nick's text but realized I didn't have my phone.

Two hundred decades since the birth of Jesus and we managed all but two without cellphones.

The light turned green, and I headed west on Abercorn, right through the retail heart of Savannah, past malls, car dealers, banks, all kinds of stores and restaurants.

Both sides of the law wanted me out of McIntosh County. Sheriff Boatwright thinks I'm a troublemaker. Bentley had an elaborate entrapment going and hoped to bring down the cartel that blew up a Coast Guard boat and killed our sailors. Both these fine gentlemen and Ricky Lee wanted me out of the way.

If I showed up in my red and white Land Cruiser, it would throw a monkey wrench in everyone's plans. But now I was driving in the perfect camouflage... an old pickup truck that no one's going to give a second look.

CHAPTER 27

"Green with Envy"

Early afternoon – Back again
From the Journal of Brendan Macbean:

William Rawlings once told me, "No one makes plans to go to Hell, Macbean. If they did, they'd pack ice."

I had not packed ice... just bottled water from Parker's when I gassed up the truck. My plan was simple. Sneak back into McIntosh County unseen. Fortunately, I encountered light traffic on the interstate. No one took notice of a guy in an old truck pulling off at exit sixty-seven. Highway seventeen offered even less traffic, and as I crossed the bridge over the South Newport River, I saw that it was low tide, the river a canyon of mud and grass, the ramps to the floating docks hanging at a steep angle.

I wondered if I should have considered the tides. In Atlanta, hundreds of miles from the ocean, we pay little attention to the state of the tide, but my instincts told me despite the depth of the water, Ricky Lee would want to get his hands on the smuggled XLR unit, which represented the biggest payday of his life, and he would allow nothing to get in his way, notwithstanding daylight and tide.

Crossing the Newport marked my official return to McIntosh County, and as I had hoped, it went completely unnoticed. I did finally see the Smallest Church in America in daylight, a tiny building no bigger than a child's playhouse, resting in a pretty clearing off the road, flanked by an American flag and a statue of Saint Mary.

But no time for tourism. I was on a mission.

I turned left on Harris Neck Road and drove its entire length without spotting a single car, man, woman, or 'possum, just a couple of horses in the field around Eagle Neck giving me the eye. The entrance to Gould's Landing was similarly deserted as was the Barbour River Yacht Club itself. I took the last parking spot on the left, facing the river with a great view of the boat-lift area and the yacht club's clubhouse.

The tide level in the river was so low the floating docks could not be seen, but I had a good view of the river itself.

It was time to settle in for the stakeout. I felt a bit conspicuous sitting behind the wheel of the old Silverado, but the truck had a generous rear seat, so I climbed in back and made myself comfortable. I slid open the sliding glass rear window for some air.

I checked my LG tablet. No wifi... no signal of any kind. I was flying blind. I powered it off and put it in my backpack.

Thirty minutes into my stakeout, I had identified the calls of a half dozen birds and named two scampering squirrels, Chip and Dale. They should have been chipmunks, but I saw no chipmunks. A green lizard skittered across the edge of the truck's bed and disappeared.

The inactivity sorely tested my faith in my instincts, but I knew that cops and detectives did this for hours and days on end, waiting and hoping... and often in vain. But the sound of an approaching motor chased that thought away.

Harkening back to my experience Sunday night when I was awakened by the sound of a Diesel engine, I knew this motor was not what I was waiting for. It grew louder, chearly heard through the open rear window.

I craned my neck and saw Stan Hizeman, the guy who lived across the road from Rawlings' place, driving a gas-powered golf cart. He drove past, right behind my truck with barely a glance. A medium-sized dog sat beside him, a prototypical rescue dog, a mixture of mongrel and mutt.

My camo must be working!

The pair pulled up to the yacht club's small clubhouse. Stan got out and walked into the building. The dog followed him with a proprietary air.

I wondered what would happen if Ricky Lee and the Cuthberts arrived while Stan Hizeman was here. Stan, the retired policeman, aware of the massive manhunt for Ricky Lee, would surely start something if he saw them.

A nervous quarter of an hour passed and finally the door to the clubhouse opened and the dog emerged followed by Stan. Stan headed for the golf cart, but the dog stopped in mid-stride and stared intently at my truck. He had picked up a scent or a sound and gave me his full attention

Stan barked at the dog in what seemed like the dog's own language. The dog turned to look at him, gave him a few wags of the tail and returned his gaze at me. Stan barked again and the dog's body language drooped, ears down, head down, tail down, He hopped on the golf cart and up on the seat.

They drove away in the direction they had come.

I suspected that Stan had come to the clubhouse to use the bathroom. Men followed habits and were predictably disposed to a fondness for the toilet that offered the best combination of comfort, privacy and especially reliability. Convenience mattered little over these other values and a man would pass up bathrooms in his own house to go to his preferred place. His wife, the lovely Linda, the winner of his Hizeman trophy would understand when he said, "Honey, I'm going down to the yacht club for a few minutes."

And why not take the dog?

My assessment reminded me that I could use a similar break. All that coffee and bottled water produced a predictable result. Unfortunately, it meant I had to leave my place of concealment. There were hundreds of trees available, and I am not above using one even if it offered nothing but convenience and reliability.

But on a stakeout, a tree wasn't a good choice. On impulse I left the truck and sprinted to the clubhouse.

What was good enough for a Hizeman was good enough for a Macbean.

The clubhouse turned out to be a one room building, big enough for a small party with two sets of sturdy table and chairs. The walls were lined with bookshelves and the shelves were full of paperback books of all types, thousands of titles, one man's lifetime reading list.

At the far end of the room a doorway led to a small walk-in closet filled with picnic supplies, a sink and microwave but no bathroom.

Another sliding glass door faced the river and I stepped out onto a deck. This was where I met Freddie Framus, the earthmover, who greeted me after my run with a wave and a twelve pack... when I discovered the piece of paper that started me on this journey.

To my left I spotted a huge cedar thicket at the north end of the building. It would have to do, I guess. But when I turned the corner, I saw a door and inside a bathroom... a very nice bathroom, cleaner than most gas station bathrooms... and showing no sign of having been recently used.

There goes my theory about men and toilettes.

A couple of minutes later I emerged renewed and refreshed.

I heard the sound of an outboard motor and saw a big boat coming up the river.

A big, white center console with a T-top. There seemed to be no one aboard, but as it got closer I saw a diminutive figure at the wheel, childlike with legs dangling below the captain's seat.

Ricky Lee, of course.

I was completely out of place. I ducked down behind the deck furniture hoping Ricky Lee would not see me.

He slowed the boat and expertly wheeled it around making a circular vortex in the water. At a gentle speed he snuggled it up to the floating dock, neatly tucking it behind the only other boat moored there.

I realized with a pang of guilt... the other boat was Green With Envy, Rawlings' little skiff, bobbing quietly right where Lily and I had tied it up a couple of days ago after our adventure.

Rawlings will never forgive me for neglecting his boat. I made a vow as soon as all this was over, I'd some kind of amends.

Ricky tied up his boat and climbed back into his chair, killed the engine, folded his arms and waited.

He didn't have to wait long. His head snapped to the right and I heard it too... the clatter of a diesel engine.

The Cuthberts were coming.

The lumbering flatbed truck turned onto the circular driveway and backed under the boat lift. With a squeal and a gasp, the driver set the brake and killed the engine. All that could be heard was the sound of Ricky Lee bounding up the aluminum gangway, his footfalls sounding like muted strikes of a kettle drum.

He approached the right side of the truck, not a stone's throw from where I squatted behind the deck chairs. In fact, if I had had a stone, I might have tried the throw. Nailing the bastard in the back of the head with a rock might feel mighty pleasant.

Apparently. he forgot his stepladder. His head came up inches shy of the truck's bed. Not much of a problem when you have giant Keith, the "Barn" Barnecki helping you, but he messed with the wrong dude Tuesday morning.

Impatiently Ricky Lee walked up to the truck's passenger door and banged his fist against it.

"Roll down your window," he shouted.

When that had no immediate effect, he banged the door again loud enough to stop nearby birdsong in mid-warble.

The window came down and a head stuck out and stared down at Ricky Lee. Donnie Cuthbert still wore the dirty bandage on his ear.

"Tell Merle to get out here and help me."

Donnie responded with a string of nonsense which I couldn't make out.

"Shut your damn mouth, Donnie and tell Merle to get out here!"

Merle Cuthbert came around the front of the truck. A big broad-shouldered man, he towered over Ricky Lee.

Ricky Lee stomped back to container number four and pointed up.

"Open her up, Merle, and get that thing out."

Merle worked the secret door's latch and lifted it up. He looked like he'd rather stick his hand into a nest of snakes, but he reached into the dark interior.

What he brought out blinded us with sparkly magic. A bright shiny box that looked to be polished aluminum. It was suitcase sized but a little too big to be a carry-on. Merle hefted it to the ground and looked back into the hidden compartment to see if there was anything else.

There was not.

Apparently neither Merle nor Ricky Lee was impressed with the sparkling beauty of the XLR's case. They paid no more attention to it than they would have a bag of spuds.

Ricky Lee picked up the XLR and said, "You boys get out of here before somebody shows up."

He turned and labored clumsily down the gangway, banging and scraping the case against the metal handrails and making more noise than a bowling ball in a cement mixer.

The big truck lurched up the slight incline, turned left and headed down the road.

Down on the floating dock, Ricky Lee wrestled the XLR into his boat. He started the engine and untied the ropes. The big center console boat floated away from the dock. Ricky Lee eased the throttle forward and the boat moved into the current of the incoming tide.

For a second, I watched the big boat head down the Barbour River toward Barbour Island... presumably he headed to a rendezvous with the cartel who paid him to steal the XLR, at a location known by only them.

He did not appear to be in a hurry. Perhaps it was the low tide. The Barbour River was a canyon of mud and the navigable water in short supply.

Then it hit me... this was the end game. Wherever the meet-up took place, everyone hoped I was somewhere else. The federal bust with agents in flak jackets and helicopters would take place out of my sight.

It rankled me.

I jumped up and ran to my truck, grabbed my backpack and sprinted down the gangway to the floating dock. Ricky Lee's boat disappeared around a zig-zag bend in the Barbour River, with only the white T-top visible above the marsh grass.

I furiously tried to remember the sequence Lily had taught me about starting the motor. Green With Envy waited, bobbing softly in the mild chop.

I lowered the motor into the water and pumped the fuel line bulb. I found the key still in the ignition and twisted it.

Nothing. Oh, the battery switch. I tried it again. The motor cranked, sputtered and moaned. Again. And again, then the motor stated with an uneven idle.

Maybe Ricky Lee wasn't in a hurry, but I was. I ignored the 'No Wake' sign and urged the throttle forward all the way. In seconds, the little green boat came up on plane and I had to jerk the wheel to avoid running into the marsh grass.

Ricky Lee's boat had left a trail of smooth water flecked with bits of foam, an ever-widening V shaped wake, which made finding the channel in the low-tide water a little easier.

The Barbour River zigzagged through the marsh. I could not see the boat I pursued because I cruised at the bottom of a giant ditch of mud. I realized that even though Ricky Lee loped along, the distance between us widened. He was already on the second zig while I finished the first zag.

Ahead I saw the bend to the right and smoothly steered my boat into it, past a mound of oysters exposed by the low tide. Quickly the next turn approached, this time to the left, followed by a series of gentle S-turns. It was fun guiding the boat even though I had no clue what my plan was.

The last stretch in the river was a mile-long widening strip of water at the end of which I could see Barbour Island. I remembered from the trip with Lily the river widened out in front of Barbour Island. Ricky Lee had already made the turn to the right and was out of my sight.

At that moment, my engine coughed, sputtered and died for a second and then came back to full life. I turned around to look at it and saw nothing that might have caused the problem.

I made the full sweeping turn into the giant lagoon, and the engine died another death. This one sounded permanent. My boat spun around idly as its momentum died.

I had run out of gas.

Ahead, I saw Ricky Lee throttle back and bring his boat to a stop.

His boat rocked idlily in the river about a thousand feet ahead of me. With his hands on his hips, he stood in the stern staring at me. Slowly he crouched down, out of sight and then stood up, holding something long and black and ugly.

The assault rifle... probably the one he had jammed into my head last night while he threatened the living daylights out of me.

He put the rifle to his shoulder. Sparks flew. A supersonic hornet whizzed by my ear. Another shot and something struck my boat a hard 'thunk.' I heard a sound like 'pat -a-pat.' More sparks. Another thunk. A bullet pierced the Plexiglas windshield shattering the GPS behind it.

I fell to the bottom of the boat.

I had not expected him to stop. He must have seen me following and instead of using his extra speed to get away, he stopped.

My backpack was within reach and I pulled it to me and wrapped my hand around the Redhawk's rosewood grips. Instead of comfort and confidence it offered me teeth chattering fear and the cold realization that I was no gunfighter. A hero might expose himself to shoot back, but I was out gunned. At a thousand feet, an AR rifle was much better than a pistol... just a bunch of words to hide the fact I was too scared to stand up and fight.

What then? Wait for him to realize I was stranded. All he had to do was throttle up and leave me behind. Surely that made more sense than shooting at each other.

His motor rose in pitch but instead of the sound fading as he drove away, it grew louder.

I gripped the butt of pistol and saw the T-top come into view.

The two boats came together.

Ricky Lee stepped up on a platform and loomed over me, the only way he could loom over anybody... a bigger boat and something to stand on.

"Macbean, I thought I told you to skedaddle."

He stepped into my boat.

"I think you run out of gas... a dumb, rookie mistake. You cityboys think there's a gas station every half mile, but not out here. Remember, I still have this rifle and most of a clip. I just need to pull the trigger to end your life.

"Now ease your hand out of that backpack and it better be empty."

I felt numb and could barely move, but I did what I was told.

"Okay, now put your hands together behind your back like you're grabbing your ass."

Ricky Lee knelt over me and slipped something around my wrists and tightened it.

"That's what they call a zip-tie. The police use these things when they do a big raid. Like handcuffs only cheaper."

My hands were tied, literally behind my back.

"I want you lie still. You may not have any pain right now, but I could kick in a couple of your ribs. So it's your choice. You going to lie still?"

I nodded.

"Okay, let's see what you got here." He picked up my backpack. "This is heavy. Wow! look what you got. She's a beauty." He brandished the Redhawk. I felt angry heat flush my face. "Well, she's mine now." He put the pistol back in the backpack and pulled out the LG tablet. "Geez, what a piece of shit. I couldn't get two dollars for it."

He flung my tablet over the side. It hit the water with a splat.

I watched all my secrets drown in salt water.

"Where's your cell phone?" I shook my head. "Left it in the truck, did you? Another rookie mistake."

Ricky Lee rummaged around in the storage in the bow. "Yeah, I can use this." He lifted out the small anchor and cut the rope above the anchor chain.

"I can use this, too." He lifted out a tiny pink and purple life jacket covered in cartoon characters. "The Doc's got grandkids... must be for them."

"Come on, Macbean. It's time to go."

He bent over, rolled me like a bag of dirt and then lifted me by the upper arm. I scuttled my feet under myself to avoid getting my shoulder dislocated and stood awkwardly.

"You're probably wondering how you're gonna get over to my boat with your hands tied. Step up on the gunnel."

I did what I was told. He shoved me hard in the small of the back. I tumbled into his boat, hitting the center console hard on my left side. Stars danced in my vision, and I lay on the deck, now like a spilled bag of dirt. I blinked and saw the pile of stuff Ricky Lee had pilfered from my boat, my backpack, the anchor and the kiddie lifejacket. And the XLR unit, gleaming and shiny, resting on the floor in the bow.

Ricky Lee worked quickly, wrapping the anchor chain around my ankles and securing it with a length of rope. He took the kiddie lifejacket and buckled it around my neck.

He stood over me like an orator.

"Okay, Macbean. You made a big mistake coming back here. Now I got to make an example of you. I can't have people saying I let you slide after I told you never to come back. So, I have a little something my daddy came up with when he worked for the old sheriff, way before Lanny "Do-Right" Boatwright became sheriff.

"You're all trussed up like crab bait for a reason. We're going up a little creek and drop you off at a place where the water ain't too deep. The anchor will keep you in place and that kiddie lifejacket will keep your head above water so you can breathe. It might take a few days for somebody to find you, if they even start looking, but it won't take long for the crabs. Think of it! Three hundred million years and the crab hasn't changed all that much. You're nothing but a piece of meat to a crab and they'll climb all over you to get to the front of the line. Little crabs no bigger than your thumbnail and big ones the size of saucers. They'll snip away at the soft parts of your body, your eyelids, ears and the skin of your neck and skull, They'll crawl up your pantlegs and find your privates."

Ricky Lee leaned down close to my ear.

"When your blood starts to seep, the little sharks will come in, some of them no bigger than a couple of feet. And bigger sharks too. Sand Sharks and Duskies too. Bonnet Heads, but they won't bother you too much... they'll come in to eat the crabs. But the Bull

Sharks and Blacktips... they want meat. Teeth like chainsaws, ripping big bites out of you."

Breathing heavily, he paused.

"Well, maybe somebody will find you after a few days. Take you to the hospital and try to figure out what parts of you to save. My guess, there won't be much of you left. The folks around here will say, 'Whatever happened to that fellow from Atlanta? The one who tangled with Ricky Lee? Dead... No, not just dead... Harris Neck Dead."

The horror of what he was telling me sank in. I was going to be devoured by marine life. It amazed me that I didn't start writhing like a madman, but although my heart pounded with fear, I lay still and watched Ricky Lee climb into his captain's chair.

Somewhere in the boat a cell phone rang. The best I could do was roll over halfway to see what was going on.

Sitting on the captain's seat behind the center console, Ricky Lee picked up a cell phone.

He stared at the screen for a second and said, "Hey, que?"

I listened to a one-sided conversation. Ricky Lee spoke fluently, but my high school Spanish only caught part of it.

I heard, "Estoy retrasado treinta minutos más o menos." "Una reportera de televisión de Atlanta." "Una pequeña celebridad."

And finally, "Okay, okay. No lo lastimaré. Lo traeré."

Ricky Lee put the cell phone back in the drink holder and turned to me. "Well Macbean, the crabs will have to wait. The boys want to meet you."

CHAPTER 28

"Mar Tranquillo"

Friday afternoon – Out in the Atlantic
From the Journal of Brendan Macbean:

My promotion from crab bait to kidnap victim greatly improved my survival chances. I should be happy about that, but my kidnapper mostly keep me in the dark about what's going on. And I lay at the bottom of the boat, hands bound and feet chained to an anchor... I saw lots of room for improvement.

Georgia's Spanish speaking population had grown significantly during my life, but my Spanish skills had stagnated since the tenth grade. I tried to parse the cell phone conversation Ricky Lee had had. My guess was that he spoke to someone in the cartel. Ricky had told them we were about thirty minutes away...'treinta minutos' but still no clue as to where.

He told them I was an Atlanta TV reporter and a minor celebrity, which was a slight exaggeration since I had not been in front of a camera for a few years and minor celebs fade quickly.

But he had been ordered him to bring me to them, thwarting his intensions of the gruesome Harris Neck Dead. Now I had to wonder... was the cartel going to offer me for ransom? I didn't know a soul who would pay much for me.

I could not see where we headed. I knew we continued down the Barbour River pointed in the direction of Sapelo Sound. The turns sent me rolling on the floor of the boat like unsecured freight. I lay just a few feet from the XLR unit, a twenty-million-dollar prize, gleaming in its polished aluminum case, scratched up from Ricky Lee's rough handling.

When the boat started rocking, I figured we were in Sapelo Sound. According to the sun we headed east. Ricky Lee sat on the captain's chair with his legs dangling, swinging his feet like Edith Ann in a big rocker. The black AR-15 lay on the seat beside him.

The headwinds and chop changed to smooth rollers and a stiff breeze. The up and down motion of the boat felt soothing, and I believed I might have even dozed a little, maybe close to thirty minutes because Ricky Lee throttled back, and the boat turned sharply.

Craning my head, I saw that we had come up against an enormous transom, the rear of a motor yacht with shiny brass letters in an arc across the broad stern.

"Mar Tranquillo."

Ricky Lee tied his boat athwart the stern of Mar Tranquillo, his bow to the yacht's starboard. A swarthy man in a Hawaiian shirt and Bermuda shorts came down a staircase on the port side of the stern. He stood on a swim platform and looked at me lying on the floor of Ricky Lee's boat.

"¿Es él? Vendarle los ojos y luego sacar esa cosa."

"Vale, jefe."

Ricky Lee produced a roll of duct tape, tore off a six-inch strip and laid it across my eyes.

I heard scraping sounds, footsteps. The boat rocked.

Another span of time passed, while I lay there in my now blinded state. I heard several voices conversing. I could not make out what was being said, but the topic grew heated.

Were they arguing about me?

The hot topic turned ugly, with shouting. A scuffle broke out... the sound of bodies crashing into furniture. Loud orders... unintelligible swearing.

Then the human storm passed, doors opened and closed leaving only silence... just the wind and water lapping against the two boats.

I had no idea what had just taken place.

More than a year ago, when I first met Daniel Conklin, I met the guy he had hired to keep him safe. He was an Israeli, a former security officer for their government. In one intense afternoon he had taught me many tricks to keep myself safe, one of those tricks I had utilized when Ricky Lee bound my hands behind my back.

"The cross-section of the human wrist is rectangular, which can be used to fool your captor." I remember his strange, accented English. "You hold your hands thumb to thumb, like this... and when they bind you, you have extra room. You, see?"

"Then when it comes time to escape, you turn your wrists, like this... palm to palm. Your left hand is as much as twenty percent smaller than the right and you try to touch your thumb to your little finger and work the left hand free. With a little luck and a sloppy tying job you might be able to work one hand free. And then, of course, you can free the other."

It took me a while and a lot of twisting, but it worked. My left hand came out and then the right. I brought my hands to the front and flexed them. I took a deep breath and pulled the tape off my eyes. I and untied the rope holding the chain around my ankles.

I was free!

I gave myself a few minutes to enjoy the sensation. And then I grabbed my backpack and drew out the Redhawk. This time I felt like a gunfighter. If mister swarthy showed up, I'd shoot him right through his Bermudas.

But nobody showed. I looked around. We were out in the Atlantic. No sight of land in any direction. Amend that. To the west you could see barely a smudge that might be land. No other vessels in sight. Not even an airliner steaking across the sky.

Location was not as important as what I would do next. The smart thing, considering I had worked my way free and I was not a kidnap victim anymore, would be to untie the boat and, like Ricky Lee had told me, to skedaddle.

And where were the feds? Wasn't it time to spring the trap? Ricky Lee had led them to the cartel, the ones responsible for blowing up the Coast Guard boat.

Where was the federals sting operation?

I wasn't ready to leave just yet.

With a deep breath to calm my nerves, I stepped up to Mar Tranquillo's swim platform and inched toward the steep staircase. The transom with the brass lettering loomed taller than my head.

I listened for any sound of movement above me. Nothing, just wind and waves. I took the first step. And another. My head poked above the level of the deck.

An open-air salon, lots of glossy wood and shiny metal, a fancy, unattended bar, lounging furniture with one overturned chair. The salon was partially covered with a roof, more stairs going to an upper deck. At the stern end of the salon, a table with the XLR unit on it, opened with the rocket launcher menacingly deployed and at the ready. Someone's laptop sat next to the launcher.

No people. I guess they all went inside.

Except Ricky Lee. He sat slumped on the floor against the bar at the end of the salon, hands behind his back his chin resting on his chest. He looked mussed up, his shirt half pulled out and a red welt on one side of his face, and a piece of duct tape across his eyes.

Hands behind his back and blindfolded?

I crept up the last of the stairs and heard some voices and noise coming through a door to the interior of the yacht… excited, foreign-language voices… it sounded like sports commentary, a TV-quality voice rapidly speaking Spanish.

Ricky Lee captured, beat up and himself now a kidnap victim still had the instincts of a predator. His head came up as he heard my approach. He weirdly kicked his short legs back and forth in an effort to free himself. I realized his hands were bound to the brass footrail at the bottom of the bar.

I pulled the tape off his eyes, and he gave me a momentary wild-eyed look.

I put my finger to my lips. He silently mouthed, "Macbean!" and then in a hoarse whisper, "Untie me. There's a knife in my pocket." He rolled over to expose his binding.

I shook my head. Old swarthy-face had done a great job of binding Ricky Lee's wrists, weaving the zip-tie in a figure eight around them and pulling the nylon strap so tight, his hands had turned red. Another nylon tie looped through his bindings and the brass footrail.

He wasn't going anywhere.

I heard joyful shouting from inside. The 'guys' were enjoying the game.

I had my own pocketknife, a slim one I bought in Switzerland with a blade like a scalpel. It sliced through the tie freeing him from the brass rail but keeping his wrists still bound.

I pulled Ricky Lee to his feet and pointed toward the stairs in the stern. He stumbled like a toddler learning to walk.

He paused at the top of the stairs. I whispered behind his ear. "You're probably wondering how you're gonna get down the stairs with your hands tied."

I pushed him. What started out as an uncontrolled swan dive became a clumsy roll. His instincts twisted his body oddly, ending in a hard landing on the swim platform. Only a miracle saved him from rolling into the water. I scrambled after him.

I wrestled his inert body over the gunnel into the other boat, untied the bow and stern ropes and stepped in myself.

The action of the waves separated us from Mar Tranquillo. No one interrupted their TV watching to see us off.

I went to work, securing the anchor chain around Ricky Lee's feet, the same chain that had been around my own ankles earlier.

I sat in the captain's chair, next to Ricky Lee's assault rifle and examined the array of dials, displays and controls. One switch, labeled "master" seemed a good place to start. I switched it on.

Lots of screens lit up. Another, "Raymarine," caught my eye. A display lit up showing my vessel right next to Mar Tranquillo, now fifteen yards away. Sixteen yards. Seventeen and drifting.

I twisted the key in the ignition. The powerful engine behind me quietly came to life making no more noise than a microwave.

I eased the throttle forward and headed west. Not fast, making a small wake on the smooth, rolling Atlantic.

When Raymarine indicated we were five hundred yards from Mar Tranquillo, I eased the throttle into neutral, swinging Ricky Lee's boat broadside to the larger boat.

Behind me Ricky Lee moaned and stirred.

I wrestled him into a seat molded in the stern of the boat. He sat awkwardly, glazed eyes wandering.

"What? Where are we?" he said in a hoarse whisper.

"We're in a boat... your boat."

On his battered face I saw a dawning awareness of his situation. He stared at the chain around his ankles, the same chain he had wrapped around my ankles, with his intentions to feed me alive to the crabs. Then he looked across the waves toward Mar Tranquillo, now about a third of a mile away.

"What in hell are you doing?"

"I just rescued you, you idiot. What were they going to do with you? Or me?"

He thought about this for a second. "Ransom. They were going to ransom both of us." Then he squinted in the sunlight. "Now they're going to kill us."

"How are they going to do that?"

"They got that thing... just like that Coast Guard boat. You saw that in the news? That was them." He pointed with his chin. "Look, Macbean... we got to get away... now! They're busy watching soccer... they do that every afternoon... watch soccer and get drunk."

"Who are they?" I asked.

"Cartel Unido... that's what they're called. 'United.' Two brothers from Cartagena and two moneymen from Panama City." Then he added, "Doctor Mudd."

"Doctor Mudd?"

"He's from Yemen... the cartel's connection to the yahoos in Afghanistan. I don't know his real name, Mahmud or something. We call him Doctor Mudd. He's a weapons expert. He fired the rockets that blew up the boat last Tuesday. I told him not to do it, but he did it anyway. Those little rockets are like nuclear weapons... just blew the toad-snot out of that boat.

"But then we couldn't get paid. Terrorists wanted to know what was busting their chops in Afghanistan and figure out countermeasures. We got a hold of one from Fort Stewart, but it only had two rockets. Normally comes with twelve, but this was a partial kit. It got smuggled out of the field trials over there.

"Doctor Mudd saw the Coast Guard boat coming at us and we all got scared they were going to board us. I told them not to do it but he did it anyway. All you got to do is put your phone camera on the target and it brackets it on the screen, identifies it... just like that. Says, 'Defender class boat. Recommends two rockets.' It goes green and you press the button." Ricky Lee makes two sounds like air-blasts. "Choo, choo... two rockets launch, ignite and in five seconds that boat is burnt biscuits. I told them not to do it. The feds are coming after us for sure now and we got nothing to sell the outfit that put up the money.

"Then we hightail it out of there and there's nobody coming after us. We got clean away and we're cruising around in Mar Tranquillo wondering how to get our hands on some more rockets. Then my guy in Fort Stewart tells me he's got another unit... brand new and it's extra inventory. Only now my guy says 'twenty million' or it ain't worth the risk. Doctor Mudd says, 'fine' and we're in business."

"Who else is on the yacht?"

"A captain and two crew. That boat belongs to one of the Panamanians. That's all the crew he has. They just run the boat."

"Women? Bimbos, bikini girls, floozies?"

Ricky Lee shook his head. "Not on this trip. The cartel guys dropped their wives off at Ponte Vedras. This trip is business... they didn't bring any babes.

"Look Macbean, I'm telling you this... they are going to hit us... as soon as they realize we got away... but we're not far enough away. Hit the throttle and get this boat out of here. They can't blow us up if they don't see us."

"Why did they tie you up?"

Ricky Lee shook his head. "I didn't see that one coming. They told me on the phone, to bring you to them. They could get some ransom for you, you're a celebrity and all. Those guys are kidnap experts. When they drove all the cartels out of Columbia, some of them went to Panama... lots of big money going into Panama since we don't have the canal anymore. Big banks, big development. That's how they became 'Unido'... United. For a while all the cartels going into one city... they're all kidnapping each other's families... like a weird cash-flow thing. They have contacts on top of contacts. They think they'll get some money out of you."

'Foolish," I said. "There's nobody who'd pay much for me."

"Well, they realized they didn't have to pay me the twenty million if they turned me into the feds."

He slumped, looking sad and pitiful sitting in the back of the boat all tied up like pig going to slaughter. I had to remind myself that Ricky Lee would cut my heart out in a second if our situations were reversed.

He shifted his shoulders and arms like trying his bonds.

"Hands tied too tight?" I asked him.

He nodded. "I can't feel 'em. No circulation. I'm going to lose my hands if you don't loosen these ties."

I smiled. "And the world would be a better place... if you lost your hands."

Then he looked hard at me.

"Macbean, I left you all tied up at the bottom of this boat. How'd you get free?"

"An old trick I learned from Houdini," I said.

"Who-da-what?"

"Harry Houdini. He was an escape artist back in the Roaring Twenties."

"So you think you saved me from those hard cases over there." Again, he pointed with his chin. "All they're going to do is roast us when they find out."

I brightened and gave him another smile.

"Yeah, that's what the holdup is. They're so interested in that soccer game; they don't even know we're gone."

I looked around. "Hey, what's this?" I spotted what I thought was Ricky Lee's cell phone sitting in a drink holder on the top of the center console. I picked it up. It was a rather clunky-looking cell phone, like a five-year-old Android type.

"Ricky, what did you call my old tablet before you chunked it into the drink? A piece of crap? This looks like your grandma's phone." I held it up like I was going to chunk it over the side.

He snarled, "You idiot... that's not a cell phone. It's a..." and he clammed up, like he stopped himself from saying too much.

"Not a cell phone? Looks like a cell phone." I pressed the home button. The screen lit up... and went straight to the main screen.

"Hmmmm... it's not asking me for a code. Didn't put a password on your phone? Sounds like a rookie mistake. Wow, I'm getting lots of bars... way out here in the middle of the ocean? It must be a satellite phone. Let's see what the call log says... Hmmm, you got a call from somebody you call 'UN1'. Like in 'Unido' a guy in the Unido cartel?" I pushed the number highlighted in blue, in a couple of seconds, I heard a ringing tone.

On the second ring somebody answered. I heard someone say, "¡Oye! Apaga la television!" and then, "Quien es?" The voice was deep and Spanish, and I imagined the guy in the Hawaiian shirt.

I took a deep breath. "English, dude. My Spanish is a little rusty."

A pause, then, "Who is it? What do you want?"

"Why this is Brendon Macbean, the minor TV celebrity from Atlanta. I'm here with Ricky Lee, your former thug slash thief slash delivery boy. You have not checked lately but me and Ricky Lee... uh..."

My Spanish returned like a migrating bird. 'Tus pollos han volado ... nos hemos ido.'"

Another pause... no translation necessary.

"Okay, Senior Drug Dealer... we are in Ricky Lee's boat about five hundred yards due west of your position. We have assault rifles and large caliber firearms." I gave my Redhawk a look. "In five minutes, we will open fire on your vessel." I thought for a minute and said, "En cinco minutos, abriremos fuego contra su embarcación."

I turned to look at Ricky Lee. "Did I say that right?"

He gave me an open-mouthed look of utter disbelief.

"Sweet Jesus, what are you doing?"

I clicked off the phone and put it back in the drink holder.

Ricky Lee shook his head and looked at me.

"This is all a setup, isn't it?"

I said nothing.

"Macbean, you're begging them to blow us up. That's what they're gonna to do.... fire off a couple of those rockets and ... boom! Couple of days ago, those idiots fired off the only two rockets we had and blowed up that Coast Guard boat. We strained our guts out trying to get those rockets and they shot them off. Then two days later, a brand new unit shows up and, uh, my Fort Stew guy calls me and... "

"You mean, Skinner? Sergeant Skinner of the Recycling Center... that's your guy?"

Ricky Lee shakes his head and then nods. "You know about him and you were prowling around at the Cuthberts' place. I thought I could scare you away. I mean, twenty million dollars... It made me stupid."

"Yeah, Ricky Lee. By now they're all in custody... Skinner and the Cuthberts. They all have families. Their lives ruined. They're all going to jail.

"You..." I pointed at him. "are going to jail. Federal prison, maximum security. I have a friend in the Justice Department that will make sure it's Florence, Colorado and not Oakdale in Louisiana."

Ricky Lee gave me a steely look with his sky-blue eyes. "I'd rather go to hell than to prison and I'll make a deal with the devil that you and me will be together the whole time."

He turned his eyes toward Mar Tranquillo.

"Looks like I'm gonna get my wish."

"The Cleaner"

Friday afternoon – Out in the Atlantic
From the Journal of Brendan Macbean:

Following Ricky Lee's eyes, I saw men moving around on the stern of Mar Tranquilo. At this distance, I couldn't see much detail, kind of like watching people at a Braves game on the other side of the stadium.

I said, "I bet they have binoculars."

The assault rifle on the seat beside me had a small optical device mounted on the top rail. I shouldered the weapon and looked through the mini scope. I saw the guy in the Hawaiian shirt looking in our direction and yes, he had binoculars. He hastily brought the binoculars down and ducked out of sight. I guess he saw me pointing an assault rifle in his direction. Heads bobbed up and down like targets in a carnival game. I saw someone bent over the table in the back where I had seen the XLR unit deployed.

Maybe the infamous Doctor Mudd, the weapons expert.

When I rescued Ricky Lee, I remember seeing the XLR launcher deployed on the table in the rear of the salon. I was in a hurry to get away. I didn't give it more than a cursory glance. But now my memory gave me a menacing picture, the warheads had a no-nonsense dull gray finish, like no one wanted to make something pretty which was going to blow things up and cause death and destruction.

The guy bent over the table... I saw him stand up.

I didn't have long to wait.

Two projectiles flew out of the back of Mar Tranquillo, arching vertically like a pair of pop-flies. At the apex, sparks like camera flashes ignited the rockets. They collected themselves, formed a sort of formation, trailing thin white smoke, a pair of mini-jet planes.

Heading straight toward us, picking up ferocious speed.

Ricky Lee twisted his head over his left shoulder. He hissed, "Jesus! God!"

Like a pair of falcons, the XLR rockets flew... only much faster than falcons.

I felt a horrible sense of miscalculation. I had deliberately placed myself in the path of certain, obvious death.

That's about all I had time for.

The XLRs screamed overhead, maybe twenty feet above us, emitting a loud sizzling sound like frying bacon.

I ducked out from under the T-top to watch their flight. The pair of rockets continued past us in a straight line for a hundred yards and began a gentle turn to the left resulting in a wide sweeping circle.

Back toward Mar Tranquilo.

Just before the XLRs reached the yacht, rockets three, four, five and six launched straight up in the air like batting practice. I saw XLRs one and two enter the salon...

White hot sun super nova, blinding ripping tearing... in a second a roar reached us like Mount Saint Helens... the roof of the yacht's salon flew straight upwards with debris starbursting in all direction. A wave of radiant heat burned my face, making me turn away, followed by a billowing ripple of a shock wave, a mini-tsunami traveling fast enough to rock the boat and make the water boil.

I turned and grabbed Ricky Lee, threw him to the floor and flopped on top of him.

XLRs three through six fell on the yacht exploding at half second intervals, the white light blinding, somehow reaching my eyes even though I kept them tightly shut and we were lying on the bottom the boat, protected by the boat's high gunnels.

Boom... flash... repeat four times.

I wondered if the other six warheads would detonate., but it was all over in a minute. Our boat shook in the waves from the explosions, but that too passed.

I could hear splashes and at first, I thought it might be struggling survivors, but no one could have survived that concentration of heat and explosions.

I peeked over the gunnel and saw bits and pieces of what used to be the yacht, Mar Tranquillo's pieces rained from the sky. I saw a dark triangle floating and realized that it was the largest piece of the boat, a few feet of its bow pointed skyward. As I watched, it slipped beneath the waves and was gone.

Other than the mess of debris on the surface, there wasn't much remaining of the yacht or the people. There was a large circle of calm water where the wreckage floated, the waves of the mighty Atlantic blown away by the explosions.

Temporarily.

In the back of the boat, Ricky Lee moaned but otherwise lay still. A whiff of corruption invaded my nostrils, a stink like a septic tank. In all the excitement accidents can happen. An impromptu and probably undiscovered yoga position confirmed my status unsullied.

The sound of a helicopter attracted my attention and pulled my eyes to the south. I spotted it immediately. And another. And a third. Three orange streaks, flying at full throttle. Beneath them I saw a flotilla of Defender Class boats, four of them, a spectrum of orange and white and sliver paint.

And another boat I recognized. Silver and yellow, a more modern Defender Class boat, from the state of Georgia Marine Patrol.

Captain Corny, Georgia State Criminal Interdiction Unit... or something like that.

He headed in our direction while the other boats cruised toward the circle of wreckage. The gaggle of helicopters circled above, making a racket.

Instinct made me shove my Redhawk back in my backpack.

Captain Corny made the same precipitous approach as he had on Lily and me two days ago, like he was going to cut us in half but this time I knew better. He spun the boat around and sidled up against my boat's left side.

His boat bristled with men, maybe a half a dozen with helmets, body armor and assault rifles. A man in the bow pointed a long-barreled machine gun at me. I swallowed hard a couple of times and practiced patience and restraint.

"Macbean! Cut your engine," he shouted.

I had the boat in neutral but didn't argue. I killed the engine.

Captain Reginald Cornelius stood a few feet away, his usual mirrored sunglasses shielding his expression.

In a more conversational tone he said, "Were you born one morning in a drizzling rain?"

I could do pop song trivia with the best of them. "Fighting and trouble are my middle name."

His eyebrows shot up. "You know the song?"

"It's a little before my time, but sure... Merle Travis, circa 1946."

His brows knitted. "What? Not Tennessee Ernie Ford?"

"About a decade later... Still before my time, but yeah... 'Sixteen Tons what do you get?'"

"Looks like I get you," he said. "You city-boys know about sunscreen? Your face is all red. And your boat's all scorched. What happened?"

"Like Icarus, I flew too close to the sun and my feathers melted." My sarcastic side coming out.

"Greek Mythology... I'm dealing with a learned man... Do you know this is a federal operation?"

"What are you doing in it then? You're state of Georgia, aren't you?"

"Local cooperation. They needed help and I volunteered. I told them I wanted you, Macbean."

"Well, you got me. Now what?"

"What's that?" He pointed at the recumbent Ricky Lee.

"Why, that's Ricky Lee Duggan... the worst badass within a hundred miles. Only now he doesn't look all that badass to me."

Captain Corny eyed Ricky Lee and wrinkled his nose.

"I smell a barn."

I said, "I guess in all the excitement, Ricky Lee has soiled hisself."

Corny grinned broadly. "Well, that makes our job easier."

"It does?"

"Certainly. In the history of Law Enforcement, no prisoner has ever escaped after he's messed his britches."

I chuckled. "Okay, Captain, but when you get in front of a TV camera, I would change the word 'history' to 'annals.'"

Corny considered this. "Yes... Macbean you are a wit."

He barked an order, "Smith, Dewar! Get that prisoner onboard."

Two of his men jumped to it. At first, I thought Corny had said, 'Onboard' but what he said was "on the board.' I understood when the two men returned with a long plastic stretcher-like device with slots and webbing.

They boarded my boat and went straight to Ricky Lee. One of the men bent over him and said, "Shit. Captain, this one has a dirty diaper."

"Well, you don't have to change him... just strap him up and bring him over."

While they were securing Ricky Lee, I glanced at the area where Mar Tranquillo had sunk. Coast Guard defender boats swarmed over the site like hungry Sharks. A large ship, well over a hundred feet, had sailed into our vicinity without me noticing.

"What is that?" I asked.

He looked over at the big ship. "Marine Recovery ship. The Coast Guard wants to recover as much of the wreck as possible."

He turned to me. "Hey, look, Macbean. These boys have a lot of work to do here, but we're going back to Brunswick. I'll get a guy to drive your boat, but would you like to ride with me?"

I accepted Captain Corny's hand and moved over to his boat. We immediately departed with Ricky Lee stashed like cargo in the back. Corny's men followed us in Ricky Lee's boat.

From the get-go Corny showed preference for full throttle. With whiplash acceleration we dashed toward Brunswick. For some reason, he assumed I was interested in the second-generation model Response Boat and babbled on about its attributes. I retained little of this... even within the cabin the operational noise was deafening.

In addition to the noise, the boat leapt and crashed repeatedly against moderate waves as it came on plane, launched itself into the air and fell back casting up huge sheets of spray. Still it was exhilarating and exhausting, there being little to hold on to.

A glance behind told me the two men driving Ricky Lee's boat could not keep up.

Corny shouted, "Don't worry about them. They know the way."

About the time I achieved some stability on the bouncing ship, Corny altered our course more in line with the direction of the waves and the boat's motion steadied.

I had never seen Saint Simon's Island from the Atlantic and it caught my interest. Around the southern tip of the island the Sidney Lanier Bridge came into sight, spanning the entrance to the port of Brunswick. A large container ship was inbound and seemed to take up the entire channel. Captain Corny set a collision course toward the huge ship but veered off to the right and entered a small creek just as we went under the bridge.

He pulled up to a dock, and his men leapt into action, putting out bumpers and securing the boat. We were greeted by a squad of khaki-dressed youths who gang-wrestled Ricky Lee's stretcher on to a gurney and off to, hopefully, a secure prison cell.

I got hustled into a golf cart. After a short ride we arrived at a building with a sign that said, "United States Coast Guard, Brunswick, Georgia."

Well, at least I knew where I was.

Inside, the air conditioning felt wonderfully cool against my skin. One of my escorts pointed to a bathroom. In the mirror I immediately saw my red face, either from the sun or the explosion. I regretted my earlier neglect not using sunscreen.

Upon exiting the men's room they took me to a conference room. It was drearily familiar, large table, large TV on the wall. A sideboard held water, soft drinks, and an ice bucket. I made myself at home and sat down with a diet cola.

The TV flickered on and a large rendition of Nick Carrillo's face appeared.

"Brendan! Thank God you're okay."

I didn't know where the camera was, so I just stared at the TV.

"I'm okay... except for a little sunburn."

"Put some Aloe Vera on it," Nick said.

"Sounds like something my mom would say."

"That's what my mom says."

"Nick, I have a lot of questions to ask you," I said.

He gave me an evasive look.

"Brendan, we didn't know you were going to be there. We ordered our agents to hold their position at three miles."

I took my time digesting that statement.

"Nick, I don't understand. Tuesday a Coast Guard boat blows up within a mile of ten thousand people and nobody sees it. What I saw could have been seen from twenty miles away. And felt."

"Second generation XLR technology. Many times more powerful," he said.

"More nasty, you mean."

Nick said, "The goal of weapons development is to increase effectiveness."

"Yeah, well..."

"We didn't know you'd be inside the radius."

Nick kept his eyes on his keyboard. "Brendan, since you were there, we need a statement from you."

"So, you're going to interrogate *me* now?"

"Not an interrogation. We want your cooperation... tell us what you did and what you saw."

"In the interest of weapons development..." I said. "How patriotic!"

"You have full immunity..."

"For how long?"

"Come on, Mister Mac. For this operation. And you have a security clearance, which means you can't talk about what happened. Surely you can see why."

So, I gave my statement, but it was more like an interrogation. There were unseen other people submitting questions through Nick. It seems our government was curious about how I inserted myself into their operation without them knowing about it. I told them that they also had Ricky Lee to interrogate, but Nick didn't react to that. They were curious why I saved him, and I had a hard time explaining that. When I thought about it, I could not rationalize any reason for putting myself into the damage radius. Or even why I snuck out of my hotel room and made such a surreptitious effort to get into harm's way. My deep-rooted reason was pride, of course. I had handed them the blueprint of Ricky Lee's smuggling operation and the whys and wherefores of how our enemies got hold of a secret weapon and used it to kill three of our servicemen and destroy a patrol boat... essentially an attack on our homeland and against our people.

Nobody ever said to me, "Thank you very much, Mister Macbean... for handing this to us on a silver platter. Now you sit back and eat ice cream at Leopold's while we take care of this nasty business."

And I never would have heard a thing about it, how it went down, and our government would have concocted a story that fit their need for secrecy and satisfied the people that their government still had things very much under control.

Even if I could never tell anyone about it, I could not let that happen. My plan had been impulsive, reckless and idiotic.

But I survived.

The statement-taking went on for over an hour before Nick called a break.

The conference room door opened, and a grinning Coast Guard sailor entered with a big bag and a gallon jug full of, what I immediately identified as sweet tea, a Southern staple. The bag had printing on it that identified its origin as "Southern Soul Bar-beque," one of the best barbeque restaurants in the area. The contents, a warm pulled-pork sandwich, coleslaw and fried okra, cold dill pickle slices and an assortment of barbeque sauces.

Heaven. I had not realized how hungry I was.

The sailor left it all on the table and I ate alone.

Thirty minutes of food-gobbling better than a cheeseburger in paradise!

My interrogators probably took a meal break too because the TV screen began a montage of scenic views of the world, which I paid little attention to.

Nicks face appeared on the TV and the questions continued, mostly covering what we had all discussed before. But the late hour and the meal break curtailed their inquisitional intensity and when we got to the desultory level, we called it quits by acclamation.

Nick said, "Mister Mac, everybody's offline now. We've arranged for you to stay at the Embassy Suites tonight. Tomorrow we'll drive you anywhere you want..."

I interrupted him. "Nick, if it's all the same to you, I'd like a ride back to the Yacht Club... near Rawlings cottage. I left my truck there. Rawling's cottage is where I want to sleep tonight."

Nick said, "Okay."

Five minutes later a young woman entered the conference room. She was petite and dressed in fatigues. The patch on her blouse read, "Kleinschmidt."

She stuck out her hand like a salesman. "Mister Macbean, I'm El. I'm going to drive wherever you want to go."

I wasn;t sure she said 'El' or 'L' the letter.

"Nice to meet you, L." I picked up my backpack which she immediately wrestled out of my hand.

"I'll help you with that, sir."

"Okay, L. Lead the way."

She also opened the door for me and set a fast pace.

I kept up. We strode out into the humid night air to a nearly new Ford Expedition. I climbed into the passenger seat.

L looked like a child in a driver's seat big enough for a basketball player. She turned to me and smiled prettily.

"Where to, Mister Macbean?"

"The Barbour River Yacht Club."

After I spelled it for her, we managed to find the address on the Expedition's console. She pressed the 'go' button and we went.

I dozed off and didn't remember much about the ride. I only know that my weary brain was awoken when the car came to a rather abrupt halt.

"What the F...." L said.

I blinked my eyes awake. In a few seconds I realized where we were and said, "It's ok. It looks like there's no road, but there is. Just go ahead slowly. You'll see it"

L moved the Expedition forward through the brick columns of Gould's Landing. She edged the car around the big tree in the middle of the road.

"Creepy…" she said. L drove until I told her to stop, at my old Silverado.

"Let me out here. Do you think you can find your way back?"

"Sure. No problem." She stared straight ahead and gripped the steering wheel.

"L, are you alright?"

"Yeah, the place is creepy, that's all." She turned and looked at me with wide eyes. "How did you ever find this place?"

I shrugged. "The same way you did, I guess."

"I mean before GPS."

"I know," I said. "Coming here at night doesn't make the best impression. You'll be alright, just follow the line."

I pointed at the Ford's console.

"Oh, and if you see a guy with a chain saw… lock the doors and keep going."

She smiled and gave me the finger. "Roger that."

I drove the Silverado to Rawlings place. Inside, I undressed in front of the washing machine, stuffed everything into it and ran upstairs naked to a hot shower and a fluffy towel. Misses Rawlings had a big bottle of Aloe Vera stuff with which I treated my sunburn.

Under the covers with the lights out, I spent a moment listening to the treefrogs. Sleep was coming on hard, but a thought kept ticking through my head in lock step with the ticking of the ancient ceiling fan.

Many years ago, the state of Ohio had invited me to witness the execution of TV Swanson, a notorious criminal with multiple murders on his slate, including two police officers and his own wife. He had been a wretched human being and the subject of my only book, a sort of 'In Cold Blood' real crime novel, no ways near as fine as the Capote book, but a modest best seller all the same. Prior to his execution I had sidled up to this monster who strained to maintain his humanity around me. By the time he received his 'hot shot' he considered me his only friend. The lesson I derived from this painful episode in my life is that there is a human soul at the bottom of any well of iniquity. Despite my Christian upbringing, I struggled to like Swanson or forgive his deeds. But I could still feel genuine sorrow at the ending of his life and the misery he caused himself and others.

Ricky Lee Duggan was another monster of this world, maybe worse than TV Swanson. He needed to be kept away from the rest of us.

And today I had participated in a calculated mass-assassination where our government had deliberately lured greedy criminals into a death trap, appointing themselves judge, jury and executioner. I had gone to extraordinary lengths to step in the middle of it.

My interrogators had thrown a question at me three times and three times I could not answer. Now it turned over in my head like an egg that would not fry.

"Why did you save Ricky Lee?"

Chapter 29 - "Maybe later. Maybe never."

CHAPTER 30

"Maybe later... Maybe never"

Saturday – Gould's Landing
From the Journal of Brendan Macbean:

I woke to brilliant sunshine pouring into the bedroom and cool, marsh-scented air gently rustling the curtains. I lay there for a moment feeling a sense of peace and forgiveness and... I don't know what the rest of what I was feeling, but I felt ready to close the books on yesterday, felt powerless to change the world and at the same time, powerful enough to let go of it all.

My huddling place in Atlanta beckoned me to return, and it felt right to answer that call.

But first I had some tidying up to do.

I gave Rawlings' cottage a thorough cleaning, washed the sheets and towels, emptied the refrigerator of perishable food and bagged all the trash. Since Thursday night's departure had been forced and hasty, I hoped if I got the place sparkling Rawlings would forgive me the rest.

Outside I made a happy discovery... Green With Envy, Rawlings' boat... someone had recovered it and brought it back. It sat on its trailer under the shed overhang, exactly where it was when I first saw it... bullet holes and all.

My fault Rawlings' boat was damaged. I made a solemn promise to set it all to rights.

I loaded the trash in the truck's bed, turned off the hot water heater and left Rawlings' cottage, making sure to close the gate. Luckily, I encountered nobody who wanted to flag me down for explanations. I made a swing by the yacht club, tossed the trash in the dumpster, and gazed one last time at the Barbour River glittering in the late morning sun.

Leaving through the brick-column gateway of Gould's Landing, I felt a complete lack of melancholy No giant dog came to say goodbye, and the place faded in my review mirror.

I had one more thing to do.

I turned left on Youngman Road and left again on Old Shellman Road. I didn't know exactly where I was going, didn't have an address, just a funny name for the place... Pleasure Bluff. Odd that the locals chose to name it that, right next to Contentment Bluff.

That's where she lived. I found it on the big map on the wall of Rawling's place. Shellman Bluff, not really a town just a name for a community that was full of tiny communities, fish camps really, places where people came to enjoy what this place had to offer. These camps had come into existence along the Broro and Julienten Rivers with an easy-going lack of planning. Dallas Bluff, Contentment Bluff, Pleasure Bluff and Shellman Bluff itself. The area was dotted with more names, bluffs and landings and points.

My destination was Pleasure Bluff. I turned left at the War Memorial onto Dallas Bluff Road and found Cherry Lane, the apparent entrance to the neighborhood where she lived.

Pleasure Bluff was home to a mix of frame houses and mobile homes. I drove around the place twice before I found her. It was a vintage single wide mobile home mounted on a block foundation. A screened porch had been added to the front. Her battered, ancient little red truck was out front with a gleaming white Jaguar parked behind it.

I parked the Silverado behind the Jag and sat there for a moment to let my pounding heart calm a bit.

What I was about to do scared me in a way that I could not identify. What I was about to see terrified me. I had to push myself to get out of the truck.

I went through the screened porch and raised my hand to knock. I saw that the door had recently been repaired. A clean plank of new wood, as yet unpainted, had been laid vertical against the jam. Marks from a crowbar on the frame of the door told of Ricky Lee's breaking and entering.

I knocked hard and heard voices behind the door. Voices and a disagreement, and some kind of a resolution.

The door opened.

Before me stood a beautiful woman. Tall and thin with snow white hair and perfect complexion, a mostly wrinkle-free face, eyes as blue as star sapphires, her expression as cold as a glacier. Lily's cheekbones, nose, hairline, a mold from which she had been cast, dressed in luxury-casual, a mature model right off a magazine cover.

"Yes?" Lily's momma's voice, regally glacial.

"Mrs. Samson?" I stammered.

"And you are?"

"Uh...," like I didn't know. "I'm Brendan Macbean."

Her frosty blue eyes gave me an examination.

"Yes, Lanny Boatwright told me about you. What do you want?"

Her mom's lack of welcome felt like a wall of frozen air. She gave me no measure of friendliness or welcome, no 'Come on in, Mister Macbean.' She let me stand outside as unwanted as a door-to-door salesman.

I took a deep breath. "I came to see Lily."

She snorted and tossed her head like a brusque and spirited mare.

"Quite impossible. Lily's not seeing anyone, especially a stranger."

"We're not strangers. I..."

She cut me off. "You met in a bar. What, three days ago? What makes you think you're anything but a stranger? We don't know you. What I *do* know about you isn't very appealing. According to Lanny, you're the reason that little bastard beat her up."

My body shook from her wave of hostility.

"Ricky Lee..."

"Yes, I know," she said. "He's dead... with all those other criminals.

I had to stiffen my knees. "Dead?"

"Yes, dead. It's all over the news. Their boat blew up. You should know... I thought you were in television."

She made it sound like I stood a grade above a tramp. But I knew he wasn't dead. It dawned on me that I was hearing the spin, the government's version of reality, what they wanted the public to know and I was sworn to not divulge a word of his real fate.

"I had not seen any news... for a while."

"Mister Macbean, I need you to leave. Lily is in very bad shape. She needs time and space to heal."

"Why isn't she in the hospital?"

She gave me a challenging look, like I had no right to ask.

"Because they discharged her. And we can't take her anywhere else because of her probation. My husband will change that, of course, now that the threat is gone. But, Mister Macbean, it's the weekend. Nothing can be done until Monday. And not that's it any of your business."

Her look softened slightly. "I can appreciate you might have feelings for Lily and you seem like a decent kind of person even if you are a journalist or whatever. Everybody loves my Lily..."

Her hand went to her pretty mouth and she stifled a sob.

"My beautiful little girl... he nearly killed her. She's not beautiful anymore. He beat her face, kicked her body. You want to know what he did to her? Three dozen stitches in her face! Her cheek-bones... her nose smashed. The parietal and temporal bones... "

She traced her finger along the side of her head. "...caved in. And he kicked her body all over the room, dislocated her shoulder. Two cracked ribs and a hyperextended knee. Bruises everywhere.

"I used to pray that the police would catch him or that he would die in some criminal thing. I'm a Christian woman but I prayed to God to take this nightmare away from us.

"What did we do, mister Macbean, to be so cursed? My beautiful baby girl... she's thirty-seven years old and we've been locked in this hell for twenty years. Her daughter... little Maggie is so pretty and such a good girl. We were so afraid Ricky Lee would hurt her. The police couldn't do anything, and that bastard kept sending us photos in the mail... pictures of little Maggie in the playground at school... or us at the mall. That little bastard was always around stalking us."

Lily's mom wiped her eyes. "Her beauty is gone, Mister Macbean. After the stitches come out, they have to go in and break all the bones again to try to put her face back together. And even then, she's going to look like a cartoon the rest of her life.

"You have feelings for her, I know. Lots of men fall in love with my little girl. She's lovely and friendly. Beyond beauty... she's been on magazine covers."

She stopped. Her hand came up and covered her face. Lily's mom wept for a while. I waited, counting her sobs... spaced apart like picking things up from the floor. Finally she straightened and wiped her eyes.

"Well, that's gone, Mister Macbean. All gone. It will be a different life for her now.

"But she has a chance for something else. We can be a family again. Lily will heal. She can be a momma to little Maggie. She can leave..." Lily's mom let her eyes drift over the rude little fish camp... I was seeing it through her eyes. This used to be her life and her first husband died and now she was married to the rich TV lawyer, Max Samson, and drove around in a gleaming white Jaguar.

She had run out of words. With tears drying on her cheekbones, she looked at me waiting for me to say something or leave.

"I understand, Mrs. Samson. I want to help her...

"She doesn't need your help. Lily has her family. We have resources you can't possibly imagine."

Lily's mom really didn't know much about me, but it hurt. Hell, this whole conversation hurt, but it was nothing to what Lily endured.

"Mrs. Samson. I wanted to know how she's doing and if there's anything I can do..."

She cut me off. "There is nothing. If you have any regard for her or us, then go back to where you came from. You don't belong here, and she doesn't need a man in her life.

What she didn't say but it rang in my head, 'She doesn't need a man... not one as needy as you.'

I took a breath. "Well, maybe later..."

Lily's mom tossed her head again, backed up a step and began closing the door.

"Maybe never."

CHAPTER 31

Epilog – Homeward Bound

Saturday – On the road again
From the Journal of Brendan Macbean:

I did not like it... not one bit. Three people in as many days told to me to go back where I came from and that I didn't belong here. They were right and it rankled me, but tonight I would sleep in my own bed.

I felt like a total pioneer navigating without electronics or GPS. No cell phone with Waze or Google Maps, just my memory of the map on Rawlings' wall. I managed to find the Coastal Highway and the Interstate, but I'm not sure I took the shortest route.

My old truck and I cruised north and came to highway 204 which took me east toward Savannah. The road became Abercorn heading into the heart of the city. From there I made it to Eisenhower and drove past Spanish Moss Motors where I bought the truck yesterday. Across the street, I found Goodwill, where I turned the truck over to a very nice Goodwill associate named Ray Charles Robinson.

After handing over the paperwork, I asked, "Can you call me a cab?"

"What, sir? You don't have a ride?"

"No... not even a phone. Poor planning, huh?"

"How far you going?"

"The Marriott Riverfront. I think it's about eight miles from here."

Ray Charles whipped out his phone, "Man, I got this. Hop in, I'll take you."

Soon we were on our way, me as a passenger and Ray Charles driving to the gently spoken directions of Lady Waze.

At the Marriott, I gave Ray Charles a hundred-dollar tip and I thought he was going to cry. I climbed out of the Silverado, kind of sorry to see it go. The doorman recognized me, and I gave him a twenty.

I was in a generous mood.

I stopped at the front desk and told the clerk I was checking out.

"Is there something wrong with the room, sir?"

"I don't think so, but I haven't seen it since yesterday morning."

That got a look. I went to my room.

Reunited with my electronics, I checked the news on my computer.

The feds had spun a very tall tale which certainly would launch dozens of conspiracy theories. Our ever-diligent government had uncovered a criminal operation smuggling high explosives out of Fort Stewart. This dangerous material was being funneled to drug dealing cartels who were in turn selling it to terrorists to be used in making bombs to use against American soldiers. Facing crackdowns both here and abroad, the smugglers made a desperate effort to ship a final, massive amount of explosives through coastal locations. A parcel of this explosive had carelessly fallen into the waters off Saint Simons Island where it was picked up by the Coast Guard boat. Coast Guardsmen routinely fished packages out of the waters, but unaware of the nature of the contents, and the package accidently detonated which destroyed the boat and killed three servicemen.

The smugglers were able to load the rest of the explosives aboard a large luxury yacht, the Mar Tranquilo, and set sail for parts unknown, Our Coast Guard found the yacht and during a gun battle on the high seas, the explosives detonated completely destroying the Mar Tranquillo and killing all on board.

The names of the dead were listed in the report, which included the cartel members and one Richard Lee Duggan, a known and wanted criminal. The names of the army insiders in Fort Stewart and Afghanistan and the Cuthberts were not mentioned.

A story like this couldn't stay hot for long without new angles. The public grows weary hearing about it otherwise. And there wouldn't be new angles, not if our government had anything to do with it.

The story omitted the existence of a secret high-tech super weapon. Just plain explosives. You ask the man on the street what happened, the answer you would get was they just plain blowed up.

But I knew Ricky Lee did not die. Messy britches although unpleasant, isn't fatal.

The story the feds threw out to the media said he had died and that gave me chills. It spoke of secret lockups and lack of due process. Ricky Lee had probably given them everything he had in terms of useful information. His rank as a small-time hood, not even on the national most wanted list placed his value to the Department of Justice as next to nothing.

With mixed feelings, I thought about what they would do to him.

The government said he died. Now they had to make that story stick. Captain Corny and his crew knew Ricky Lee survived the destruction of Mar Tranquillo and had to become co-conspirators. How were they silenced?

For me it was over. I had finished up one hell of an investigation. I could tell nobody but Daniel Conklin and my own secret journal. It was now the government's problem.

And I'm heading home... where I belong.

Reuniting with my Land Cruiser pleased me more than I expected. The valet brought it around, gleaming and shining with recent detailing, clean as a whistle inside with a tantalizing fragrance. The seat moved smoothly to suit my personal preference. My cell phone and laptop clicked into their docking stations.

I took a second to enjoy it.

"TLC!" I commanded. It took her a moment to wake up.

"Boss! Where have you been? I've been so worried... "

My explanation must have bored her.

"Boss, you lost me with, 'I left the Land Cruiser with the valet.'"

"Okay, well, anyway I'm fine. Just a little sunburn."

"You should use sunscreen. You know that."

"You sound like my mother."

"A smart woman. You should listen to her."

"But now I have you to take care of me..."

She purred like a stretching cat, "Yes darling, I'll take good care of you."

"TLC, call Connie Garza."

"Brendan!" Connie greeted me loudly. "Are you coming home? Where are you?"

"Connie, I'm coming home. Uh, I'm just leaving Savannah. I should be home this evening. How are things there."

"Peaceful, quiet. Same old, same old," she said. "I put all your mail on the kitchen counter. Oh, hey... you got a package."

"Really, what kind of package?"

"Just a package... like the thing in the song...'brown paper packages tied up with string...'"

"Really? It's tied up with string? Sounds a little old fashioned."

"Weird too. No address on it."

"Where'd it come from?"

"I don't know... no address. Like somebody wrote your name with a Sharpie and dropped it off."

"It was in my mailbox?"

"No, left it on the porch. It feels like a book."

I shrugged. I get books all the time.

"Okay, I guess I'll see you and Jose tonight."

"We won't be here, Bren. We'll go home. Unless you want me to sneak back here later for some hanky-panky."

"Jose is a retired Marine. He'd kill me. Besides, I'll be tired."

"Okay. I left a chile relleno in the fridge with some rice."

"Thanks, Connie. You're wonderful."

"You better believe it, Bren. You have a good time in Savannah?"

"I had a blast." For some reason I thought that was funny and chuckled.

"Bren, you sound happy. It's been a long time since you sound happy. You meet a girl?"

I stopped laughing. "Yes, Connie. I met a girl."

"She pretty?"

"Pretty... she was beautiful, Connie."

"Hmm, now you don't sound so happy. What happened?"

"Long story. I'll tell you later."

"Okay, Bren. You drive safe, okay?"

"Okay."

The interstate between Savannah and Macon has little to offer. Perhaps it was the bland drive or perhaps it was the mantle of melancholy that settled over me. I drove without a memorable thought all the way past the Dublin exit.

Atlanta traffic starts just before you get to Macon. All the commerce from seaports and the agricultural heart of the South funnels into the junction of two interstates feeding into Atlanta.

I timed my arrival in the big ATL just right. Cresting the hill at Cleveland Avenue the entire city skyline spread out before me, thousands of panes of glass reflecting sparkles of red, orange, yellow, a looming thunderstorm on the northeast horizon dramatically contrasting rays of the setting sun.

Atlanta welcoming me home... where I belong.

That again... how many times do I need to hear it? Glenn Frey's song, 'You Belong to the City' banged around in my head.

I easily traversed downtown and found north I-75 to the Northside Drive exit. The pace slowed as I neared Vinings, the charming community within Greater Atlanta. When I drove along the serpentine brick wall that bordered my neighborhood. A lump formed in my throat like I had been away a month.

My house at the bottom of the hill brought another lump. A brick two story, in a neighborhood of big houses on modest-sized lots, way too big for me but it was my first house. I lived in condos until Bettye and I got serious. I bought this beautiful house with the idea we'd share it, foolishly ignoring the certainty that she'd never leave Paris. Well now it was my comfort zone, where I belonged, and I never intended leaving.

I parked in the garage and entered through a hallway that connected to the kitchen. There I saw the stack of mail Connie had left for me and the mysterious 'brown paper package, tied up with string.'

When I saw my name written on it my knees buckled.

It was Bettye's handwriting.

I knew what it was... her book, her memoir about her battle with cancer, "Un Jour de Plus." One more day... now a New York Times best seller.

I reverently tore open the package and there on the dedication page, it said, "To the love of my Life, my soulmate, Brendan Macbean. Without your unwavering love and steadfast wisdom, I never would have had the strength to live 'one more day.'"

My eyes filled with tears.

Below the dedication, Bettye wrote a note in her neat script:

My dearest Brendan,

When you left, I cried for days. I did not have the courage to say the words to you, but you needed to come home. You gave yourself to my cause but we both know you do not need to be a caretaker for an old woman. Cancer took away my beauty and my youth. You need a woman who is young and beautiful like you. She is out there waiting to love you. Because I know you will not look for her, please promise me that you will keep your heart open for when she finds you. Know that until I draw my last breath, I will love you always.

Bettye

The End

Author's Note

Jean and I discovered the community of Shellman Bluff soon after we learned we were going to be grandparents. Since our grandchildren were to be born and raised in Savannah, we wanted to live much closer than Atlanta. Like Macbean, we discovered a hidden gem on the Georgia Coast, a place of natural beauty with interesting, kind and generous people.

Our only hesitation was the contrast to what we were used to. Jean, a native Atlantan and I, having spent over forty years in the Big ATL, we wanted to assure ourselves we could hack the rural life, in a county with no traffic lights and no corner grocery. Learning to guide a boat through the salt water marsh would have to come later, but could city folk sleep at night without streetlights and traffic noise?

We bought the cottage in Gould's Landing and used it as our weekend getaway. Our experience morphing from city dweller to rural gentility provided the grist I needed to write this story.

Gould's Landing and the Barbour River Yacht Club are real as are the Barbour River, Barbour Island, Blackbeard and Sapelo Islands and Harris Neck itself, and described herein with only slight embellishment.

People often ask writers where their characters come from. Well, they come from life itself, the wonderful assortment of wild and wooly folks you run into every day. Unfortunately, you can never really know another person, including the one you look at in the mirror. An author often assembles the best characters from piece-parts of everybody they've met.

Within the pages of Harris Neck Dead my friends and neighbors might notice a few locals showing up now and then. The place just wouldn't be the same without them.

I met Doctor William Rawlings at the library in Smyrna, Georgia, many years ago. An intelligent and brilliant writer, had at that time written a handful of novels and I had one of my own, Beneath Juliette. We shared a table at a literary conference, Murder Goes South, held at the library. We struck up a friendship and stayed in touch over the years. Doctor Rawlings agreed to appear in my novel as the catalyst to this adventure as long as I made him younger and more handsome than he is in real life. Since he is younger than I am and already darn good looking, I saw no purpose acceding to his request. He does not own a cottage in Gould's Landing, so there's no need to come looking for it.

My good friend Ricky McDonald agreed to donate his physical description from which I made my villain. When I told him he might be the villain he said, "Good. Make me one mean SOB." In real life, Ricky Mac is the kindest, most generous person you will ever encounter and nothing like the mean SOB in my story.

Every other character is completely fictitious, made from the storehouse of piece-parts I have rattling around in my skull.

I give my final and most sincere acknowledgement to my children, Kira and Luke. They have my deepest love and respect and have provided me with some of the greatest moments of my life, simply by being the wonderful, real characters they are.